PRAISE FOR ALI HAZELWOOD

"A literary breakthrough. . . . *The Love Hypothesis* is a self-assured debut, and we hypothesize it's just the first bit of greatness we'll see from an author who somehow has the audacity to be both an academic powerhouse and [a] divinely talented novelist."

—*Entertainment Weekly*

"Contemporary romance's unicorn: the elusive marriage of deeply brainy and delightfully escapist. . . . *The Love Hypothesis* has wild commercial appeal, but the quieter secret is that there is a specific audience, made up of all the Olives in the world, who have deeply, ardently waited for this exact book."

—*New York Times* bestselling author Christina Lauren

"With her sophomore novel, Ali Hazelwood proves that she is the perfect writer to show that science is sexy as hell, and that love can 'STEM' from the most unlikely places. She's my newest must-buy author."

—Jodi Picoult, #1 *New York Times* bestselling author of *Wish You Were Here*

"Funny, sexy, and smart. Ali Hazelwood did a terrific job with *The Love Hypothesis*."

—*New York Times* bestselling author Mariana Zapata

"Gloriously nerdy and sexy, with on-point commentary about women in STEM."

—*New York Times* bestselling author Helen Hoang on *Love on the Brain*

"STEMinists, assemble. Your world is about to be rocked."

—*New York Times* bestselling author Elena Armas
on *Love on the Brain*

"This tackles one of my favorite tropes—Grumpy meets Sunshine—in a fun and utterly endearing way. . . . I loved the nods toward fandom and romance novels, and I couldn't put it down. Highly recommended!"

—*New York Times* bestselling author Jessica Clare
on *The Love Hypothesis*

"Pure slow-burning gold with lots of chemistry."   —PopSugar

"A beautifully written romantic comedy with a heroine you will instantly fall in love with, *The Love Hypothesis* is destined to earn a place on your keeper shelf."

—Elizabeth Everett, author of *A Lady's Formula for Love*

"Smart, witty dialogue and a diverse cast of likable secondary characters. . . . A realistic, amusing novel that readers won't be able to put down."   —*Library Journal* (starred review)

"Hilarious and heartwarming, *The Love Hypothesis* is romantic comedy at its best. . . . A perfect amalgamation of sex and science, sure to appeal to readers of Christina Lauren or Abby Jimenez."

—Shelf Awareness

"With whip-smart and endearing characters, snappy prose, and a quirky take on a favorite trope, Hazelwood convincingly navigates the fraught shoals of academia."   —*Publishers Weekly*

Love,
Theoretically

ALI HAZELWOOD

BERKLEY

NEW YORK

BERKLEY
An imprint of Penguin Random House LLC
penguinrandomhouse.com

Copyright © 2023 by Ali Hazelwood

Penguin Random House supports copyright. Copyright fuels creativity, encourages diverse
voices, promotes free speech, and creates a vibrant culture. Thank you for buying an authorized
edition of this book and for complying with copyright laws by not reproducing, scanning, or
distributing any part of it in any form without permission. You are supporting writers and
allowing Penguin Random House to continue to publish books for every reader.

BERKLEY and the BERKLEY & B colophon are registered trademarks of
Penguin Random House LLC.

ISBN: 9780593638859

The Library of Congress has cataloged the Berkley Romance
trade paperback edition of this book as follows:

Names: Hazelwood, Ali, author.
Title: Love, theoretically / Ali Hazelwood.
Description: New York: Berkley Romance, 2023.
Identifiers: LCCN 2022046963 (print) | LCCN 2022046964 (ebook) |
ISBN 9780593336861 (trade paperback) | ISBN 9780593336878 (ebook)
Classification: LCC PS3608.A98845 L75 2023 (print) |
LCC PS3608.A98845 (ebook) | DDC 813/.6—dc23
LC record available at https://lccn.loc.gov/2022046963
LC ebook record available at https://lccn.loc.gov/2022046964

Printed in the United States of America
1st Printing

Book design by Daniel Brount

To all my readers, from the AO3 days to where we are now.
The Adam and Olive cameo is for you. ❤

PROLOGUE

I N MY LIFE I HAVE EXPERIENCED REGRET, EMBARRASSMENT, maybe even a touch of agony. But nothing, absolutely *nothing* prepared me for the ignominy of finding myself in a bathroom stall, pressed against the arrogant older brother of the guy I've been pretending to date for the past six months.

It's an award-winning, rock-bottoming low. Especially when coupled with the knowledge that *Jack Smith* is saving *my* ass. When he picks me up by the waist to maneuver me around the cramped space, gravity-defyingly strong, I'm not sure what's worse: the fact that his hands are all that prevent me from crumpling like a scrunchie, or the mortifying amount of gratitude I feel toward him.

"Settle down, Elsie," he says against the skin of my cheek, terse as usual, but also incongruously soothing. He's close—too close. I'm close—too close. Not *nearly* close enough? The sweet oblivion of death. "And stop fidgeting."

"I'm *not* fidgeting, Jack," I say, fidgeting.

But after a second I just give in. I close my eyes. Relax into his chest. Feel the scent of him in my nostrils, anchoring me to sanity. And wonder which one, out of my millions of asinine life choices, led me to this moment.

1

WAVES AND PARTICLES

Twenty-four hours earlier

ALL THROUGHOUT MIDDLE SCHOOL, MY HALLOWEEN COS-
tume was the duality of light.

I made it with a marker, drawing a bunch of circles and zigzag lines all over one of Dad's white undershirts I'd rescued from the trash can. In hindsight, the production value was so low, not even the physics teacher managed to guess what it was. I never minded, though. I'd walk around the hallways hearing Bill Nye's voice in my head, his beautiful explanation of the ways light could be two different things at once, depending on what others wanted to see: a particle *and* a wave.

It seemed like a winning idea. And had me wondering if I, too, could contain two—no, a whole multitude of Elsies. Each one would be crafted, custom tailored, carefully curated with a different person in mind. I'd give everyone the me they wanted, needed, craved, and in exchange they'd care about me.

Easy peasy, photons squeezy.

Funny how my physics career and my people-pleasing career started around the same time. How I can draw a straight line from baby's first quantum mechanics concept to my current job. Actually, to *both* my current jobs. The day one, in which I earn next to nothing by hatching physical theories that explain why small molecules cluster together like cliques of mean girls during lunch hour. And the other one, in which . . .

Well. The other one, in which I pretend to be someone else, at least pays well.

"Uncle Paul will try to rope us into a threesome, again," Greg tells me, soulful brown eyes full of apologies, and I don't hesitate. I don't act annoyed. I don't shudder in revulsion thinking about Uncle Paul's sewage breath or his oily comb-over, which reminds me of pubic hair.

Okay, maybe I do shudder a little bit. But I cover it up with a smile and a professional "Got it."

"Also," he continues, running a hand through his messy curls, "Dad recently developed severe lactose intolerance but refuses to ease up on the dairy. There might be . . ."

"Gastrointestinal events." Understandable. I'd resist giving up cheese, too.

"And my cousin Izzy—she's known to become physically aggressive when people disagree with her over the literary value of the Twilight Saga."

I perk up. "Is she pro or against?"

"Against," Greg says darkly.

I love *Twilight* even more than cheese, but I can withhold my

TED Talk on why Alice and Bella should have left all those idiots behind and ridden off into the sunset.

Team Bellice 4evah.

"Understood."

"Elsie, I'm sorry. It's Grandma's ninetieth. The whole family will be here." He sighs, breath smoky white in the night air of this icy Boston January. "Mom's going to be at her worst."

"Don't worry." I ring the doorbell of Greg's grandmother's town house and offer my most encouraging smile. He hired me to be his fake girlfriend, and he'll get the Elsie he wants me to be: reassuring, yes, but also gently bossy. A dominatrix who doesn't like to wield a whip—but could if necessary. "Remember our exit strategy?"

"Pinch your elbow twice."

"I'll say I'm feeling poorly, and we'll duck out. And when the threesome offer comes, heavily imply that I have gonorrhea."

"That wouldn't deter Uncle Paul."

"Genital warts?"

"Mmm. Maybe?" He massages his temple. "The only good thing is that my brother's coming."

I tense. "Jack?"

"Yeah."

Stupid question. Greg only has the one. "I thought you said he'd be gone?"

"His work dinner got canceled."

I groan inwardly.

"What?"

Shit, I groaned outwardly. "Nothing." I grin and squeeze his arm through his coat. Greg Smith is my favorite client, and I will see him through this evening unscathed. "Let me handle your family, okay? It's what you pay me for, after all."

It really is. And I'm grateful every day that I've never had to remind him. Many of my clients wonder more or less openly what other services I might offer, even though the terms of service in the Faux app are pretty explicit. They clear their throat, stroke their chin, and ask, "What *exactly* is included in this . . . fake-girlfriend rate?" I'm often tempted to roll my eyes and knee them in the nuts, but I try to not take offense, to smile kindly, and to say, "*Not* sex."

I also—to answer the standard follow-up questions—don't kiss, frot, dirty talk, get naked, do butt stuff, give BJs, HJs, TJs, and whatever other Js might exist that I'm not aware of. I don't let them pee on me or fondle my feet, nor do I facilitate and/or allow orgasms in my general vicinity.

Not that there would be anything wrong: sex work is legitimate work, and people who engage in it are just as deserving of respect as ballerinas, or firefighters, or hedge fund managers. But ten months ago, when I graduated with a Ph.D. in theoretical physics from Northeastern, I figured that by now I'd have a reasonably remunerated academic position. I did *not* imagine that at twenty-seven I'd be paying my water bill by helping adult men pretend that they have dating lives. And yet here I am, fake-girlfriending my way through my student loans.

Not to kill anyone's buzz, but I'm starting to suspect that life might not always turn out the way you want. An unavoidable loss of faith: there are only so many times one can be hired to project the idea that a client is a charming, well-adjusted, emotionally available human being capable of holding on to a medium-term relationship with an equally high-functioning adult, in order to . . . Well, it varies. I've never asked Greg why Caroline Smith is so obsessed with the idea of her thirty-year-old son having a significant other. Based on snippets of overheard conversations within the Smith Cinematic

Universe, I suspect it has to do with the massive estate that will come into play once the matriarch dies, and with the belief that if he provided the first great-grandchild, he'd be more likely to inherit . . . a diamond-studded water hose, I assume?

Rich people. They're just like us.

But Greg's nosy mom is still much better than his brother, who's bad news for a whole bunch of reasons that do not bear contemplating. Frankly, it's a relief that *she* is my target. It means that when the front door of Smith Manor opens, I can focus solely on her: the withholding, PVC-hearted woman who manages to air-kiss us, fuss with Greg's hair, and push two full glasses of wine into our hands all at once.

"How's life in finance, Gregory?" Caroline asks her son. He downs half of his drink in a single gulp—I suspect because I've heard him explain that he does not, in fact, work in finance. At least four times. "And you, Elsie?" she adds without waiting for a reply. "How are things at the library?"

Following Faux's guidelines, I tell my clients nothing about myself—not my full name, not my day job, not my true opinions on cilantro (excellent, if you enjoy eating soap). And that, in a nutshell, is what fake-girlfriending is about. It initially seemed sketchy that people would pay for a fake date in the age of Tinder and Pornhub, and that they'd pay *me*—unremarkable Elsie Hannaway of the medium everything. Medium height. Medium-brown hair and eyes. Medium nose, butt, feet, legs, breasts. Pretty, yeah, sure, but in a medium, nondescript way. And yet, my medium mediumness is the perfect blank slate to fill. An empty canvas to paint on. A mirror, reflecting only what others care to project. A bolt of fabric that can be custom tailored to—well. I'm sure everyone's tracking the metaphor.

The Elsie that Caroline Smith wants is someone able to fit in with people who use *summer* as a verb, not flashy enough to attract a better catch than Greg, and with the nurturing instincts to take care of the son she might love but cannot be bothered to know. Children's librarian seemed like a great fake profession. It's been fun scouring online forums in search of charming anecdotes.

"Today I found three Goldfish crackers in our best copy of *Matilda*," I say with a smile. *Or at least, Reddit user iluvbigbooks did.*

"That is *hilarious*," Caroline says without laughing, smiling, or otherwise displaying amusement. Then she leans closer, whispering as though her son, who's a foot away, cannot hear us. "We are *so* glad that you're here, Elsie." *We,* I believe, includes Greg's dad, who stands silently next to her, popping three cubes of colby jack into his mouth with the vacant smile of someone who's been dissociating since 1999. "We were *so* worried about Gregory. But now he's with you, and he's never been happier." *Has he, though?* "Gregory, make sure to spend lots of quality time with your grandmother tonight. Izzy is taking pics with her Polaroid to give her at the end of the night—make sure you're in *all* of them."

"I'll make sure he is, Mrs. Smith," I promise, weaving my arm through Greg's. I break that promise fifteen seconds later, at the end of the glitzy hallway. He downs what's left of his wine, steals two large gulps of mine, and then stage-whispers "See you in ten minutes" before locking himself inside the bathroom.

I laugh and let him be. I feel protective of him—enough to break Faux standard protocol and agree to repeat fake dates, enough to want to defend him from muggers and pirates and his extended family. Maybe it's that his first sentence to me was a panicky "My mother won't stop asking why I don't date," followed by a hesitant, frazzled explanation of why *that* wasn't going to happen anytime soon—an explanation that hit too close to home. Maybe it's that he always looks like how I feel: tired and overwhelmed. In another timeline we'd be best friends, bonding over the unavoidable stress ulcers that will soon ravage the linings of our stomachs.

I find the empty kitchen, duck inside, and watch the red swirl down the drain as I pour what's left of my glass into the sink. A waste. I should have just refused it, but that would lead to questions, and I don't want to explain that alcohol is a dangerous, glycemic terrorist and that my struggling pancreas does *not* negotiate with—

"Not to your taste?"

I jump. And yelp. And almost drop the glass, which probably costs more than my graduate education.

I thought I was alone. Wasn't I alone? I *was* alone. But Greg's older brother is in the room, leaning against the marble counter, arms crossed over his chest. Those unique multicolored eyes of his are staring at me with the usual inscrutable expression. I'm standing between him and the only entrance—either I overlooked him, or he bent the space-time continuum.

Or I mixed him up with the refrigerator. They *are* similarly sized, after all.

"Are you okay?" he asks.

"I—yes. Yes, sorry. I just . . ." I force a smile. "Hi, Jack."

"Hi, Elsie." He says my name like it's familiar to him. The first word he ever learned. Second nature, and not just a bunch of vowels and consonants he's barely had reason to use before.

He doesn't smile, of course. Well, he *does* smile, but never at me. Whenever we're in the same room, he's an imposing, sky-soaring, stern presence whose main pastime appears to be judging me unworthy of Greg.

"Don't like the wine?"

"That's not it." I blink, flustered. There's a tattoo on his forearm, just peeking out of the rolled-up sleeve of his shirt. Because *of course* he's wearing jeans and a plaid shirt, even though the Evite specifically asked for semiformal.

But he's Jack Smith. He can do whatever he wants. He probably has a permit carved in those ridiculous biceps of his. Stamped on the blue quarter of his right eye, the one that sticks out like a sore thumb in the chestnut of his irises.

"The wine was great," I say, collecting myself. "But there was a fly in it."

"Was there?"

He doesn't believe me. I don't know how I know, but I know. And he knows that I know. I can see it, no—I can *feel* it. There's a tingle at the base of my spine, liquid and sparkly and warm. *Careful, Elsie,* it says. *He'll have you arrested for crimes against grapes. You'll spend the rest of your life in federal prison. He'll visit once a week to stare through the plexiglass and make you uncomfortable.*

"Izzy must be looking for you," I say, hoping to get rid of him. "She's upstairs."

"I know," he replies, *not* heading upstairs. He just studies me— attentive, calm, like he knows something secret about me. That I floss once a week, tops. That I can't figure out what the Dow Jones is, even after reading the Wikipedia entry. Other, scarier, *darker* things.

"Is your girlfriend here?" I ask to fill the silence. He once brought someone to a family thing. A geologist. The most beautiful woman I've ever seen. Nice. Funny, too. I wish I could say she was out of his league.

"No."

Silence, again. More staring. I smile to hide how aggressively I'm grinding my teeth. "It's been a while."

"Since Labor Day."

"Oh, right. I forgot."

I did not forget. Before today, I've met Jack twice, as in two times, one and then another, and they're both stubbornly wedged in my brain, as pleasant as spinach leaves stuck between molars.

The first was Greg's birthday dinner, when Jack and I shook hands and he nodded back at me tightly, when he spent the night giving me long, searching glances, when I overheard him ask Greg, "Where did you meet her?" and "How long has it been?" and "How serious is this?" with an inquisitive, deceptively casual tone that sent an odd shiver down my spine.

So Jack Smith wasn't a fan. Okay. Fine. Whatever.

And then there was the second. Late in the summer, at the Smiths' Labor Day pool party, where I didn't swim. Because there's no way to hide my pod in a bikini.

I'm not embarrassed to be diabetic. I've had nearly two decades to make peace with my overactive immune system, which has way too much fun destroying necessary cells. But people's reactions to the knowledge that I must pump insulin into my body on the reg can be unpredictable. When I was diagnosed (at ten, after a seizure in the school gym that earned me the cruel but uncreative nickname of Shaky Elsie), I overheard my parents chat, low whispers behind the hospital room's divider curtains.

"Not this, too." Mom sounded exhausted.

"I know." Dad sounded the same. "It's gotta be on us. Lance is flunking out of high school. Lucas is going to be arrested for fistfighting in the Walmart parking lot any day now. Of course the one easygoing kid we got turns out to have *something.*"

"It's not *her* fault."

"No."

"But it's going to be expensive."

"Yeah."

I don't blame my parents: my brother Lance *did* eventually flunk out of school (and now makes an excellent living as an electrician), just like Lucas *did* end up being arrested (albeit behind a Shake Shack, and for possession of drugs that are now legal). Mom and Dad were tired, overwhelmed. A little poor. They'd hoped for a break, something easy for once, and I was truly sorry I wasn't it. To make it up to them, I've tried to make my health issues—and any other subsequent issues—as ignorable as possible.

I find that people like me better if they don't have to expend emotional energy on me.

That's why I didn't swim at the Smith Labor Day party, opting to sit on a blanket and eat a slice of cake, an artfully arranged smile on my face. Why I miscalculated the carbs I ate and the insulin I'd need. And why I stumbled across the lawn of the Smiths' Manchester-by-the-Sea vacation home high on glucose, vision blurry, head pounding, trying to remember where I'd put my phone so that I could adjust my bolus, and—

I walked right into Jack.

Literally. I didn't see him and stepped into his chest like it was a supermassive black hole. Which it wasn't. A black hole, that is. Plenty supermassive, though.

"Elsie?" *Ugh.* His *voice.* "You okay?"

"Yeah. Yeah, I . . ." *Am going to puke.*

He cupped my cheek, scanning my face. "Should I call Greg?"

"No nee—" Pain knifed through my head.

"I'm calling Greg."

"No—*don't* call Greg, please."

He scowled. "Why?"

"Because—" *Because good fake girlfriends are low maintenance. They smile, don't have strong opinions on cilantro, and never, ever drag you away from a pool party.* "Can you—I need to go to the restroom and—my phone—"

A moment later I was in a bathroom that looked like a luxury spa, purse in my lap. And I'd love to say that I don't remember how I got there, but there's a floating memory in my head, a memory of strong arms picking me up; of being carried, buoyant as a bird; of warm breath on my temple, murmuring words I cannot recall.

And that, unfortunately, was that. Was Jack kind and helpful? Yup. Did he believe the story I later made up about not wanting to bother Greg with my migraines? Doubtful, considering his skeptical, cold, insistent look. Maybe he suspects I'm on drugs. Maybe he's afraid I'll taint the Smith line with my weak headache genes. *Surely* he believes his brother can do better.

But it doesn't matter. Jack's not my target—his mother is. Which is good, because I don't have the faintest idea who the Elsie that Jack wants is.

It's unprecedented. I'm a pro at picking up cues, but Jack—he gives me *nothing*. I don't know what to amp up, what to tone down; what to hide and what to fake; what personality to sacrifice at his altar. It's like he's trying to puzzle me out without changing me— and that's impossible. That's not how people are, not with me.

So when he asks "How have you been, Elsie?" with a tone that feels just a touch too inquisitive, I smile as neutrally as possible.

"The usual. Fantastic." *Not about to collapse on you, for once.* "You? How are things at work?" He's some kind of PE teacher, Greg mentioned. Unsurprising, since he's built like someone who has a CrossFit decal on his car and drinks protein shakes while reading

Men's Health's powerlifting column. The other Smiths are lithe, insubstantial brunettes. And then there's this sandy-haired brick house, a foot taller than his tallest relative, all masculine features and cutting deep voice. My theory: overworked nurse, hospital crib switch-up. "Having a good semester?"

He grunts, noncommittal. "Haven't murdered any of my students. Yet."

A surprisingly relatable sentiment. "Sounds like a win."

"Not to me."

Shit. He's making me smile. "Why do you want to murder them?"

"They whine. They don't read the syllabus." Syllabi for PE? My gym teacher's entire curriculum was shame-spiraling us for failing to climb the rope. Education's making strides. "They lie."

I swallow. "Lie about what?"

"About several things." His eyes gleam, and his lips twitch, and his shoulders hulk under his shirt and—

I used to think—no, I used to *know* that light-haired guys weren't attractive. Middle school? Everyone went after Legolas, but I was an Aragorn girl. "Which *Game of Thrones* House Are You" BuzzFeed quiz? Never a Targaryen. I hate that I look at Jack Smith, with his good jaw and his good dimples and those good hands, and find him handsome.

Maybe I just won't look. Yes, excellent plan.

"Excuse me," I say politely. "I bet Greg's looking for me." I turn before he can reply, immediately feeling like I managed to free myself from a gravitational singularity.

Phew.

The living room's a couple of twists and turns away, large but crowded, pretty despite the overabundance of naval paintings and aggressive leather furniture. I spend a few minutes reassuring Greg's aunt that we'll consult her before choosing a caterer for the wedding; pretending not to notice Uncle Paul licking his lips at me; amiably chatting with an assortment of cousins about the weather, traffic, and bad *Twilight* takes. The birthday girl is opening presents by the fireplace, telling one of her daughters-in-law, "A coupon for a mud bath? Lovely. It'll feel like practice for when I'm lowered in my grave and you all fight over my money."

It's on brand: the first time I met Millicent Smith, she put both hands on my shoulders and told me, "Having kids was the worst mistake of my life." Her eldest son was standing right next to her. I have yet to ascertain whether she is a malevolent hag or just unintentionally cruel. Either way, she's my favorite Smith character.

I wander away with a smile, winding up at the half-played Go board in the corner of the room. It's been here ever since my first visit, the wooden squares and porcelain stones incongruous amid the coastal decor. Greg is chatting with his dad, and I wonder if we'll leave soon. I have thirty-three Vibrations, Waves, and Optics essays to grade, which will surely have me wishing for a violent death. A Fundamentals of Materials Science Scantron exam to write. And, of course, a job talk to prepare. I want—no, I *need* to nail it. There's no margin of error, since it's my way out of spending my nights fake dating and my days exchanging emails with sexxxy.chad.420@ hotmail.com about whether his chinchilla's gluten allergy should release him from the Physics 101 midterm. I'll have to rehearse it a minimum of eleven times—i.e., the number of dimensions according to M-theory, my favorite über-string version—

"Do you play?"

I startle. *Again.* Jack stands on the other side of the board, dark eyes studying me. All his relatives are here—why is he wasting precious family time to pester his brother's fake girlfriend?

"Elsie?" My name, again. Said like the universe made that word for him alone. "I asked, do you play?" He sounds amused. I hate him.

"Oh. Um, a bit." Understatement. Go is mind twisting and punishingly intricate—therefore, many physicists' extracurricular activity of choice. "Do you?"

Jack doesn't answer. Instead he adds a few white stones.

"Oh, no." I shake my head. "It's someone else's game. We can't—"

"Black okay?"

Not really. But I swallow and hesitantly reach for the stones and set them down. My pride plays a nice little tug-of-war against my survival instincts: I won't conceal my Go skills and let Jack win, but for all I know losing will transform him into a fire-breathing bison and he'll incinerate a load-bearing wall. I don't want to die in a house collapse, next to Jack Smith and his threesome-obsessed uncle.

"How's Greg?" he asks.

"He's over there, with your cousin," I say absentmindedly, watching him place more stones. His hands are stupidly large. But also graceful, and it makes no sense. Also makes no sense? There are two chairs, but we're not sitting.

"But *how* is he?"

In my humble experience, siblings at best tolerate each other, and at worst spit gum in one another's hair. (Mine. *My* hair.) Jack and Greg, though, are close—for undivinable reasons, given that Greg's a likable human disaster full of Sturm und Drang, while Jack . . . I'm not sure what Jack's deal is. There's a dash of bad boy there, a hint of mystery, a dollop of smoothness. And yet a touch of hunger, a raw, unrefined air. Mostly, he looks *cool*. Too cool to even *be* cool. Like maybe in high school he skipped the school dance for a Guggenheim fellow's art exhibition and somehow still managed to get elected prom king.

Jack looks distant. Uninterested. Effortlessly confident. Charismatic in an intriguingly opaque, inaccessible way.

But he does care for Greg. And Greg cares for him. I heard him say, with my own two ears, that Jack is his "best friend," someone he "can trust." And I listened without pointing out that he can't really *trust* his *best friend* Jack that much, or he'd be honest with him about the fake dating—because I'm a supportive fake girlfriend.

"Greg's good. Why do you ask?"

"When we talked the other day he sounded stressed about Woodacre."

About . . . what? Is this something Greg's girlfriend should know? "Ah, yes," I fib. "A little."

"A little?"

I busy myself with the stones. I'm not winning as easily as I expected. "It's getting better." Everything does with time, right?

"Is it?"

"Very much." I nod enthusiastically.

He nods, too. Less enthusiastically. "Really?"

Jack's actually not *bad* at Go. How have I not wiped the floor with him yet? "Really."

"I thought Woodacre was in a couple of days. I figured Greg'd be upset."

I tense. Maybe I should have asked Greg for talking points. "Oh, yeah, true. Now that you mention it—"

"Remind me, Elsie." He takes a tiny step closer to the board, towering over me like a towering tower. But I'm not short. I *refuse* to feel short. "What's Woodacre, again?"

Crap. "It's"—I try for an amused expression—"Woodacre, of course."

Jack gives me a *Don't bullshit me* look. "That's not an answer, is it?"

"It's . . ." I clear my throat. "A thing Greg's working on." The extent of what I've been told about Greg's job? That he's a data scientist. "I don't know the details. It's complicated science stuff." I smile airily, as though I don't spend my life building complex mathematical models to uncover the origins of the universe. My heart hurts.

"Complicated science stuff." Jack studies me like he's peeling off my skin and expects to find a banana rotting inside.

"Yeah. People like you and I wouldn't understand."

He frowns. "People like you and I."

"Yeah. I mean." I hold his eyes and put down another stone. "What even *are* numbers—"

I snap my mouth shut. We must have reached for the same square. My fingers brush against Jack's, and something electric and unidentifiable licks up my arm. I wait for him to pull away, but he doesn't. Even though it was *my* turn. Wasn't it *my* turn? I'm pretty sure—

"Well, if it isn't a draw."

I yank back my hand. Millicent is next to me, staring at the board. I follow her gaze and nearly gasp, because . . . she's right.

I just *not*-thrashed Jack Freaking Smith at Go.

"It's been a long time since Jack hasn't won a game," Millicent says with a pleased smile.

It's been a long time since I haven't won a game. What the hell? I look up at Jack—still staring, still furrowing his brow, still judging me silently. My brain blanks. I panic and blurt out the first thing that comes to mind. "There are more legal board positions in Go than the atoms in the known universe."

A snort. "Someone's been telling me since he was barely out of diapers." Millicent glances shrewdly at Jack, who is *still. Staring. At. Me.* "You and Elsie make for a very good couple. Although, Jack, my dear, she should still sign a prenup."

I don't immediately understand what she's saying. Then I do and turn crimson all over. "Oh, no. Mrs. Smith, I'm—I'm dating Greg. Your *other* grandson."

"Are you sure?"

What? "I—yes. Of course."

"Didn't seem like it." She shrugs. "But what do I know? I'm a ninety-year-old bat who frolics in mud." I watch her shuffle toward the canapé table. Then I turn to Jack with a nervous laugh.

"Wow. That was—"

He's *still* staring. At me. Stone faced. Intent. Sectoral hetero-chromic. Like I'm interesting, very interesting, very, *very* interest-ing. I open my mouth to ask him what's going on. To demand a rematch to the death. To beg him to quit counting the pores in my nose. And that's when—

"Smile, guys!"

I whip my head around, and the flash of Izzy's Polaroid instantly blinds me.

"MY PARENTS' ANNIVERSARY NEXT MONTH SHOULD BE THE last time I need to take you along." Greg signals right and pulls into my building's parking lot. "After, I'll tell Mom you broke up with me. I begged you not to. Serenaded you. Bought you my weight in plushies—all in vain."

I nod sympathetically. "You're heartbroken. Too inconsolable to date someone else."

"I might need to find solace in a Spotify playlist."

"Or frost your tips."

He grimaces. I laugh, and once the car stops I lean against the passenger door to study his handsome profile in the yellow lights. "Tell her that I cheated on you with the Grubhub delivery guy. It'll buy you longer moping rights."

"Brilliant."

We're silent while I think about Greg's situation. The reason he even needs a fake girlfriend. What he felt comfortable telling *me*, a stranger, and not his own family. How similar we are. "After this is done, if you need . . . if you *want* someone to talk to. A friend. I'd love to . . ."

His smile is genuine. "Thanks, Elsie."

I'm barely out of the car. Ice crinkles under the heel of my boot as I turn around. "Oh, Greg?"

"Yes?"

"What's the Woodacre thing?"

He groans. His neck tips back against the headrest. "It's a silent meditation retreat our boss is forcing us to do. We're leaving tomorrow—four days of no contact with the outside world. No email, no Twitter. He got the idea from a Goop newsletter."

Oh. "So it has nothing to do with . . . complicated science?"

He gives me a desperate look. "The opposite. Why?"

"Ah . . ." I close my eyes. Let mortification sink its fangs into my brain. "No reason. Have a good night, Greg."

I close the passenger door, wave half-heartedly, and let the frigid air pop into my lungs. The North Star blinks at me from the sky, and I remember tomorrow's job interview.

It doesn't matter if tonight I made a fool of myself with Greg's punch-worthy brother. Because with just a sprinkle of luck, I might never have to see Jack Smith again.

2

NUCLEAR FISSION

From: sexxxy.chad.420@hotmail.com
Subject: Re: Re: Re: My chinchilla

Hey Doctor H.,

I understand you don't care about Chewie McChewerton's gluten allergy, but what about the fact that last night I got a DUI? Does that get me out of the Physics 101 midterm?

Sincerely,
Chad

From: McCormackE@umass.edu
Subject: can't come to class

pls find attached a pic of my vomit this morning

Emmett

. . . .

From: Dupont.Camilla@bu.edu
Subject: Merchant of Venice reflection paper

Dr Hannaday,

I was wondering if you could quickly give feedback on what
I wrote regarding the imagery of the lead casket. Please
find the word doc attached.

Sincerely,
Cam

. . . .

From: michellehannaway5@gmail.com
Subject: ELSIE CONTACT ME ASAP YOUR BROTHERS ARE
BEING UNREASONABLE AGAIN AND I NEED HELP I TRIED TO
CALL LAST NIGHT BUT NO ANSWER

[this email has no body]

. . . .

From: Monica.Salt@mit.edu
Subject: MIT Interview—Faculty Position

Dear Doctor Hannaway,

I wanted to say once again how excited I am that you'll be interviewing for a tenure track position in the physics department here at MIT. We are extremely impressed with your CV, and have narrowed down our choice to you and another candidate. The search committee and I are looking forward to getting to know you informally tonight, at dinner at Miel, before your on-campus interview starts tomorrow.

If that's okay with you, I'd like for the two of us to meet alone a few minutes before the dinner at Miel to chat a bit. There are a few things I'd like to explain.

Best,
Monica Salt, Ph.D.
A.M. Wentworth Professor of Physics
Department of Physics, Chair
MIT

My heart sparks with excitement.

I set my tea on the kitchen table and click Reply, to assure Monica Salt that yes, absolutely, *of course*: I will meet her whenever and wherever she wants, including the plains of Mordor at two fifteen a.m., because she holds the key to my future. But the second my hand closes around the mouse, excruciating pain stabs my palm and shoots up my arm.

I screech and jump out of my chair. "What the fu—?"

"Where are they? *Where are they?*" My roommate staggers into the kitchen, wearing onesie pajamas and a Noam Chomsky sleep mask pulled up to her forehead. Also: swinging a plastic baseball bat like a madwoman. "Leave now or I'll call 911! This is trespassing!"

"Cece—"

"A misdemeanor *and* a felony! You will be arrested for battery! My cousin is taking the bar this year, and she will sue you for *millions* of dollars—"

"Cece, no one's in here."

"Oh." She windmills the bat a few more times, blinking owlishly. "Why are we screaming, then?"

"The fact that your porcupine decided to impersonate my mouse *might* be related."

"Hedgehog—you know she's a hedgehog."

"Do I."

She yawns, tossing the bat back into her room. It misses, bouncing emptily across the chipped linoleum floor. "Smaller. Cuter. Quillier. Also, Hedgizabeth Bennet? Not a porcupine name."

"Right. Sorry." I cradle my hand to my chest. "The searing pain had me a tad out of sorts."

"It's okay. Hedgie's a kind soul—she forgives you." Cece picks her up. "Do you? Do you forgive Elsie for misspeciesing you, baby?"

I glare at Hedgie, who stares back with beady, triumphant eyes. That malignant sentient pincushion. *I'm going to fry you up with scallions*, I mouth.

I swear to God, her spines puff up a little.

"Where were you last night?" Cece asks, blessedly unaware of our interspecies war. I wonder what it says of me that my best friend's best friend is a hedgehog. "Faux? That Greg guy?"

"Yup."

"How'd it go?"

"Good." I suddenly recall *not* crushing Jack Smith like an egg. "Well, fine. Yours?"

Cece and I got into fake dating during the financial and emotional dark ages of our lives: graduate school. I was down to two pairs of non-mismatched socks, living off computational cosmology theorems and instant ramen. In hindsight, I was perilously close to developing scurvy. Then, on a dark and stormy night, as I contemplated selling a heart valve, my former friend J.J. texted me a link to Faux's recruitment page. The caption was a laughing emoji, the one with tears shooting out of the eyes, and a simple Check this out! It's like that thing we did in college.

I frowned, like I often do when reminded of J.J.'s existence, and never replied. But I did notice that the hourly rates were high. And in between TA'ing Multivariable Calculus, forming an opinion on loop quantum gravity, and trying not to punch my all-male fellow grads for constantly assuming that *I* should be the one making *their* coffee, I found myself making a profile. Then interviewing. Then being matched with my first client—a dorky twenty-year-old who gave me a pleading look and asked, "Can you pretend to be my age? And Canadian? We met in eighth grade at summer camp, and your name is Klarissa, with a *K*. Also, if anyone asks, I am *not* a virgin."

"Are they likely to ask?"

He considered it. "If they don't, could you casually bring it up?"

It turned out not to be *that* bad, so I asked Cece if she wanted to try it, too. I swear I don't secretly hate her. It was just the only thing I could think of upon realizing that we'd both made the stupidest of career choices (i.e., academia). We're overeducated and too poor to survive—as evidenced by our crappy apartment, full of exposed wiring and scary spiders that look like the love children of murder hornets and coconut crabs. If we had a sitcom-like group of friends, we'd hold an asbestos-removal party. Sadly, it's just us. And the barely avoided scurvy.

"So." She steals my tea mug and hops on the counter. I let her: no need for caffeine after the sheer agony of a thousand needles. "They sent me to this guy."

"What's his deal?" Meaning: *What deep-seated, soul-scorching trauma dragged this poor sap out of the primordial swamp and made him shell out wads of cash to pretend he's not alone?*

"He's one of yours."

"Of mine?"

"A scientist."

Cece is a linguist, finishing up her Ph.D. at Harvard. We first met when her former roommate moved out: apparently, Hedgie had chewed her way through his boxer briefs. Also apparently: blasting "Immigrant Song" while making poached eggs on Saturday mornings is not something normal people put up with. Cece was desperate for someone to help with rent. I felt as if I'd just been skinned alive, and was desperate not to be living with J.J. Two desperate souls, who found each other in desperate times and desperately bonded—over the fact that I could scrape together seven hundred dollars a month, was not attached to my underwear, and owned a set of noise-canceling headphones.

Frankly, I lucked out. Roommate feuds are a pain, what with the passive-aggressive notes and the aggressive-aggressive Windex poisoning. I was ready to bend, twist, and carve my personality a million different ways to get along with Cece. As it turns out, the Elsie that Cece wants is conveniently close to the Elsie I am: someone who'll companionably pig out on cheese while she complains about academia; who, like her, *chooses* to use children's Tylenol because it tastes like grape. I do have to fake an appreciation for avant-garde cinema, but it's still a surprisingly relaxing friendship.

"What kind of scientist is he?"

"Is there more than one kind?"

I smile.

"Chemist. Or engineer? He was . . . handsome. Funny. He made a joke about mulch. My first mulch joke. Popped my mulch cherry." Her tone is vaguely dreamy. "He just . . . seems like someone you'd *want* to date, you know?"

"*I'd* want to date?"

"Well"—she waves her hand—"not *you* you. You'd rather walk into the sea with stones in your pockets than date—though that's because of your basic misconception that human romantic relationships can only succeed if you hide and shape yourself into what you think *others* want you to be—"

"Not a misconception."

"—but other people would *not* ban Kirk from their chambers."

"Kirk, huh?"

I initially feared that Cece would abysmally fail at fake-girlfriending. For one, she's way too beautiful. Her wide-apart eyes, pointy chin, and Cupid's-bowy lips might be unconventional, but she looks like the sexiest, most stunning bug in the universe. Secondly: she's the opposite of a blank slate. A thing of nature who pees with the door open and eats Chex Mix as cereal, full of lurid anecdotes about dead linguists' sex lives doled out with a charming lisp. I barely let any of my personality come through, but she *bombards* people.

And it did turn out to be a problem: clients like her way too much.

"What do you tell them when they ask you to date for real?" she asked me one night. We were splitting a bag of Babybels while watching a Russian silent movie in eight parts.

"Not sure." I wondered if the guy who offered me seventy bucks to have sex in his nearby parked car qualified. Probably not. "It's never happened."

"Wait—really?"

"Nope." I shrugged. "No one ever asks me out, really."

"No way."

I let the cheese melt in my mouth. On-screen, someone had been sobbing for twenty-five minutes. "I don't think people see me as dating material."

"They're intimidated. Because you're a genius. And pretty. And nice. Hedgie loves you, and she's the best judge of character. Also, you know *lots* about the Tadpole Galaxy."

Fact-check: none of this is true—except for the last bit. Sadly, listing random facts about star clusters four hundred million light-years away is not considered love interest material.

"Kirk the Scientist asked if he could hire me again," Cece says now. "Next week. I said yes."

I try to sound casual. "Faux has a one-date policy."

"I know. But you broke it, too, for Greg." She shrugs, trying to look casual. Lots of casual going on. Hmm. "Of course, I might cancel, since by next week you'll have your fancy MIT job, and I shall retire from the fake-dating scene to become your kept BFF."

I sit back in my chair and—I want it bad, *so bad*, I moan. My way out of fake-girlfriending. Above all, my way out of the crappiest, lamest circle of academia: the one of adjunct professors.

I know that I sound dramatic. I know that the title conjures lofty images. *Professor*? Has prestige, nurtures minds, wears tweed jackets. *Adjunct*? Pretty word, starts with the first letter of the alphabet, reminds one faintly of a sneeze. When I tell people that I'm an adjunct professor of physics at several Boston universities, they think that I made it in life. That I'm adulting. And I let them. Take my mom: she has lots to worry about, between my idiot brother and my other idiot brother. It's good for her to believe that her daughter is a fully operational human being with access to basic healthcare.

Not good for her? To know that I teach nine courses and commute between three different universities, translating into some five hundred students sending me pics of the weird rash on their crotch to get their absence excused. That I make so little money, it's almost *no* money. That I have no long-term contract or benefits.

Cue mournful violin sonata.

It's not that I don't like teaching. It's just that . . . I *really* dislike teaching. Really, really, *really*. I'm constantly drowning in the ever-swallowing quicksand of student emails, and I'm way too screwed up to shape young minds into anything that's not aberrant. My dreams of physics academia always entailed me as a full-time researcher, a blackboard, and long hours spent pondering the theories on the equatorial sections of Schwarzschild wormholes.

And yet here I am. Adjuncting and fake-girlfriending on the side. Teaching load: 100 percent. Despair load: incalculable.

But things might be turning around. Adjuncts are cheap labor, the gig workers of academia, but tenure-track positions . . . oh, tenure tracks. I shiver just thinking about them. If adjuncts float like buoys in the open sea, tenure tracks are oil rigs cemented into the ocean floor. If adjuncts open Nickelback concerts, tenure tracks headline Coachella. If adjuncts are Laughing Cow wedges, tenure tracks are pule cheese, lovingly made from the milk of Serbian Balkan donkeys.

Point is, I've been academia's disposable fake girlfriend for a while now, and I'm exhausted. I'm all done. I'm ready to graduate to a real relationship, ideally something lasting with MIT—who'll put a 401(k) and a ring on it.

Unless they choose the other physicist they're interviewing. Oh God. What if they choose the other physicist they're interviewing?

"Elsie? Are you thinking about whether they'll hire the other candidate?"

"Don't read my mind, please."

Cece laughs. "Listen—they won't. You're the shit. All those years in grad school spent thinking about multiverses and binomial equations and . . . protons?" I lift my eyebrow. "Fine, I have no idea what you do. But you forsook a social life—and oftentimes personal hygiene—to *elevate* yourself above the sea of mediocre white men that is theoretical physics. And now—one job opening this year, *one*, and out of hundreds of applicants, you're in the final round—"

"*Two* job openings. I didn't get an interview for Duke—"

"Because Duke's a nepotistic swamp and the position was already earmarked for the chair's cousin's son's girlfriend's llama, or whatever." She hops off the counter and sits across from me, reaching out to cup my hand. "You're going to get the job. I know it. Just be yourself during the interview." She bites her lip. "Unless you can be Stephen Hawking. Is there any way you could—"

"No."

"Then yourself will do." She smiles. "Think of the future. Of your livable salary, which will allow us to hire some brawny lad to come lift the *top* part of the credenza onto the *bottom* part of the credenza." She points at the hutch in the corner of the living room. Cece and I hit a wall mid-assembly. Three years ago. "And of course it will keep me in the cheese lifestyle I am accustomed to."

It's easy, with Cece, to smile and let myself believe. "Unlimited pecorino romano."

"And all the insulin your worthless pancreas desires."

"Concrete bricks. To squash the Raid-resistant crab-hornet spiders."

"A little plasma TV for Hedgie's terrarium."

"Matching 'academia sux' tattoos."

"A golden toilet."

"A golden *bidet*."

We gasp. Then laugh. Then I sober up. "I just want to be paid to contemplate cosmological models of the observable universe, you know?"

"I know." Her smile softens. "What does Dr. L. say about your chances?"

Laurendeau—or Dr. L., as I'd never dare to call him to his face—was my Ph.D. advisor and is the person to whom I owe every single bit of my academic success. He's just as involved in my career as he was before I graduated, and I'm constantly thankful for it. "Optimistic."

"There you go. How many days is the interview going to be?"

"Three."

"You start today?"

"Yup. Informal interview dinner tonight." I think about the chair wanting to meet me early. Is it promising? Inauspicious? Weird? No clue. "Teaching demonstration tomorrow. Research talk and a final reception the day after. Various meetings with faculty members scattered throughout."

"Did you prep?"

"Is 'prep' rocking myself? Contemplating my own mortality? Sacrificing a live creature to the gods of academia?" I glance at Hedgie, who looks dutifully cowed.

"Have you stalked the search committee online?"

"I haven't been given their names or a detailed itinerary yet. It's just as well—I need to answer emails. And buy pantyhose. And call my mom."

"No, no, no." Cece lifts her hand. "Do *not* call your mom. She'll just dump all her problems on you. You need to focus, not listen to her bitch about how your brothers are punching each other over the last hot dog."

"Woman—they're considering fratricide over a woman." The Hannaways: prime *Jerry Springer* material.

"Doesn't matter. Promise me that if your mom calls, you'll tell her about the interview. And that your childhood was mediocre, at best."

I mull it over. "How about I promise to avoid her for a few days?"

She squints. "Fine. So you're going out for the pantyhose?"

"Yup."

"Can you stop by the store to get me cereal?"

I don't really have time for that. But what doesn't kill you makes you stronger. Or makes you resent your pathological inability to set boundaries, one of the two. "Sure. What kind—"

"No!" She slaps her hand on the table. "Elsie, you have to learn to say *no*."

I massage my temple. "Will you please stop testing me?"

"I'll stop when *you* stop putting others' needs in front of yours." She sets down her—*my*—empty mug and picks up Hedgie. "Gotta pee. You still want to borrow my red dress for tonight?"

I frown. "I never asked to borrow your—"

"And I'll also do your makeup, if you insist."

"I really don't need—"

"Fine, you win—I'll pluck your eyebrows, too." Cece winks. Hedgie glares, parrot-perched on her shoulder. The bathroom door closes after them.

The clock on the wall says six forty-five. I sigh and allow myself a small indulgence: I double-click on the Word doc on the upper left corner of my screen. I scroll to the bottom of the half-written manuscript, then back to the top. The title, *A Unified Theory of Two-Dimensional Liquid Crystal*, waves wistfully at me. For a handful of seconds I let my imagination run to a near future, one in which I'm able to set aside time to complete it. Maybe even submit it.

I sigh deeply as I close it. Then I self-consciously trace my eyebrows and go back to answering emails.

ACADEMIC JOB INTERVIEWS ARE FAMOUSLY OPTIMIZED TO ENsure the candidate's maximum suffering. So I'm not surprised when I get to Miel and find out that it's a multi-fork, Lego-portioned, *May I recommend a 1934 sauvignon blanc* type of restaurant.

I observe a minute of silence for the expensive, excellent cheese I'll order but not enjoy while busy hustling for my future—bleu d'Auvergne; brie; camembert (significantly different from brie, despite what the heathens say). Then I step into the restaurant, newborn-calf wobbly on my high heels.

There were no pantyhose at the store, which means that I'm wearing thigh highs—a fitting tribute to the burlesque that is my life. I'm also 56 percent sure that I shouldn't have let Cece talk me into her crimson-red sheath dress or her cardinal-red lipstick or her lava-red nail polish.

"You look like Taylor Swift circa 2013," she told me, pleased, finishing side-curling my hair.

"I was aiming more for AOC circa 2020."

"Yeah." She sighed. "We all were."

I reach for my phone. Under the inexplicably vulva-shaped cracks on the screen—the iTwat, Cece calls it—I find a last-minute email from my advisor:

> You'll make a fantastic impression. Remember: more than any other candidate, you are *entitled* to this position.

His trust is like a hand on my shoulder: reassuringly warm and uncomfortably heavy. I shouldn't be this nervous. Not because I've got the job in the bag—I've got *nothing* in the bag, except death, federal student loans repayment, and three-year-old Mentos crusted in lint. What I *do* have is lots of practice showing people that I am who they want me to be, and that's what interviewing is all about. I once convincingly played a lovesick ballerina, kneeling in the middle of a crowded restaurant to propose to a balding middle-aged man who smelled like feet—just so he could refuse me in front of his work archrival. I should be able to convince a handful of MIT professors that I'm a decent physicist. Right?

I don't know. Maybe. I think so. Yeah.

I'll just focus on the fake-girlfriending protocol. APE, Cece and I call it. (Well, *I* call it APE. Cece just shakes her head and asks, "What's wrong with scientists? Were you all, like, bullied in high school?") First, *assess* the need: What is it that the person in front of me wants to see? Then, *plan* a response: How can I become what they want? And lastly, *enact*—

"Dr. Hannaway?"

I turn around. A dark-haired woman studies me as I mentally rehearse how to human. "Dr. Salt?"

Her handshake is strong. Businesslike. "It is nice to meet you in person."

"Likewise."

"Come—let's go to the bar."

I follow her, a little starstruck. Dr. Monica Salt wrote the text-book on theoretical physics—literally. *The Salt* has been sitting tight on my shelf for over a decade. Nine hundred pages of excellent content. Bonus: it squashes the hornet-crab spiders like a dream.

"Dr. Hannaway?" She sounds assertive. Charismatic. Badass. Like I wish I felt.

"Elsie, please."

"Monica, then. I'm happy you applied for the position. When I saw your CV, I thought for sure some other university would have snatched you up by now."

I smile, noncommittal. *Yep, that's me. Beating off job offers with a stick.*

"Your dissertation on liquid crystals' static distortions in biaxial nematics was brilliant, Elsie."

I feel myself flush. Sex does nothing for me, but maybe this is my kink: being complimented by leading scholars in my field. Hot, huh? "You're too kind."

"I can hardly believe how much your work has already affected our understanding of non-equilibrium systems and macroscopic coherent motion. Liquid crystals are a hot topic in theoretical phys-ics, and you've positioned yourself as an expert."

I am thoroughly flattered. Well, almost thoroughly: there is some-thing in her tone that has me on edge. Something odd. Nudging.

"Your discoveries are going to have long-ranging impact on many fields, from displays to optical imaging to drug delivery. Truly impressive."

Like maybe there's a *but*?

"I cannot overstate how impressed I am with the scientific out-put you've produced in such a short period."

There's definitely a *but*.

"You'll be an asset to whatever institution you choose, and MIT would be the perfect home for you. I want to be honest and admit that based on what I have seen, *you* should be the person we hire."

... But?

"But."

I knew it. I knew it. I *knew* it, but my heart drops to the bottom of my stomach anyway.

"Elsie, I asked you to meet alone because I feel that it would be better if you knew about the . . . politics that are currently at play."

"Politics?" I shouldn't be surprised. STEM academia is 98 percent politics and 1 percent science (the rest, I suspect, "I Should Be Writing" memes). "What do you mean?"

"You might have several job offers, and I want to make sure that you choose us despite . . . whatever might happen during your interview."

I frown. "Whatever might happen?"

She sighs. "As you know, in the past few years there has been some . . . some acrimony, between theoretical and experimental physicists."

I hold back a snort. *Acrimony* is a nice ten-dollar word to say that if the Purge were announced at this very moment, three-quarters of the world's experimentalists would ring the theorists' doorbells with their freshly sharpened machetes. Of course it would all be in vain: they'd find the theorists long gone, already swinging their scimitars in the experimentalists' front yards.

Yes, in this much-visited scenario of mine, we theorists have the cooler weapons.

We're just different breeds. Apples and oranges. Dwarves and elves. Cool scientists and less-cool scientists. We theorists use math, construct models, explain the whys and hows of nature. We are *thinkers*. Experimentalists . . . well, they like to fuck around and find out. Build things and get their hands dirty. Like engineers. Or three-year-olds at the sandbox.

Theorists think they're smarter (spoiler alert: we are), and experimentalists think they're more useful (re-spoiler re-alert: they are *not*). It makes for some . . . Yeah. Acrimony.

Monica, thank the universe and the subatomic particles it's made of, is a theorist. We exchange a long, loaded, understanding look. "I am aware," I say.

"Good. And you might have heard that Jonathan Smith-Turner has recently joined MIT?"

I stiffen. "I had not."

"But you *are* familiar with Jonathan Smith-Turner. And with his . . . article."

It's not a question. Monica is wise and fully aware that there is no dimension, no parallel universe, no hypothetical self-contained plane of existence in which a theoretical physicist wouldn't know who he is.

Because Jonathan Smith-Turner is an experimentalist—no, *the* experimentalist. And several years ago, when I was in middle school and he was probably a grown-ass man who should have known better, he did something horrible. Something unforgivable. Something abominable.

He made theoretical physicists look dumb.

Driven by what I can only assume was bitterness, an overabundance of free time, and involuntary celibacy, he set out to prove to the world that . . . actually, I don't know what he wanted to prove. But he wrote a scientific article on quantum mechanics that was just full enough of jargon and math to sound like it was written by a theorist.

Except that the article was completely made up. Bogus. A parody, if you will. That turned into a prank when he submitted it to *Annals of Theoretical Physics*, our most prestigious journal, and waited. Rubbing his hands together evilly, one can only assume.

And that's where things went wrong. Because despite undergoing supposedly rigorous peer review, the article was accepted. And published. And it stayed published for several weeks, or at least until shit hit the fan—in the form of a blog post by someone likely affiliated with Smith-Turner, back in the olden times when blogging was a thing.

"Is Theoretical Physics Pseudoscience?" had been the title. The post, which detailed how Smith-Turner had gotten a bunch of nonsense published in the most respected theory journal, was even worse. "Has the field of physics lost its way? . . . Is it all made up?" And my personal favorite: "If theoretical physics is gibberish, is it fair to compensate theorists with federal tax money?"

I'm not being needlessly dramatic when I say that it was a whole thing. On Facebook. On the news, including *60 Minutes*. Even Oprah talked about it—the Jonathan Smith-Turner Affair, the Theoretical Hoax, the Physics Scandal. Einstein rolled in his grave. Newton puked up his apple. Feynman quietly stepped in a tank of liquid helium. Young Elsie, who in her early teens already knew what she wanted to be when she grew up, seethed and growled and boycotted all coverage of the topic, declaring a ban on all media in the Hannaway household. (The ban was unheeded, as the Hannaway household tended to forget young Elsie existed; her parents were probably too busy trying to stop her brothers from egging the neighbor's shed.)

Mainstream interest blew over soon enough. *Annals of Theoretical Physics* pulled the article and apologized for the oversight, a bunch of theorists in improbable sweaters and spray-on hair took to

YouTube to defend their honor, and Jonathan Smith-Turner never spoke publicly on the matter. Thankfully, the amount of mental energy normies like to expend on physics is limited.

But the hoax was a humiliating, devastating blow, and the field never quite recovered—all because of a stupid prank. Over a decade later, theoretical physics funding has been slashed. Theory job openings are decimated. The running joke is still that theoretical physics is akin to creative writing, books have been written on how theorists are exploitative wackjobs, and Google's main autofills for *theoretical physics* are: *Not real science. Nonsense. Dead.*

(Slanderous. Google is slanderous and we should all switch to Bing.)

And yet it gets even worse—for two reasons that make all of this personal to me. First, one of the major downfalls of the article was that the theoretical physics community, needing to save face, quickly found a scapegoat: they formally censured the chief editor of *Annals*—the academic version of pushing someone into a paddle cactus bed and leaving them for dead.

That editor was Christophe Laurendeau—my mentor.

Yup.

The second reason is that, regrettably, Smith-Turner and I operate in the same subfield of physics. Our work on liquid crystals partially overlaps, and I occasionally wonder if that's reason enough for me to switch to some other topic. Black holes? Lattices? Quantum supremacy? I'm still debating. In the meantime, I've been on a boycott. For years I've refused to care about what Jonathan Smith-Turner is doing—I've refused to read his papers, to acknowledge his existence, to even mention his name.

In hindsight, I probably should have kept tabs.

"Naturally," Monica is saying, "Jonathan is a talented experimentalist and an asset to the department. He joined us last year—moved from Caltech with sizable grants to lead the MIT Physics Institute. We're lucky to have him." Her expression makes it abundantly clear she believes no such thing. "The position you're interviewing for is a joint one. Half of your salary will be paid by my department, half from the Physics Institute. Which is headed by Jonathan. Who, in turn, strongly favors the other candidate we are interviewing." Monica sighs. "I cannot tell you who the other candidate is, for obvious reasons."

My fingers tighten around the glass. "The other candidate is an experimentalist, I assume."

"Yes. And a previous collaborator of Jonathan's."

I close my eyes, and it sinks into me that—*shit.*

This interview, it's a pissing contest. Theorists vs. experimentalists. Physics Department vs. Physics Institute. Monica vs. Jonathan.

Hiring Committee: Civil War.

"If I get the job, would Jonathan Smith-Turner be my superior?" There may be a limit to what I'm willing to compromise for protected research time, health insurance, and bottomless cheese-purchasing power.

Monica shakes her head energetically. "Not in any meaningful way."

"I see." Relief warms my belly. Very well. "Thank you for being straightforward with me. I'll be equally straightforward: Is there anything I can do to be chosen over the other candidate?"

She studies me, serious for a moment. Then her face breaks into a fierce grin, and that—*that* is my tell. That's how I know who the *me* Monica wants is: a champion. Her tribute to the Hunger Games of physics. A gladiator to take on Jonathan Smith-Turner, the entitled STEMlord she despises.

Well, I can do that. Because I happen to despise the very same guy.

"This is what you need to know, Elsie: most of the faculty members you'll meet during the interview—including Jonathan—have already decided which candidate they'll recommend for hire, based on whether they prefer a theorist or an experimentalist. They already know whether they'll vote for you or for George, and there isn't much we can do to change their minds."

My eyebrow arches before I can yank it down. I don't think Monica meant to let slip that Jonathan Smith-Turner's candidate's name is George, but I'm the diametrical opposite of surprised. *Of course* he'd want to hire a man.

"But," she continues, "there are a handful of professors who straddle the line between theoretical and experimental. Drs. Ikagawa, Alvarez, Voight. They're part of Volkov's research team and follow where he leads. Which means that Volkov is going to be the deciding vote. My advice is, talk to him during the dead times of your interview. If possible, tailor your presentations to suit his interests. And . . . I don't know that Jonathan might try to give his candidate an advantage and make you look bad, but . . . be wary of him. Be very careful."

I nod slowly. And then I nod again, inhaling deeply, untangling my overwhelmed thoughts.

Yes, academic interviews are optimized to ensure the candidate's maximum suffering—but this is situation-room-level politicking, more than I prepared for. I'm a simple girl. With simple needs. All I want is to spend my days solving hydrodynamic equations to calculate the large-scale spatiotemporal chaos exhibited by dry active nematics. And maybe, if possible, buy life-compatible levels of pancreatic hormones at reasonable prices.

But—I bite my lower lip, thinking quickly—maybe I *can* do this.

I'm a great physicist, a pro at giving others what they want, and once I get this job, it'll be just me and my science. And being selected over Smith-Turner's candidate? It'd be like avenging Dr. L. and theoretical physics, even just a little. What a lovely, heartwarming thought.

"Okay," I tell Monica. I met her all of ten minutes ago, but we're looking at each other like lifelong allies. That accelerated camaraderie that comes from plotting a murder together. Jonathan Smith-Turner's, of course. "I can do that."

She's pleased. "I know this is unorthodox. But you're the ideal candidate. What's best for the department."

"Thank you." I smile, projecting self-assurance I don't quite feel. "I won't let you down."

She smiles back, at once warm and steely. "Very well. Let's go. The rest of the search committee should be here." I follow her to the entrance, head spinning with new information, trying not to walk like a T. rex. "Ah, there they all are."

The people nestled in the waiting area are, it pains me to say, embarrassingly easy to identify as physicists. It's not the cargo pants or the sweater vests or the widespread uncombable hair syndrome. Not the eyeglass chains, worn unironically. It's not even that they're all men, in line with the hyperabundance of dudes in my field.

It's that they're having a physics pun-off.

"What's the best book on quantum gravity?" an elderly gentleman in transition lenses is asking. He looks like a benign version of the Penguin from *Batman*. "The one that's impossible to put down! Get it?"

The laughter that follows sounds genuine. Ah, my people.

"Everyone." Monica clears her throat. "This is Dr. Elsie Hannaway. So pleased that she's joining us tonight."

I smile warmly, feeling like I'm auditioning for a reality show.

Academia's Got Talent. Dancing with the Profs. The Bachelor (of Science). I'm greeted by the hesitant, awkward handshakes of those who feel more at home staring at a whiteboard than exchanging physical contact, but I don't hold it against them. I'm the same; I've just learned to hide it a bit better.

Several faculty members are familiar to me, both theorists and experimentalists, some just by name, others from conferences and guest lectures. Penguin turns out to be Sasha Volkov, and he gets a wider smile than the others. "I am a fan of your articles on dark matter," I say. It's not a lie—Volkov's a big deal. I'm familiar enough with his work to kiss his ass a bit. "I'd love to chat about—"

"Dr. Hannaway," he interrupts me, all sharp consonants and round belly, "I have a very important question."

Oh? "Of course."

"Do you know what the formula for a velociraptor is?"

I scowl. The *what*, now? Is he *quizzing* me on something? The formula for the—*oh.*

Oh, right.

I clear my throat. "Is it, by any chance, um, a distanceraptor divided by a timeraptor?"

He regards me icily for a second. Then he breaks into a slow, pleased, belly-deep laugh. "This one"—he points at me, glancing at Monica—"I like this one. Good sense of humor!"

Clearly, the Elsie that Volkov wants doles out physics dad jokes. I'll have to build a repertoire.

"I think we're all here. We should head for the table—oh." Monica stops, staring at someplace high behind my shoulder. Her expression hardens. "There are Jonathan and Andrea. Better late than never."

I take a deep breath, bracing myself for this meeting. I can be nice to Jonathan Smith-Turner. I can be polite to this waste of academic space. And I can make him cry by getting this job.

My eyes hold Monica's for a fraction of a second, a silent promise, and then I turn around, ready to be perfectly pleasant, ready to shake the asswipe's hand without saying *Yikes* or *I hate you* or *Thank you for ruining physics for us, dick.*

And then I stop.

Because the person who just came in—

The person standing in the entrance of the restaurant, snowflakes melting in his light hair—

The person unbuttoning his North Face coat—

—is none other than Jack Smith.

3

CHAIN REACTION

BLINK STUPIDLY—ONE, TWO, SEVEN TIMES.

Then I blink again, for good measure.

Why is Jack here, brushing snow off his parka, shrinking the entrance to half its size with his overgrown shoulders? Is it keto night at Miel? Did he get lost on his way to a calisthenics convention?

I'm debating whether to ignore him or briefly wave at him when Monica says, "You're late." She sounds chiding. And she looks a lot like she's talking to Jack, who checks his wristwatch (a wristwatch, in *this* year of our lord) and calmly replies, "I was in the lab. Must have lost track of time."

"I had to pry him off the optical tweezers," the blonde next to him—Andrea?—butts in.

Monica all but rolls her eyes. I glance back and forth between them, disoriented. Does Jack know Monica? Are they SoulCycle buddies? What's he late for?

"Since you're finally gracing us with your presence, this is Dr. Elsie Hannaway, one of the candidates for the faculty position. Elsie, this is Dr. Andrea Albritton, an associate professor in the department. And Dr. Jonathan Smith-Turner, the head of the MIT Physics Institute."

I almost look around. I almost scan the restaurant in search of the elusive Jonathan Smith-Turner. But then I don't, because Jack is staring down at me, looking exactly how I feel.

Confused. Puzzled. Concerned for Monica's mental health.

"You've got it wrong," he tells her with that good voice he has, shaking his head, amused. "Elsie's not a . . ."

He trails off, and his demeanor switches: the amusement dissolves. Something twitches in his ridiculous superhero jaw. The frown between his eyes deepens into a W—for *What the everloving fuck?* I can only assume.

Jack Smith's always stubbornly, peculiarly unreadable, but right now I can safely guess that he's *pissed.* He wants to curse me. Slaughter me. Feast on the tender marrow of my bones.

Though he does none of that. His expression switches again, this time to a polite blank as he offers his hand. I have no choice but to shake it.

"Dr. Hannaway," he says, voice rich and disturbingly familiar. His skin is Boston-in-January-with-no-gloves cold. Calloused. Scary. "Thank you for your interest in MIT."

"Dr. Turner," I manage around the catch in my throat.

"Smith-Turner." The correction is a punch in the sternum. This can't be. Jack Smith and Jonathan Smith-Turner *cannot* be—

"But call me Jack."

—the same person.

"Dr. Hannaway goes by Elsie, *Jonathan*," Monica says archly.

Jack ignores her tone. "Elsie," he says, like he's trying it out for the first time. Like he didn't use my name just last night, over the sole game of Go I haven't won in years.

Shit.

I wait for one of us to acknowledge that we already know each other—in vain. My mouth remains closed. His, too. Brown eyes stay on mine, and I feel as pinned as an exotic dragonfly.

This is wrong. Jack Smith is a PE teacher. Greg told me so when we met at that coffee shop to plan our backstory. Right?

"And I have a brother. Older. Three years," Greg says, setting down his mug. "I won't tell him that I hired you, but he's great, unlike . . . well, my other relatives."

I nod, typing Brother *in my Notes app.* Close, *I add. "May I have his name and something about him?"*

"Something about Jack?"

"That I can bring up when we meet? Something like 'Greg talks about you all the time. You're a hippotherapist, right? And you love soap carving! How lovely that you met your spouse while climbing Machu Picchu.'"

Greg shakes his head. "Jack's not married."

"Any partners?"

"No. He doesn't really date."

My eyebrow lifts at Greg, who immediately shakes his head.

"Not like me. He . . . has friends, women that he . . . But he's very clear about not being interested in relationships."

I nod. Type Stud? Yikes. *"Your mother doesn't hound him about settling down like she does you?"*

"It's complicated." Greg's expression is almost guilty. "But no. Mom doesn't really care what he does. Let's see, something about Jack." He drums his fingers. "He comes across as a bit rough around the edges,

like he doesn't care about anything but his job, but—he's nice. Kind. For instance, he was the only person who showed up for my Jesus Christ Superstar recital back in high school." He sighs. "I played Peter."

"The only person in your family?"

"The only person in the audience. Did lots of clapping." Greg shrugs. "And he's freakishly smart. Likes board games. Recently moved back to Boston from California."

"What's his job?"

"He teaches. Phys—"

A loud sound from a nearby table makes us start. A toddler, slamming her fist on the table, yelling at her mom, "Not banana— cookie!"

"Sweetie, you've been sick."

"I'm not sick. I—" Suddenly, there's a puddle of vomit on the front of her shirt.

Greg and I exchange a look before he continues, "Also, um . . . he plays sports with his friends. Stuff like that."

I nod and write down, PE teacher. Monopoly? Gym bro? Not the target. Nonissue.

Until now.

Suddenly, Jonathan Jack Jesus Christ Superstar Smith-Turner, who plays board games and teaches something that starts with *phys-* and is most definitely *not* physical education, is a big fucking issue.

Impossible. Insane. I must be on *Punk'd*. General relativity was right: I've time-traveled back to the early 2000s. A camera crew and Uncle Paul are hiding behind that pretentious potted fern in the corner. The interview was a setup. My entire life is a joke.

"Hey, Jack," Volkov asks from behind me, all sharp, eastern European sounds, "with great power comes . . . ?"

"Great current squared times resistance," Jack murmurs, eyes planted on me. I shiver hot and cold while everyone else laughs. As usual, Jack is inaccessible; I have no idea what's happening in his brain. As usual, I feel like he's skinning me like a clementine, seeing all my squishy, secret, hidden bits.

How hard will Cece murder me if I puke all over her dress?

"MIT party?" The hostess smiles. "Let me show you to your table."

I turn around clumsily, as if wading through water. My brain won't stop flipping its fins. So Jack's a physicist—bad. An experimentalist—bad. *The* experimentalist—bad. He wants to hire some George dude—bad. He knows me as a librarian his brother's dating—bad. He never liked me—bad. He thinks I made up my Ph.D.—badder—and am conning MIT into hiring me—baddest.

"Don't let him get to you," Monica whispers in my ear.

"W-what?"

"The way Jonathan was looking at you, like you're trying to smuggle a full bottle of shampoo through TSA—definitely one of his power plays. Ignore him."

Shit—what if he narcs me out to Monica? To Volkov? Oh God, am I going to have to explain to my future colleagues about my side gig? About Faux? I bet filet mignon goes great with anecdotes of that debt collector who threatened to shatter my kneecaps. "Okay." I smile weakly. I'm in deep shit—ten feet under, I estimate.

No, fifteen. Rapidly digging when Monica notices that I'm sitting far from Volkov and says, "There's a terrible draft here. Can someone switch with me? Elsie, would you mind?"

Musical chairs ensue. She maneuvers until I'm between her and Volkov. Excellent. Less excellent? Jack, right across from me. He's folding himself in his chair, twice as broad as the experimentalist riffling through the menu next to him. He stares like he's about to deseed me like a pomegranate.

I try to think about a single way this interview could have started less auspiciously, and come up empty-handed. Maybe if Godzilla stepped into Miel and started grazing on the orchid centerpiece.

I glance toward the entrance. Is Godzilla about to—

"Where are you currently, Elsie?"

I whip my head to Jack. His gaze is on me and only me, like we're alone in the restaurant. In Boston. In the Virgo galaxy supercluster. "I . . . don't understand the question."

"Your workplace. If you currently work."

My cheeks heat. "I teach at UMass Boston, Emerson, and Boston University."

"Ah." He stuffs entire worlds in that single sound—none of which I care to visit. "Remind me, is UMass ranked as a Research One institution?"

My nostrils flare. I remember what my mom always says (*You look like a piglet when you do that*) and make a conscious effort to relax. "Research Two."

Jack nods like he didn't already know and takes a carefree sip of his water. I wonder what would happen if I kicked him under the table.

"You really must move to a Research One institution, Dr. Hannaway." Volkov gives me a look of fatherly concern. "There's simply no comparison. More resources. More funds."

You don't say. "Yes, Dr. Volkov."

"And are you on tenure track, Elsie?" Jack asks.

"An adjunct." I am *totally* going to kick him. In the nuts. It's the only acceptable use of my foot.

"I am so jealous of adjuncts," Volkov murmurs distractedly, staring at the entrée page. "They have mobility. Flexibility. Keeps you young at heart."

I paste a smile on my face. "So much flexibility." Offering to forward him the biweekly op-eds the *Atlantic* runs on how we are the underclass of academia seems rude, so I silently wish him an unpassable kidney stone.

"And where did you get your Ph.D.?" Jack asks.

"Northeastern."

"Northeastern, huh?" He nods, pensive. "Great school. A friend used to be there."

"Oh. In the Physics Department?"

"No. Library Science."

A rush of heat sweeps over me. *Does he mean—*

"Jonathan, I emailed you Dr. Hannaway's CV and several of her publications," Monica says sweetly. "Did you not receive them?"

"Perhaps they got flagged as spam." He doesn't take his eyes off me. "My apologies, Dr. Hannaway." He crosses his arms over his chest and leans back, preparing to study me at his leisure. He's wearing a dark-green henley in this fancy-ass restaurant. Underdressed, *again*, like his entire brand is Instagram lumbersexual and he can't risk being spotted wearing business casual. "Do you have any siblings?"

Where the hell is he going with this? "Two."

"Sisters?"

"No."

"Odd. You look uncannily similar to someone my brother used to date. I believe her name was . . ." He taps his finger on the table. "Pity I can't recall."

I flush, looking around shiftily. Most people are too busy deciding what to order with department funds to pay attention. I bury my face in the menu and take a deep breath. *Ignore Jack Smith. Jack Turner. Jack Smith-Turner. Do not go on a rampage and stab him with your salad fork.*

Actually, what I need is to explain to him the situation. That I'm not a con artist. Get him off my case. Yes, I need to—

"Jack, how's the ferroelectric nematic experiment going?" someone asks from the other end of the table.

"Great. So great, I've been considering a leave of absence." He makes a show of tapping his chin. "A couple of years backpacking, maybe."

Volkov laughs. "No luck, then?"

"Nope." His brow furrows. "We're doing something wrong. Can't figure out what, though. How's Russia this time of year, Sasha?"

More people chuckle. "If you feel you must leave us, who are we to stop you?" Monica mutters. I scowl into the salads page: Jack has no business going from total asshole to charmingly self-deprecating.

"Things will turn around, Jack. You know that experimental physics is . . . experi-*meant* to be hard." Volkov snickers at his own joke. "Theoretical physics, too. Doesn't it sometimes make you . . . *theory*-eyed, Dr. Hannaway?"

Laugh, I order myself. *Be charming. Be convivial. Top of your game.* "It sure does."

"Good one," Jack says. "Sasha, have you heard the one about Schrödinger's girlfriend?"

Volkov rubs his hands. "No, do tell!"

"It's my favorite. Schrödinger's girlfriend is simultaneously a librarian *and* a theoretical—"

I snap my menu shut, embarrassment and anger pounding up my spine. Am I having a rage stroke? Is my nose bleeding? "Excuse me for a moment." I stand, forcing myself to smile at Monica and

Volkov. I need air. I need to regroup. I need a second to think about this mess of a situation without Jack jabbing at me. "I, um, petted a dog earlier. I'll wash my hands and be right back."

Volkov seems pleased at my sudden concern with hygiene. "Yes, yes, good idea. *Lather* safe than sorry." He guffaws like he's on nitrous oxide. I love a good pun; I really do. But not when my one chance at financial freedom is being sabotaged by my fake boyfriend's evil brother.

I'm several feet away when Jack's voice makes my stomach twist. "You know, I petted a *cat*. I think I'll join Dr. Hannaway."

The restrooms are across the restaurant, at the end of a long, dimly lit hallway decorated with ficus and monochrome pictures of Paris. I left the table first and should have a considerable advantage, but Jack catches up with me in a handful of steps, without even the grace to look winded.

I brace for him to say something devious and offensive. It'll be my excuse to trip him—who needs sex when you can watch Jack Smith face-plant on the floor? But he remains silent. Strolls by my side, grossly unconcerned, like he doesn't have a worry on his mind. *One of his power plays*, Monica said earlier, and I grit my teeth, wishing I had some power to bring to the playground. If I get this job, I'm going to make his life impossible: put his science equipment in Jell-O, cut my nails on his desk, lick the rim of his cup when I have a cold, sprinkle tacks on his—

End of the hallway. He opens the door on the left—men's restroom—and I head to the right—ladies'. Free from this pain, finally. Except that I make a crucial mistake: I turn around for one last resentful glance, and Jack's standing there. With a waiting expression.

Holding the restroom's door open.

I exhale a low, confused laugh. Is this an invitation? To the men's restroom? To . . . to what, sit on the urinals for tea and hors d'oeuvres? Is he *bananas*?

No. *I* am bananas. Because for reasons that warrant a brain scan and comprehensive neuropsychological evaluations, I take him up on it. I barely glance around to make sure that an MIT chancellor is not coming down the hallway, and step inside.

The bathroom's deserted—no one around to witness my lunacy. The place stinks, like someone dipped their post-gym crotch in a bucket of citrus disinfectant. There's the pitter-patter of a dripping faucet, and my reflection in the full-body mirror is a lie: the slender woman in the sheath dress is too flustered, too livid, too *red* to be mild Elsie Hannaway of the accommodating ways.

I turn around. Jack lingers by the door, as ever studying, appraising, vivisectioning me. I start a mental countdown. Five. Four. When I reach *one*, I'm going to explain the situation. In a calm, dignified tone. Tell him it's a misunderstanding. Three. Two.

"Congratulations," he says.

Uh?

"On your Ph.D."

"W-what?"

"A noteworthy accomplishment," he continues, serious, calm, "given that less than twenty-four hours ago you weren't even working on one."

I exhale deeply. "Listen, it's not what you—"

"Will you be leaving your post at the library, or are you planning on a dual career? I'd be worried for your schedule, but I hear that theoretical physics often consists of staring into the void and jotting down the occasional mathematical symbol—"

"I—no. That's *not* what theoretical physics is about and—" I screw my eyes shut. Calm down. Be reasonable. This can be fixed with a simple conversation. "Jack, I'm not a librarian."

His eyes widen in playacted surprise. "No way."

"I am a physicist. I got my Ph.D. about a year ago."

His expression hardens. He steps closer, and I feel like a garden gnome. "And I assume Greg has no idea."

"He does. I—" Wait. No. I never told Greg about my Ph.D.— because it was irrelevant. "Well, okay. He *doesn't* know, but that's only because—"

"You've been lying to him."

I'm taken aback. "Lying?"

"You're playing a twisted game with my brother, pretending to be someone you're not. I don't know why, but if you think I'm going to let you continue—"

"What? No. This isn't . . ." I can't believe that the conclusion he's come to is that I'm catfishing Greg. *As if.* "I *care* about Greg."

"Is that why you hide things from him?"

"I don't!"

"What about when you passed out in my arms and begged me not to tell him?"

I wince. "It was not *in* your arms, just *near* your arms, and that was—I didn't want to bother him!"

"What about the fact that you didn't know he was about to go on a trip." Jack is icily, uncompromisingly furious at the idea of me mistreating his brother. "You don't seem to care what his job entails. What his problems are. What his *life* is."

"Neither does the rest of your family!"

"True." He scowls. "But irrelevant."

I almost run a hand down my face before remembering Cece's *Ruin your makeup and I'll skewer you like a shish kebab.* God, I'm going to have to explain to Jack the concept of fake dating. He won't believe it's a real thing—men with nice baritones and hints of tattoos and perfectly scruffy five-o'clock shadows are just *not* the target demographic of Faux. Jack probably has legions of women standing in line for the opportunity to partner-stretch hamstrings with him—let alone *real* date. And what are the chances he won't use my side gig against me during the interview? Subzero kelvin. "Listen, I know it *looks* like I'm lying to Greg, but I'm not. I can explain."

"Can you?"

"Yes. I'm a—" My brain stutters, then freezes as something occurs to me: if I told Jack about the fake dating, I'd be outing not just myself, but also Greg.

Yes, Jack and Greg are close. No, Greg did not tell Jack about Faux, and it's not my place to do so. I could avoid saying *why* Greg has decided to hire me, but would that matter? Jack would know that Greg is hiding something. That there's something to prod, to investigate, and . . .

"It's just—I don't know how my family would take it." Greg rubs *his palm in his eye, looking like he could use a deep-tissue massage and forty hours of sleep.* "They might be complete assholes about it or *be great or try to be nice and instead end up being massively invasive and . . . I'd rather not tell them, for now. I'd rather they not know that there's something to tell."*

I can hear Greg's words as I glance up. Jack's dark eyes are stern. Expectant. Inflexible.

I'd rather lick the urinals than tell this guy any of my secrets. "Actually, I *can't* explain, but—"

Two voices—male laughter, loafer steps right outside the bathroom. We both wheel around to the entrance.

"Someone's coming," I say unnecessarily. Shit. What if it's someone from our party? I shoot Jack a panicked look, fully expecting to find him gloating. Instead his face takes on an urgent, calculating look, and things I do *not* expect happen.

His huge hand lifts. Splays across the small of my back. Pushes me toward the closest stall. He wants to *hide* me?

"What are you—"

"Go," he orders.

"No! I can't just—"

I must hesitate too long, because Jack's hands close around my waist. He lifts me effortlessly, like I weigh less than a Higgs boson, and carries me inside the stall, depositing my feet on the rim of the toilet. My brain blanks—*no thoughts, head empty*—and I don't have the faintest idea what's going on. What is he—

The stall door closes.

The bathroom door opens.

Two men enter, discussing quantum advantage. "—scale the error correction by the number of qubits?"

"You don't. Scaled-up system behavior is erratic. How do you account for that?"

Shit. Shit, *shit*—

"Calm down," Jack murmurs against the shell of my ear, like he knows that I'm on the verge of popping an aneurysm.

"They're from the MIT table," I whisper under my breath.

"Shh." His giant paws tighten around me, as if to contain me and my panic. They span my waist. Our size difference sits somewhere between absurd and obscene. "Settle down."

I feel dizzy. "Why am I standing on the toilet?"

"I figured you'd rather Dr. Pereira and Dr. Crowley keep on chatting about superpolynomial speedups and not see your heels under the stall. Was I wrong?"

I close my eyes, mortified. This is not my life. I'm a discerning scientist with insightful opinions on spintronic tech, not this blighted creature clinging to Jonathan Smith-Turner's shoulders on top of a latrine.

Oh, who am I kidding? This is exactly my brand. Improbable. Cringeworthy. Botched.

"Settle down," Jack repeats, gruffly reassuring. We're way too close. I want his breath to be garlic and sauerkraut, but it's vaguely minty and pleasantly warm. I want his skin to smell ridiculous, like mango tanning mousse, but all my nose picks up on is *nice, clean, good*. I want his grip to be creepy and knee-in-the-groin worthy, but it's just what I need to avoid slipping in the toilet. "Stop fidgeting."

"I'm not—" Pereira and Crowley are still talking physics—*can't believe all the fuss with the quantum Hadamard transform*—with the added background of a stream trickling. Oh God, they're peeing. I'm eavesdropping on one of the world's foremost solar neutrinos scholars *peeing*. I can't come back from this, can I?

"Elsie." Jack's lips graze my cheekbone. "Calm down. They'll leave as soon as they're done, and you can go back to the table. Laugh at Volkov's puns till he votes for you. Tell a few more lies."

"I'm not *lying*." I pull back, and our eyes are at the same level. The slice of blue in the deep brown is icy, weird, beautiful. "I can't explain, but this is . . . *not* the way you think it is. It's . . . different."

"From what?"

"From the way you think it is."

He nods. Our noses nearly brush together. "That was remarkably articulate."

I roll my eyes.

"Monica will love to hear about your secret librarian identity—"

"No!" I barely keep my voice down. "*Please*, just call Greg before you talk to Monica. He'll explain."

"Convenient, given that I can't get in touch with him while he's on his retreat, and he won't be back until your interview is over."

Shit. I'd forgotten about Woodacre. "There must be a way to reach him. Can you tell him it's an emergency? That, um, he left his porch light on? You need his alarm code to go turn it off. Save the environment."

"No."

"Please. At least—"

"No."

"You're being absolutely *unreasonable*. All I ask is that you—"

"—do you think about the girl? Hannaway, right?" one of the urinal voices asks. We both instantly tune in.

A mistake, clearly.

"CV's real good. Her two-dimensional liquid crystals theories . . . good stuff."

"I remember reading her paper last year. I was very impressed. Had no idea she was that junior."

"Right? Makes you wonder how much of it is her mentor's." A vague hum of agreement that has my hands tightening around the balls of Jack's shoulders. *None*, I want to scream. *It was my model.* "She's young and beautiful. Which means that she'll get pregnant in a couple of years, and we'll have to teach her courses."

It's like a punch in the sternum, to the point that I almost slip butt-first into the toilet. Jack stops me with a hand between my shoulder blades, arm contracting around my waist. He's frowning like he's as disgusted as I am. Though he's not. He can't be, because Pereira, or maybe Crowley, adds:

"Doesn't matter. I'm voting for Jack's candidate. He's got influence, and he *hates* theorists."

"He does? Oh, yeah. Can't believe I forgot that article he wrote."

"It was brutal, man. And hilarious. Wouldn't want to be on *his* bad side."

A hand dryer goes off, muffling the rest. Jack's still holding me, eyes on mine, foreheads near touching. My nails dig into his chest—made of some granite-Kevlar blend, engineered by a task force of experimentalists to exude heat. He's a sentient weighted blanket, and I—

I hate him.

I've never hated anybody: not J.J. Not the Film Appreciation 101 professor who nearly failed me for saying that *Twilight* is an unrecognized masterpiece. Not even my brother Lucas, who had me convinced that I was adopted for over six months. I'm mild mannered, adaptable, unobtrusive. I get along with people: I give them what they want, and all I ask in return is that they not actively dislike me.

But Jack Smith. Jonathan Fucking Smith Fucking Turner. He's been hostile and unpleasant and suspicious since the day we met. He has shat upon my field and destroyed my mentor, and now stands between me and my dreams. For that, he lost the privilege that I afford every human being: to deal with the Elsie he wants.

The Elsie he's going to get is the one *I* care to give him. And she's pissed.

"I *want* this job, Jack," I hiss over the hand dryer. I actually *need* this job, but—semantics.

"I know you do, Elsie." His voice is low pitched and rumbly. "But I want someone else to get it."

"I know. *Jack.*"

"Then it seems like we're at an impasse. *Elsie.*" He articulates my name slowly, carefully. I'm going to lean forward and bite his stupid lips bloody.

No, I won't, because I'm better than that.

Or am I?

"You do not want to come at me," I hiss.

"Oh, Elsie." His hands on me are incongruously gentle, and yet we're on the verge of the academic equivalent of nuclear warfare. "I think it's exactly what I want."

The dryer turns off into silence and saves me from committing aggravated assault. "They left," I say. "Let me *go*."

His mouth twitches, but he deposits me on the floor in some ludicrous reverse–*Dirty Dancing* move. His hands on my waist linger, but as soon as they leave me I'm scampering out of the stall, heels clicking on the tiles. I nearly lose my balance. With Jack's scent out of my nose, the stench of the place hits me anew.

"Talk to Monica if you want to," I bluff, turning back to him. "You'll see the good it does you."

"Oh, I will." He's clearly about to smile, like the angrier I get, the more amused he becomes. A never-ending vicious cycle that can end only in me holding his head in the toilet bowl.

"It's my word against the word of the guy with a decade-long agenda against theorists, after all."

He shrugs. "Maybe. Or maybe it's a physicist's word against a librarian's."

I scoff and stalk to the entrance, suddenly confident in my stilt shoes, determined not to be in his presence a second longer. But when I reach the door, something ticks inside me. I whip my head back to Jack, who's standing there like K2, studying me with an interested frown, like I'm an exotic caterpillar about to pupate.

God, I hope he has itchy, purulent ass acne for the rest of his natural life. "I know you have despised me since the very first moment we met," I spit out.

He bites the inside of his cheek. "You do?"

"Yes. And you know what? It doesn't matter if you hated me at first sight, because I've hated you long before we ever met. I hated you the first time I heard your name. I hated you when I was twelve and read what you'd done in *Scientific American*. I've hated you harder, I've hated you longer, and I've hated you for better reasons."

Jack doesn't look so amused anymore. This is new to me—talking to others like the *me* I really am. It's new and different and weird, and I freaking *love* it.

"I'm really good at hating you, Jack, so here's what I'm going to do: not only am I going to get this job, but when we're colleagues at MIT, I'm going to make sure that you have to look at me every day and wish that I were George. I'm going to make you regret every single little jab. And I'm going to single-handedly make your life so hard that you'll regret taking on me, and Monica, and theoretical physics, until you cry in your office every morning and finally apologize to the scientific community for what you did."

He is *really* not amused now. "Is that so?" he asks. Cold. Cutting.

This time I'm the one to smile. "You bet, *Jonathan*."

I open the door. Leave the restroom.

And I don't glance at him for the rest of the evening.

4

ENTROPY

S O. JUST TO GET THIS STRAIGHT. YOU, ELSIE 'I'M ALLERGIC to peanuts but I still ate Mrs. Tuttle's homemade brittle because I didn't want to hurt her feelings, have you seen my EpiPen?' Hannaway—you told Jack Smith . . . all *that*?"

I've kicked off the red dress, and I'm neurotically pacing in the glory of my thigh highs, striped cotton underwear, and insulin pod. I should be cold, but my anger burns toasty from within, like the plasma core of the sun. "It's a minor allergy, Mrs. Tuttle is very elderly *and* our landlady, and yes, I did—because Jack *deserved it*."

"I don't doubt it." Cece lies back on the couch, watching like my meltdown is the apotheosis of entertainment. Hedgie lounges in her lap with a schadenfreudey, demonic gleam, clearly getting a serotonin boost from my impending demise. "That article he wrote was such a huge deal, every academic field still talks about it. Even linguistics. How did *you* not know what he looked like?"

I rub my eyes. My fingers come back soot black. "I was engaging in an academic boycott."

"Maybe not your most fortunate idea."

"If someone wrote a hoax paper saying that adjectives suck, you'd boycott them, too."

"I'd straight up murder them. And I'm proud of you for finally yelling at someone—a most pleasing moment in your career. But my question is, how are you going to do"—she waves her hand inchoately—"all that?"

"Do what?"

"Hatch out of the yolky egg of adjuncthood. Get the job. Make Jack rue the day he was born. What's the plan here?"

"Right. Yeah." I stop pacing. Massage my temples. "I have none."

"I see no flaws in that."

The only response I can think of involves kicking the top part of the credenza. I do just that, then proceed to limp around with a swollen pinky toe.

"I've never seen you like this, Elsie."

"I've never *felt* like this." I'm a Large Hadron Collider: atomic particles smash angrily about my body, building up the energy to burn Jack to a crisp. Or at least cook him well done. I can't remember the last time I experienced so many negative emotions. "I should have known. I always had a bad feeling about him, and last night—that's why he's so good at Go. He was a physicist all along, that—that *piece of Uranus*—"

"Science insult. Nice."

"I bet he thinks in *Fahrenheit*—"

"Ooh, sick burn."

"—and spends his free time flying to Westminster Abbey to dance on Stephen Hawking's grave—"

"Hawking's *dead*?"

"—and won't even bother calling Greg to ask for an explanation, because he's a sadistic, egotistical, ignorant black hole of sh—"

"Elsie, babe, do you need us here for this, or should we go to our room to mourn Stephen?"

I stop pacing. Cece and Hedgie are staring, heads tilted at the same angle. "Sorry," I say sheepishly.

"Not gonna lie, it's kinda fun to see you soapbox it all out, geyser-style. I'm sure there are some serious health benefits to this. But before you pull a machete out of your butt crack and begin the rampage, let me point out, this Smith-Turner dude? He cannot touch you."

"He may not be able to knee me in the groin or poison my tea with a vial of measles, but—"

"He also cannot interfere with your interview."

"If Jack tells Volkov or Monica, I—"

"Pff." She waves her hand. "He won't."

"He won't?" I squint at Cece. Is she placating me? I wouldn't know—I never need placating.

"First, admitting that he knows you from a nonacademic setting would create a sizable conflict of interest. They'd force him to recuse himself from the search committee. He'd lose the ability to influence the other members."

"Oh." I nod. First slowly, then not. "You're right."

"Plus, you're not contrabanding cigars or organizing illegal cock-fights. You told a small, irrelevant lie about your personal life to a passing acquaintance. For all Jack knows, you're in the witness protection program. Or you misspoke when you were first introduced. Or you and Greg have a role-play kink you expand out of the bedroom: you pretend to be a librarian at his grandma's birthday, he spanks you with Billy the IKEA bookcase, orgasms are had. Consensual, Swedish, and above all: private."

"That's . . . intense."

"I've been watching HBO with Mrs. Tuttle's password. Point is, Jack's not telling anyone shit. Can you imagine if he went to Monica and brought up random details of your romantic relationships that he thinks should be disqualifying? HR would have a field day. Don't you watch the harassment-prevention webinars?"

"I—they're mandatory."

Cece's eyes narrow. "Yes, but do you watch them, or do you let them play while you do integral calculus and browse cheese porn on Pinterest?" I flush and look away, and she sighs. "Here's a recap: Jack can't ask you about your personal life."

"He already has."

"But he can't tell *others*. It would be, as the kids say, a bad look. And, as the lawyers say, illegal. Plus, Monica the badass chair would kick him in the nuts. She seems nicely predisposed to nut kicking."

I exhale. "You're right." I celebrate my relief by rolling down my thigh highs. Small miracle: no holes yet. "So he's bluffing. Posturing. Just like I am."

"Yup." Cece bites into her lip, suddenly pained. "With one minor difference."

"Which is?"

"If his posturing doesn't work, he's still an MIT professor. If yours doesn't . . ."

I groan and drop onto the lazy chair. "If *mine* doesn't, it's one more year in the adjunct pit." No research time. Students calling me Mom and insisting their dogs ate their computers. Rationed insulin. And, of course, the longer I spend without a tenure-track job, the less appealing a candidate I'll be. I hate vicious cycles, and academic ones are the most vicious of all.

"Hey!" Cece comes to kneel next to me, setting Hedgie on top of my chest. "Clearly Jack knows you have a shot at the job, or he wouldn't try to intimidate you. And Kirk said that scientists—"

I sit up. "Kirk? The new Faux guy?"

"Yeah." Is she blushing, or is it just the poor lighting? We need new bulbs. Also needed: money for new bulbs. "He said that scientists get mean when they feel threatened."

"Hmm." What if Jack really does think I have a better shot than George? I ponder the possibilities until Hedgie rolls on her back, quills stabbing my right boob. "I'm going to boil you and eat your soup with udon noodles," I murmur.

Cece frowns. "What did you say?"

"Nothing! Just . . . You're right. Thank you for talking me down."

She smiles, and I feel a surge of affection for her. "See, that's the reason scientists need the humanities. You guys lack big picture."

"We don't—"

"Plus, you morons are training the machines to become our robotic overlords." She pats my head. "Have you told Dr. L. about this?"

I groan, once again sapped of my will to live. "I sent him an email. He wants to see me in his office tomorrow morning."

"*Before* your teaching demo? Can't you just have a call?"

"He doesn't like phones."

"Hmm. High maintenance."

He's not. Dr. L. only wants the best for me, and given everything he's done, waking up one hour early is the least I can do. Or *two* hours, accounting for traffic.

The first thing I do once I'm in my jammies and my "Physics: why shit does stuff" Snuggie is contact Greg. I already tried from the Uber, after spending dinner debasing myself by using my hard-earned physics Ph.D. to make up puns for Volkov—my serial killer origin story. I wonder if Jack tried to call his brother, too, and I snort at the idea. Clearly he's decided that I'm after the Smith trust funds, like some skank from the *Dynasty* reboot. He probably just called his nosy mom and Uncle Paul the Perv, and they're all about to descend on Greg like a horde of goblin sharks.

But Greg is unreachable. I send him a text he won't see. I set the iTwat aside, wondering if Jack's phone is cracked, too. Probably not. Next time I see him, I should smash it into the sidewalk and correct the situation.

What a plan.

With a sigh, I pull out my 2013 MacBook Pro. (*Decrepit*, Cece calls it. I prefer *vintage*. Still, the number of high-performance computing simulations I've been able to run in the past year is zero.) In love and war everything's fair, and this is bloodshed. So I allow myself something not quite kosher: I look up the competition.

The physics community is weirdly sized: not so small that we're all bosom friends, not so large that we can overlook someone's existence. Especially someone good enough to make the final round of an MIT interview. Take me: my claim to fame, what got me on Monica's radar, is my dissertation—a bunch of mathematical formulas that predict the behavior of two-dimensional liquid crystals. They are special, multitudes-containing materials, with properties of both liquids and solids, of mobility and stasis, of chaos and organization. Like me, basically. And my favorite part about them is that the very multitudes they contain may have led them to play a key role in the origins of life, by helping build the first biomolecules on Earth.

Riveting, I know. Just wait for the movie adaptation.

But it did get some buzz, because what Monica said is also true: the possible applications of my research are nearly infinite. For my work, I got one of those *Forbes* STEM awards that only people *not* in STEM care about, and I was interviewed on a couple of podcasts downloaded by more than just the host's extended family. One of my *Nature Physics* articles was even featured on the cover. The research groups at Northeastern started giving me covetous glances and stopped asking me to make coffee—only fair, since I don't even drink it. Cece got me a "Great women of science" T-shirt with my portrait sandwiched between Alice Ball's and Ada Lovelace's. My parents . . . Well, my family didn't react to any of it, because they were busy dealing with a tax audit or something. But Dr. L., who's family in any way that counts, patted me on the back, told me that I was the most promising theorist of my generation, and assured me that I'd have my pick of tenure-track positions out of grad school.

And any other time, it might have even been true. But these times are unprecedented—hiring freezes, systematic defunding of higher education, adjunctification. And a few weeks ago, when the *Forbes* journalist contacted me to do a "where are they now" follow-up story, I had to tell her that no, it wasn't a mistake: I hadn't published in months, my research had stalled, and I had *not* been able to get a cool job at a top institution. In fact, I was lucky to find *any* job. Even one whose description is *academia's little bitch*.

George the Chosen Experimentalist, though . . . I have no idea what *his* claim to fame is, and he doesn't ring any bells. So I google the devil I know: Jack. He has a Wikipedia entry—I refuse to give it hits on principle—and a Google Scholar page—which I *must* click on, but do so while gagging. I try not to notice how much I have to scroll down to get to the bottom of his publication list, mutter "Show-off," then start combing through his coauthors.

I find a Gabriel. Gayle. Giovanni. Gunner (really?). Georgina Sepulveda, a physics superstar whose work I've been stanning for years (I choose to think she collaborated with Jack under duress and donated all proceeds to the local animal shelter). After a minute, I come across the elusive George—George Green. He's on two low-impact articles—both recent, both with Jack. There's next to no online trace of him, but he just finished his postdoc at Harvard and posts on physics subreddits under his real name.

"Seriously?" This guy's being interviewed? Whatever strings Jack had to pull, I'm going to cut them one by one with my poultry shears. His mediocre love child doesn't stand a chance—

My phone rings. I jolt and immediately pick up—Greg. *Finally.*

"Hey! I—"

"I need your help."

I swallow a groan. "Hi, Mom." I've made a lethal mistake.

"The situation is *dire.* You need to rein in your brothers."

After two and a half decades of APE, I can safely state that the Elsie my mom wants is a droid. She's powerful, mobile, financially soluble. She successfully quenched her earthly needs and lives in a state of perennial prosperity. Her main purpose is to score prestige points when Aunt Minnie brags about her son who almost finished law school. Her secondary purpose? To intervene when two idiots decide to embark on months-long feuds over stuff that, historically, has included:

- who gets the front seat in the car
- who deserves the piece of cake with the frosting bootie at Cousin Jenna's baby shower
- who's taller (they are identical twins)
- who's more handsome (see above)

- whose birth year, according to the *Guinness World Records* book, has more recorded python attacks (see above!)
- who gets to pick the dog's name (we never had pets)

This is a noncomprehensive list. Over the years, the feuds have become more rabid, Dad more absent, Mom more reliant on me for cleanups. "You can't be your family's janitorial staff," Cece tells me once a week, but I do my best to make Mom happy, even though of all the Elsies people want, hers is the fakest—and the one with deepest roots. I have, after all, cursed my way into it, tirelessly and painstakingly.

"How are you, Mom—"

"*Overwhelmed.* Lucas and Lance are at it again. Almost came to fists after their soccer game."

"Over the result?"

"Over *Dana.*"

I rub my temple. "They both agreed to stop dating her."

"They did. But Dana needed a ride somewhere."

"Who did she call?"

"Lucas. Lance slashed his tire. The neighbors are starting to talk. You *need* to stop them."

"I did, Mom. Two weeks ago. A month ago. Three months ago." I've been holding a series of conflict mediation seminars in my parents' basement. They mostly consist of me reminding my brothers that murder is illegal.

"Well, do it again. Come over tomorrow."

I physically cringe. "I'm sorry. It's not possible."

"Why?"

"I—" No. No *I* statements. Too personal. "This is a stressful, busy time. The semester just started and . . ." Do I tell her? I shouldn't. But maybe she'll want to know? "I'm interviewing for a job."

"You have a job."

"This is a better job."

"Your job is *already* a better job."

I consider bringing up concepts like relativity, gig economy, and insulin resistance. "This is even better."

"Let's hear it—what is it?"

"Professor."

"So you'd go from being a professor to being a professor."

Needless to say, I don't bother telling my parents about the pendulous nature of my job situation. Or . . . anything else. "I'll call them tomorrow morning, okay?"

She grumbles for five more minutes and guilts me into calling tonight, then switches to complaining about something related to toxic deodorants that she saw on Facebook. I hang up to a notification—not Greg, but some guy looking for a fake girlfriend for a Valentine's Day group date. I decide on the spot to personally blame Faux for tonight's shit show and chuck the iTwat into the laundry hamper.

What's the plan here? Cece asked.

I have a grand total of zero ideas, which means that I'm going to have to annihilate Jack Shitwipe Smith-Turner the old way: by excelling at my job.

I sigh deeply. Then I pull my ancient Mac onto my lap, click on my teaching demonstration, and rehearse the crap out of it.

5

GRAVITATIONAL CONSTANT

N THE MAJOR MOTION PICTURE OF MY LIFE—A LOW-BUDGET slapstick tragicomedy—Dr. Christophe Laurendeau's role would be played by one of those old-school French actors who often star in Cece's movies. He shouldn't be hard to cast: a long-faced man who looks at once stern and wise, wears only turtlenecks, and never stops being handsome, not even in the tail end of his sixties, when his hair goes ash gray and his skin wrinkles into sandpaper. His office smells like chamomile tea and old books, and whenever I'm here (daily for the five years of my Ph.D., weekly since I graduated), he does the same thing: unfolds his tall, razor-thin frame from behind his desk and instructs, like it's my first time on the Northeastern campus, "Sit down, please. In that green chair." His English is never anything but perfect, even if his accent is still Disney strong. "How are you, Elise?"

It's something I learned not to wince at, the way he always uses the wrong name. In Dr. L.'s defense, he called me Elise on our first meeting, and I never bothered to correct him. I did consider asking him to switch to Elsie when he took me out for dinner after I defended my dissertation, but I chickened out.

Aside from Cece, Dr. L. was the only human being who acknowledged me getting my Ph.D.—a matter of circumstances, I tell myself. After the Smith-Turner hoax almost killed his career, I was his first mentee in many years, which meant no close labmates. The theoretical physics research group at Northeastern was not quite fond enough of women in STEM to celebrate one. And my family . . . They couldn't make the two-hour drive because of Lance's adult league game—and, likely, because I never fully managed to convey to them what grad school is, though Mom once asked if I was done with that paper I had to turn in (i.e., my dissertation), which I took as a win.

So Dr. L. took me out to a fancy restaurant, just the two of us, where the hostess gave me an inquisitive *Daughter, granddaughter, or sugar baby?* look. And when he looked at me over a dinner that cost half my rent and said, "You carried yourself well, Elise. I am proud of you," the rare spark of initiative died out. If I had Dr. L.'s approval, he could call me whatever he liked.

And that's the story of my doctoral work: bookended by someone else's name.

Elise, I've come to believe, is the Elsie that Dr. L. wants—a brilliant theoretical physicist with an illustrious job that will garner her the admiration of the scientific community—and while she might not be who I *am*, she's who I *want* to be.

Too bad that her existence is antithetical to this other guy's.

"Jonathan Smith-Turner." Dr. L.'s mouth is a thin line. His eyes, hurt. "A disgrace."

I nod.

"The likes of him taint physics and academia."

I nod again.

"It is apparent what needs to be done."

More nodding, in full agreement.

"Clearly, you must withdraw your application."

Hang on. Maybe not *full* agreement. "Withdraw . . . my application?"

"I cannot allow you to work in the same department as that *animal*."

"But I . . ." I squirm and lean forward in the chair. So much for elegance and poise. "I need the job."

"You *have* a job."

"I cannot adjunct for one more year."

"But you are an adjunct *professor*. You should be *proud* of your current employment."

Throughout my Ph.D., I expected to graduate and then move on to a research-only position. Those tend to come with better pay than adjuncts, health insurance, and a blessedly low number of student emails claiming the sixth grandparent's death of the semester. As someone with . . . whatever the opposite of a calling for teaching is, it seemed like a no-brainer. My passion, my joy, my talent—they all fit into three simple words: two-dimensional liquid crystals.

Laurendeau was against it, saying that research-only positions are not prestigious enough. I initially disagreed (who cares about prestige if I can do what I love *and* purchase pancreatic hormones?) and for a while worried that he wouldn't help me find the kind of job I wanted. Professorships aside, most academic postings are not advertised online, but obtained through professional networks of peers and advisors. In the end, it didn't turn out to be an issue: Dr. L. said that he respected my wishes and reached out widely to all his colleagues to let it be known that I was looking for a research position.

Not *one* person was interested in hiring me. And when no tenure-track professorship was available, either . . .

"I used my connections to find you your current jobs, Elise," he tells me, eyes full of concern. "Are you having issues with them?"

I'm instantly swimming in guilt. Dr. L. pulled strings. He called up old colleagues—reached out to people who turned their backs to him after the Smith-Turner censure. Swallowed his pride for *me*. "No! The commute between different campuses is time consuming, but . . ." I start biting into my cuticles, then remember that I stopped three years ago. With the help of Cece and a spray bottle. "But nice. The variety." I smile.

He smiles back, pleased, and I feel a heady sense of relief and affection. Dr. L. is my one ally in the Red Riding Hood forest of academia. If it weren't for him, I'd never have gotten into grad school to begin with. My heart squeezes as I remember senior year of college. My low grades. My mediocre GRE scores blinking on the screen, and the knowledge that I couldn't afford to retake it. J.J.'s careless "Hey, what's up?" whenever we crossed paths.

I remember the sense of dread I felt compiling my applications and sending them to fourteen—*fourteen*—schools, and then, over the following weeks, the weight sinking in my stomach, centimeter after centimeter. Other students were being flown out for on-campus interviews, and my email pinged with nothing but spam and Mom's requests that I take care of my brothers.

It was the shortest winter of my life, and yet it crawled at a snail's pace till the end of February, when I finally knew that it just wouldn't happen. Becoming a physicist was the only thing I ever wanted, and it would never come true because of a stupid mistake.

Until Christophe Laurendeau contacted me.

"I was going through some . . . personal issues," I told him during our first meeting, hoping to explain the dip in my grades. "Just relationship stuff."

"I see." He assessed me, inscrutable. "I trust that everything is resolved."

"It is. For good." *No more relationships*, I hoped he would read between the lines, and when he nodded with a pleased smile, I thought maybe he had.

"Theoretical physics, if pursued seriously, is hardly compatible with . . . personal issues."

It sounded good to me. Ever since learning that the universe is subject to rules that can be described and understood, I'd had *one* dream. *One* constant, throughout the iterations of Elsies I carefully constructed for others. If it weren't for Dr. L., I'd be left without it, and that's why I'll forever trust him.

But paying for insulin out of pocket for one more year . . .

"Elise, it is my responsibility to look out for you," he's saying, voice full of worry. "You deserve better than to work with Jonathan Smith-Turner—"

"He's not in the Physics Department," I blurt out. It is, technically, the truth.

Dr. L. squints. "What do you mean?"

"Ja—he's the head of the Physics *Institute*. He's . . . *barely* part of the search. I might never meet him again." I wrap a hand around a green armrest. Okay, this one's a lie. But small. A lielet.

"I see." He nods silently, fingers stroking his chin. "In that case . . ."

I'll forever trust Laurendeau with my career, but his salary *is* six figures. He hasn't taken a bus since the late eighties, and I bet the credenzas in his house are all neatly assembled.

"Do not withdraw, then. But be careful. You know what that man did," he admonishes. The Smith-Turner Affair is, surprisingly, not a taboo topic. Laurendeau is nothing but open about his contempt. "If I hadn't been tenured, I would have lost my faculty position. And he nearly destroyed my reputation. If it hadn't been for him, I would have been awarded grants in the past sixteen years. I would have had the funds to keep you here, working with me."

One more reason to hate Jack. My jaw sets. "I know."

"Very well, Elise," Laurendeau says, holding my eyes a little too intensely. "Now that I think about it, you winning the position over his handpicked candidate might be an opportunity in disguise."

"An opportunity?"

He slowly breaks into a smile. "For revenge."

6

ANODE AND CATHODE

From: Bobbylicious@gmail.com
Subject: thermo paper

omg I forgot to write it can I turn it in late? im sorry i was at wedding last weekend and got soooo high i've been out of it for the whole week.

. . . .

From: kelsytromboli@umass.edu
Subject: No fair!

A B- on my Vibrations paper? Offensive. I'm emailing the Dean about this.

No rest for the adjunct.

As in, contractually: adjuncts cannot take time off. Since I'll be busy interviewing, I prerecorded lessons and scrambled to find instructors to cover my classes. But I need to reply to students' messages—while fantasizing about "accidentally" misspelling my email in next year's syllabus. When I arrive on the MIT campus, I'm still answering the odd *May I have an extension* email. The one thing adjuncting has done for me is hone my teaching skills, so I'm not too nervous about today's demonstration.

That is, till Monica meets me at the entrance of the physics building and tells me darkly, "You'll be evaluated by me, Volkov, and Smith-Turner."

Instant. Stomach. Knot.

"I see." Maybe it's like figure skating at the Winter Olympics, where the highest and lowest scores get automatically tossed out?

"But don't worry." She darts up the stairs, and I struggle to keep up in my pencil skirt. (The thigh highs are proving surprisingly comfortable, if . . . drafty.) "I've seen your student evals—you're an excellent lecturer." She takes a right and guides me through a series of doors. "You'll be teaching a graduate class, and the Ph.D. students will be asked to weigh in and give their impressions of you. Keep that in mind and do the thing where you make them feel important. Stupid questions don't exist, yada yada." She stops outside a closed door and bites her lip. "There's something else."

"What is it?" I'm a little winded.

She clears her throat. "I *really* tried to get your demonstration to be for another group of students."

Oh? "Why?"

"Because the faculty member who teaches this one—"

"Dr. Hannaway!" We both turn. Volkov is waddling toward us, grinning like we go way back and he used to babysit me. "Do you know the one about the radio that only works in the morning?"

I force myself to smile. God, I'm tired. "The AM radio?"

He laughs, delighted. Monica discreetly rolls her eyes, opens the door, and gestures me inside, our coaching session cut short.

The first thing I notice is Jack—which is unsurprising. He's a giant mountain of muscles, after all, and there's probably a physics equation that explains his annoying habit of becoming the center of mass of every room he burdens with his presence. He's standing behind the podium, tinkering with the computer, wearing jeans and a T-shirt, as though the world outside is not relapsing into an ice age. The lines of his tattoo curl around a biceps that frankly no one, *no one* who doesn't work out for a living should have. I still can't tell what the ink's supposed to form.

In theory, it's a scene I know well. The few minutes leading up to the start of class: students enjoying the last few seconds with their phones, the instructor scrambling to pull up the PowerPoint against all IT odds (missing cables, incompatibility issues, never-ending Windows 10 updates). In practice, there are about twenty pairs of eyes in the room, and they're all fixed on Jack with a mix of admiration, respect, and awe, like he's the dominant turkey of the mating season.

Okay.

So the MIT grad body fanboys over Jack.

Fantastic.

"—whether it's true or not," a young man with faded green hair is saying, "that Christopher Nolan uses you as a consultant on all his movies?"

Jack shakes his head, and I see the muscles cording his neck. Breaking news: necks have muscles. "I will not be blamed for *Tenet*, Cole," he replies, and everyone laughs.

I hate him. Though that's not news. What *is* news is how he looks in my direction and politely says, as though last night I didn't threaten to feed his rotting corpse to the earthworms, "Welcome, Dr. Hannaway. I started the monitor for you." He's smiling, but there's an edge to it. A challenge. Like he's asking me to jump into a puddle that's actually twenty feet deep.

"Thank you." Our arms brush together on my way to the podium. I remember his hands, warm, unwavering around my waist, a hushed *settle down* murmured against my temple, and I suppress a shiver.

Have I mentioned that I hate him?

"Good morning, and thank you for having me," I say once my PowerPoint is loaded. The class is (predictably) 90 percent male and (predictably) made of students who are around my age.

It's complicated, being a woman in STEM. Even more so when you're young and unproven. And even *more* so when you have a semi-pathological need to get along with others. As the only female grad in my department, I've had ample opportunity to contemplate the tightrope that those who are not white cishet men tread in academic spaces.

Do I want to be seen as a congenial, affable colleague? Yes, and thanks to a lifetime of APE, I know the exact combination to achieve that: charming self-deprecation, modesty, humorous tangents, admitting to doubt and fallibility. It's not rocket science (incidentally, a branch of experimental physics I'm obliged to scoff at). Using jokes and simple examples to be a charismatic, engaging speaker is a pretty textbook way to come across as a likable guy.

Guy being the operative word. Because when you're a woman talking about your research, there are anywhere between one and a million STEMlords ready to exploit every little weakness—every little sign that you're not a lean, mean science machine. The *you* people want is sharp, impeccable, perfect enough to justify your intrusion in a field that for centuries has been "rightfully" male. But not *too* perfect, because apparently only "stone-cold bitches" are like that, and they do not make for congenial, affable colleagues. STEM culture has been a boys' club for so long, I often feel like I can be allowed to play only if I follow the rules men made. And those rules? They downright suck.

Like I said, a tightrope. With a bunch of crocodiles throwing their maws open in wait for fresh meat.

Well. Here goes. I make my smile a combination of warm and self-assured that doesn't exist in nature, and say, "Since this class deals with current topics in physics, I've prepared a lecture on Wigner crystals, a highly discussed—"

A groan.

Did someone groan?

I look around, puzzled. Students stare at me expectantly.

I imagined it.

"Wigner crystallization occurs when electron gases that live in a periodic lattice—"

"Excuse me?" Cole. Of the green hair. "Dr. Hannaway, are you going to talk about the topic of Wigner crystals from a theoretical perspective?"

"Great question. Mostly theory, but I'll give an overview of the experimental evidence, too." Next slide—and perfect segue. "Once we achieved the ability to create large inter-electronic distances, Wigner crystallization—"

"Excuse me." Cole. *Again.* "A question."

I smile patiently. I'm used to this. The last time I presented at a conference, some dude *well, actually*'d me before I even pulled up my PowerPoint. "Of course, go ahead."

"My question is . . . what's the point of this?"

Several people laugh. I sigh internally. "Excuse me?"

"Isn't it a bit useless, talking about theories for hours?" He talks slowly but earnestly. Like he's Steve Jobs unveiling a new phone. "Shouldn't we focus on the *actual* applications?"

I open my mouth to ask who hurt him—*Did Michio Kaku bully you, Cole? Did Feynman steal your lunch money?*—but my eyes fall on Volkov. He's giving me an interested look, like he's curious to see how I'll deal with this shitgibbon. Next to him, Monica's lips are flat and resigned. And behind her . . .

Jack.

Who never bothered to sit. He leans against the wall, arms crossed over his chest in a casual *Yeah, I work out* way, staring at me like a brown recluse spider on steroids. His sharp, unyielding eyes miss nothing, but whatever emotion I managed to squeeze from him last night is gone, and I'm back to having no clue what he's thinking. He's like a closed book.

No, he's like a book on fire. *Fahrenheit 451*—no words to read, just ashes and the abyss.

Everything clicks together. I fill in the blanks of my interrupted conversation with Monica: it's Jack who teaches this class. Jack, who has lots of opinions about theorists. Jack, who indoctrinated his students into believing that people like me are the enemy. Jack, whose sexual fantasies likely involve me failing to defend my discipline to two dozen hostile dudes. I bet he gets off to recordings of me mispronouncing *syzygy* at the eleventh-grade science fair.

This is a setup. The teaching demonstration was always going to be my *Titanic*—the ship, not the high-grossing motion picture.

Except that, no.

I hold Jack's eyes and give him my sweetest, most feral smile. *You underestimated me*, it says, and he knows it. Because he half smiles back and nods minutely—devious, ready, coiled. *Have I, Elsie?*

It's on.

"You make a really good point, Cole." I set down my clicker and wander from behind the podium. "Theoretical physics *can* be a waste of time." I take off my suit jacket, even though it's cold. I glance down at my abdomen to make sure the bump of my pod is not visible. *I'm basically one of you. Two, three years older? Look, I'm sitting on the table. Let's be friends.* "Who would agree? Show of hands." It takes a few seconds of exchanged *Is this a trap?* looks, but 80 percent of the hands are up in no time.

That's when I raise my own, too.

They laugh. "Aren't you a theorist, Dr. Hannaway?" someone asks.

"Yes, but I get it. And please, call me Elsie." *I'm not like a regular theorist. I'm a cool theorist.* Yikes. Erwin Schrödinger, avert your eyes. "It *is* unfair that most of the physicists who win Nobel Prizes or become household names are theorists. Newton. Einstein. Feynman. Kaku. Sheldon Cooper got the seven-season spin-off show, but Leonard? Nothing." People chuckle—including Volkov. Jack's slim smile doesn't waver. "The advantage of theory is that we trade in ideas, and ideas are cheap and fast. Experimental physicists need expensive equipment to troubleshoot every step, but theorists can just sit there and write"—I add a calculated shrug—"science fan fiction." It's an actual insult I got when I went to a Harvard social as Cece's plus-one. From a philosophy grad who, after three beers, decided to mansplain to the entire bar why my publications didn't really count.

The things I do for free food.

"Theorists *hide* behind fancy math," Cole says. *Sweet summer STEMlord. I promise you're not as edgy as you think.*

"What I don't get is . . . what's the point of building abstract theories that are not even bound by the laws of nature?" says the guy next to Cole. He's wearing a long-sleeved tee that reads "Physics and Chill" in the *Shrek* font. I kinda love it.

"Experiments are way more useful." Another dude. In the first row.

"You only care about what *might* be, but not what actually *is*." Dude, of course. This time from the third row. "The possible applications are always an afterthought."

Many students nod. So do I, because I can read them like a large-print edition. I know the exact Elsie they want.

Time to bring this home.

"What you guys are saying is that theoretical physics doesn't always end in a product. And to that, all I can say is . . . I agree. Physics is like sex: it may yield practical results, but often that's not *why* we do it." *At least that's what Feynman once said. He's also on record as calling women worthless bitches, but we'll let it slide since his quote made you laugh.* "How many of you are experimentalists?" Almost all hands shoot up, and Cole's the highest. I'm depressingly unsurprised. "The truth is, you guys are right. Theorists *do* focus on mathematical models and abstract concepts. But they do it hoping that experimentalists like you will come across our theories and decide to prove us right." *Ugh.* I want a shower and a bar of industrial-strength soap. "And that's why I want to talk with you guys about my theories on Wigner crystallization. So that I can hear your opinions and improve through your feedback. I don't know when theorists and experimentalists became rivals, but physics is not about competition—it's about collaboration. You're free to make up your mind, and I'm not going to try and convince you that *you* need my theories. I will acknowledge, however, that *I* need your experiments." Am I laying it on too thick? Nope. Well, yes. But the grads love it. They nod. They murmur. A couple of them grin smugly.

It's my cue to unsheathe my warmest smile. "Does that answer your question, Cole?"

It does. Cole's ravenous ego has been sufficiently fed with scraps of my dignity. Oh, the things I do for healthcare and pension funds matching. "Yes, Elsie. Thank you for addressing my concerns."

Dickbag. "Excellent." I push away from the table and walk back to the podium. "I'm *so* excited to tell you about Wigner crystallization. Feel free to interrupt again at any point, because what you take out of the lecture, that's what matters." A beat. Then I deliver my final blow. "Unless you multiply it by the speed of light. In which case it *energies*."

Aaand, scene.

I lift my eyes just as Volkov starts wheezing. Beside him, Monica gives me a delighted look: her gladiator, making her proud. I allow the students a few seconds to groan at my cheesy, dorky pun that they secretly love because—who doesn't? "Thank you, I'll be here all week." Groans turn into chuckles.

And that's when I let myself look at Jack. My chin lifts, just a millimeter. *I told you you'd regret taking me on, Dr. Smith-Turner.*

Jack stares back, expressionless. Not smiling. Not frowning. Not gritting his teeth. He just stares, in what I really hope is a reassessment of my threat to his physics domination plan. To his precious George. It's fleeting, and I'm probably imagining it, but I could almost swear that I spot a twinkle in the blue slice of his eye.

I shelve it as a win and get started with my talk.

AFTER THE TEACHING DEMONSTRATION I COULD USE A NAP, but my day is booked full. I have a meeting with the dean of the School of Science, a pleasant guy who sips coffee from a tentacle mug that has me pondering his porn preferences. Then there's an informal lunch with two physics profs—clearly a couple having a lovers' spat, which results in me staring at my salad while they bicker over someone named Raul. Afterward I get a five-minute bathroom break (spent figuring out whether my insulin pod is acting up or I'm just a dumpster fire of paranoia) followed by one-on-one interviews.

One-on-ones are, of course, what I'm best at. It's simple math: being the Elsie one person wants is much easier than negotiating between the Elsies twelve different people demand. These interviews are ostensibly for me to ask questions about the department that will help me decide whether to accept an offer, but let's not forget that (1) my current job situation is a bukkake of shit, and (2) carrying out interviews qualifies as academic service, and academics hate service with the intensity of a thousand quasars.

Luckily, I'm a pro at making people feel like time spent with me is not wasted. Dr. Ikagawa uses inflatable yoga balls instead of chairs—not ideal in a pencil skirt, but conducive to bonding conversation over our core and upper-body routines. Dr. Voight has been on hold with his dental insurance for hours, and when I let him spend our fifteen minutes fighting them on the phone, he looks like he could kiss me. I trap a mosquito that's been infesting Alvarez's office and make a lifelong friend. I workshop Dr. Albritton's syllabus; laugh with Dr. Deol about his son's third-grade teacher, who still thinks Pluto is a planet; nod as Dr. Sader sips on a Capri Sun while rambling about dark matter being not a clump but a smoothly distributed wavy superfluid.

It's going well, I tell myself as a gangly grad student tasked with escorting me around takes me to my seventh interview of the day. *I am projecting affability. Collegiality. Desirabili—*

"Here it is," she says in front of a black door.

I stare at the name plaque for a second. Briefly consider defacing it. Resist my base impulses and tell her, "I think there might be a mistake. My itinerary says that my next meeting is with Dr. Pereira."

Was I looking forward to it after what I overheard last night? No. But since I cannot report him or his buddy to HR without admitting that I broke into a restroom, I was fully ready to make him uncomfortable with passive-aggressive questions about whether he'd be willing to take over my classes if I were to start a family.

It's not like I'm ever getting his vote, anyway.

"There was a change to Dr. Pereira's slots. Jack—I mean, Dr. Smith-Turner—is going to be your last interview."

Maybe I was a baby-seal clubber in a past life. Or a Wall Street CEO. It would explain my luck. "Are you sure?"

"Yeah." She clears her throat. "Dr. Hannaway, I wanted to say . . . you're such an inspiration. When you won that *Forbes* award—well, hardly any physicist ever does, not to mention women. Also, I was in your teaching demonstration today. You were so poised and assertive. Cole's a huge prick, and . . ." She flushes. "Anyway, it was inspiring."

"I—" I flush, too. "I don't know what to—" She scurries away before I can stammer the rest of the sentence.

Was she making fun of me? Does someone *really* find me inspiring? Even though I spend my life pretzeling my personality to avoid being hated? Even though I am the fraudiest of impostors?

It doesn't matter. I sigh and knock on the worst door in all of Boston. "Come," a deep voice says, and I resignedly let myself in.

I don't look around Jack's office. I refuse to care if it's well lit, or wallpapered in brocade, or a pigsty—though, tragically, I do notice that it smells nice. Soap and books and wood and coffee and Jack, the scent of him but in intense, deconstructed notes. Because apparently I know his scent by now, which makes me want to tear my olfactory glands out of my nostrils. Bah.

There's a free chair in front of the desk. I make a beeline for it as he keeps typing on his computer.

And typing.

And typing.

And—wait for it—typing.

Ten seconds go by. Thirty. Forty-five. He has yet to acknowledge me, and the same antagonistic tension from last night bubbles inside me, filling the office. I know exactly what he's doing—*power plays*—and while I cannot stop him, I refuse to let him upset me.

Okay, I refuse to let him *know* that he upsets me.

I don't look around. I don't tap my foot. I don't show impatience or annoyance at his rudeness. Instead I take the iTwat out of my purse and start doing what he does: minding my own damn business.

Dr. Hannaway,

It's Alan, from Quantum Mechanics. I wanted to let you know: I don't really like it. Quantum Mechanics, that is. It's kind of boring. But I don't blame you, it's not your fault. Like, you didn't come up with subatomic particles. (If you did, I apologize). But don't shoot the messenger, right? LOL. I was wondering, could you make your classes more fun? Maybe we could watch a few Quantum Mechanics movies? Just some advice.

Best,
Alan from Quantum Mechanics

Mrs. Hannaway,

What do you mean, federal law prohibits you from discussing my son's grades with me? I pay for his tuition. I demand to know whether he's doing well. This is unacceptable.

Karen

. . . .

Hi Ms. Elsie,

If I skip class to bring my dog to the groomer, does it count as an excused absence?

Halle

PS: I wouldn't ask, but he really needs a haircut.

I roll my eyes, and that's when I notice: Jack's no longer typing. Instead he's leaning back in his chair, those arms that probably have their own Wikipedia entry (top read in all languages, all day, every day) crossed over his chest. His tattoo remains an obscure mystery, and he stares at me silently, as cloudy and impenetrable as usual. How fitting.

I glance at the clock on the wall and inadvertently take in about half of the office, which is large and sunny and tastefully furnished. There's a cactus by the window. Hmph. I've been here for three minutes.

"Are you bored?" he asks, with his stupid, beautiful voice.

"No." I smile, murderously pleasant. "You?"

He doesn't answer. "I believe we're meant to use this time to interview."

"You seemed busy. Didn't want to interfere."

"I was replying to an urgent email." I doubt it. I think he was writing the next great American novel. Making a grocery list. Messing with me. "We're supposed to get to know each other better, Elsie." My name. *Again.* From his lips. That tone, timbre, inflection. "How am I to make a decision on your hiring otherwise?"

Everyone knows exactly where you stand when it comes to my hiring. I almost say it, but I don't want a repeat of last night in the bathroom. I don't want to lose control. I can be calm, even in the face of Jack's portentous dickishness. "What would you like to talk about?"

"I bet we can find something. Blood type? First pet? Favorite color?"

"If you're trying to hack my online banking security questions, you should know there isn't much to steal."

His mouth quirks, and I think something nonsensical: *I'd hate him less if he weren't so handsome. Even less if he were as charming as a morgue. And even* even *less if I could read him, just a little.* "If you'd rather use the time to rest, feel free."

"Thank you. I'm not tired."

"Really? It seems tiresome, being you."

I frown. "Tiresome?"

"It can't be easy"—he taps his finger lightly against the edge of the desk—"this thing you're always doing."

This thing I—what does he mean? He's not referring to . . . He doesn't know about the APE. About the different Elsies. "I'm not sure what you're talking about."

He nods affably, like I said exactly what he expected me to, and disappointed him in the process. He doesn't break eye contact, and as usual, I feel he's stripped a layer of skin off me. Naked, in the worst possible way. I find myself adjusting the hem of my skirt—which is already at a perfectly acceptable length. It was fine this morning in Dr. L.'s office. It was fine on a yoga ball. Why do I feel weird *now*?

"Relax, then. My grads tell me that chair is quite comfortable."

"Is Cole one of your grads?"

"Cole is, I believe, Volkov's." He must notice my surprise, because he adds, "But I wouldn't worry. The Feynman sex quote really had him."

The way he says it (*Feynman sex quote*), all perfect vowels and hard consonants, makes me hot and cold and wanting to look away. Which I stubbornly refuse to do. "This *is* a comfortable chair." I lean back, mimicking his pose. *I'm not intimidated. You're not intimidated. We're both unintimidated.*

"I slept in it once, after a forty-eight-hour experiment."

"I'm *not* going to fall asleep."

"You could."

"Yeah. And you could take out a permanent marker and scribble something on my forehead."

His head tilts. "What would I scribble?"

I shrug. "'Do not hire'? 'Albert Einstein sux'? 'I hate theorists'?"

He steeples his hands. "Is this what you think? That I hate theorists?" He finds me amusing. Or boring. Or pitiful. Or a mix. I wish I could tell, but I shall die in ignorance.

"Your students sure seem to."

"And you think I'm the reason?" He sounds genuinely puzzled by that. The *audacity*.

"Who else?"

He shrugs. "You're discounting a simpler explanation: students interested in experimental physics are both more likely to have pre-conceived notions about theory *and* more likely to choose to take a class taught by me. Correlation does not equal causation."

"Of course." I smile politely. I'm calm. Still calm. "I'm sure the fact that someone they look up to—*you*—notoriously hates theorists has no impact on their view of the discipline."

"Do I?" His head tilts. "Notoriously hate theorists? I regularly collaborate with them. Respect their work. Admire several."

"Name one."

"You." He pins me with his stupid, hyper-seeing look. "You are very impressive, Elsie."

My stomach flips, even though I know he's lying. I just . . . didn't expect this specific lie. "I doubt you know anything about my work."

"I've read every word you've written." He looks serious, but he must be mocking me.

What do I do? Mock back. "Did you enjoy my middle school diary?"

A hint of a crinkle appears at the corners of his eyes. "It was a little Justin Bieber heavy."

"You broke into the wrong childhood bedroom—I was all about Bill Nye."

His mouth twitches. "One of the popular kids, were you?"

"Not to brag, but I also played the tuba in the marching band."

"Lots of competition, I bet." He has a dimple. Only one. Ugh.

"*Tons.* But I had an in. Through the D&D Club."

His laugh is soft. Relaxed. Lopsided. Different from the unyielding expression I've come to expect from him. Even more breaking news: I'm smiling, too. Yikes.

"I bet you weren't half as cool," I say, pressing my lips together, assessing him. The broad shoulders. The strange, striking eyes. The casual confidence of someone who was never picked anything but first during PE. Jack was no marching tuba. "You held the heads of people like me in the toilet bowl. Occupied the janitor's closet with the cheerleaders."

"We mathletes often do," he murmurs, a little cryptic. "Your models are elegant and grounded. It's clear that you have a very intuitive grasp of particle kinetics, and your theories on the transitions to spherulitic structures are fascinating. Your 2021 paper in the *Annals*, in particular."

My eyebrow lifts. I don't believe for a second that anything he's saying is true. "I'm surprised you read the *Annals.*"

He laughs once, silent. "Because it's too advanced for me?"

"Because of what you've done to Christophe Laurendeau."

The detached nothingness of his expression slips. Morphs into something harsh. "Christophe Laurendeau."

"Not a familiar name? He was the editor of the *Annals* when you pulled your stunt. And, more recently, my mentor." Jack's eyes widen into something that looks beautifully, unexpectedly like shock. *Splendid.* I exploit my advantage by leaning forward in the seat, resist the temptation to adjust the hem of my skirt, and say, "No theorist has forgotten about the article. It might have been fifteen years ago, but—"

Wait. Something doesn't add up.

Jack's three years older than Greg, which makes him about five years older than me. Thirty-two or thirty-three. Except that . . .

I study him narrowly. "The hoax article came out when I was in middle school. You must have been . . ."

"Seventeen."

I shrink back in the chair. Was he some sort of wunderkind? "Were you already doing your Ph.D.?"

"I was in high school."

"Then why—how does one submit a paper to a higher education journal at *seventeen*?"

He shrugs, and whatever emotion he was showing a minute ago has been reabsorbed into the customary blank wall. "I didn't know there were age limits."

"No, but most seventeen-year-olds were too busy begging for hall passes or rereading *Twilight*—"

"*Twilight* and Bill Nye, huh?"

"—to focus on cloak-and-dagger ploys that involved writing offensive, unethical parody articles whose only purpose is to deceive hardworking scholars *and slander an entire discipline*." I end the sentence practically yelling, nails clawing the armrests.

Okay. Maybe I'm not *super* calm. Maybe I could use some deep breaths. De-escalate. How does one de-escalate? I don't know. I'm usually *already* de-escalated. Unless Jack's around, that is. Jack, who's sitting there, relaxed, all-knowing. Punchable.

I close my eyes and think of my happy place. A warm beach somewhere. No one is fair haired and massive. Cheese is heavily featured.

"You know what puzzles me?" Jack asks.

"The entire gamut of human emotions?"

"That, too." I look at him. Take in his self-deprecating smile when there isn't a single self-deprecating bone in his body. "But here's the thing: whenever the article comes up, what everyone asks is how I could do such a *horrible* thing. Why did I write it? Why did I submit? Why did I set out to humiliate theoretical physics?"

"As opposed to? What chianti vintage you celebrated your evil triumph with? The breed of the mandatory supervillain white cat you were stroking? The decibels at which you cackled?"

"As opposed to why it got accepted."

I know exactly where he's going with this. "It was a fluke."

"Maybe," he concedes. "But here's the thing: if a theoretical geologist wrote a bullshit article saying that the inner core of the earth is made of nougat, and the foremost authority in the discipline, say, the *New England Journal of Rocks*, decided to publish and endorse the article, I wouldn't be so quick to chalk it off as a fluke. Instead I'd investigate whether there is a systemic problem in the way theoretical geology papers are assessed. Whether *the editor* made a mistake."

I swallow. It goes down like broken glass. "I am willing to acknowledge that the system is fallible, if you stop pretending that you acted out of concern for the injustice of the peer-review system and admit that you maliciously exploited its loopholes because you wanted to . . . You still haven't answered, actually. Why did you do it?"

"Not for any reason you think, Elsie."

I bite my lip to not bark at him to stop using my name. "Not to pull an epic prank and become famous among the lab bros?"

"No." I wish he sounded defensive or offended or—anything at all. He's just matter-of-fact, like he's saying a simple truth.

"And not the same reason you want to hire an experimentalist over me?"

He draws back, looking surprised. Disturbed, even. "You think I don't want to hire you because you're a theorist?"

I almost snort and say, *Yes, of course*, but then I remember my first meeting with him, back in the summer. The way he looked at me a little too hard, hesitated a little too long before shaking my hand. "Well," I concede with a small shrug, "I suppose you do come by your dislike of me honestly."

He huffs out a laugh and shakes his head. "Again, with this supposed dislike."

"I heard you talking to Greg about me." I ignore the way his eyes widen, almost alarmed. "Asking him how quickly he planned to get rid of me." I pull on the hem of my skirt again, and his eyes dart to my knees, lingering for a moment before ricocheting away. I should probably stop doing that. I need a new nervous habit. Nail biting. Fidget spinners. I've heard great things about crystal meth.

"I've never said—"

"Oh, it's fine." I wave my hand. "You have every right to your opinion of me. You think I'm not good enough for him. I don't care." Much.

He bites the inside of his mouth. His paw-like hand reaches out to play with something on his desk—a 3D-printed model of the Large Hadron Collider. "You make lots of assumptions about my thoughts," he says, setting it down. "*Negative* assumptions."

"Your thoughts are clearly negative."

"It might be connected to the fact that you've been insincere with my brother for months."

I sigh. "We can navel-gaze about how abominable a girlfriend I am till Betelgeuse explodes, but there are a few things you don't know about me and Greg, and until—"

"There are *many* things I don't know." He drums his fingers on his desk, slow, methodical. I cannot look away. "I spent hours last night trying to home in on this, and I'm not any closer to sorting you out. For instance, why would you lie about your job? You're an adjunct, not Jeff Bezos's accountant. And the fact that not only are you a physicist, but you're interviewing *here* . . . My first instinct would be to assume that it has something to do with me."

"I—"

"But I saw your face last night. You had no idea who I was. So back to square one. Why the lie? And what else have you lied about?

How have you kept it up for months without Greg realizing it? How will he react when he finds out? And above all, how will *you* react when he finds out?" He stares at me like I'm a hexagonal Rubik's cube. I picture him lying in a bed too small for his frame, wondering all sorts of things about me, and nearly shiver. "Are you in love with my brother, Elsie?"

I swallow. "This is a very intrusive question."

"Is it. Hmm." He shrugs graciously.

"And anyway, Greg is thirty years old. He doesn't need you to run his life."

"Greg is thirty years old, and you are the first person he's been in any kind of romantic relationship with." His eyes harden. "Considering the lies you've been feeding him, it seems that he *does* need someone looking out for him."

"If you just *called* him—"

"He won't be back until Sunday."

"Have you *tried* to get in touch with him?"

"No." His eyes darken. "I'm not going to tell my brother that his girlfriend is secretly a liquid crystal theory superhero on the phone. I'll do him the favor of breaking his heart in person."

"So you can pat him on the back? Say 'there, there'?"

"I'm serious, Elsie."

I cock my head, picturing an empty auditorium. Greg dressed like the apostle Peter. A single person in the audience, clapping loudly after every song. *My best friend.* "You really care about Greg."

"Yes," he says like he's talking to a child, "I care about my brother."

"It's not a given, you know."

"Do you not care about your siblings? Or do your siblings not care about you?"

I shrug, remembering my phone calls with them this morning

LOVE, THEORETICALLY

after they didn't bother answering the phone last night. Lucas picked up half-asleep. Not only didn't he recognize my voice, he also asked, *Elsie who?* "I don't think they are fully aware that I exist in a corporeal form," I murmur, almost thinking out loud. I regret it instantly, because Jack nods in a way that has me wondering if he's filing away the information. Future ammo?

"I'm sorry your brothers are assholes." He sounds surprisingly sincere. "But given your history with lies, you can't blame me for being concerned about mine."

"You didn't know that I was lying when we first met."

"No, I didn't." Jack's expression sharpens. He straightens and leans forward, elbows on his desk. The entire room shifts and thickens with tension. "I did know, however, that there is something about you. That you tirelessly study people. Figure out who they are, what they want, and then mold yourself into whatever shape you think will fit them. I've seen you play half a dozen different roles for half a dozen different situations, switching personalities like you're channel surfing, and I still have no idea who *you* are. So I think it's within my right to be concerned for my brother. And I think it's within my right to be curious about you."

I freeze.

Did he just—

He didn't. He doesn't know *me*. I must have misheard. Misinterpreted. Misunderstood. Mis—*fuck*.

"I—" My hands tremble, and I slide them between my thighs and chair, like a child. I feel bare. Head spinning, I blurt out, "I don't know what you—"

The phone rings. Jacks lifts one finger to signal me to wait and picks up. "Smith-Turner. Hi, Sasha. Yes. She's here. She was just about to . . . Ah. I see. Yeah. No problem. I can take care of it." I'm too shaken by what he just said—*mold yourself into whatever shape you think will fit*—to eavesdrop. Which makes it all the more stupefying when Jack says, "Volkov's in the middle of something and cannot give you a tour of the department." The faint, crooked smile reappears. "But don't worry, Elsie. I'm happy to take over."

7

ELECTRICAL RESISTANCE

I REPEAT TO HIM "THERE'S NO NEED" SO MANY TIMES, THE words lose meaning like in a tongue twister. It's all in vain.

"Jack, I'm sure you have lots of things to do," I say as he ushers me out of his office, arm brushing against mine.

"Like what?"

"Um." Make necklaces out of baby teeth? Deadlift an anvil? "Work?"

He slides his key in the back pocket of his jeans and sizes me up from five feet above me. I feel ridiculously overdressed, even though I'm the one wearing proper professional attire. "I can make the time to show around a potential future colleague."

Don't snort, Elsie. Don't snort. "There really is no need—"

He tuts. "If you keep repeating that, I'll figure that you don't want to hang out with me."

I don't. But I'd love to hang you.

He pushes me down the hallway with a hand between my shoulder blades, and for a second his many feet and inches and pounds feel tantalizingly, inexplicably inviting. I'm tired. A little weary. I could sink against him and . . .

Whoa.

I think I'm getting woozy. Maybe I need to eat. I shouldn't, though. I had vitamin-enriched gummy rabbits between interviews to keep my blood sugar from dropping—unwise, letting yourself get hangry when you're with someone you daydream of slaughtering at baseline. I take out my phone, meaning to check my glycemic levels. Except Jack is staring at it, eyes on the crack splitting the lock screen. (A selfie of Cece and me laughing as we hold up a block of cranberry goat cheese. It was on New Year's Eve, before we spent four hours watching a Belgian movie about cannibalism, then one more hour discussing its emotional throughline. I wanted to die. The cheese was good, though.)

My glucose monitor looks fine, but I want to check my pod. I need a minute alone. Maybe I can pretend I forgot something in Jack's office? I turn around to give the door one longing look, and my eyes fall on his nameplate.

"Where's the *Turner* from, anyway?" Jack gives me a curious glance. I suspect that his leisure pace is faster than my full-on sprint, but he slows down to match me. How gracious. "Greg's last name is just Smith."

"Turner's my mom's last name."

"And Greg didn't take it?"

"See, this seems like the exact type of information that someone who's in a loving relationship with my brother would already have." Okay. That's not *untrue*. "Where was Volkov supposed to take you?"

I take my itinerary out of my minuscule pocket. I have to unfold it about twenty times, which seems to amuse Jack. Dick. "Wait. It says here that Dr. Crowley was going to give me the tour." I look up, hopeful. "You don't need to—"

"Crowley—and Pereira—are no longer on the search committee."

"What?" The very two assholes I overheard in the bathroom? "Why?"

"Something came up. They had to step back." He says it in a monotone, like it's not weird that two faculty members would pull out in the middle of a search. "But I'm happy to take over." He holds my eyes, final, blue-quartered. "What does the schedule say?"

Dammit. "Tour of the labs."

He huffs a laugh. "You sure you want to see those? They're crawling with experimentalists."

I stifle an eye roll. "I'd *love* to see the labs. Like I said, I firmly believe in the collaboration between experimental and theoretical physics, and I value . . ." Jack's eyebrow lifts (subtext: *You're full of shit*), and I trail off.

"Should I just show you the offices, Elsie?"

I press my lips together (subtext: *Stop saying my name*). "Yes, please."

The thing about theoretical physics is, it mostly involves thinking. And reading. And scribbling equations on a chalkboard. And contemplating a hemlock salad when you realize that the last three months of your work don't jive with the Bekenstein-Hawking formula. While writing my dissertation, I spent the bulk of my time in my apartment, staring at the wall, trying to make sense of the segregation of crystals into chiral domains. Every few hours Cece would poke me with the Swiffer to make sure I was alive; Hedgie was perched on her shoulder, eagerly awaiting the green light to feast on my corpse.

We theorists don't really do labs, and the fanciest equipment we need is computers to run simulations. I've never even worn a lab coat—except for the year J.J. made me dress like a sexy neurosurgeon for a Halloween party. Even then, it was 80 percent fishnets.

"Conference rooms are that way." Jack points to the right. His forearm is corded with muscle. What workout even targets those? "About sixty percent of the department focuses mostly on theory. More, if you include hybrid faculty like Volkov." He gives me a sideways glance. "Nice job with the puns, by the way. Did you spend hours googling dad jokes?"

Only about twenty minutes. I'm a skimmer. "Tell me, do you feel safe here?"

"Safe?"

"If over sixty percent of faculty are theorists, there must have been instances of . . . slashed tires? Defaced mailbox? Giant dumps on your desk? Unless you sent every theorist an apology Fudgie the Whale on your first day."

Is that an eye crinkle again? "I'm not the most popular guy on faculty. And I have yet to be invited to the department's weekly happy hour. But most people are civil. And again, I have nothing against theorists."

"Sure. Some of your best friends are theorists."

He holds my eyes as he unlocks a door, and the single dimple makes a reappearance. "This will be your office, Elsie. If your pun game stays on point."

My fantasies of filling Jack with candy and taking a bat to him— do I need sugar?—are derailed by the high window overlooking campus. And the beautiful desk. And the matching shelves. And the giant whiteboard.

God, this office is *spectacular*. I could sit here every day. Take in the hardwood smell. Sink into a comfortable chair MIT procurement purchased for me. Let my brain crunch away connections and expand my theories for hours.

Finish my manuscript—the one that's been on pause for over a year.

I shiver in pleasure at the idea. Unlike at my apartment, no coconut-crab bugs would try to crawl in my mouth. My life would see a 900 percent reduction of *May I pay this class's tuition in Dogecoins* emails. And the salary . . . I'd have personal finances. Real ones, not just dimes I forgot in my winter coat the previous year.

I want this office. I want this job. I want it more than I have ever wanted anything, including that Polly Pocket set at age five.

"Do you need some privacy? A mattress? Emergency contraception?"

I whirl around. Jack is leaning against the doorjamb, the set of his shoulders relaxed, his frame filling the entrance. He stares at me with that lopsided smile that almost has me forgetting that we hate each other.

"It's . . ." I clear my throat. "A nice office."

"Just nice? You looked on the verge of something there."

I collect myself. "No, I . . . What's the teaching load for the position, again?"

He studies me, assessing, and I face away. I've had enough of him for today. "Do you enjoy teaching?"

"Of course," I lie, running a finger over a wooden shelf. It's not even dusty.

"You don't," he says, pilfering truths out of my skull. "Maybe you did before having to teach ninety classes a week, but not anymore." It's not a question. "The teaching load is two classes per semester."

I palm the filing cabinet. "Not too bad."

"You do know that there *are* physics jobs that require no teaching?"

"I can get grants. Buy out my classes so I don't have to teach."

"Grants are rare for theory. It'll take you months to apply, years to hear back. Wouldn't you rather be a full-time researcher?"

I turn around, hands on my hips. "I'm okay with you not wanting me to *get* this job, but I draw the line at you not wanting me to *want* it."

His mouth twitches. "Seems to me like you want to *want* it a little too much."

"Jack, here you are." A young woman stomps at the door of my—okay, *the*—office. She's only a few inches shorter than Jack, with long dark hair and an accent that I cannot place. She is gesticulating. A lot. "They did it *again*."

"Did what?"

"Overrode my booking of the tokamak. Can you believe it? Third time this month, what the fuck? I had it for next week, then bam, kicked from the calendar. All that bullshit about how the reactor is available to all MIT personnel? They *clearly* don't mean grad students. How am I supposed to fuse the plasma—in my fucking pressure cooker?"

"Michi." Jack sounds unfazed.

"If they want me to superheat gases in my bathtub and blow up my roommate's Pomeranian, I will fucking do it, but the entire point of being employed by MIT was not having to coalesce my own antimatter! This is the worst goddamn place in the universe, and I'm going to quit this program. I should have stayed at Caltech. I should have gotten into Grandma's squirrel feeders business—"

"Michi," Jack interrupts, his voice just a touch firmer. "This is Dr. Elsie Hannaway, one of the candidates for the open faculty position. Dr. Hannaway, Michi is one of my grads."

Michi had *not* realized someone else was in the room. The way she turns beet purple is a dead giveaway, and so is her appalled, wide-eyed expression.

I run a quick APE: Michi's smart, motivated, overworked. She likes and trusts Jack (so maybe not *that* smart?). She's mortified her rant was overheard. Judging from her quivering lower lip, she's about to burst into tears.

Uh-oh.

"That sucks," I say quickly. The Elsie she needs commiserates. "I hate it when labs double-book." I've never booked a lab in my entire life. But. "How hard is it to set up a functioning Google calendar?" Very, I assume. But Michi's lip un-quivers. She un-purples.

"Right?"

"It's not just MIT. Every place is like that. I was a grad until a year ago, and we were always the last to get access to equipment." If by equipment you mean colored chalk. "It gets better after you graduate."

The lip re-quivers. "It does?"

"I promise." I smile reassuringly. My weakness is women in STEM. I want to protect them from the structurally unequal hellfire of academia. "In the meantime, I'm sure Jack will be happy to intercede."

Jack's scowl broadcasts his unfamiliarity with the concept of happiness. "I'll make sure you have access, Michi." He says *Michi*, but he's looking at me. Glaring, to be precise. And when Michi scurries away with a nod, he pushes from the door and walks right up to me, a vertical line between his brows.

It's almost a physical shock, redirecting from Michi—open-book, see-through Michi—to Jack. He's the usual blank brick wall of question marks, and I want to tear out my hair. His hair. *All* hair. Why does he have to be so frustrating? Why does he have to be the most unreadable—

"The real girl who wished to be a puppet," he murmurs, low and rumbly.

"What?"

"I can actually watch you do it."

"Do what?"

"Analyze people. Turn yourself on and off."

I take a terrified step back. A combative step forward. I can't read him for shit, and he's in my head? "You know, Jack, we all interact differently with different people. It's called code-switching, a totally normal social skill—"

"Code-switching has nothing to do with *erasing* who you are and twisting what's left of you. Have you ever even booked a lab? What equipment were you denied?"

"Listen, it worked. Michi was about to cry. I anticipated her needs, and there were no tears."

"You *lie*, Elsie. Every single one of your interactions is a lie." He crosses his arms and looms. We're supposed to be on a tour of the department. I feel like he's taking a tour of *me*. "Is this what you do with Greg, too? You *code-switch* a conjured, nonexistent persona he fell in love with?"

"No." Jesus. Greg needs to get his ass back from yoga camp as stat as possible.

"Are you doing it with me, too?" His scowl deepens.

"What? No!" *I can't even read you!*

"Are you turning yourself into what *I* want? Is that why whenever I'm with you, I . . ." His voice trails off, or maybe it doesn't. Maybe I've just reached critical mass.

I'm dizzy. My heart's a drum in my ears. There's a single droplet of cold sweat running down my spine, and I'm sure, absolutely positive that fighting with Jack has burned the last of my glucose molecules.

My blood is 0 percent sugar. Fun.

"Elsie?"

Vision's blurry. Where's the wall? I gotta lean against the—

"Elsie?" Hands. Muscles. Bones. Warmth. I'm pressed against something and—"Elsie, what the hell is going on?"

"Sugar." So nice, not having to stand anymore. I feel *so* light. "Fast-acting carbs. Juice or soda or . . . candy. Can you . . . ?" There's warm, smooth skin under my palm. Then I'm deposited on top of the desk—my desk—my future desk—God, I really hope I get this job—I'll put that Bill Nye figurine I like to pretend J.J. didn't give me by the computer—my Alice and Bella Funko Pops on the cabinet—a plant on the windowsill—something vicious and carnivorous—a Venus flytrap, maybe—I'll feed Jack's cactus to her—I'll feed *Jack* to her—

"Here."

My eyes flutter open. I suspect Jack was gone for a peaceful moment, but now he's back. To witness my misery. Like those arsonists who return to the crime scene to masturbate—

"Elsie. Take it."

There's a bottle in front of my nose, full of a dark liquid. I pry it from his hand and take several long gulps. Instant bliss.

Well, not instant. Not bliss, either. It takes a few minutes for my blood sugar to stabilize. Even then, I still feel like a cadaver. A bad one that you get when you're in med school and show up late for anatomy lab.

Should I drink more? I check my glucose level on the iTwat—shit, my pod malfunctioned *again*. Delivered too much. Blood sugar's under seventy milligrams. I'll take two more sips, then wait two minutes, then—

"You have diabetes."

I look up. Oh, right. Jack's still here. Watching me with a half-hawkish, entirely concerned expression. Taking up most of my future office in that visceral, present way of his. I need to get going with that Venus flytrap purchase.

"Mm-hmm."

"Type 1?"

I nod.

"Why didn't you tell me?"

I take another sip of my soda—which, I'm slowly realizing, is *not* Coke—and laugh. "Why would I tell you? So you can slip Werther's Original in my tea?"

"Funny you mention that." He doesn't seem to be having fun. "Since I've met you exactly five times so far, and during two of those you suffered from some diabetes-related complication that required my help."

"Eight more and I get a free sub?"

He snorts a laugh. "With this level of self-sabotaging, you don't need outside help."

I evil-eye him half-heartedly, too tired to bicker. "The only two times I've had glycemic attacks in the last year were in your presence. Maybe your superpower is making my pod malfunction."

"You need to tell Monica."

"Monica's not going to like me any less because I have diabetes." I think?

His eyes harden. "You think I want you to tell her to diminish your chances? You're shitting on your chances all on your own, with the fainting around and the easily disprovable lies. I'm concerned about your *health*."

"I take full responsibility for my health, and it doesn't affect my work. I'm not required to share my status to—"

"You almost *passed out.*"

"My pump *malfunctioned*. It's old and shitty and I need a new one. But they're prohibitive without health insurance, so."

Does he look guilty? Maybe. Maybe it's just resting frown face. "Does Greg know about the diabetes?"

How socially acceptable would it be for me to burst into Greg's corporate bonding retreat and drag him back to Boston by the ear? "He doesn't need to know."

Jack's lips thin. "Is this part of your game?"

"My what?"

"This weird thing. Where you delete and remake yourself?"

"You are *obsessed.*" And disturbingly right. "Are you into conspiracy theories? Lizard people? Fictional Finland?" I take another sip. "God, this is bitter." The label on the bottle is in a foreign language. "What *is* it?"

"Volkov's favorite drink."

"What?"

"He has his brother send a few cases over from Russia that he rations and cherishes like liquid gold. That's the last bottle."

I'd do a spit take if I could bear to drink another sip. "*What?*"

"Don't worry. I'll mention that you *really* needed it, Elsie. He won't mind much."

"No. No, no, no. Don't tell him. Do *not* tell Volkov. I'm gonna find an import store. Buy a replacement. Where did you get this from? I can . . ."

I trail off. Jack's dimple is back. He's smiling.

Evilly.

"It's not really Volkov's, is it?"

He shakes his head.

"I hate you," I say without heat.

"I know." He grabs the bottle, takes a sip. Scrunches his nose in an almost cute way. Does he know my lips were right there? "Disgusting. I stole it from the student lounge. Only non-diet soda I could find."

"You just *stole* from a grad student?" I laugh.

"Yeah. An unexpected low."

I laugh harder—must be that sugar high. "How do you sleep at night?"

"I have a really firm mattress. Great for spinal health."

Laughing again here. And so is Jack. I take the bottle back and sip again. I guess we're both vaccinated. What's the harm? "God, this tastes like paint thinner."

"Or a plankton isopropyl alcohol smoothie." Oh my God. I'm laughing even *more*. Do I have permanent brain damage? "Are you going to be okay?" His voice is suddenly softer. More intimate. He's really standing closer than we need to be. At least he'll catch me if I fall again.

"Yeah. I just need a second to recover." Last sip. Is this compost juice growing on me? Maybe it's just this place. The midafternoon sunlight warming the hardwood floor. The shelves waiting to be filled with my books. "And another second to marvel at the splendor of my future office."

Jack shakes his head and smiles, almost wistful. "Sorry, Elsie. It won't be your office."

The thought is bloodcurdling. "You're *not* sorry. And you don't know the future. I'm outpunning you, Jack. The teaching demonstration—it went really well. And I didn't even steal Volkov's mother's milk. I have a *chance*."

He studies me for a long moment, silent. Then asks again, "Will you be all right?"

"Yeah, I just need a second to—"

"No, I mean . . . will you be okay? If you lose Greg—because I *will* tell him about you. And if you don't get this job. Will you still be . . . fine?"

I can't immediately decipher his tone. Then I do and burst out laughing.

He's *worried*. He seems genuinely worried about my well-being and state of mind. Which is surprisingly nice and maybe a tad amusing, until I realize why: he's convinced that I'll fail. And that makes me feel . . . something. A mix of anger and fear and something else, reminiscent of the carefree joy that comes from dancing on the graves of enemies who dared to underestimate me.

"What will *you* do if I get this job, Jack?" I lean forward. My face is a couple of inches from his. "Pull out your hair? Ask for the manager? Leave the department and become a Zumba instructor?"

He doesn't pull back. Instead he watches me even more intently, like I'm a critter in the palm of his hand, and I contemplate the possible scenarios, the same ones that must be filling his head, too.

Jack Smith-Turner and Elsie Hannaway. Esteemed colleagues. Office neighbors. Academic foes.

Oh, I could make his life so hard. Spread the rumor that he wraps his entire mouth around the water fountain. Put a nest of killer cicadas in the lowest drawer of his desk. Push him outside bare-eyed during an eclipse. The sky's the limit, and I want to see him suffer. I want to see him lose. I want to see him sweat it. I want to see him cry, because he lost and I won.

But perhaps I won't.

Because: "If you get the job . . ." He leans close. That slice of eye burns bright blue, and his mouth curves. "I'll make do."

"While crying yourself to sleep because I'm not George?"

"Not everyone wants you to be someone else, Elsie." He's wrong about that, but I can smell his skin. It's good in a way that's primeval. Almost evolutionary. I hate it. "And I definitely wouldn't want you to be George."

"And why is that?"

He presses his lips together. He's even closer now. Surprisingly earnest. "It would be a waste."

"A waste of *what*?"

"Of you."

My heart skips. Stumbles. Restarts with a gallop. What does he even—

"Jack! Dr. Hannaway—here you are. My meeting just ended." Volkov appears in the doorframe. "I'm so sorry for running late."

Jack has taken a step back. "No problem," he says, looking at me. "I just hope you wore something reflective."

A moment of silence. Then Volkov registers the pun and starts wheezing. "Oh, Jack, you—you—" He chortles. Jack's already walking out of the room, but he stops in the door for a long glance and a low "Goodbye, Elsie." After a beat, he adds, "It was a pleasure."

8

FRICTION

WHAT DO YOU MEAN, YOU THINK WE SHOULD LEAVE *them be?*"

Mom's voice is so shrill, I glance around to make sure no one overheard her through the phone. Dr. Voight waves at me before slipping inside the auditorium—the one where I'll give my research talk in fifteen minutes—and my stomach flips, omelet-style.

"It's just . . . Lucas is very stubborn. Short of locking him in my dishwasher, I'm not sure how to stop him from acting up." I hasten to add before Mom asks me to do just that, "And I think he'll be okay if we give him space to sulk."

"What about Thanksgiving?"

Uh? "What *about* Thanksgiving?"

"What if he's not done *sulking* by Thanksgiving? Where do I seat him? What if he doesn't show? Your aunt will say that I don't have my family under control. That *she* should host next year! She's been trying to steal this from me for *decades*!"

"Mom, it's . . . January."

"And?"

I spot Jack and Andrea coming my way, laughing, Michi and a gaggle of grads in tow. He's one whole head taller than the crowd—like at every single Smith gathering—and wears a gray long-sleeved henley that manages to look simultaneously like the first thing he found in the laundry hamper *and* a high-end piece tailored to showcase that protein is his favorite macronutrient.

Haute couture by Chuck Norris.

I wish he didn't nod at me with that stupid smirk. I wish he wasn't amused by my glare.

"If by November things aren't better, I'll . . . look into rope restraints and cheap storage space, I promise. Gotta go, Mom. I'll call you back tonight, okay?" I hang up to find a good luck email from Dr. L., who hasn't quite mastered text messaging yet, and smile.

At least *someone* cares.

"I'm so, so sorry about yesterday," Monica says, arriving in a flurry of clicking heels. Her eyes knife into Jack's monstrous shoulders, and I do love how committed she is to despising him. Truly warms my high-risk cardiovascular system. "I left you with Jack for so long. I had no idea Sasha was late—men. *So* unreliable."

"Not a problem." It's not even a lie. Last night I managed to put in two solid hours of email answering before dinner, and I didn't even doze off when Cece told me all about the recent breakthrough in her analysis of "The Odessa Steps" (i.e., act 4 of the 1925 silent movie *Battleship Potyomkin*). We've watched it together before—multiple times, since I made the rookie mistake of pretending to love it the first. But last night I was considerably less tired than usual, and my theory is that Jack's the reason.

Here's the deal: things between him and me are unsalvageably bad. I'll *never* conjure an Elsie able to please him, especially since he's figured out my APE strategies. And as much as I hate knowing that there's someone out there whom I cannot win over, it also lets me off the hook. With Jack, I don't *need* to be someone else, because I *can't* be someone else. It's unsettling, and disturbingly baring, and also . . . relaxing.

Basically, I had fun with Jack Smith-Turner. A phrase never before uttered by a human tongue.

Have I been doing it all wrong? Maybe instead of getting people to think that I'm worth their time, I should stop giving a shit about them? Hmm. Food for thought.

"On the positive, everyone who's had one-on-ones with you *adored* you, Elsie." Monica grins. "And the students—*glowing* feedback. I think we got this in the bag. You just need to nail this research talk."

No pressure. "On it." I smile.

Her hand settles warmly on my shoulder. "You'll be such a wonderful asset to the department."

Ten minutes later, after Monica has introduced me to a packed auditorium (I suspect mandatory attendance), I can still feel the weight of her fingers. She mentioned the Forbes 30 Under 30, the SN 10: Scientists to Watch, and the Young Investigator Prize, and everyone clapped. People look between me and my slides. No one seems to be nodding off yet. I'm talking about the models I created, some unpublished material I haven't had a chance to write up yet, and . . .

God. I fucking love it.

The thing is, I'm good at it. Really, genuinely good. Anything else I've ever been praised for—*You're so pretty, Elsie, so interesting to talk to, so funny, so extroverted, so introverted, so kind, so understanding, so pleasant, so thoughtful, so levelheaded, so insightful, so crazy, so carefree, so disciplined, so intense, so laid-back*—is made up. A product of fog machines and carefully angled mirrors that reflect what *others* want me to be. But physics . . . I didn't fake my way into physics. And I love talking about it to other people—not something I've been able to do over the past year, since I teach approximately seventy bajillion classes and my students are still at the "apple falls on head" stage of physics. I sometimes try to involve Cece in my work, but every time I mention liquid crystals, she giggles and whispers, "My Preciousss." Which is okay. It's not exactly a party topic, but physicists? They're into it. Experimentalists love the applications, and theorists love to wonder what they were up to during the big bang, whether they're the real origin of life on Earth, if they can be added to a smoothie.

It's a win-win.

". . . this was phase two of the model—let me know if it's not *crystal* clear." I deliver the first of my three scheduled puns to a roomful of chuckles. If the world is a just place, this prostitution of my sense of humor will buy me Volkov's vote. "Now, moving on to the third."

Jack's in the fourth row, paying me an uncomfortable amount of attention, writing something in a notebook. At best, he's doodling cool *S*'s—at worst, drafting an online petition to dissuade MIT from hiring a diabetic slug who pilfers imported sodas and catfishes impressionable young men. He has something planned. I know it. He knows it. We both know it, and that's why our gazes meet and hold so often. But I've practiced this talk so much, I could give it while getting my crotch waxed. *Whatever you're plotting, I'm ready for it,* I think at him the next time our eyes catch. He smirks back his familiar, uneven smile.

I carry on and wait for the shoe to drop. And wait. And wait. And . . .

It doesn't. Jack doesn't raise his hand to ask an unintelligible four-part question. His students don't jump out of their chairs to stage an anti-theory flash mob. Once we get to the Q&A, I peek at the ceiling, fully expecting a bucket of pig's blood. Nothing.

Just Dr. Massey, raising his hand from the left side, saying, "What a deeply fascinating model, Dr. Hannaway. Some of the experimentalists here would really benefit from your collaboration." He points at a middle-aged man sitting in front of him. "Toby, you're working on nematics."

"No, not me. It was Dr. Deol."

"No, Deol's particles. Maybe Sasha?"

The room devolves into a chicken coop, everyone talking over everyone until Volkov interrupts: "Wasn't it Dr. Smith-Turner?"

He turns around with effort, looking for someone, and I pray he misspoke. I pray there's another Smith-Turner in the crowd. I pray for a quick and merciful ending. But: "Jack, you've been stuck on your nematics experiments, right? You could use this model, correct?"

I dare to glance at Jack, expecting to see him frown. To scoff. To lash back. But he says, "Indeed, I have. And indeed, I could." He smiles a little, pleased in a way that's not bitter enough for my taste.

I just knocked this talk out of the park. Jack should be sobbing. Why does he look almost . . . admiring?

His eyes hold mine again. I glance away first and take the next question.

. . . .

"YOU ARE A MOST IMPRESSIVE YOUNG SCIENTIST," VOLKOV TELLS me, pausing to pop a bacon-wrapped mushroom in his mouth. "A rising star, with a bright career ahead of you."

"I'll make sure to buy sunglasses." I watch him cackle his way to the canapés table, hoping he won't be back.

The interview went well, but I'm ready for it to be over. This shindig at Monica's place is the homestretch: ostensibly, an informal reception meant to convey the amiable culture of the department and the convivial rapport among its faculty members. But I've been to tons of these back at Northeastern, and all they manage to show is that we academics are awkward, resentful nerds unable to interact with our colleagues without liters of ethanolic lubricant.

Which have by now been distributed. The room ranges from buzzy to outright drunk. The conversation from PS5 games to gossip about the grad students. (Cole is universally loathed, had a soul patch phase, once tried to organize an orgy in the spectroscopy lab. I should introduce him to Uncle Paul.)

Monica's house is fancy and sprawling, and I shouldn't be shocked: she *is* a big shot—of course she has KFC buckets of money. Many of those who manage to stick around academia till the full professor stage do, right? It's just . . . the income difference between tenured faculty and people like me is gaping. Maybe scholars move up from the poverty line and forget all about how they used to jerk awake to coconut-crab roaches crawling on their skin. Maybe there's a switch in the brain that teaches people the difference between hors d'oeuvres and amuse-bouches and makes them want to drop serious cash on cow skull wall decor?

I sip the club soda I pretended to splash with gin and mutter, "God."

"Pretty sure God left this department years ago," someone whispers above my ear.

I turn and—it's Jack. Of course it's Jack. The electron to my nucleus, constantly spinning around me in the most annoying of orbits. He's so close I have to tilt my chin, and from this perspective it strikes me again how handsome he is. Like a picture in an airport store that sells fancy perfume.

"Stop frowning," he orders, and at first I automatically smooth my forehead.

Then I frown harder. "Don't tell me what to do."

"Come on, Elsie." The corner of his lips twitches. "I didn't even ask you to smile."

He's standing in the door, one hand on each side of the doorframe. His biceps brushes against my hair, but I won't step out of reach. I was here first. Also, I'm clearly twelve. "Did you need something?"

"Just checking in. Making sure you've eaten enough."

I roll my eyes. "I did. Thanks, Daddy." My blood sugar is at 120 milligrams. I'm killing it.

"Thought so, since you're not lying facedown on Monica's"—he glances at the rug beneath my feet, and his nose scrunches—"dead Dalmatian?"

"I think it's cowhide?"

"Ah. That explains the skulls on the wall."

"They really . . ." I clear my throat. "Tie the whole room together?"

"You think she killed them herself?"

"Why? Afraid you're next?"

"Of course. Monica's terrifying."

I laugh. There's nothing Jack can do to make me look unhirable now. We're just two friendly archenemies chatting at a party. No one's paying attention to us, which feels oddly nice. Isolating but restful. Because Jack expects nothing from me.

"Are you and Andrea dating?" I ask, because I can and I'm curious.

"No." He seems surprised. "Why?"

I shrug. "I see you together a lot." That's who he was chatting with while Volkov soapboxed about competitive duck herding.

"We're friends, we collaborate, we're the only two faculty members under thirty-five." He takes a sip of his beer. "I don't date much."

Right. That's what Greg said, too. What bugs me is—I'm positive that Andrea, an otherwise brilliant woman, thinks Jack's a nice guy. And that Michi thinks he's a good mentor, judging by how comfortable she feels interacting with him via meltdowns. About anyone else, these would be green flags, but I know better.

"So," I say, "your nematics experiments are going poorly?"

"Indeed. How did you know? Oh, right. You were there when Volkov announced my repeated failures to obtain decent results to a three-hundred-person auditorium." The self-deprecating smile is back, and so is the dimple. I don't want to laugh again, but . . . it's hard. I've had a long day.

"I kind of liked it. In fact, I think I had an orgasm when it happened."

"I bet." His eyes darken around the blue wedge.

"On a scale from taking a CrossFit class to writing parody articles as a form of activism, how mad are you that someone suggested you use a model of mine?"

"What's a CrossFit, and why would I be mad? My lab discussed the application of your model in our meeting today."

I lean back to search his eyes. "What?"

"Michi bragged to everyone that you guys are friends. She followed you on Twitter, I think."

"I don't have Twitter."

"I did tell her you probably aren't @SmexyElsie69—"

"Wait, are you serious? Are you really going to apply my model?"

"Of course."

"But it's a purely theoretical model."

He shrugs. "We've been stuck for months. And it's brilliant. And like I told you *multiple times*, I've always incorporated theoretical models and collaborated with—"

"Stop." I turn to face him directly and get half-wedged under his arm. We look like we're about to embrace. In a *Game of Thrones*, stab-you-while-I-hug-you way. "Listen, I . . . Stop this, please. I don't know what you want from me. I've been adjuncting for a year, and it sucks so much—so, *so* much. I just want a job in a good department to continue with my research."

"You deserve it," he says quietly. I feel the words for irony. Find no trace.

"Stop it," I repeat. "I don't know what game you're playing, but—"

"Game?" He scowls. "I just said that I hope you get the opportunity to continue your work, because you clearly *are* one of the great minds of our generation."

I tense. "I don't need your condescending praises."

"I—" He shakes his head. His hand comes up to my chin, straightens my face to better study me. Which he does, for endless seconds, before asking, "What happened to you, Elsie?"

"Excuse me?" I feel flayed alive when he looks at me like that. Stripped to my bones.

"Every time I mention that I admire your work, you become dismissive and combative."

No, I don't. Or do I? "Maybe if you didn't spend half your time reminding me that I'm on par with a skanky villain from a mid-2000s CW show, I—"

"I am able to multitask." He sounds . . . not upset, but on his way. Not his usual detached self. "I can admire you as a scientist and at the same time resent what you're doing to my brother."

"Allegedly doing to your brother. And . . ." Am I being needlessly antagonistic? No. No, Jack and I *are* antagonists. Insulin and glucagon. Rey and Kylo Ren. Galileo and the entire Catholic Church, circa 1615. "It's hard to believe that you respect me when all I know you for is dissing the very people who do my job *and* advocating for George to be hired."

"That has nothing to do with you, and everything with George— who you know nothing about."

"Right. Maybe if I met him and heard all about his one and a half publications, I'd withdraw my application in cowed admiration."

Jack's eyes widen. "What?" He bites the inside of his cheek. "Elsie. You're operating on some pretty big assumptions—"

"Elsie. Here you are." Monica crosses the cowhide toward us. She looks at me. Then at Jack. Then at me again. "I thought you might need some saving," she murmurs in my ear. Judging from his half smile, Jack heard, too.

"I was just making sure she still wants to work with us after Christos put his hand down his waistband while trying to convince her that cereal is technically soup." Jack's tone is once again amused. Relaxed.

"He does make some valid points," I interject before Monica field-dresses Jack on the cowhide. "Monica, this evening has been so lovely. Thank you so much for having me in your beautiful home."

"But of course. Have you met my family?"

"Your husband, yes. His research is *fascinating*." He's an evolutionary biologist. We teared up together over the tawny frogmouths, who mate for life and let themselves starve by the body of their dead partner. Good times.

"What about Austin, my son? He just got home. He's staying with us—currently between . . . careers. Looks like spending hundreds of thousands of dollars to major in golf management was not a good investment." Her smile is tight. "Did you know Jack and Austin hang out?"

"Oh." I look between Jack and Monica, who seem to find the fact, respectively, amusing and teeth-grind worthy.

"We play basketball at the same gym," Jack explains. His voice vibrates through me, like he's *very* close.

"On Sunday nights. Right during our family dinner—which Austin hasn't attended in weeks."

"Maybe you should install a hoop in your living room." He points at the wall. "Right there, between those two fossils?"

"Maybe *you* should install a hoop up your—oh, there he is. Austin, dear, let me introduce you to our guest of honor."

A tall man resentfully stops staring at his phone to come to us. He's handsome in a common, forgettable kind of way, and initially I think that's why he looks vaguely familiar. But as I watch him exchange a friendly handshake with Jack, I realize it's more than that. I'm positive that I've seen him before. Where, though? I cannot place him. One of my students? No. He must be in his late twenties.

Then it hits me. When Monica says, "Austin, this is a future potential colleague, Dr. Elsie Hannaway."

Because Austin's response is to give me the once-over, snort, and then say, "No, she's not."

And that's when it occurs to me that the last time I met Austin Salt, he offered me seventy dollars to have sex with him.

9

ESCAPE VELOCITY

Fuck.

Fuck, *fuck*, fuck.

It was my fifth or sixth date through Faux, four years ago, and Francesca, the app manager, was scrambling to find someone last minute. "The client doesn't even want a preliminary meeting," she told me over the phone. I was running across campus, from an astroparticle seminar to an Intro to Physics TA meeting, frantically dodging gaggles of undergrads. "All he needs is 'arm candy'—his words. It's the formal inauguration of a new golf course, and he wants to impress his boss. If someone asks, you met through friends a couple of months ago and work in insurance. Background check's good, and he'll pay extra for short notice—you in?"

Rent was due in a week, and I had a grand total of two rotten bananas in the fridge. So I wore one of the three cheap cocktail dresses Cece and I had gone halfsies on, watched a winged eyeliner tutorial, and in the cab ride to the suburbs, got myself carsick editing a fellowship application due the following day.

Austin had gelled-back hair and answered the phone with "Talk to me." Not a bad client as much as an absentee one. "Arm candy" seemed to be code for *pretty wallpaper*, which meant that my job was to sit at our table, smile widely when he introduced me as Lizzie, and wonder why the fancy asparagus crepes were decorated with strawberries. There was lots of downtime, which I used to do some grading, phone hidden under the expensive linen tablecloth. At the end of the night he gave me a ride. We chatted about the hows and whys of golf till we got downtown, at which point he offered me seventy bucks to have sex with him. I said no.

To be fair, he started lower. And to be fairer, I had to say no several times (peppered with a few yeses when questions veered to "Are you serious?" and "Are you saying people pay you to just look hot next to them?" and "Are you really going to act like a bitch?"). I wasn't too scared, because we were on a non-deserted sidewalk. I turned on my heels and ignored him as he yelled, "You're not even that hot! Your tits are tiny and your makeup is shit!"

The following day I told Francesca, who made a gagging noise on the phone, asked the million-dollar question ("God, Elsie. Why *are* men?"), and blocked him from the client database. For the following fake dates, I made an effort to do better makeup and use push-up bras. As a people pleaser *and* a graduate student, I was primed to take all sorts of constructive criticism to heart.

And that was the end of it.

Or just an intermission? Because when Austin looks at me and snorts and says, "No, she's not," the temperature around me drops. I look into Austin's resentful eyes, and my nerves screech. My brain ices over and then shatters into a million tiny razor-sharp fragments that crash noisily into my skull.

I know that I am fucked. Well and truly fucked.

Monica gasps. "For God's sake, Voight's about to spill his wineglass on my Fendi chair." She scurries away, and I cannot breathe.

"What are you doing here?" Austin takes a step closer, and the smell hits: he's been drinking. I'm going to puke in the cow skull.

"Hi, Austin. How are you?" I sound solid, I think. Self-assured, but he ignores me.

"Honestly, it's a good move. You kind of sucked as a hooker."

My shoulder blades make sudden contact with something hard and warm. I must have physically recoiled. And pushed back into—

Jack is behind me. Witnessing all of this. Cross-referencing notes about how terrible I am with Austin. Shit. *Shit*—"What did you just say?" he asks.

"You ever hire her?" He points at me with his chin.

I can't see Jack's face, but I hear the frown in his voice. "Elsie is a physicist."

Austin laughs. It blends seamlessly with the chatter in the background, because people are still eating. Drinking. Arguing. While my professional life falls apart. "Dude, no way. Elsie here is, like, an escort."

Anger bleeds into my panic and I stiffen. "This is incorrect," I hiss. "Not that there would be anything wrong with it, but Faux is a fake-dating app, which you'd know if you read the terms and conditions you agreed to when you signed up. But you're too busy whacking balls around with a crowbar to learn basic literacy *or* how to treat your fellow humans with respect. Step away from me, or—"

"At least I'm not some kind of hooker who doesn't even bother to fuck her clients—"

"Hey." Jack's palm closes around my arm and pulls me back into him, like I'm an unruly child who might walk into traffic. His voice is low and menacing, and I feel it reverberate through my own skin. "Austin. You heard her. She asked you to step away."

Austin lets out an ugly laugh. "This is *my* house."

"Then go to your room and play with your Transformers figurines. Leave her alone."

"Jack, I *paid* her to go out with me. You don't understand—"

"I understand what I'm seeing, so listen to me, asshole." Jack's tone is chilling. Terrifyingly calm. Austin pales and takes a small step back, and I almost feel sorry for him. "You're harassing a woman who asked you to get out of her personal space while she's at a work function. Because she rejected you."

"But I *paid* her to—"

"I don't *care*. She asked you to leave. Get the fuck out of my sight."

Austin doesn't *want* to leave. It's clear in his flared nostrils, in his twitching jaw while he stares at the place above my shoulders where Jack has taken up residence. But he doesn't stand a chance: after a few frustrated seconds he mutters "Fuck this" and finally, *finally* takes a step back.

My heart starts beating again.

"And one more thing," Jack adds.

Austin swallows. "What?"

"If you say *anything* about this, to *anyone*, including your mother, I'm going to make sure you regret it for a long, *long* time. Understood?"

Austin presses his lips together and nods once, tight. Then he disappears into the crowd, into another room, and—

I free my arms and turn around, meaning to . . . I don't know. Thank Jack? Explain myself? Play off what just happened as a fever dream?

Problem is, he's staring down at me. Watching me with sharp, inflexible eyes that miss nothing, and—

He sees everything. Every molecule I am built of—he could list it, describe it, reproduce it in a lab. He sees the rebar structure in me, and I . . . I see nothing. I understand nothing.

I still have no idea what he wants me to be.

"Jack," I say. A barely there whisper, but he can hear me. He can hear *everything*. "Jack. I . . . I just . . ." I shake my head. And then I can't stand to be seen anymore, so I take a step back and weave my way through the room, looking for Monica to make my excuses.

10

INERTIA

N HINDSIGHT," CECE MUSES WHILE NIBBLING PENSIVELY ON A piece of gouda, "we should have seen this coming. Boston's population is seven hundred thousand. Say half are men, and half of that twenty-one to forty—Faux's target demo. Now, Faux's not cheap, and the masses are getting poorer while Jeff Bezos ruthlessly profits off my desperate need for one-day shipping of dill-pickle lip balm. So maybe only a fourth of the dudes can afford to hire us. And of that fourth, half is either in a happily committed relationship or . . . has morals. Now, consider that we've been doing this for about four years, fake-girlfriending an average of two clients a month. If we crunch the numbers . . ." She looks at me expectantly. I consider pretending I'm not a human calculator, then give up.

"Ninety-six men." I sigh. "And their family and friends. In a pool of twenty-one thousand."

Cece holds a carrot to Hedgie, who takes a delicate nibble. "Which makes the probability of us coming across someone we met through Faux in our private lives . . . ? Time to nerd out, nerd queen."

"Bayesian probability? Or frequentist?"

Cece's grin is my favorite of hers, with the tongue sticking out of her teeth. "Doesn't matter. The point is, it's possible that in our quixotic quest to make enough money to pay our taxes—something Jeff Dill Pickle Bezos is *not* asked to do, by the way—we . . ."

"Fucked up?"

"A good assessment."

I let my forehead slide to the table. It's cold, and sticky with something that might *not* be Hedgie's urine. "What if Austin tells his mother that I'm some kind of con woman who tricks her clients into . . . into . . ."

"Into *not* fucking her? Did he look like he might want to talk to Monica?"

"I . . ." Once Jack was done with him, he just looked scared. Shitless, one might add. But also angry, and angry people do angry, stupid things. Like climbing on top of a toilet in the men's restroom with Jack Smith-Turner's hands pressed into their waist. Or forgetting to monitor their glucose levels. God, what a shit show of an interview. At least the most disgraceful moments happened behind the scenes—yay for semiprivate humiliation. "I don't know."

"Either way, as a mother myself," Cece says with a meaningful glance at Hedgie, "if my douchebag kid came to me whining that the rising star of theoretical physics denied him an eighty—"

"Seventy."

"—seventy-dollar hand job—the *audacity* of that bitch—I'd exclusively be angry at my douchebag kid."

I straighten and sigh again. The gouda's predictably gone, so I pick up the carrot and take a small bite, avoiding Hedgie's corner.

Though, why, really? How bad could toxoplasmosis be? Not nearly as painful as the way Jack stared at me after everything. Like he could break me down into the smallest diatomic molecules with a look and a handful of words.

Better take my chances with the salmonella.

"I need to talk to Jack. Explain what Austin said."

Cece scoffs. "You don't owe him anything."

"He helped me, though. Without him I—"

"He stood up for you when some shit-faced manboy verbally harassed you—Elsie, it's the bare minimum. The bar's so low, you could pick it up and beat him with it."

Okay. So maybe I don't *need* to talk to Jack. I want to, though. I want to explain to him that . . .

That what? Really, what? He must have put together that what I'm doing with Greg is similar to what I did with Austin. And if he hasn't . . . didn't I decide two days ago that I don't care what he thinks of me? That he's a lost cause anyway? If I don't get the MIT job, I'm never going to meet Jack again. And if I do . . . we'll be cordial, distant enemies. He's still the nutsack who turned seventeen and decided to declare war on an entire discipline—*my* discipline. So he's the one guy I can't read, the one person who can't be APE'd. All the more reason to never voluntarily interact with him again.

I just don't know why it's scorched into my stupid brain, that last glance he gave me as I stepped out of Monica's home. And the earlier one, when he grabbed my chin and studied me like I'm something unique. My own Cartesian coordinates.

What happened to you, Elsie?

I square my shoulders. "You're right. Greg's the one I need to talk to." Warn him that Jack might ask questions. Give him time to prepare answers. Greg's the reason I was keeping secrets all along. He's the one who deserves protecting. "In the meantime, no more Faux." I look at Cece. "Should you quit, too? You'll be on the job market once you're done with your thesis—what if this happens to you, too?"

"It won't be until next year. We might be dead by then."

"Would be nice, wouldn't it?"

We exchange smiles. "I must say, the situation *is* making me reconsider Faux. Then again, the number of dollars in my bank account is making me reconsider my reconsiderations." She taps her chin. "It's a good reason to keep working with Kirk."

I frown. "Kirk?"

"Yeah, that guy who—"

"I know who Kirk is. I just thought . . . You've been talking about him a lot. And you refer to him by his first name."

"How else should I refer to him?"

"Historically, your clients have been, you know . . . Big Nostrils Jim. Not Anderson Cooper. Doomsday Prepper Pete. Anchovy Breath One. Anchovy Breath Two. Deep V-Neck. Anchovy Breath Three—"

"I get the gist."

"Kirk is always just Kirk, which has me wondering if . . ."

"Whoa." Her eyes widen dramatically. "Am I being *attacked*? In my own *home*?"

"No. I just—"

"At my own *table*?"

I shake my head. "No, I—"

"On my own *chair* that I retrieved from the curbside and that used to have bedbugs and maybe still does?"

"No! I didn't mean to—" I notice Cece's sly smile. "You're evil."

She laughs. "Is Greg still on that hippie retreat where you pay to weed their flower beds? When's he coming back? And when is the search committee voting on the candidates?"

Is she trying to change the topic? "I have no idea. I don't even know if George has already been interviewed. Greg should be back by the weekend, but he'll have tons of messages, and . . ."

"And he'll see a million texts from you. He'll call the second he turns on his phone. You'll calmly explain what happened, and you'll come up with a plan together. Don't worry about it, okay?"

I nod.

As it turns out, Cece is right—I do get a call from Greg the moment he comes back to civilized society. But she's also wrong, because things don't go the way she predicted. Not at all.

Not even a little bit.

MY FIRST THOUGHT WHEN I READ *UNKNOWN BOSTON NUMBER* is that I'm going to be offered the job. It must be the sheer depth of my desperation making an optimist and a fool out of me. For a moment, I see myself holding back tears as I accept an appointment letter. *I would like to thank the Academy, my roommate, and the girl who runs the WhatWouldMarieDo account—my rocks during the harrowing years of grad school. I owe this to you.*

It makes the fall back to reality that much harder.

"Do you know someone named Gregory Smith?" Whoever's on the other end of the line sounds so angry, I briefly forget how to talk.

"Um—"

"I sure hope so, because there are forty unread texts from you on his phone. And if you're his stalker . . . you'll still do. He was brought here an hour ago for emergency dental surgery, and we need someone to come pick him up."

"Pick him . . . up?"

"Yes. It means that you come here. Get him. Then take him

where he lives." She's speaking very slowly. If I told her about my doctoral degree, she would *not* believe me. "With a vehicle such as a car. Or a wheelbarrow, for all I care."

"I—I don't own a car. And I don't know where he lives. Can't you call him an Uber and—"

"Honey, he's drugged out of his mind. I cannot let him walk out of here alone—he just mumbled something about walking into the Charles River to hang out with Aquaman."

I close my eyes. Then I open them. I glance at the lecture I've been preparing, then at the time (6:42 p.m.), then at Hedgie glaring at me from the kitchen counter.

I sigh and hear myself ask, "Where are you located?"

11

CENTRIPETAL FORCE

F GREG WERE A DOG, HE'D BE PEEING ALL OVER THE WAITING room.

In my twenty-seven years, no one has been happier to see me. He leaps (albeit sluggishly) out of his chair, tries (and fails) to spin me around, effusively compliments my stained "May the Mass Times Acceleration Be with You" shirt, and finally sandwiches my face in his palms and says, "I'm about to blow your mind, Elsie. Did you know that quinoa is not a grain? It's like, a sprout. Oh my God, let's do the Harlem Shake!"

Behind the reception counter, the nurse shakes her head and mutters, "High like a hot-air balloon."

"I—thank you for calling me." She looks less pissed than she sounded on the phone, but more exhausted. The place smells like mint, potpourri, and that air hygienists blow into the mouth during cleanings.

"Sure. Get this idiot out of my waiting room, please. I gotta go home and feed my own brood of idiots."

"Of course." I smile reassuringly at Greg, who's petting a strand of hair that escaped my bun. "Like I said, I don't know his home address. Do you have it in your paperwork? Or I could bring him to my place—"

"I've got it."

I turn to the door even though I'm well familiar with the voice—from the past three days of interviewing, from my worst fears, from that weird, intrusive dream I had last night. Greg's already running to his brother, giving him the same unabashed welcome he gave me.

My first thought is a familiar one: *I can't believe they're related.* If they played siblings in an HBO Max miniseries, I'd call bullshit on the casting director. My second is, of course, *Fuck.*

Fucking fuck. Why is *he* here?

I look to the nurse. "Did you . . . did you call *both* of us to pick Greg up?"

"Yup. Because the first person I called was his mom, who told me she'd be here in fifteen and then canceled because of a mani appointment." Her lifted eyebrow is 100 percent judgment. I blame her 0 percent. "I decided to hedge my bets."

"Right," I say. Greg yaps on about his fantabulous quinoa discovery, and I don't want to meet Jack's eyes. I cannot bear for him to see me, not after yesterday's mess at Monica's and that last look. "Understandable." I smile weakly at the nurse. Then I turn, meticulously keeping my eyes on Greg. "Your big bro's here to take you home, so I'm leaving. I'll call tomorrow when you're feeling better, and—"

"Oh, no." Greg looks at me like I'm pouring liquid glue on a brown pelican. "You *can't* leave. That'd be *awful!*"

"But—"

"You have to come!"

"I suggest you do what he says," the nurse tells me. "His tooth was abscessing. They pumped him *full.*"

"Greg, I—"

"Come on, Elsie. I'll pay the usual rate—"

"No. No, *no*, I—" Shit. *Shit.* I chance a look at Jack, expecting to see . . . I don't know. A sneer of disgust. The usual smirk. A SWAT team barging from behind him to handcuff me for solicitation. But he's waiting patiently, hands in the pockets of his jeans, the dark blue of his shirt pulling out the color in his eye. He's not wearing a coat, because he's physically unable to feel cold. Born without thermoreceptors—a tragedy. "Sure. I'll come for a bit. Let's go, Greg." I turn to the nurse, whose interest perked up at *usual rate.* "Is there anything we should know?"

"Here are his meds—starting tomorrow morning. Just put him to bed to sleep the drugs off. And don't let him make any major life decisions for the next four to six hours—no puppy adoption, no MLMs. Also, I googled it: quinoa's a seed."

Greg gasps. "We should get a puppy!"

Jack presses his lips together, but the dimple is right there. "My car's this way. I'll drive you to the humane society."

Buckling Greg up in the back seat of Jack's hybrid SUV takes so long, I contemplate never having kids. As the other not-under-the-influence adult, I'm probably expected to ride in the passenger seat next to Jack, but . . .

Nope.

"I'll sit in the back in case Greg needs anything."

Jack's look clearly says, *I know you're avoiding me,* because of course he does. He knows *everything*—and what he doesn't know is his for the taking, because I'm translucent. Fun.

I realize how bad an idea this was twenty seconds into the ride: whatever they gave Greg is messing with his working memory. He's able to focus only on what's right in front of his eyes, and catastrophically, 70 percent of his field of view happens to be me.

The other 30 is, of course, Jack.

"You guys, this is fun. Is it not fun? Just the three of us. No Mom, no Dad, no Uncle Paul."

"Very fun," Jack says, navigating out of the lot.

Greg's head lolls back against the seat. "Jacky, you can ask Elsie all those things you wanted to know. Hey, Elsie." He attempts to whisper in my ear, though it comes out slurred and very loud. "Jacky has a thing for you. Like, he stares all the time. And he asks so many questions about you."

"Oh, Greg." This is mortifying. "That's . . . *really* not what's happening."

In the front seat, Jack's silence is quietly, painfully loud.

"Full disclosure, Jacky," Greg continues with a loopy grin, "I made up all the answers. I dunno if she likes to travel, if she wants kids, if she's into movies. Like, how'm I s'posed to know?"

Jack's expression through the rearview mirror is sealed. "She has a thing for *Twilight*, I've discovered."

Greg is *delighted*. "The vampire or the wolf—"

"Greg, how was the retreat?" I interrupt him with a smile.

"Sooo mandatory. But then my tooth exploded in my mouth, and I got to leave early. Hey, you know how sometimes there are shoes on the power lines? Who *puts* them there?"

"Um, not sure. Listen, do you remember if you got a chance to check your texts on your way to the dentist? Or your email? Or listen to your voicemails?"

He stares at me with an intense, solemn expression. I tense with anticipation as his eyes go wide. Then he says, "Oh my *God*. We should play I Spy!"

I sigh.

Fifteen minutes later, after Greg claims to spy a bear, P. Diddy, and a can of garbanzo beans, we park outside a pretty Roxbury house carved into two apartments.

"Where are your keys, Greg?" I ask.

"I've got a spare," Jack says, finishing in twenty seconds a parallel parking job that would have taken me twenty minutes and my whole dignity. "Just make sure he doesn't wander into traffic."

I'd like to think that Greg's place is what mine and Cece's would be like if we managed to lift our credenza, could afford non-bedbugged furniture, and were less prone to frolicking in our own filth. It's simple and cozy, covered in knickknacks that remind me of Greg's personality and his quirky sense of humor. Jack dwarfs the entrance, but he doesn't seem out of place. He obviously spends time here, because he knows exactly where to find the light switch, how to raise the thermostat, which shelf to set the mail on.

"Cutlet!" Greg yells, fisting Jack's shirt. "Cutlet—where is she?"

I look around, expecting to see a cat slinking closer, but it's just us in the apartment—me idling, Jack relentlessly inching Greg toward a bedroom. "On my desk at work. Let's go take a nap, G. Sounds nice, right?"

"Did you water her? Has she changed? Does she still remember me?"

"I watered it. Her. She looks the same. Not sure she remembers you, since she's nonsentient—like most cactuses. How 'bout that nap?"

"Can I have a drink first, please?"

"Elsie, could you get him some water while I put him to bed?"

"Milk! Did you know that milk comes from nipples?"

Jack and I exchange a brief *Isn't coparenting fun* glance, and I rush into the kitchen. I can't find the actual glasses, so I pour the milk into a Bonne Maman jar. I'll bring it to Greg, then leave in an Uber the second they disappear into the bedroom. I have my lecture to prep. Cece doesn't know where I am. I can't be alone with Jack. Yes, perfect.

"Here you go," I tell Greg, who's being herded to his bedroom while humming "Gangnam Style." "You only have almond milk— technically *not* from a nipple." I hand him the jar and—big mistake. Huge. Because Greg sips none percent of it before spilling the entirety of it on Jack's shirt.

I gasp. Greg laughs uproariously while yelling something about the milk being back on nipples. Jack gives his brother a patient, ever-suffering-dad smile. "You having fun?"

"Soooo much. Hey, remember when we switched Mom's yogurt with mayo?"

"I do. It was genius—your idea, of course."

"And Mom puked."

"She was pissed. Come on, let's go to bed."

"I got grounded for a day. But you got grounded for two weeks, because she kind of hates you."

"Worth it." Jack smiles, like he doesn't mind being told that his mom hates him. Greg tries to embrace him, and Jack stops him. "Bud, I'll get non-nipple milk all over you."

"Why don't I get him into bed?" I take Greg's arm, pulling him with me. "Go find something clean."

The bedroom is just a tad messier than the rest of the place, the bed still unmade from Greg's last night in Boston. He's narrating a documentary on the environmental toll of almond production, which makes cajoling him into lying down marginally easier. I don't turn on the lights, and he falls quiet while I'm untying his shoe.

Thank God he's asleep. I'll be out of here in a minute and—

"I like you, Elsie."

I look up from Greg's boot. His eyes are closed. "I like you, too, Greg."

"Remember how you said we could be friends?"

"Yeah."

"I want to be friends."

My heart breaks a little. *Not when you snap out of it and check your email, you won't.* "Awesome. Let's be friends."

"Good. Because I like you. Did I mention it?"

"Yup."

"Not *like* like you. I don't know if I can *like* like people."

"I know," I say softly. I pull the boot off and get started on the other.

"But you're cool. Like . . . a Barbie."

"A Barbie?"

"You're not blond. But there's one of you for every occasion."

Something catches the corner of my eye and I turn. Jack. Standing in the doorframe. Listening to us. His expression is dark, his brow is furrowed, and his chest is . . .

Bare.

He's taken off his soiled shirt, and for some reason I am physically unable to look anywhere but at his body. Which has me realizing that I was totally wrong about him.

He is . . . well, he *is* big. And well muscled, *very* well muscled. And I can see all the . . . all that stuff that people always talk about—

the bulk, the mass, the abs, the biceps and the triceps stretching under the ink. But he's not made the way I thought he'd be. I expected a gym rat body with 0.3 percent body fat and bulging veins, but he's a little different. He's real. Imperfectly, usefully strong. There's something unrefined about him, as though he stumbled upon all this mass by chance. As though he's never even thought about taking a mirror selfie in his life.

Something warm and liquid twists behind my navel, and the feeling is so rare for me, so unfamiliar, for a moment I barely recognize it. Then I do, and I flush hotly.

What is *wrong* with me? Why do I find the idea of someone *not* going to the gym attractive? Why can't I stop *staring* at him, and why is he staring back?

Jack clears his throat. He turns to reach for something to wear in Greg's dresser, and whatever's happening between his shoulder blades looks like a religious experience.

"Elsie," Greg mumbles from the bed. I'm grateful for the reminder to look away. "Is soy milk from a nipple?"

"Oh, um . . . no." My voice is hoarse. Breathing's hard, but marginally easier once Jack walks out of the room. "Soy's a bean."

"You're so wise. And full of layers. Like . . ."

"An onion?"

"Like a yogurt with the fruit on the bottom."

I smile and drag a quilt over him. "Let's play a game. I'll go in the living room, and we're both going to count however high we can. Whoever counts highest wins." I have vague memories of Mom making Lucas and Lance do this. Of course, like everything with Lucas and Lance, it always devolved into them fighting over who could count the highest and waking up the entire house.

"What a shitty game." Greg yawns. "I'll kick your ass."

"I bet." I close the door between thirteen and fourteen. Jack's waiting on the green Lawson couch, wearing a too-tight hoodie that's probably tentlike on Greg. The mysteries of genetics.

He doesn't look up. He sits motionless, elbows on his knees, staring at one of Greg's colorful, artsy wall prints with a half-vacant, all-tense expression.

My stomach sinks.

He's pissed. *Really* pissed. I've seen him amused, curious, annoyed, even angry last night with Austin, but this . . . He's *furious.* Because I'm here. Because he thinks I extorted his brother. Because I overfilled the milk jar. There's going to be a whole messy confrontation, and after the last three days, I'm not even sure I want to avoid it.

"Listen." I take two steps toward him, one back, two forward. If we have to argue, we might as well be close. Keep the volume down to avoid waking Greg. I run my sweaty palms over the back of my leggings. "I know I haven't been exactly . . . truthful. And I assume you're figuring out what's going on between Greg and me. But this entire shit show is reaching a quantum-entanglement, spontaneous-parametric-down-conversion, decoherent stage. And I'm asking you to wait till Greg feels better to have a frank conversation with him."

Jack opens his mouth, no doubt to unleash his wrath, and then . . .

He doesn't.

Instead he closes it, shakes his head, and covers his eyes with his hands.

Oh, fuck. What *is* this?

"Jack?" No answer. "Jack, I . . ."

I debate what to do for a moment, then go sit next to him. If he starts yelling now . . . well. R.I.P. my eardrum.

"It's okay," I say. "Greg's not sick or anything, I promise. Nothing bad is—"

"He told me." Jack straightens his back, eyes once again on the print. "I should have known."

"Known what?"

"When he was . . . I'm not sure. Fifteen? He was still in high school. I came back from college during break." His throat works. "He took me aside and said that he was worried. That he couldn't imagine ever wanting to be in a romantic relationship. And I told him he shouldn't worry. That it was still early and he'd find someone. That it was normal to be nervous before becoming sexually active. That he should just keep an open mind. And then I . . ." Something jumps in Jack's jaw. He closes his eyes. "And then I asked to watch *Battlestar Galactica* together. Like a total fucking asshole."

I never came out to anyone in my family, Greg once told me. *I think I tried, once. Kind of. But then I chickened out and . . . I don't know. It's better this way.*

"Have you ever heard of the ace/aro spectrum?" I ask gently. I'm being gentle to Jack, apparently.

He shakes his head, eyes still closed.

"It's . . . well, some of it is what Greg told you. But there's more. Lots of complexities. There are good resources online that you might want to look up before you guys have another talk. And he . . . I think he's still trying to figure himself out." *Many of us are*, I nearly add. But it's more of myself than I'd rather show.

"Fuck." Jack turns to me. His expression is . . . *Devastated* is the only word that comes to mind. If he started slapping himself, I wouldn't be surprised. "He should have punched me in the face."

I open my mouth. Close it. Then think, *What the hell.* "Would it make you feel better if *I* punched you in the face?"

His eyebrow lifts. "Would it make *you* feel better?"

"Oh, a lot."

He lets out a silent, wistful laugh, and my heart squeezes for both Smith brothers. "Jack, you were a kid. And ignorant. And an asshole. And . . . okay, you're still two of these things." I lift my hand. It hovers for a few seconds by his shoulders while I contemplate the insanity of me voluntarily offering physical and emotional comfort to Dr. Jonathan Smith-Turner. Endothermic hell must be supercooling. "Your apology isn't mine to accept, but I know Greg cares about you as much as you care about him." His shoulder is tight and warm under my palm. Solid.

"He was paying you to pretend he was in a relationship. So my family would get off his back?"

I press my lips together and nod. He swears softly.

"If it makes any difference, he wasn't paying me to . . . Not that there would be anything bad with it, but we didn't . . ." I flush under his eyes.

"Fuck?"

I flush harder and nod. I'm usually pretty matter-of-fact when it comes to sex. Not sure why Jack brings out the blushing adolescent in me. "It's a . . . performance of sorts. I do it for lots of men. Like Austin—who, by the way, was by far my worst client. By parsecs. Greg's the best, of course." I glance away. I'm babbling, but it's weird to talk about Faux with someone who's not directly involved in some capacity. "And Greg and I . . . we became friends. I know it's unbelievable, given that he paid me and that I made up an entire backstory for myself, but I would have done it for free. For him. If I could afford it. Except that . . ."

"Adjuncting doesn't pay for shit?"

I laugh. "Pretty much."

Jack sighs and leans against the back of the couch. "Why didn't you tell me? When we met at the restaurant?"

"It wasn't my thing to tell, you know? You were going to ask why he'd hired me. And I was going to have to waffle, and . . . We should probably stop talking about this. So you can have the conversation with him. Once he's not so, um, focused on quinoa and nipples."

He nods. And then he does something unexpected. Revolutionary. Gobsmacking. Universe rocking.

He says, "I'm sorry, Elsie."

It takes me by surprise. So much so that I blurt out a "For what?"

"For accusing you of lying to my brother. Over and over."

"You did, didn't you?" I cock my head and observe him for a moment. His strong, handsome face looks pained. "Does it hurt?"

"What?"

"This apology." He glares at me, and I laugh. "Was it your first? Did I pop your apology cherry?"

"Apology retracted." His expression shifts into something inward. Like he's finally processing an important, crucial, weighty piece of information. Like something's shifting in his worldview, and the universe around him needs to be adjusted for it. I wonder what that might be till he focuses back on me and says, "You and Greg never dated. He doesn't . . ." There is something hesitant to it, like he needs to hear me confirm it. To make sure it's true, sculpted into stone.

"Nope. He's not into me, never has been." I nearly roll my eyes. "You happy?"

"Yes." His tone is dead serious, and I snort, standing up. Time to leave.

"Shall we Grubhub champagne and cupcakes? Celebrate that I won't be polluting the shades of the Smith estate?"

He gives me an odd, long look. "You think that's the reason I'm happy?"

"What else?"

He shakes his head but doesn't elaborate. Instead he stands, too, following me to the coatrack by the entrance. "Did Greg ever tell you I was a physicist?"

"Nope. Well, yes, but it didn't register, because projectile vomiting was involved—don't ask. He also didn't know *I* was a physicist, because we're usually stingy with personal details. Fake last names, fake professions. An extra layer of protection, you know?"

"We?"

"There are several of us. Fake daters, that is. We work for this app, Faux. Available for Apple and Android—Android version's *so* buggy, though." I need to stop babbling. Jack's looking at me like I'm a Higgs boson about to give him a lap dance.

"Is that how Austin found you?"

"Sadly, yeah." I bite my lower lip. "Do you think he told Monica about my alternative academic career yet?"

"He won't."

"How can you be sure?"

"After you left, I . . . followed up with him." Jack's features are a bland mask. Unreadable as ever. "You'll be fine."

"How do you know?"

"Trust me."

I have no idea what that means. I want to ask, but his tone

sounds final, and anyway . . . "Shouldn't you *want* Austin to tell Monica? So George will get the job? And you guys can bro out in the MIT restroom? Do aromatherapy together and discuss who has the biggest Hadron Collider?"

"George will get the job anyway. And we won't be doing that." A wild dimple appears.

"Everyone knows yours is larger, anyway." His eyebrow cocks and I turn to the coatrack. Shit, did I say that out loud? "I can't believe your mom refused to pick Greg up for a mani. What a jerk."

"She's not."

"She totally *is* a jerk. Come on, who—"

"I meant, she's not my mother. And she wouldn't appreciate you saying otherwise."

"Okay, edgelord. That's a bit dramatic. We all have issues with our parents, but—"

"Caroline is not my mother. Not biologically, nor in any other way."

I turn back to him. "What?"

"My mother is dead. Greg is my half brother."

I stare at him for a long stretch. Then I close my eyes. "Fuck."

"Fuck?"

"Fuck." I scratch my head. "I just hate it when I act like an asshole without even wanting to."

He laughs. "Don't worry. Like you said, she's a jerk. Dad's no better."

"Still, I'm sorry about your mom. I didn't know."

"I'm not surprised." He shrugs in his impossibly tight Suffolk hoodie. "No one talks about her."

"That explains it, though."

"Explains what?"

"Why Greg's such a sweetheart and you . . ."

Dimple: on. "And me?"

I look away, flushing. "Nothing. Anyway." I rummage in my coat pockets for my phone. "Greg's settled down, so I'm going to call an Uber—"

"So," Jack asks conversationally, "what came first?"

I look up. "Uh?"

"The fake-girlfriend enterprise?" He sounds genuinely curious. "Or the myriad of different Elsies you impersonate? Was it on-the-job training, or had you been . . . *modifying* yourself before?"

"I don't—" Oh, there's no point in arguing with him. Not when he's not even wrong. "Listen, now that we've ascertained that I'm not some gold digger threatening the Smith gene pool, could you stop?"

"Stop . . . ?"

"This weird"—I gesticulate between us—"anthropological character study of me. Fine, you got me. I want people to like me, and I give them the *me* they want. I enjoy getting along with others. Gasp. Report me to the authenticity police for aiding and abetting."

"It's easier like that, isn't it?"

"What is?"

"Never showing anyone who you really are." He watches me calmly. Patiently. In the soft light of the apartment, his eyes are dark all around. Sometimes I hear a car running, but the traffic here is not nearly as loud as at my own apartment. "That way if something goes wrong, if someone rejects you, then it's not about *you*, is it? When you're yourself, that's when you're exposed. Vulnerable. But if you hold back . . . Losing a game's always painful, but knowing that you haven't played your best hand makes it bearable."

I hide my fist behind my back, clenching it tight at the unsolicited psychoanalysis. My nails bite into my palm. "Bold of you to assume that the real me is my best hand."

That stupid, crooked half smile is back. "Foolish of you to think it isn't."

"Come, now." I force myself to smile sweetly. "We both know you're only mad because I've never been the Elsie *you* wanted."

"Is that so?" He looks like he was put on this stringed plane of reality as an omniscient entity. I'm angry, and he needs to stop talking like he *understands*.

"It's your own damn fault, Jack."

"Why?"

"Because *you*"—I point my finger in his face—"don't give me *anything*. Everyone else does. Something to latch on to, something I can use to be the person they want. But you're not putting out signals. And that's why you're not getting the VIP treatment like everyone else. So quit whining, please."

"I see." His hand, warm and calloused, closes around my wrist and pulls my index finger from his face down to his chest. He covers the back of my hand with his palm, and what the hell is he—?

"Have you considered that maybe you're already the way I want you to be? That maybe there are no signals because nothing needs to be changed?"

I scoff. Here he is, the Jack I've come to know and loathe. "Right. Sure."

"Once again," he says, tone oddly gentle, "what happened to you, Elsie?"

"Seriously? What happened to—" My hand is still under his. I lift my chin, bringing our faces that much closer. "*This* is what happened to me, Jack: a little over six months ago, I go meet my date's family for the first time. And maybe we aren't really together, but you know what? It doesn't matter. What matters is that since the very start, my date's brother is an absolute *prick*. He keeps staring at me like I'm Ginger Spice crashing the royal wedding. He asks his brother questions about me because he thinks I'm inferior and unworthy. He acts unfriendly and suspicious whenever I'm around. I think we can both agree that given the opportunity, he'd want to change *the shit* out of me."

The last part comes out more aggressively than I meant, but— whatever. I'm mad now, growing exponentially madder as I watch Jack nod slowly, as though considering my words. "Well, that's an interpretation." Heat radiates through me from his grip. It warms my belly, licks up my spine, reminds me how close we've somehow gravitated.

"It's facts," I hiss.

"You're a physicist, Elsie. You should know better than to throw around the word *fact* when quantum mechanics exists."

"What's *your* interpretation, then?"

He says nothing for a long moment, as if collecting his thoughts or deciding whether I'm worth his words. Then something shifts. The air in the room becomes thicker. His Adam's apple bobs, his eyes fix on mine, and he starts talking.

"A little over six months ago, I go to a family birthday expecting the usual night of misery. I'm only there for my brother, because I can count on two fingers the relatives I care about, and he's one of them. We usually stick together, but this dinner is different. My brother brings a date. A woman he's never spoken about—weird, since we talk nearly every day. The family, especially his mom, are thrilled." Jack's grip on my hand shifts. Softens. My fingers are still on his chest, half-pressed against his heart. My own has begun to thump in a hesitant, bracing way.

"She's beautiful, the girl. Really beautiful. There are lots of beautiful women in the world, and if you can believe it, it's not something I usually notice, but I'm paying more attention to her than I otherwise would. Someone pulls Greg away before he has a chance to introduce me yet. But I watch her touch my grandmother's Go board and pick up one of the stones the traditional way, index and middle finger. I watch her sneak a bite of cheese. At some point, I'm almost sure she says something that no one but me understands as a Heisenberg principle joke. And then, when my brother comes back . . . that's when it starts for me. Because I watch her run interference between him and my family in a way I've never managed—and believe me, I've tried. I've spent thirty years of my life trying to protect him from their bullshit, and this girl. She just does it better. I've never seen him so . . . *happy*'s not the right word, but he seems at ease. And as the night goes on, I can't stop looking at her, and I realize something: she's hypervigilant. Constantly thinking two steps ahead. Anticipating others' needs, like people are equations that need to be solved in real time. It's subtle, but it's there, and . . ." He shrugs, free hand coming up to scratch the back of his neck. Like he's still puzzled. My chest is getting heavy, the air in my lungs suddenly leaden.

"That night I get home. Go to bed. Cannot sleep till I admit to myself that I'm jealous. Or envious. A mix. My brother's settling down, keeping secrets, and we're close, so I'm not used to it. And the girl . . . Maybe it's how *good* she is with the person I care about the most. Maybe I have a type, and she just happens to embody it. But . . . well, I'm reacting to her more than I can remember ever doing. With anyone. I'm having some . . . complicated feelings, but I force myself to get over them. Push them out of my head. I am, briefly, successful. Then there's Labor Day.

"She passes out in my arms. No explanation. She acts like nothing happened, and goes back to that personality twisting of hers. She does beg me not to tell Greg, though, and it has me wondering if this is not a solid relationship." His voice is getting lower, deeper, and his eyes move into the middle distance, like he's taking a step backward inside himself. Our hands must have shifted, because my palm is flat under his. I wonder whether he's aware. I wonder why I don't pull free. "And that's when I realize how much of a piece of shit I am. Because she's obviously good for my brother, but I am *relieved* that their relationship might not go anywhere. And I'd love to lie to myself and come up with a valid excuse, but the truth is, it's because I'm a shithead. It's because I want her for myself. I want to . . . I don't even fucking know. I want to take her to dinner, make sure she's relaxed, make sure she doesn't feel like she *needs* to think two steps ahead. I want to know why she can hold a Go stone. And I really, *really* want to . . . well. I'll spare you the graphic details. I'm sure you can imagine."

His smile is small and rueful. My stomach is tight, tied in a million knots, and I'm hot. Hot all over.

"Avoiding her is the best course of action. I don't mind skipping family functions, and my brother never talks about her. It's like he forgets that she exists, which is weird, because I can't *stop* thinking about her. I ask questions, even though I shouldn't. I have a couple of really *wrong*, really *messy* dreams—about my brother's girlfriend. When I see her again after a while, at my grandmother's birthday, it's not any better. It's *worse*—but I'm never going to act on it. It'll go away, I know it. When I find out that she's not who she said she is, I'm mad—*really* mad, because Greg's the best person I know and does *not* deserve this shit. But I'm also a little relieved." He looks at me again. "You know why, Elsie?"

There's something disarmingly, devastatingly self-confident about Jack. About the way he laid out all these facts without hesitating, as though owning his feelings is first and second nature. I study the glint of the lamp hitting his golden hair and wonder why this man would even bother thinking of me. He's figured out my entire game. I came to him empty handed.

My muscles feel numb. I shake my head with difficulty.

"I'm relieved because whatever thing I have for her, it'll go away. It won't survive knowing that she lied. Except that I didn't account for having to watch her talk about physics, or read her work. I didn't account for having to spend two days with her and finding out that she is . . ." He smiles at me. Gentle. Resigned. "Spectacular."

There is a loud noise, but neither of us looks that way. We're locked too tight into each other, bound to whatever this thick, starved, voracious moment between us is.

Until we hear, "Guys, why *does* pee smell bad after you eat asparagus?"

I glance at Greg, who is—

"Naked!" I yelp, twisting my neck to turn away.

"Dude." Jack's voice is hoarse. He's shaking his head. "Where the hell are your clothes?"

"Lost them. Hey, remember when we tried to see who could piss the farthest away?"

Jack winces and takes a step away from me. His hand holds on to mine for just a second longer, and then, all of a sudden, the room is cold and drafty.

"I should probably . . ." I start.

He gives me a weighty look. "Go home."

"Yup." I find my phone while Jack whispers "Let's take this to the bathroom, buddy?" and I slip out as I hear something about "asparapee."

No, thank you.

The second the front door closes behind me, I slump against it. I take a deep breath and stare for a long, long time at the glow of Christmas lights the neighbors forgot to take down.

12

COLLISION (INELASTIC)

From: Dupont.Camilla@bu.edu
Subject: Macbeth reflection paper

Dr. Hannaday,

I'm focusing my paper on Lady Macbeth as the fourth witch. Some parts of the text support this interpretation— do you mind taking a look at what I have so far? The file is attached.

Sincerely,
Cam

. . . .

From: martinash3@umass.edu
Subject: who is cute

U doc u cute u really cute u sooooo cute

. . . .

From: martinash3@umass.edu
Subject: Please disregard

Dr. Hannaway,

My roommate accidentally ate the wrong batch of
brownies and locked himself in the bathroom with my
phone. Please ignore any emails I might have sent.

Cheers,
Ashton

. . . .

From: greenbermichael12@emerson.edu
Subject: Thermo paper

Extension plz.

The following week is soul-crushingly busy, with both the run-
of-the-mill grind of adjuncthood and catching up on the work I
missed during the interview. No worries, though: in between proc-
toring exams and teaching the wonders of the Fraunhofer diffrac-
tion, I still carve out opportunities to agonize over whether I got the
job, when I'll know whether I got the job, how I'll know whether I

got the job, and who'll tell me whether I got the job. See? Excellent multitasking skills. Almost as though I'm not a human disaster juggling several subclinical mood disorders at any given time.

The iTwat becomes my faithful companion, lest I miss a call, an email, a text message, a Vatican smoke signal informing me that my days of pain are gone:

Welcome to MIT, Elsie, says Monica's disembodied voice, ready to groom me as her successor.

You're now part-icle of the Physics Department, Volkov guffaws, hands on his belly.

I hear you stole George's job, Jack tells me, clucking his tongue from a whole foot above me, smiling only with those beautiful, genetically improbable eyes of his. *You and I should really learn to get along.*

It's all in vain. Whenever I pick up, it's telemarketers. Phishing scams reminding me to pay a warranty on the car I do not own. Lucas, calling to bitch about Lance. Lance, calling to bitch about Lucas. Mom, calling to bitch about Lucas and Lance. On one memorable occasion, Dana calling to ask my opinion on whether my brothers would agree to have sex with her at the same time. "Why's everyone so into threesomes all of a sudden?" I ask, and then hastily walk away when the secretary of the UMass Biophysics Department looks up from the exams she's archiving.

I try to call Greg, but he doesn't pick up or answer my texts, which sends me into an additional spiral of anxiety: I've ruined his life. He'll hate me forever. But I can't force him to accept my apology, so I sublimate the nervous energy into refreshing my email: a beloved, if fruitless, hobby. No mit.edu address appears in my inbox—just students on the verge of mental breakdowns at 11:34 on a Wednesday night because they forgot whether chapter 8 will be covered on the test (*Pls pls pls say no, Dr. H.*). Because it's grad school application season, a few even make it to office hours to ask for recommendation letters. When I point out to a Boston University senior that he failed my class, he blinks confusedly and asks, "Is that a no?"

On Thursday night, halfway through loading the dishwasher, Cece catches me trying to unlock the home screen with my elbow.

"That's it." She picks up the iTwat and slides it in her pocket. "I'm confiscating this till tomorrow."

"No. No, please! I really need it." I sound defensive and whiny. What a combination. "It's my Linus blankie."

"You've developed a transitional object in your late twenties?"

"A what?"

"Security blankets, teddy bears, you know. That stuff kids latch on to when they're anxious, they're called transitional objects."

"Where do they transition you to?"

She gives me a consternated look. "The merciless ravages of adulthood."

It actually helps, not being able to stalk the social media of the entire MIT search committee for one evening. Monica posts only about the papers her grads publish, anyway. Volkov hasn't been active since 2017, when he retweeted a "Thank God Newton wasn't under a coconut tree" meme. George, if that's his real account, is all about pics of his lunches (which look annoyingly delicious). Jack, of course, is not on social media.

Which is fine. Because he's in my head—plenty. Not that I know *why*. First, I'm not sure I believe anything he said. Second, I'm almost sure I don't believe anything he said. Third, he's still the guy who wrote that hoax paper, and fourth, he wants another candidate to get the job. Fifth: no. Just no. Sixth, if I believed anything he said, three, four, and five would still be valid.

"No. I didn't see him during the rest of my interview," I tell Dr. L. when I visit him in his office.

He smiles, pleased. His turtleneck is the same dark gray as his hair. "Very well, Elise. And what about your talk? Did you change it like I told you?"

Dr. L.'s feedback can sometimes be a tad out of touch. For instance, I don't think that writing the entire history of liquid crystals research on a slide in 8.5-point font is a good idea, but:

"I did," I lie. When he smiles again, I savor knowing that I pleased him, but the moment I step out of his office, guilt sweeps over me. For deceiving him. Or maybe . . . maybe for having admitted to myself that I find Jack, who ruined my mentor's career, attractive—*viscerally* attractive, in a way I didn't think I was able to notice.

It occurs to me on Friday night that the attraction has little to do with him being tall or handsome, and everything to do with how perceptive he is.

Jack sees *me*—a puppet who maybe, just maybe, is a real girl after all.

And *because* he sees me, I cannot interact with him safely. And that's why I'm not willing to think about the things he said to me. The way he looked. The dimple. His hand sliding up the inside of my thigh, warm, inexorable. *Elsie. You know what I want to do to you?* I shake my head. *I'll spare you the graphic details. I'm sure you can imagine.*

Okay—yes, there have been dreams. *A* dream. Graphic. Detailed. A little sweaty. But no, nope, no. I have other things to get an ulcer over. Time's arrow. Climate change. The lack of government accountability and transparency. My professional future. I can choose what to stress about, and Jack's not it.

That's what I tell myself until Saturday night, when it all comes to a head.

"SOMETIMES I WONDER WHY I WASN'T BORN IN THE EARLY SEV-enteenth century, which really hinders my ability to wear a ruff in public and practice leech-based medicine. Or in ancient Rome, where I could have spent my days in a socially acceptable cycle of reclining, eating, puking. But then I experience wonders like this in IMAX, and I know, I just *know*, that I was meant to be alive in this day and age. My reward for an upright, leechless existence."

I blink at Cece, eyes still bleary from three hours in the theater. When we walked inside, the sun was up and the last week's worth of snow had finally melted. Now it's pitch black, and Cece's catching a whole new batch of flakes with her tongue, like the Florida-born dork she is.

I do love her. Quite a bit. And that's why I sacrificed my precious Saturday afternoon to the gods of Faking It and spent it watching the original version of the famed 1968 Kubrick masterpiece, *2001: A Space Odyssey*. One hundred and sixty excruciating minutes of solar system screen saver pics set to . . . Vivaldi, maybe?

With movies like this, who needs waterboarding?

"Wasn't it amazing?" She beams.

"It sure was lots of things."

Cece is not too high on the cinematography to notice my tone. "You didn't like it?" She frowns. "I do agree that the 'Dawn of Man' scene where the ape looks at the bone was *dearly* missed."

"Um, yeah. That's it."

She steps in front of me, cocking her head. Bundled up in her red maxi coat, she looks about sixteen. "You didn't enjoy the movie?"

It's easier like that, isn't it? Never showing anyone who you really are . . . When you're yourself, that's when you're exposed.

For a split second, what Jack told me flashes through my head, a too-catchy tune earworming around. It's nothing I hadn't known, but once put into words, it got harder to ignore—a brusque shift from procedural to semantic knowledge.

Say I considered it. Cece, after all, is my closest friend. I could smile, slide my arm under hers, pull her toward the T station, and say conversationally, *I didn't like the movie. I have no idea what even happened. My favorite character was the evil computer, and twenty minutes in I was on the verge of letting out the piercing shriek of a million Brood Ten cicadas. Also I'd love to never again watch the director's cut of literally anything—in fact, I'd rather spend an afternoon staring at my student loan portal, the one that makes me burst into tears once a month. And since we're at it, the other day I caught your hedgehog defecating on my pillow. My tea is next.*

The thought of admitting any of this makes my right side ache. That ulcer, probably.

I still slide my arm under Cece's, but what I say is, "It was sublime. The journey of man's consciousness into the universe. The eventual passage of that consciousness onto a new level." It's a line from Roger Ebert's 1997 review of the movie. I memorized it this morning.

"Unparalleled." She beams, then squints. "It's the job—that's why you're blergh."

"I'm not blergh. Am I blergh?"

"Yes. Are you worried about the job?"

"No."

"No?"

"Well," I concede, "yes."

She stops me in the middle of the sidewalk. "You'll get it. You did great."

"I'm . . ." Cece's in a good mood from watching slo-mo space ballet, and I don't want to spoil it. I smile. "Very optimistic."

"Maybe we should watch another movie when we get home." She tugs at my sleeve. "Something light and funny. *Modern Times*? Or *The Great Dictator*? Laughter is the best medicine."

"I think antibiotics are the best medicine. Unless it's a viral infection, in which case—" I stop because someone behind me is saying my name.

The worst thing is, I know exactly whose voice it is, because it's burned into my auditory cortex in a way that signifies certain neural damage. But I turn around anyway, and there he is.

Jack.

In his black North Face coat, which is familiar by now. With his broad shoulders and light hair and inexplicable, gut-felt presence. Taking up more room than he should on the sidewalk, looking at me as though I'm the ghost of Nikola Tesla and meeting me by chance in downtown Boston is unforeseen but very welcome.

"Oh," I croak. Shit. Shit? *Shit. Why* is he here? "Um . . ."

"It's *hi*." God, his voice. That lopsided smile. "That's what you say when you meet someone, Elsie."

"Right." I swallow. "Hi."

My first thought is that I've conjured him. By thinking about him forty times a day—up to and including seconds ago.

The second: I must be cursed. All I want is to excise Jack from my life, but I'm just like the *Australopithecus afarensis* in *2001*: trying to frolic in the prehistoric veldt, forever doomed to be hunted by an alien monolith. (I think? I dozed off.)

The third: he's not alone. There's a tall woman by his side, with long braided hair and deep-red lips. They were clearly in the middle of laughing about something. When Jack stopped to talk to me, she bumped against him and never moved away.

He's on a date.

With someone else.

Jack's out on a date with someone, and it feels like a stone in my belly.

"One of your grads?" the woman asks, entertained. Her dark skin is immaculate, and she looks familiar in the way very beautiful people often do.

"No." Jack has yet to look away from me. "Not quite."

"Hi." Cece interrupts with her most charming grin. "Clearly Elsie is experiencing a breakdown in the social pragmatic skills necessary to introduce us, so . . . what's your name, tall gentleman?"

"Jack."

"Nice to meet you, Jack." She thrusts out her hand, which disappears inside his. I stare, half-paralyzed. "I'm Celeste, Elsie's most favorite person in the whole world."

"Are you?" His eyes slide to mine. "Must be nice." He's still half smiling, like this is making his Saturday night.

"Well, you know, it's hard work. Lots of cheese sharing. And I did just take her to watch *2001*, which she *loved*."

"Oh my God!" The Most Beautiful Woman in the World is delighted. "We were in there, too."

"Stunning, right?"

"A masterpiece. Despite Jack's commentary on the predictability of the 'evil space Siri's' arc."

He lifts one eyebrow. "I got bored."

"You *always* get bored at the movies." She presses her shoulder against his. "I have to confiscate his phone and poke him awake."

"Because you always take me to see boring movies."

She pinches his arm through the coat. "If it were up to you, we'd only watch *Jackass*."

"It was once."

"Once too many."

He shrugs, unbothered. I cannot stop looking at the two of them framed by the snowflakes. The easy banter. Jack's obvious affection. The woman's fingers, still around his sleeve. Something slimy and cold presses behind my sternum.

"So," Cece butts in, "how do you guys know Elsie?"

"I don't, actually," the woman says with a curious look at Jack. "How do *you* know Elsie, Jack?"

His eyes are fixed on me again. "She dated my brother. Among . . . other things."

The atmosphere changes instantly. The air was already icy, dense with the promise of snowstorms, but the temperature drops colder as people parse the meaning of Jack's words.

First there's Cece, who knows that I don't date, not for real, and is putting together where she last heard the name Jack. She scowls and takes a protective step closer, ready to defend me against my most recent archenemy, kitten-hissing-at-a-bison style.

And then there's the woman. Her expression morphs, too, into something knowing and intrigued. "You're Greg's girlfriend. *That* Elsie." She looks between me and Jack once, twice, and then holds her hand out to me. "I've heard so much about you. It's really nice to meet you. I'm George."

My brain halts.

"Well, Georgina. Sepulveda. But please, call me George." Her smile is warm and welcoming, as though I'm a dear friend of Jack's whom she's been dying to meet.

"Georgina Sepulveda," I mouth, barely audible. The name unlocks a drawer in my brain, full of scientific papers, TED Talks, conference addresses. Georgina Sepulveda, young physics hotshot. I'm a fan of her work. She doesn't *look* familiar—she is.

"Yup, that's me." Her hand is still outstretched. I should take it. "I work with Jack."

"George," Jack warns.

"Okay, technically not *yet*. But I'll start at MIT next year. What? Come on, Jack. I got the formal offer, sent back the signed contract this morning. I can tell people." She gives me a conspiratorial look. My stomach churns. "You're a librarian, right? I *love* libraries."

Next to me, Cece sucks in a breath. Meanwhile, I nod. It must be an automatic reaction, because all my neural cells are busy, sluggishly processing what I just heard.

Georgina.

George.

MIT.

Formal offer.

No. No, no, no. There is lead in my belly. Blood thumps in my ears, and—

I take a step back, and for a split second my mind skitters to a place far away: my apartment. The computer I left on the bed. The half-written manuscript on it—the one I was finally going to finish when I got the MIT job.

But I didn't get it. George did, George who's with Jack, and it's over.

I gave it my all, and it wasn't enough.

"Elsie," Jack starts. He must have moved, because George and Cece have disappeared behind him. His throat bobs. "Unsuccessful candidates are not notified until all paperwork is complete."

I shake my head and he falls silent. His eyes are full of compassion, of sincere, heartbreaking sorrow. I cannot bear to watch it.

I turn around slowly. Step away just as slowly, barely taking in the sidewalk. The man walking his husky. The group of students feigning excitement for an upcoming Truffaut retrospective. I walk past them and I walk some more, unhurried, like everything's going to be fine.

Everything will be all right.

I'm at the red crosswalk light when I hear, "Elsie?"

It's Cece, calling from where I left her behind. I ignore her.

"Is everything okay?" George. "Shit, did I do something?"

Cece doesn't answer her. "Elsie, let's . . . let's just go home."

Silence. Then Jack: "Elsie. Come back, please." He sounds like his eyes looked, and it's simply intolerable.

The crossing light turns green. I take a deep breath, let the cold air fill my lungs, and start running.

13

ANNIHILATION

RUN ONE BLOCK.

One and a half.

Two.

Snowflakes stick to my skin. My lungs burn. My pod catches on the waistband of my leggings, and yet it feels good.

I'm no athlete. I've only ever run for the bus and passing PE grades, but this is nicely all-consuming. I focus on the slap of my boots against the sidewalk, the oxygen that's never quite enough, the taste of iron in the back of my throat. My thigh muscles clench, protest, but the feeling of getting away makes up for it. The snow thickens, forming a tunnel, a cocoon to tune everything else out. I'm making my way through a wormhole to a separate point in space-time. A different timeline, in which I'm not a failure, I won't spend one more year without healthcare and the money to live like a fucking human being, I won't disappoint my mentor and my friend and—

Fingers close around my wrist. I lose my balance. Stumble. Fall on my face—no, not quite. Something stops me. Strong hands on my waist straighten me, set me on my heels, and then Jack is towering in front of me, the colossus of everything that's wrong in my life. I want to scratch my nails down his face and see him in as much pain as I am in right now.

I could. We're virtually alone. Hundreds of feet away from Cece and George—

Shit. I just ran away from them like I'm fucking bananas. Like I'm an entire fruit salad.

"You weren't supposed to find out like that," he says, barely winded. I cannot breathe. Fuck this shit—I'm never exercising again. "She has no idea you were the other candidate. You were supposed to be notified on Monday—"

"Fuck you," I spit out.

Jack is taken aback, and so am I. Did not expect for that to come out of my mouth, but in desperatio veritas. We share a second of surprise, then he collects himself. "It was never going to be you, Elsie." His tone is not unkind, but it's not compassionate, either. Like he knows I could take neither. "Volkov and his team were never going to vote for you, because—"

I walk around him, but he grabs my wrist.

"—*because* it was never a fair competition. I told you that George would get the job—"

"It was just *posturing*!"

"It was not. I told you as much as I could without divulging confidential information. This entire search was mishandled, and making you aware of who the other candidate was was a huge misstep on Monica's part—"

"Well, clearly I had no clue who George *really* was."

He exhales. "Elsie." A flake settles on his cheekbone, right under the slice of blue. It instantly melts. "Elsie, you never stood a chance."

"I hate you."

"That's fine. Hate me. But know this: it was a bad-faith interview." He takes a step closer. His warmth makes the chill bearable, and I hate him for it. "Elsie. I am sorry."

"Bullshit."

"Elsie—"

"Do you even realize what this means for me? For you it's—it's *The Hunger Games*, The Academe Edition, but this is my lousy future and everything I've worked toward for my *entire adult life*. I *needed* that job."

"I know."

"No, you *don't* know." I press my hands against his chest and push him away. He doesn't budge, which makes me *explosively* mad. "You don't know what it feels like to have a chronic condition and no health insurance! To have to be *perfect*, to have to be *on* all the time because everyone around you expects you to be! And it's *pretty fucking hard* to be perfect when you're working fifteen-hour days for no money at a job you hate! You're not experiencing any of that, so you don't fucking *know* how I—"

"You're terrified. You're overwhelmed. The job market is at its worst, and you don't know if there'll be openings next year. Believe me, I can relate—"

"Oh really? *You* can relate? With your long and arduous trek into STEM academia as a white, wealthy man?"

He leans forward. His hand closes around my upper arm. "Do you think I'm *happy* about this?"

"You got *exactly* what you wanted!"

"I did." His face hardens. "And a bunch of things I did *not* want, too."

"Oh yeah? Like what? Humiliating another theoretical physicist? Installing your girlfriend down the hall so you can get laid between classes—"

"*Enough.*"

I recoil. His voice is harsh, and it gives just enough pause to process the words that just tumbled out of me.

Oh God. Oh my God. I know Georgina Sepulveda. I know her work. I know how incredibly shitty academia has always been to me, a woman in physics, and I just did the same to *another* woman in physics. A woman in physics whom I've admired for years.

What the hell did I just do? Who the fuck is this person inside me? "I'm *so* sorry." My hand flies to my mouth to muffle a sob. "I—I'm so, *so* sorry. It's not even true. None of it. I've read her articles. She's amazing and—"

"It's okay." Jack's expression is back to soft. Like I'm not the protocluster of all assholes.

"No." I shake my head. "No, she doesn't deserve any of it, and—fuck. *Fuck.*" My throat burns with guilt and something that feels a lot like shame. My cheeks are icy and wet. Very wet. I press the heels of my palms into my eyes, but the tears keep coming.

"Elsie, it's okay. You have every right to be upset—"

"No. It's *not* okay. I'm being unreasonable and none of this is Georgina's fault, and as terrible as you are, it's not your fault, either. I'm the one who fucked up the interview, and—" Another sob. He heard this time. No way he didn't. "You shouldn't let me talk to you like this."

He is silent for a moment. Then I feel him take a step closer. He doesn't touch me, but his coat brushes against mine, a muted, swishing sound.

"I like it, actually."

I look up. There's a faint smile on his lips. "You like being yelled at?"

"I like to see *you*. When you're not trying to be someone else."

I'm actually hiccuping, like a three-year-old with a bruised elbow at the monkey bars. I bite the inside of my cheek to make it stop, but it's a lost battle. Like my entire stupid life. "I can't imagine why."

"I like rare occurrences."

I need to leave. I can't stand here, shivering, being snowed on in the middle of the sidewalk. With Jonathan Smith-Turner. Bawling like I'm on an onion farm. But crying my heart out and thoroughly humiliating myself in front of a professional rival takes up all my energy, which means I can't leave.

"It's cold," he says, like he's reading my mind. "I live five minutes from here." I sniffle, unsure how to answer. *Bully for you?* But then he adds, "Come over." I must have shown some kind of reaction, because he continues, "Not for anything you're thinking. Come over so I can warm you up. I want to explain what happened with the search."

"No. I—" I'm not . . . No.

"I'll answer your questions. Tell you exactly what happened."

"I can't—"

His hand comes up to cup the back of my head, like he wants to make sure that our eyes are locked for this. That we understand each other. "Elsie, if I let you go right now, you're just going to replay the whole interview in your head and reach the misguided conclusion that it's your fault you didn't get the job. And you're never going to let me talk to you again." His expression is painfully honest. How does he know all this stuff about me? *I* don't even know it.

"Maybe I'll just blame it on you." I sniffle.

He huffs out a laugh. "There she is."

"I'm sorry. I know you want to help, but I just—I can't talk now. I'm crying."

"That's fine."

"No, it's not fine. Because I almost never cry"—a sob—"which m-means that I have no idea how to stop."

"Then you can cry forever."

"*No.* I d-don't want to cry. And I left Cece b-behind. And I need to tell Dr. L. that I didn't get the job. And you need to let Georgina k-know where you are. And I'm f-fucking freezing. I hate this city, and I hate being a physicist, and I hate Volkov's stupid p-puns, and—"

His arms are wool and iron around me. Perfectly warm, perfectly solid. It's several more moments of crying before I realize that he has pulled me against him. That this is a *hug.* His lips, dry and warm, press against my forehead as though he cares, as though all he wants is to comfort me. Low murmurs warm my frozen skin, soft sounds that I cannot immediately decipher.

"Shh. It's okay, Elsie. It's going to be fine."

I want to believe him. I want to sink into him more than I've ever wanted anything else. I want to bury my face in his black coat and make it my own personal wormhole. Instead I keep crying huge, silent tears, curl my fingers into the fabric of his sleeve, and hold on tight.

This, *this* is the worst. My lowest yet. And not only is Jack Smith-Turner witnessing it, I also don't have it in me to mind too much.

So when he says, "Let me get you warm. Let me do this one thing for you," and his hand slides down to take mine, I allow him to guide me wherever he wants.

14

CENTER-OF-MOMENTUM FRAME

HIS CONDO IS LARGE, ESPECIALLY FOR DOWNTOWN.
Two-story, 90 percent windows, open floor-y. There might even be a color scheme, dark blues and warm whites, but I can't picture Jack using the word *palette*, so I chalk it up to chance. Still, the place is clean and uncluttered enough that I automatically take off my shoes at the entrance, then pad my way after him to the open-plan kitchen, hoping Jack won't notice that my socks match in pattern (stripes) but not color (pink and orange).

I wish there were hints that he's a closeted brony, or an avid collector of genital casts, but this place screams *I might be an unmarried man in his thirties, but it's not because I don't have my shit together.*

Then again: he might be unmarried, but he's not quite single.

I sit gingerly at the wooden dining table and eye a bowl of fresh fruit; books and printouts of journal articles stacked neatly on the breakfast island; Jack's large back, his muscles bunching under green flannel as he putters around the stove, quickly types something on his phone, and sets a mug on the counter. The snow is picking up, giant flakes swirling under the streetlight, and getting home is going to be a bitch. I could splurge on an Uber. Shouldn't, though.

This is weird. So, *so* weird.

I should be too devastated to feel awkward, but like I said, I'm an excellent multitasker. Able to experience the existential dread seeping into my unemployed bones *and* to fantasize about crawling into a golf hole out of sheer embarrassment. Even worse, I'm so damn cold. I wrap my hands in the tear-sticky sleeves of my cardigan, slide them between my thighs, and close my eyes.

I take a slow, deep breath.

Another.

Another.

Seconds or minutes later, porcelain clinks against the wood. I blink up and Jack's forearm is there, with its roped muscles, and the light hairs, and that cut of tattoo peeking from under the rolled-up sleeve. I've seen him half-naked, and I still don't know what it's supposed to be.

"Hot chocolate," he says gently, as though I'm a skittish kitten.

It smells delicious, of sugar and comfort and heat. I watch a handful of marshmallows float happily around the top, and my mouth waters.

"Do you know," I start, then shake my head and fall silent.

Food can be such an ordeal when your pancreatic cells have left the chat. I remember my last year of middle school, at Chloe Sampson's birthday party—the most *amazing* sheet cake with buttercream frosting. Before eating a slice, the diabetes-havers (i.e., me) needed to know exactly what was in it, to counteract it with the appropriate dose of insulin. But who knows what's in a slice of Costco cake? Not me. And not Mrs. Sampson. And not the Costco website or the customer service hotline, which Mrs. Sampson called while fifteen starving teenage girls glared at me for holding up the party, and . . .

Well. The point is, I've learned to say no to unexpected sugar, no matter how tasty looking. People don't like nuisances.

"Thank you, but I'm not thirsty."

"You need the carb count?" Jack sets the package with the nutritional info beside it. "To adjust your bolus?"

I tilt my head. "Did you just use the word *bolus*?"

"Sure did." He takes a seat right across from me. Even the chairs in *his* house look too small for him.

"How?"

"I went to school. I know words." He seems amused.

"You went to school for words like *centripetal* and *brittleness* and *Rosseland optical depth*. The only people who know stuff about basal insulin and bolus are doctors."

"How fortunate, then."

"*Medical* doctors. And people with diabetes."

He stares for a moment. Then says, "I'm sure others do, too. Families of people with diabetes. Friends. Partners." His voice is deep and rich, and I need to look away from the way he's studying me.

So I take out my phone and quickly check my insulin, pretending I can't feel his eyes on me. I lift my T-shirt to make sure that the pod didn't get dislodged in the single act of exercise I engaged in during the last decade, and . . . Honestly, I can't remember the last time I did this in front of someone who isn't Cece. I want to ask Jack if he read up on diabetes after finding out about mine, but it's possibly the most self-centered thought I've ever had.

I have about forty new notifications across five apps. All from Cece.

CECE: Where are you?

CECE: We're going to the Starbucks across from the theater to wait for you guys to come back.

CECE: Pls, let me know you're okay. I know this sucks but I'm with you. We can do this. We'll move into a basement. I'll pick up more Faux dates, you'll be my sugar baby.

CECE: Jack texted George and told her you're okay. She seems to think he's trustworthy but idk. He looks like an oak tree on steroids with a six-foot-eight wingspan. Is he even human?

CECE: Elsie? 👀

I answer with a quick I'm fine. With Jack. Go home, please. When I look up, Jack is staring.

I clear my throat. "Bad-faith interview. What does it mean?"

His expression darkens. "That would be any interview in which the outcome is, for whatever reason, predecided. Like positions that are advertised as open when they're meant for a specific candidate."

"The MIT position was created for Georgina?" I feel a pang in my chest.

"More complicated than that. The position was originally left vacant when James Bickart—an experimentalist—retired two years ago. He was, I believe, three million years old."

I chuckle despite myself. "Sounds about right."

"You know the type. Lots of tweed. Lots of distrust toward computers, lots of opinions on girls who wear nail polish despite the distraction of their male peers. I was still at Caltech, but I heard some stories. The position should have been refilled immediately, but there were issues with the budget. Then my grants and I moved here." He pushes the forgotten mug closer. I'm impatient to hear more, but I take a sip to please him. The warmth spreading into my stomach is delicious. "I offered to help fund the position to hire another experimentalist—not out of some deep hatred for theorists, if you can believe it. I was hired by MIT to beef up their experimental output. Experimentalists are currently outnumbered, and we were filling a specific position. I mentioned the opening to George, and she told me she was interested in applying. She's at Harvard right now, and physics academia is an old boys' club everywhere, but . . . Harvard's *bad*. So she sent in her materials, and . . . You said you're familiar with her work. As you can imagine, everyone knew it was going to be her from the start."

I can imagine it very well. Her thesis experiments were stepping stones to massive advancements in particle physics. Georgina is the epitome of inspiring.

"Then you applied. And Monica was so impressed by your CV, she decided to bring you in despite the committee recommending against it. It was pointed out to her that there was nothing you could have done during the interview that would have gotten you the job, but she insisted, reasoning that George already had an excellent position at Harvard and might decide not to accept an offer." He sighs. "Even if George weren't a rock star, you have to understand: she and I were in grad school together. We've had half a decade longer than you in the field. Half a decade worth of scientific output, publications, grants."

You're the ideal candidate, Monica told me the first night we met, but I wasn't. I simply wasn't. "Why did Monica . . . ?"

"She tried her all to hire a theorist. And I have to admit, she played her cards well by choosing you as her candidate." He leans forward. I drag my eyes up to his. "Elsie, I was there for the final vote. George won, because she was best qualified, but everyone in the department was impressed with you. Which doesn't surprise me, after I saw your talk and read your articles."

"Right." I press my fingers into my eyes. "My articles."

"They're excellent. And also . . ."

I look at him. "Also?"

He wets his lips, like he needs time to phrase something. "Sometimes, when I read them, I can almost hear them in your voice. Your personality." He shakes his head, self-effacing, like he knows he's being fanciful. "A turn of sentence here. A formula there."

I thought we'd agreed that I don't have a personality, I'm tempted to say. But I'm too tired to be bitter, and Jack . . . he's been nothing but kind. I try for a smile. "I can't blame you for voting for her."

"I didn't."

My eyes widen.

"I recused myself."

"Why?"

He opens his mouth, but the words don't come immediately. "I had a . . . conflict of interest."

"Because of George."

He smiles faintly. "Because of you, Elsie."

I have no idea how to interpret this. So I just don't. "Aren't you and Georgina . . . ?"

He cocks his head, confused. God, he's going to make me say it.

"Together. Aren't you two together?"

He laughs. "No. But we *are* close friends. And unlike Dora, her wife, I'm scared enough of her to let her drag me to see movies that bend the space-time continuum and feel several hours longer than they actually are."

"Oh." Oh. "During the interview, did she . . . know about me? That I was the other candidate?"

"Not until a few minutes ago. I wasn't allowed to tell her who the other candidate was."

"It's just . . ." I scratch my neck, where heat is slowly creeping up. "Earlier, when I introduced myself, she seemed to know who I was."

He freezes—a millisecond of hesitation—then resumes with his casual, stone-strong confidence. "I did talk to her about you. But that was long before your interview. I told her that Greg was finally seeing someone. And that I was struggling."

"Because you disapproved."

"Elsie." His tone is patient but firm. "I understand if you are uncomfortable with what I told you. But I've never lied to you, and I'm not going to start now." His eyes hold mine like a vise. "I was attracted to someone I shouldn't have been attracted to. I felt guilty and frustrated, and I confided in George." There's a frog in my throat. An entire ecosystem. Five astral planes. Something glows and pulsates inside my stomach, and I don't know how to even *begin* to respond. Luckily I don't have to, because Jack adds, "Greg wanted to meet with you this week. I asked him not to."

"Why?"

"Because I had to tell him that you wouldn't get the job. He wasn't sure he wouldn't slip up, and . . . I was planning to be the one who explained everything."

I feel myself smile. "Not a good liar, is he?"

"I'm surprised he didn't blurt out about your arrangement on your first date."

"Yeah." Me too, actually. "How is he?"

"Good. Fine. The tooth healed. We talked about . . . him. Honestly, he didn't insult me nearly as much as he should have."

"Lucky for you, you found me." *Your resident nutjob. Screaming abuse on the sidewalk.*

"Elsie." He's doing that intense eye-holding thing again. "It's fine."

Nothing about this is fine, and it likely won't be for a long time. But I nod anyway and stand. "Right. I . . . Sorry, again. Thank you for explaining everything. And for the hot chocolate. I should go home before the snow gets bad."

He turns to one of the million windows. "Looks bad already."

It does. The outside's a whiteout of flurries, and my post-crying-jag exhaustion is swallowing me whole. Maybe I can throw a smoke bomb and disappear into the quantum vacuum. "Before it gets worse."

He stands, too. "I'll drive you."

"What? No. The roads aren't safe. I'll just take an Uber."

He lifts one eyebrow.

"With Cece," I add, checking my phone. "No need to put you in danger if . . ." I trail off and go through my texts.

CECE: George assumes you're staying with Jack???? Does she know something I don't?????

CECE: Uber surge pricing is insane. George offered to drive me home, but we need to leave now or the snow will strand her car.

CECE: Pls text me to reassure me that he's not making sausages out of your small intestine.

I squeeze my eyes shut for a second. *This is fine. It's okay.*

"You need a new phone," Jack says quietly, glancing at the cracked screen.

I need a new job. "I'll take the bus, actually."

"You think buses are running?"

"Hopefully." I attempt a smile. He's been nothing but kind, and he deserves a smiling, less-than-depressive Elsie. "Unless you'd like me to camp out on your couch," I joke.

"Nah. You can take the bed," he says without pause. Like he's been thinking this through.

He can't have been. "You're not serious."

"I'll even change the sheets."

"I . . . Why?"

He shrugs. "It's been a while."

"I meant, why do you—"

"Because you're cold, Elsie." He steps closer, and I can feel the hot glow of his skin. "Because you had a rough night, and probably a rough month. Because it's not safe. And because I like having you around."

I should probably try to process this, but I'm so, so tired. "Do you have a spare room?"

"I do. No bed in it, though, and according to my friend Adam, my air mattress 'sucks ass.'"

"Is that where you keep the skeletons of theorists?"

He smirks. Doesn't deny it. "I'll take the couch. That's where I fall asleep reading theory articles every night, anyway."

Maybe it's a jab, but it makes me laugh. I glance at the sectional, which could comfortably house three of him and looks cozier than my childhood bed. I'm really not in the position to refuse this, though I make a last-ditch effort. "I wouldn't want to put you out."

"Elsie."

I hate it when he says my name like that. A little stern, amused, annoyed. Like I should be past my bullshit, even though I'm neck deep, drowning in it. "Okay. Thank you."

"Do you need insulin? There's a pharmacy down the block."

Apparently I now discuss my meds supply with Jonathan Smith-Turner. Wild. "I just changed my pod. I'm good."

He nods, and then . . . I guess it's happening. I'm staring at his back and following him up the L-shaped staircase, like the neutron star of helplessness I've been reduced to. I try to picture waking up tomorrow. Squirting his toothpaste on my finger. Making my way downstairs, nonchalantly complimenting his orthopedic pillow, then throwing out a *Laters!* before venturing out into the blinding white.

I'm in the awkwardest timeline, but a proper freak-out will have to wait until I have enough energy.

"Bathroom's in here," he says once we reach the upstairs landing. He rummages in a linen closet, then plugs a night-light into the wall. For me.

My heart squeezes.

"That's my office." He opens a door. "And here's the bedroom."

Jack has a headboard, unlike other, more basic people (me). And a blue comforter, dark sheets that match the rug, and a bed that's probably a few notches above king. Emperor? Galactic dominator? No clue, but I bet he had it custom-made. I bet the woodworker took a good look at Jack and said, "We'll need the wood of a thousand-year Huon pine for a monstrosity like you. I shall head to Tasmania on my skiff at first light."

The rest of the room is tidy and uncluttered—no dirty boxers draped over the leather chair by the window, no Clif Bar wrappers on the floor. The window takes up the entire east wall, and there's one single piece of art: a framed picture of the Large Hadron Collider. The endcap of the Compact Muon Solenoid—a futuristic, mechanical flower.

It's beautiful. I know that Jack did some work at CERN, and maybe he took it himself—

"I'll change the sheets," he says, brushing past me toward the dresser, and I realize that I've been staring.

"Oh, don't. I'm not exactly picky, and . . ." I clear my throat. Whatever, it's fine. "We can both sleep in here. I mean, the bed is huge."

He's giving me his back, but I see the moment the words land. The drawer is half-open, and his movements stutter to a stop. Muscles tense under his shirt, then slowly relax. When he turns around, it's with his usual uneven smile. "Seems like a lot for you," he says. A bit strained, maybe. There's no dimple in sight.

"A lot?"

"Going from running away from me to sleeping in the same bed, in under one hour."

I flush and look at my toes. "I'm sorry. I didn't mean to run—I just . . . And I'm not, like, coming on to you." I'd love to sound sharp and indignant, but it's just not where I'm at.

"We've established that you don't *need* to come on to me, Elsie. Do you want something to sleep in?"

"Oh." I shake my head. "I'm good. I'm wearing leggings, anyway. I figured that if I had to suffer through *2001*, I could at least be comfy."

"I thought you loved the movie." I give him an appalled look.

Jack leans against the dresser, arms crossed. "It's what your friend said," he explains.

"Oh, no. I mean, she thinks I do. She thinks I'm into artsy movies, but I don't really . . ." *Tell her the truth.*

I think Jack can read my mind. "Does she know how much you like *Twilight*?" he asks with a small, kind smile.

"No way." I laugh weakly. "If anything, she might suspect I enjoy it ironically."

"Ironically?"

"Yeah. You know, when you like something because it's bad and love making fun of it?"

He nods. "Is that why you enjoy *Twilight*?"

"I don't know." I sit on the edge of the mattress, gripping the soft comforter. "I don't believe so, no." I ponder. "I like simple, straightforward romance stories with dramatic characters and improbably high stakes," I add, surprising myself a little. I didn't know this before putting it into words, and I feel like Jack has beaten me to some part of myself. Again. "Also, I like to imagine Alice and Bella ending up together after the movie is over."

"I see." As ever, he files away. Then he pulls something that looks like sweats and a tee from under his pillow and heads for the door. "If you change your mind or get cold, just look around. You'll find something to wear."

"Are you giving me permission to rummage around your bedroom? Like you have nothing to hide?"

He lifts one eyebrow. "What would I hide?"

"I don't know." I shrug. "A giant tentacle dildo. Viagra. A diary with a pink locket."

"None of that would be worth hiding," he says, the most quietly confident man in the entire world. "I'll be downstairs if you need anything, okay?" The door closes with a soft click, and I'm right here.

In Jack Smith-Turner's bedroom.

Alone with his pillows and his CERN wall art and probably the desiccated livers of twelve theorists. Plus, a whole lot of falling snow.

I quickly update Cece on the shit show that's my life, then slide under the covers on what I hope isn't Jack's side, groaning in pleasure.

I have a really firm mattress. Great for spinal health.

He sure does, and it's perfect. I immediately relax, enveloped by the comforter and a nice, dark scent that I'm not ready to admit is Jack's. I could stay here forever. Barricade myself. Never face the consequences of my own failures.

Cece replies (This is so weird??? But good night???), and I notice that my battery is at 12 percent. I glance around for a charger, find none, then notice the nightstand. Jack gave me permission, right? So I open the drawer, bracing myself for . . . I don't know. Cock rings. Thumbs. A copy of *Atlas Shrugged*. But the inside is surprisingly mundane: tissues, pens, keys, a flashlight with a few batteries, coins, and a white piece of paper that I cannot resist picking up.

It's a photo. A Polaroid. Blurry, with a Go board and a handful of people clustered around it. Only one face is fully in focus. A girl with brown hair and even features who frowns at the camera and—

Me. It's *me*.

The photo was taken at Millicent Smith's birthday party. A game ends in a draw; Izzy yells at people to smile; all the Smiths turn toward her.

Except for the tallest. Who keeps looking at me, *only* at me, a faint smile on his lips.

"Oh," I say softly. To whom, I don't know.

I lean back against the pillow, staring at the picture pinched between my fingers. Lights still on, contemplating the fact that my furrowed brow resides in Jack's nightstand, I drift off in a handful of seconds and dream of nothing.

WHEN I WAKE UP, THE ALARM CLOCK SAYS 3:46 A.M., AND MY first conscious thought is that I didn't get the job.

I failed.

It happened.

I'm in the worst-case scenario.

The scene of me finding out from George runs on a loop in my brain for several minutes, each replay spotlighting a different mortifying detail.

I ran away in the middle of a conversation like a child.

I left my closest friend alone in a snowstorm.

I said terrible, unfair things.

I don't make the decision to prowl downstairs, but once I'm there, I know it's where I need to be. The lamps are off and the snow is still falling, but enough light comes from the street to make out the contours of the place. Of Jack, who lies on his back on the sectional, a thin blanket draped over his lower half. His eyes are closed, but he's not asleep. Not sure how, but I know it. And he knows that I know it, because when I step closer, he doesn't move, doesn't open his eyes, but he does ask, "Do you need something?" His voice is scratchy, like he did sleep at some point.

"No," I lie. Which, of course, he knows. He knows *everything*.

"Want me to bring you up some water?"

"No. I . . ." I'm awake, but not fully. Because I kneel beside the couch, my head just inches from his, and ask, "I . . . Can I tell you something?"

His eyes finally open. He looks at me, and my hair is probably a mess, I am *surely* a mess, but I need to say this. "I don't . . . What I said about George getting the job because she's your girlfriend. Or friend. Because of some weird political intrigue—it was unfair of me. Despicable. And I don't believe it. And I just—it was awful of me to—"

"Elsie." His tone is even and deep. "Hey. It's okay. You already apologized."

He doesn't get it. "I know, but of all the things that happened today, it seems like the shittiest. And I cannot control any of this—not my career tanking, not whether I'm going to have health insurance or make rent—but I . . . I *can* control the way I react. So I'm sorry I said it. About George. And about you. And . . . people do it to me all the time. In the last year of my Ph.D., I got this stupid award. When I walked into the student lounge the following day, other students were saying that it was only because I was a woman, and . . . I felt like total shit, and I really didn't *think* they were right, but for a second I wasn't sure, for a second they made me doubt myself, and I just—I don't want to be like *them*. I—"

"Hey." Jack shifts and then does something I don't fully understand. He—

Oh.

Somehow, he pulls me up. And somehow, I'm on the couch. *Lying* on the couch. Next to *him*. My head nestles under his chin, his arms surround mine, our thighs tangle together. I open my mouth to say something like *What the hell?* or *Oh my God* or *?!??*, but nothing comes out.

Instead, I burrow deeper.

"Assholes," he says.

I'm still asleep. This is a dream. A nightmare. A blend. "Who?"

"The people who didn't like you winning the *Forbes* award." How does he know that's the award I was talking about? "You should report them."

"For what?" I ask against his throat. He's warm and smells nice. Like sleep. Like clean. Like he could easily change my sink, save kittens stuck in a tree, extinguish a fire. "For being dicks?"

"Yes. Though HR would call it sexual discrimination and building a hostile work environment."

"It's not that simple," I mumble.

"It should be." His chin brushes my hair every time he speaks, and I remember trying to mention what happened to Dr. L. The way he commiserated with me but also said that it would be better if I just forgot it happened and focused my energies on physics.

"What would *you* do if your students said something like that?"

"I'd make sure they can never have a career in physics."

The words vibrate from his skin through mine, and I know he means it. I don't have a single doubt. And that's how I start crying again, like a stupid Versailles fountain, and how his hold on me tightens, legs twisting further with mine. His fingers twine in the hair at my nape and press me deeper into him, shielding me from the cold and everything that's bad.

"I just . . ." I sniffle. "I *really* wanted a chance to finish my molecular theory of two-dimensional liquid crystals."

"I know." His lips press against my hair. Maybe on purpose. "We'll figure out a way."

There is no we, I think. And Jack says, "Not yet, no," with a small sigh that lifts his big chest. "It'll be fine, Elsie. I promise."

He cannot. Promise, that is. There are no reliable sources, no known quantities. We're in a sea of measurement uncertainty. "Maybe this rejection will be my supervillain origin story."

He chuckles. "It won't."

"How do you know?"

"Because this is not your character arc, Elsie. More like a . . . character bump."

I laugh wetly against his Adam's apple. I need to go back upstairs. I've never slept with anyone, never even considered it. I can't control what I do at night—what if I move too much or snore or take up too much space? A cover hog is the Elsie no one wants. But with Jack I have nothing to lose, right? We're past all that. "I can't believe I woke you up at four and you didn't murder me."

"Why would I murder you?"

"Because. It's late."

"Nah. I'm kind of into it." He yawns against the crown of my hair.

"You'll really enjoy the thrill of frequent nighttime urination as a senior citizen, then."

"It's not that." I think he might be about to conk out. "This . . . It fits nicely in a bunch of really weird fantasies I have about you."

I remember the picture in his nightstand. His earnest face in Greg's apartment. I'm breathing the same air as Jack Smith, but I don't feel scared or unsafe.

Just comforted, really. Warm and so sleepy.

"Do these fantasies involve giant tentacle dildos?" I'm yawning, too. Fading fast.

"Of course." I can hear his wry smile. "Way more outlandish stuff, too."

"Milkmaid role-play?"

"Wilder."

"It's furries, isn't it?"

"You wish."

"You have to tell me, or I'll picture necrophilia and dismemberment."

"In my weird fantasies, Elsie . . ." He shifts me till our curves and angles match up. Perfectly. "In my fantasies, you allow me to keep an eye on you." I feel his lips at my temple. "And when I really let go, I imagine that you let me take care of you, too."

It does sound outlandish. "Why?"

"Because in my head, no one has done it before."

I fall asleep huddled in the curve of Jack's throat, wondering whether he might be right.

15

HEAT TRANSFER

THERE ARE NO CURTAINS, AND I WAKE UP FIRST.

The morning light is blinding white, as painful as a million naked mole rats gnawing at my eyeballs. Judging from the slow, rhythmic breath chuffing against the back of my neck, it's something Jack has gotten used to.

I feel rested. Warm and cozy. At some point in the night I must have turned around in his arms, because my back is pressed against his chest. His hand is under my shirt, splayed flat against my belly, fingers brushing my pod, but not in a creepy, sexual way. He's just trying to keep me close so that we both fit under the thin blanket. It should feel like being spooned by a piranha, but it somehow works, and . . .

Maybe it *is* a bit sexual. Because there's something *very* hot, very, *very* hard, very, very, *very* big pressing against my ass.

Jack probably needs to pee. Don't men get hard in the mornings when they need to go to the bathroom? It's a pee erection. A peerection. Yup.

Still, I should leave.

I try to slip out from under Jack's massive biceps, but he resists in his sleep. My heart races when he hums something into my nape, fingers gripping my hip. That hard *thing* pushes into me, trying to nestle farther between the cheeks of my ass, and I gasp.

"You smell so good," he growls into my skin, and all of a sudden I'm glowing with heat and embarrassment and something else, something new and pulsating and unfamiliar. I squirm around the feeling. Oh God. Is this—am I *turned on*? He's barely awake, and I bet he thinks I'm his pillow girlfriend or whoever he slept with last, and I'm here, all hot and—

"Elsie," he nearly grunts. His arm tightens around my waist, then abruptly relaxes.

He's still fast asleep. And this time, when I wiggle away, he lets me go. I'm running upstairs, flushing cherry red, and he's once again breathing evenly.

It's okay. It's fine. Kind of creepy that I'm even thinking about this, since he's asleep. In the bathroom, I brush my teeth (yup, with my finger), wash my face, and reassure Cece that I haven't been sex trafficked.

My inbox is bloated with emails. The highlight:

From: melaniesmom@gmail.com
Subject: Melanie

Melanie is a good person and did not mean to copy that essay from the internet, she told me so, and I believe her because I raised her and in my household we do not condone lies. She was framed (her roommate has a vendetta against her, ever since the menstrual cup incident). Please let my daughter resubmit her assignment.

Melanie's mom

I sigh, twice, then stress-snoop in Jack's cabinets. Finding some Rogaine or antifungal meds or prescription-strength deodorant would humanize him, but there's only toothpaste (wintergreen—disgusting) and soap. So I sit back on the edge of the tub and spend an unspecified length of time thinking of a way to let Dr. L. know that I failed.

I failed *him*.

By the time I crawl downstairs, Jack's moving around the kitchen, phone lodged between shoulder and ear, laughing softly and saying, ". . . since you're staying three days, we—"

He turns around. When he notices me standing at the bottom of the staircase, his smile fades. Yes, I'm still wearing the Northeastern shirt I slept in, and yes, my hands are swallowed by my cardigan, and yes, I can't help stacking my feet on top of each other.

Clearly, I'm bringing sexy back.

"Need to go—see you next week." Jack puts down his phone, then slides a mug of coffee across the kitchen island. For me, I assume. Which means that I have no choice but to make my way there and take a seat on a stool.

He looks a bit disheveled, the back of his hair sticking up, stubble longer than last night, shoulders and arms filling the worn T-shirt, but he still has that air about him. Amused. Confident. Unbothered. I wait for him to mention that we slept together—*We. Slept. Together.* But he doesn't seem to be inclined to be a dick about it.

"Hey," he says.

The peerection (trademark pending) is gone. I think. I can't really see. He probably used the bathroom downstairs and—

Not the point, Elsie. Focus.

"Hey." I take a sip of my coffee—disgusting, as coffee always is. I set down my mug, open my mouth to apologize again about last night, about the state of the world, about the cluster of atoms that shapes my very existence, when he says, "Can I make you breakfast?"

"Oh." I shake my head even as my stomach growls. "I'm fine, I—"

"May I please watch you eat something?" Bam, dimple. "It'll be good for my mental health."

I'll just take this day for what it is: me marinating in a puddle of embarrassment. "If you have a piece of toast, that'd be great. Thank you."

He nods, slips a slice of whole grain in the toaster, and then asks a really odd question. "Why aren't you a full-time researcher?"

I blink. "What?"

"You got your Ph.D., then went straight to adjuncting. Most people try to squeeze in a full-time research position like a postdoc, especially if they're not passionate about teaching."

After years of hearing Dr. L. talk about Jack, it's surreal having *Jack* bring up Dr. L., however obliquely. "I did think of it, but there weren't any in the area. Theorists don't exactly swim in funding . . ."

"What about other places? You want to stay in the Boston area?"

"Yes. Well, I don't *want* to, but I should. For my family."

"Are you close? Do they have health issues?"

"No. And no. Just, my mom and my *brothers* are . . ." Shit shows. Complete, utter shit shows. Like me. "I *can't* leave."

He nods. Like he doesn't fully understand, like he understands too much. "You realize that your skill set would be of interest to more than theorists, right? Your work is highly translational. Experimental physicists would fight to have you on their teams."

They didn't, though. Dr. L. asked around widely, and no one was fighting. No one was even politely arguing. "Like who?"

He holds my eyes for a beat too long, and—

"No." I shake my head. "No."

His mouth twitches. "I do have the funding."

"No."

"And the need."

"Nope."

He's fully smiling. Like I'm his personal entertainment center, amusing him in 4K and Dolby Surround. "We could negotiate salary."

"No. *Nope.* No. I'm *not* going to work for you."

"Why?"

"I'm not going to grade your tests and bring you coffee—"

"I have three TAs." He looks pointedly at my full mug. "And I'm happy to take care of *your* coffee . . . You don't even like coffee, do you?"

I squirm in the stool. "I . . ."

"Oh, Elsie." He shakes his head in mock disappointment and takes away the mug. "I thought you were above sparing my feelings."

"You were really nice to me last night, and . . ." I clear my throat. "Anyway, I can't work for you."

"Why?"

"Because you are *Jonathan Smith-Turner* and almost destroyed my entire field." *And Dr. L. would kill me*, I don't add, but I still feel a stab of guilt for being about to literally break bread with my mentor's archenemy.

"Okay." He shrugs, setting a glass of water and toast in front of me. "Disappointing. But it does give me free rein to ask something else."

"Ask what?"

"Can I take you out?"

The words don't immediately compute. For several seconds they float in my brain like driftwood, aimless, unparsable, and then their meaning dawns on me. "You mean you want to . . . murder me."

He winces. "Once again, what happened to you?"

"You asked to *take me out*—"

"For a date."

"Oh." I blush. "Oh." I scratch the side of my nose. "Um . . ."

Jack's eyebrow lifts. "You seem more alarmed by dinner than murder."

"No. Yeah. I mean, it's just . . . Why?"

"You know, I'm growing concerned about your language comprehension skills." The corner of his mouth is quirking up, and I cannot take this anymore.

"Stop it," I order.

"Stop what?"

"Being *amused* by me! I don't understand why you'd want to . . . We've done nothing but butt heads since the day we met." I cover my eyes with both hands. "Why are you suddenly being so nice? Giving me shelter, offering me a job? I just . . . Is this some fetish of yours? Some people get off on armpit sex, you enjoy messing with me and—"

"Look at me, Elsie." His voice snaps me to attention. Jack has moved around the island and is leaning against it, next to me. The back of his finger taps gently against my hand, grounding me. A silent *Shut up, will you.* "You done spiraling?"

"I'm *not* spiraling," I lie. "Jack, believe me. You don't want to spend time with me."

He nods, thoughtful. "What else don't I want?"

"I'm serious. For one, I'm technically still fake-girlfriending your brother."

"Didn't know it worked as a verb. Cute."

"And you hate the personality-switching thing."

"That won't be a problem." His eyes gleam. "Since I also enjoy calling you on your bullshit."

My cheeks heat. "We have *nothing* in common. What would we even talk about?"

"We could spend two weeks just on liquid crystals. Or you could tell me about *Twilight*. Your erotic Bill Nye fan fiction phase. Stream of consciousness would be fine, too. I'd love to know what you're thinking."

"I think a lot about how much I hate you," I say with no conviction.

"I think a lot about how much you hate me, too." His smile is tender. "When's the last time you had someone in your life you could be completely honest with, Elsie?" Asked by anyone else, it would be a patronizing question. Because it's *him*, it just feels genuine.

"I . . ."

Maybe my parents, when I was very young. But I can't remember a single moment in the past two decades in which I wasn't context dependent. In which I didn't feel the need to cut myself into pieces, serve the one I thought others would want on a silver platter. There have been easier people, like Cece. People who knew most parts of me, like Cece. Even people who recognized the pleaser in me and encouraged me to stop, like Cece.

Okay: there has been Cece. And I'm grateful. But even with her, I've never been fully sincere. I've always been scared that honesty would be the deal breaker.

"It's been a while," I say. But Jack already knew that.

"Then you're overdue."

This is . . . terrifying.

"No," I say firmly, shaking my head. "Thank you for the offer, but I'm not interested."

Disappointment darkens his eyes, but I can barely take it in before a phone buzzes—his.

"Shit," he mutters. But he looks away and picks it up, and after a heaving sigh he says, "I need to leave." He grabs a sweater from the couch. "Let's go. I'll drop you off first."

I slide to my feet. "I can take the bus. The storm's over, so—"

"Elsie." Hand against my back, he pushes me to the entrance.

"No, seriously. You've already done so much . . ." He takes a soft, cozy black hat and slides it over my head. It's not mine, but it feels great. And apparently I'm not awake enough to insist that I don't need a ride *and* button up my coat at the same time. "It's fine, I can even take an Uber and . . ."

He notices my shaking hands and gently brushes them away to do my buttons himself.

"Elsie, it's fine. I get it. You don't want me to take you out." He gets to the highest button. His knuckles brush against my down-turned chin. "At least let me take you home."

JACK'S A CONFIDENT DRIVER, RELAXED EVEN IN BAD WEATHER conditions, with the roads not quite clear and other cars swaying. I sink into the heated seat he turned on for me and remember the time I swerved to avoid a squirrel, almost causing a multivehicle crash.

The squirrel turned out to be a Wendy's paper bag, but it's fine. I'm good at other things. Probably.

"Feel free to pick up," I say, pointing at Jack's phone. It's been buzzing nonstop in the cupholder, a weird techno soundtrack to NPR's world news segment.

"It's not a call," he says, looking straight ahead.

More buzzing. "Are you sure?"

"Yeah. Just an incessant barrage of texts."

"Oh. It sounds . . . urgent."

"It isn't. Not by any sane definition of the word." He sighs, uncharacteristically defeated. "Do you mind if I stop somewhere before taking you home? It's on the way and it'll take a minute."

"No, it's fine," I say—only to regret it when he pulls up a disturbingly familiar driveway. "This is . . . Isn't this . . . ?"

Jack kills the engine. "Regrettably, yes."

"I . . ." Should he be bringing me here, considering . . . literally everything? "Do you want me to, um, hide in the trunk or something?"

"It's ten degrees. The car will get cold pretty fast."

"So I should hide in the bushes?"

He looks at me like he's going to stage an intervention for my tenuous grasp of the second law of thermodynamics. "Come on. It'll be a minute."

Outside feels like Hoth, and my butt actively mourns the toasty warmth of the seat. It's considering a commemorative bench when the front door opens to the cruel, menacing, cutthroat glory of the most terrifying Smith.

Millicent.

"Well, well, well," she singsongs, standing cross-armed. She's wearing simple black pants and a cardigan, but even in a casual outfit there's something intensely *matriarchal* about her. I cannot picture her ever having been anything but ninety and rich. "Look who's not dead."

"You know," Jack says from my side, in that ever-amused tone of his, "I have many regrets in life."

"I'm certain you do."

"But teaching you how to text is the biggest."

Millicent waves her hand. "When you were three, I had to drive you to the ER because you stuck a purple crayon up your butthole. *That* should be your biggest regret."

Jack herds me inside the foyer with a gentle push on my lower back, like touching me casually is an established thing we have going on.

"You took your sweet time, considering the money you could inherit when I croak." Millicent holds her cheek up for Jack to kiss her. He refuses, instead enveloping her in a bear hug that she pretends to bristle at but clearly loves.

"I told you," he says, "just get buried with it."

"I'm being cremated."

"I hear paper burns great."

She scoffs. "Keep on this way, and I'll just will my entire fortune to Comcast." She whirls around and marches down the glitzy hallway. Jack heads the same way, unperturbed, somehow managing not to look out of place despite being a mountain of muscles in a Caltech hoodie. After a moment of consideration, I decide to follow him.

Better not be alone. Wouldn't want to be accused of stealing an ashtray.

We step into the same kitchen where Jack caught me lying about the wine two weeks ago. I watch him walk to a cupboard, hold Millicent's eyes as he opens it, take out a bag of sugar, set it on the table, cross his arms, and ask, "Was this your life-or-death emergency?"

Millicent beams. "Why, yes. I just could *not* reach it, and I *so* hate bitter coffee."

I glance at the cupboard. Which is . . . not high.

"Glad I was able to come to your aid on this very urgent matter." Jack nods politely, stops for a quick peck on his grandmother's cheek, then saunters to the door. His hand finds the usual spot on my back, and he gently pushes me out of the kitchen, clearly ready to leave, when—

"But since you're *already* here, you should really stay for coffee."

Jack's arms drop to his sides, and he turns around.

"Millicent," he says, stern. Amused. Must be a rich people thing, calling grandmas by their names. "Like I mentioned last week, and the ones before, you don't need to *trick* me into spending time with you."

"Oh, Jack. But I have been burned. *Many* times."

"When was the last time you asked me to come over and I didn't?"

"Three years ago. On my birthday. It could have been my last."

"But was it?"

"Hindsight, shmindsight." She stares remotely into the distance. "I waited and waited for my one bearable grandchild to show up—"

"I lived across the country."

"—but alas, you'd left me. Abandoned me. Moved to the West Coast in search of something elusive. A Nobel Prize, perhaps?"

"I called you *every day* for seven years."

"How's that Nobel Prize coming along, anyway?"

He sighs. "You don't have to trick me," he repeats, and this time she grins at him, impish and mischievous, and I remember that she has always been my favorite of Greg's relatives.

"But it's more fun this way."

I suspect this is an interaction they've had multiple times. I suspect Jack is trying to not smile. "I'm taking Elsie home. Then I'll come back and—"

"Elsie?" Millicent turns, as though noticing me for the first time. "Elsie." She takes a step toward me, and I stop breathing, trying to make myself inconspicuous. Who needs oxygen? I'll just photosynthesize from now on. "Why is *Elsie* so familiar?"

I gulp. Comically.

"Ah. Yes. You beat Jack at Go."

"We . . . tied, actually." I glance at Jack, who's smiling like my discomfort puts him in a good mood.

"Indeed." Millicent's eyes laser-focus on me, and I wonder what I should say if she asks why I'm here. What's the cover story? "You don't look too good."

"Oh. I . . ."

"She had a rough night," Jack says mildly. "Let her be."

Millicent nods knowingly. "Dear, whenever they can't get it up, they sit on the edge of the mattress with their heads between their hands and whine like babies and turn it into *our* problem, but—"

I gasp. "Oh, no. No, no, that's not what we—"

"She just found out she didn't get a job," Jack explains, unruffled. "But thank you for the vote of confidence."

"If you say so." Millicent seems unconvinced. Then her eyes light up with a glimmer of recollection "Wait. She's not *yours*, is she? She's the girlfriend of the one who always looks like he just stress-ate a crab apple over a trash can."

Jack rolls his eyes. "You mean Greg? My brother? Your grandson?"

"How would I know? I have four children and seven grandchildren. How many names do you expect me to memorize?"

"Eleven would be a good start."

"Bah." Her eyes fix on me, sharp. "She *is* his, though."

"Not really," Jack says. "It's a long story."

"Perfect. You can tell me over coffee. Two sugars as always, Jack?"

"Yup." He turns to leave again. "I'll have it when I come back from taking Elsie—"

"Nonsense. Elsie must stay, too. I simply *cannot* let her leave."

"Yes, you can, because kidnapping is a serious felony offense."

"Pssh."

"I'm driving her home and—"

"It's fine," I interrupt. They both look at me, stunned by my capacity for speech. "I don't mind staying."

"See? She doesn't mind!" Millicent claps her hands and drops any pretense of helplessness, pulling three mugs from a cupboard that's much higher than the one with the sugar. Jack hesitates, though. He takes a step closer and scans my face for traces of my little untruths.

"Really," I say only for Jack's ears, "it's fine."

"Fine? Spending unremunerated time with *two* Smiths?"

Staying perfectly suits my yellow-brick quest for the lesser evil, because it allows me to postpone informing Dr. L. of what happened or even dealing with the consequences of it. As long as I'm here, time is suspended. The past is set, and I didn't get the job. Any future, however, is possible: AOC will rise to power to forgive my student loans. My pancreas will produce its own insulin. I'll retire to the countryside, live off the land, and spend my days thinking about the kinematics of crystal-rich systems.

And Jack knows, because his bullshit detector works like a charm: he sees that I really want to stay and pulls back a chair for me; then our coats are off, we're sitting across from each other, and I'm glancing around to avoid noticing that he's focusing on me like I'm the key to understanding the free-fall acceleration of antimatter. Millicent begins transferring fancy jam thumbprint cookies from a fancy box to a fancy plate. I scan the wrapping for nutritional values, finding none.

"So," she asks conversationally, "how long have you two been doing it?"

I gasp so hard, I nearly choke. Jack calmly pours his coffee, unruffled. "We're not," he says.

"You're not what?"

"Doing it."

Millicent looks between us. "Not even a little bit?"

"Nope."

"Are you sure?"

"I think I'd know if we were." Jack piles sugar in his mug, and I want to fling myself into an active volcano.

"I certainly hope so. Oh well." She shrugs quaintly. "I guess it's for the best. You were always so protective of your brother—it would be a tad out of character for you to seduce his girlfriend."

"Let's not use the word *seduce* before eleven a.m., 'kay?" Jack stands and starts moving around the kitchen. "And let's talk about something else, since Elsie's in the middle of an anoxic event."

I *absolutely* am. My organs are shutting down.

"What else shall we discuss? I am but a helpless elderly lady. Nothing ever happens to me. Ah yes: the neighbors' dog has been defecating on my lawn again. I'm considering hiring someone to go defecate on theirs. Would either of you be interested?"

"I'm a bit busy," Jack says. A second later, a steaming mug appears in front of me. Jack cages me from behind, one hand next to mine on the table, the other fussing with something papery. He steeps a tea bag in the hot water, and I feel his chest brushing against my back and hair as he says, "But Elsie *is* in the market for a new job."

I twist around to glare at him, but he's already back to his seat. Millicent, on the other hand, is giving me an expectant look.

"I—sorry, I . . . I can't, and . . ." *It's probably illegal?* "Sorry."

"Second job offer she's refused this morning," Jack murmurs.

"Mmm. Picky. No matter, I'll ask my other grandchildren, then. Perhaps strongly hint that their inheritance will depend on it?"

"Less *helpless elderly lady* and more *bitter old hag* territory," Jack says fondly.

"Perhaps. What's with the tea?" she asks Jack.

"Elsie doesn't like coffee."

"Oh." There's something loaded in that *oh.* "You could have said so, Elsie."

"No, she couldn't." Jack's eyes hold mine from above his mug. The dimple appears, making my heart stutter. The air between us smells like Earl Grey, raspberry jam, and early Sunday morning. "But we're working on it."

My phone is long dead, there are no clocks in the kitchen, and I have no clue how long we sit at the table. I'm occasionally part of the conversation, but neither Millicent nor Jack asks much of me, and it's nice, being in this Smith limbo of sorts. Focusing on the way Jack and his grandmother interact, a combination of teasing and deep, utter love for one another. I don't think I've ever been in a room so full of honesty before, but I'm positive that not a single lie has been uttered since I came into this house. It's exhilarating, but in a stomach-dropping way. Like a roller coaster, or eating blue cheese.

Jack and Millicent, I discover, spend part of every weekend together—preferably through an ambush. "Last week's 'life-or-death emergency' was that she needed Bitcoin explained to her," he says dryly. It's obvious that he doesn't mind.

"I also don't get Bitcoin," I say after a long sip of tea—the third hot drink Jack's made for me in twelve hours. Not sure how this is my life.

"See?" Millicent smiles triumphantly. "Greg's maybe-girlfriend is on my side."

Jack and Millicent know more about each other's lives than any relative of mine ever did about me. She tracks with no difficulty names, places, events he mentions, and in turn he doesn't miss a beat when she announces that she'll wear a green dress to the Rutherford dinner, or after she complains that she finished her show and has nothing to watch.

"You did not finish it," he says.

"I did."

"I got you twelve seasons of *Murder, She Wrote*. You cannot have watched them in one week."

"There are no more episodes on the TV."

He stands with a sigh. "I'm going to switch the DVD. Be right back."

I open my mouth the second he disappears, ready to fill the silence with some comment about the weather, but Millicent is already giving me one of her piercing looks. "You're not a librarian, are you?"

I clear my throat. "No. I'm sorry I lied. It's a long story, but—"

"I'm ninety—no time for long stories. What is it that you do, then?"

I fidget with the tea tag. "I'm a physicist."

"Like Jack."

"Sort of. Not really." I keep my eyes on the mug. The state of my career is a sore point. "He's a world-renowned professor. I'm just an adjunct. And he's an experimental physicist, while I'm—"

"A theorist." She nods. "Like his mom, then."

I look up and blink at her. "His mom?" Is Millicent getting confused? Like Grandma Hannaway before passing, when she'd mix me up with her least favorite sister and yell at me for stealing her apron? "You don't mean the one who . . ."

"Died. Well, of course. He only ever had the one." She scoffs. "It's not as if Caroline was eager to take over. Heartbreaking, watching those two boys grow up so close. Same house, same family. One with a mother, the other without."

"Oh." I shouldn't ask any of the questions buzzing in my head. Millicent is clearly under the impression that Jack and I are something we're not, or she wouldn't disclose this. But . . . "How old was Jack?"

"When Grethe died?" *Grethe.* "About one. My son remarried just a few months later. They had Greg soon after. You see, for the first few years, it was me who insisted that we tell Jack nothing about Grethe. I thought he could have a normal life, believing that Caroline was his mother and he had lost nothing. But Caroline was never fond of him, and . . . well, it was her right to refuse. I shouldn't have interfered. Because I made it worse: a few years later he got into some trouble like children often do, and Caroline screamed at him, 'Don't call me Mom—I'm not your mother.' It was a moment of weakness. And Caroline did feel guilty afterwards. But by then, Jack knew." She sighs. "Hard to explain to a nine-year-old that everything he believes is a lie. That he shouldn't call Mom the woman his *brother* calls Mom." Millicent massages her temple. "Jack seemed to take it in stride. Except that he stopped calling his father Dad, too. I became Millicent. And ever since, he's been very distrustful of lies. Very preoccupied with . . . boundaries. More than is healthy, I believe." She busies herself stacking mugs on top of the empty cookie plate. For the first time since I met her, she looks her age. Frail, old, tired. Her mouth is downturned, bracketed by deep lines. "And yet Jack and Greg grew up thick as thieves, despite all that. The one saving grace."

I remember Jack taking care of Greg after the dentist, and my heart squeezes. I try to picture them as kids, picture Jack being anything but his tall, assured, authoritative self, and fail miserably.

"Are you sure she . . . Grethe." I want to ask if Turner was her last name. The reason Jack's a Smith but not *really* a Smith. "Are you sure she was a theorist?" Physics runs in Jack's family, when the only thing that runs in mine is eczema.

"Why do you ask?"

"Just . . . Jack doesn't seem to like theorists very much."

Millicent gives me a look. "He likes *you*, doesn't he?"

She speaks like I'm the least sharp cookie in the jar, and I flush. "But he once wrote an article that—"

"Oh, *that*." She chuckles, like it's a fond family memory. First day of kindergarten, meeting Goofy at Disneyland, and that time her grandson sent an entire field of study into a tailspin. "That had nothing to do with theoretical physics. He was just a teenager acting out, angry because of what he'd found out about Grethe. But he's a man now. A good one. Too bad I can't leave him my money, or he'll just divide it up between the rest of my ungrateful family."

"What had he found out about Grethe?" Was the entire Smith-Turner Hoax about his mom? Did he . . . hate her? Was it some sort of revenge on her for . . . for what? Dying? It's too ridiculous. "Did he write the article because of her?"

I must be asking too many questions. Millicent's expression shifts, first to guarded, then to vacuous. "I forget," she says with a ditzy shrug, even though she doesn't. Millicent, I'm certain, hasn't forgotten a single thing in her life—not Greg's name, and certainly not what led Jack to be who he is today. "Jack will tell you. When you've been together long enough."

"No, we . . . Really, Jack and I are *not*—we're not *doing* it," I say. My brain cringes so hard, it folds in on itself.

"Oh, I know. This is something else altogether, isn't it?"

"It's nothing at all. We're not even friends."

"Right." Her tone is almost . . . pitying? "Well, you'll figure it out in your own time."

"Figure out what?"

"DVD player's all set," Jack announces, emerging in the doorway, "and I've left detailed instructions on how to switch to the next season, since the ones I wrote last week are gone."

"Oh, yes. I had to throw the notepad at your aunt Maureen when she said my green pullover was too bright."

"Of course, you *had to.* Can I drive Elsie home now? Or is the abduction still ongoing?"

Millicent huffs. "Do take her, please. I'm sick of both of you. You're not nearly as entertaining as Jessica Fletcher."

She kicks us out as unceremoniously as she welcomed us in, making a symphony of faux-irritated noises that are belied by how hard she clings to Jack's hug.

"I'll stop by later to shovel some snow," he promises.

"Fine, but do not come in. I'll be busy with my show."

"I know." He kisses her forehead. "Be good till next weekend. Have fun writing spite wills."

"I shall," she says defiantly before slamming the door in our faces.

"Does she really?" I ask on our way to the car. The snow crunches under our feet.

"What?"

"Write wills for spite."

"Probably."

"Why?"

"Pettiness. Boredom. Loneliness. When I was sixteen, my father made a comment about her roast being dry, and she pledged a million dollars to a bunny shelter."

"God. Why?"

"It's a vicious cycle. Most of my family does seem to gravitate around her because of the money, which is why Millicent wields it like a weapon. But that doesn't endear her to the family members who are normal human beings and believe that threatening to vengefully pledge your estate to JPMorgan Chase just to make a point might be pushing it too far."

"Is Greg one of the decent ones?"

"Greg's the most decent, but he prefers to avoid Millicent altogether. He likes it when people get along, which cannot happen if she's in a given quantum space."

"Like Pauli's exclusion principle." We exchange a smile next to the passenger seat of the car. "You like her, though."

"She's an absolute monster. But she does burrow into you after thirty or so years," he says fondly. "Like a tick."

I laugh, my breath a gust of white in the space between us. "Should we explain to her that I wasn't really dating Greg?"

"Nah. Millicent's too busy launching feces wars to care about any of that."

"You . . ." I try to sound casual. "Do you always call her Millicent?"

"It's her name."

"I mean, why not Grandma, or Gram, or Granny, or Mawmaw—"

"Mawmaw?"

"Whatever. Babushka. Maternal Forebear."

Jack's expression goes inscrutable. "It's good, calling people by their names. It minimizes misunderstandings." I think I see a split second of hesitation, like maybe he's thinking of saying more, but it's fleeting, swiftly gone in the glistening snow. "Come on. I'll take you home before your roommate sends out an Amber Alert."

I nod, because I do need to sort out the mess that is my life in a Smith-free space. But then something occurs to me: the rest of my life is going to be a Smith-free space.

A Jack-free space.

I'll probably never see him again. Why would I? The circles we move in are a Venn diagram with little overlap. Maybe we'll meet at a physics conference two years down the road, when I'm still an adjunct teaching forty classes a week and he's workshopping his Nobel lecture. But my arrangement with Greg is likely over, which means that this is it. The last time I'll see Jack. This man, this maddening, impossible, space-taking man who seems to know me despite all that I do to *not* be known, will be gone from my life.

I should be eager to go back to simpler times, when I used to spend zero hours a week in his company and my brain wasn't made of guacamole, but . . . what a *waste*. What a surprisingly terrifying perspective.

And that's why I stop him with a tug on the sleeve of his coat. Why I open my mouth and say with no forethought, no premeditation, and a lot of reckless panic, "Youcantakemeout."

It comes out with no pauses or intonation, just a bunch of sounds smooshed together. Which Jack, judging by the knot between his brows, did not understand.

I clear my throat. Take a deep breath. "If you still want to. And if it's okay with Greg. You can take me out."

Jack just stares, motionless, reactionless, for way too long. "Take you out . . . in the mob way?"

"No. No! That's not at all what I—" I blush. I'm cold and tired and my head hurts and I have no idea what I'm doing and why won't he *understand*? "I can come to *your* place. I can take *you* out."

He nods. Slowly. "In the mob way."

"*No*, I—" I notice it, the amused gleam in his eyes, like he knows *exactly* what I'm trying to say. I press my lips together, because I don't want to encourage him, I don't want to smile, but I'm about to. "I hate you."

"Sure you do."

"Why is everything so difficult with you?"

"I like to keep you on your toes."

"Listen—let's hang out," I say. This feels foolhardy. Ill advised. Exciting. "Just . . . try. See what happens. Would that be okay?"

"It would," he says after a brief pause. "Under one condition."

I frown. "Making demands already?"

"Always." His mouth twitches, but he's back to his opaque self. "If we do this . . . when you're with me, I need you to be honest. No pretending you're someone else. No trying to be whatever you think it is that I want. You say what you think. And when you can't, at least let yourself think it. No lies, Elsie." His jaw sets. "Just you."

I nod. And then I realize that I have no idea how to do that, and I laugh, a little sad, a lot terrified. "I can try."

He nods. "That's enough for now."

"You should be honest, too," I add. "No lies on your end, either."

"I don't lie often," he says simply. Hearing it makes me think of what Millicent said about his past, and my heart clenches. I've seen Jack being brutally, needlessly honest. Lying, not so much. "And I can't see myself lying to you."

"You don't even know me."

"I don't," he admits. He studies my face for several moments, like he cannot stop on the cover or the first page, like he needs to read the whole book every time. Then he leans into me, and the icy chill of the morning melts away in his heat. My eyes catch on his cheekbones. The line of his jaw, so sharp it could cut a heart. His lips are full and upturned, a start of that lopsided smile of his that makes me angry and weak-kneed, and . . .

He bends to murmur in the shell of my ear, "I'd like to, though." My hairs rise, my spine coils like a silent bowstring, and for the first time in my entire life I'm thinking of kisses, of skin, of waking with Jack this morning, of his hand between my shoulder blades, of the ink on his arm, of his lips, which look full and soft, and he hasn't shaved in a while and he smells *good* and—

A click. Behind me. Jack straightens and pulls the passenger door open. That tension inside me is still buzzing. I feel almost dizzy.

"Get in," he orders, low and hoarse and maybe not really to me.

I slide into the seat, and it sinks in that this might be real. Happening *outside* my head.

Me, taking a shot at being *myself.*

16

FUNDAMENTAL FORCES

From: Glass.Abigail.2@bostoncollege.edu
Subject: Thermo 201

Hiya! I haven't come to class this semester because I can't find the room. Where do we meet, again? Could you draw me a map? Thx.

"Egregious."

Dr. L. says the word with soft *g*'s and mysterious vowels, like English is a French language that the Americans are just borrowing. I'd find it amusing, but it's our first meeting since relaying my job news and I can't feel anything but anxiety. He asked me to come over, and I really didn't want to, what with the snow and the crock of shit that's my schedule. And yet here I am.

"Egregious, that they'd choose another candidate," he repeats. "Perhaps an appeal is in order."

"Knowing who the winning candidate is, I doubt there are grounds."

"Georgina Sepulveda, you said?"

I nod.

"And who would that be?"

I'm taken aback that any living physicist wouldn't know of her work. But Dr. L. can be narrow minded when it comes to experimentalists. Maybe rightfully so?

"She's behind the Sepulveda model. A brilliant particle physicist. And she was a Burke fellow years ago." I look down at my knees. Then back up to Dr. L.'s deep scowl. "I'm sorry, Dr. Laurendeau. I know this is disappointing, but—"

"I wonder if Smith-Turner influenced the search, after all."

My hand grips the armrest of the green chair. "He . . . I doubt it."

"We cannot put it past him, can we?"

I clear my throat. "I'm convinced that he did not—"

"Elise, you want Smith-Turner to get his comeuppance just as much as I do, don't you?"

My stomach sinks and I lower my eyes, mortified. Dr. L. spent the last six years counseling me, and here I am. A screwup. Cavorting with the asshole who nearly ruined his career.

Not being the Elsie he wants.

I need to go back to it. To Elise—hardworking, undeterred, laser focused. "This is a huge setback, but I'm . . . regrouping," I say, trying to sound optimistic. "In terms of finding a job for next year, I—"

"But you have a job. Several, in fact."

"Yes. Absolutely." I take a deep breath. "But these adjunct gigs are time consuming and leave me little time for research. And I really want to finish developing my—"

"There is always time for research. One must want to find it."

I close my eyes, because this one hurts like hell. The Elsie he wants almost slips away, but I hold strong. "You're right."

"Could you not simply teach fewer classes?"

I breathe slowly. In and out. "Financially, that's not a possibility."

"I see. Well, sometimes money must take second place."

I grip the armrest, feeling a gust of frustration that he'd think me *greedy* for wanting to buy insulin and live in a place without mutant moths. It's immediately swallowed by guilt. This is Dr. L. I wouldn't even know the Nielsen-Ninomiya theorem if it weren't for him.

I take a deep breath, forcing myself to mention the idea that's been swelling in my head since my morning at Jack's. While there is no dimension in which me working for him would be feasible or appropriate, maybe there is *some* promise in what he said. "Someone recommended that I consider a postdoctoral fellowship or another research-only position."

Dr. L. looks at me, alarmed for a split second, and then sighs. "We have been over this, Elise."

"Right. But we talked about theorists. Maybe some experimentalists might be interested in—"

"Unfortunately, no. I asked widely, and I am very sorry, but no suitable physicist was interested in hiring you as a researcher," he says, and my stomach sinks even more.

I lower my eyes to my jeans. God, I'm an idiot. A total fucking idiot.

"Elise," he continues, tone softer, "I *know* how you feel." He circles his desk, coming to stand in front of me. "Remember when you started your doctorate? How helpless you felt? How I guided you through developing your algorithms, publishing your manuscripts, making a name for yourself within the physics community? I can help you now, too."

I think about all the things he's done for me. All the things I owe to him. I wonder where I'd be without him, and come up empty.

"Do you trust me?"

I nod.

I DON'T GET A FORMAL REJECTION FROM MIT TILL WEDNESDAY night.

I'm in the middle of what's rapidly becoming a semesterly endeavor: relearning Noether's theorem to be able to teach it to a mostly snoring classroom at eight a.m., only to forget it once again by the time my nine thirty thermo lecture comes around.

My brain is a colander.

When the iTwat rings, I look up. Cece is writing her MILF (manuscript I'd like to finish) on the couch, but she meets my eyes.

"I'm sorry it didn't work out," Monica tells me after a long explanation that includes the words *institutional fit* four times. I appreciate the call. Academic rejections are often one-line emails. More often, tumbleweeds.

"It's not your fault, Monica," I say.

"Or is it?" Cece mutters, which has me smiling.

"I understand the situation," I add, just to see Cece sprain an eye-rolling muscle.

"I want you to know," Monica says, "that new positions will be opening soon."

I thought I'd left my hope bloody and beaten on the side of the road, but apparently it's still breathing. "Next year?"

"In three to five years. Several theorists are set to retire, and the dean won't dare close the tenure-track lines. I hope you'll apply again."

Go on without me, my hope says, contemplating six more semesters of Noether's theorem. *I'll only slow you down.* "Of course I will."

"And let's keep in touch. Grab lunch once the semester is over."

"I'd love that."

"Fantastic. Was there any feedback you'd like to give me regarding the search?"

Jack's voice rings in my ear: *You say what you think. And when you can't, at least let yourself think it.*

Okay. Well. *Monica, you know that highly irregular meeting we had before my interview? Maybe you should have told me that I had no chance. Also, you overdid it with the cow decor. Also* also, *your son is a psycho, and I hope he dislocates his dick while publicly humping a fire hydrant.*

"Just, thank you for everything you've done. I appreciate it."

Jack might have a point. Contemplating the truth is a nice, cheap thrill.

By the time I hang up, I have two new emails—one from a student asking for my credit card number to buy fifteen hundred live ladybugs, one from Greg.

Hey Elsie,

I've been wanting to get in touch, but Jack said it was better to wait, and . . . well, I hear you're now in the know. Sorry you didn't get the job. But it's so cool that you're a physicist. What are the chances? Maybe Jack can help you find something else? He has tons of connections!

Anyway, would you like to get lunch in the next few days to debrief? I'll buy!

-G

PS: I have been informed that I attempted to urinate on/ near you. I am deeply regretful of my actions.

I'm considering my sudden lunch popularity—take that, middle school bullies—and almost don't notice Cece sitting next to me at the table. "Hey." She's eating croutons straight from the bag, picking them out with chopsticks. As per my usual policy, I don't ask. "How do you feel?"

"I feel . . ." What a good question. "Like all the plot balls that I was juggling have dropped to the floor. And I have no idea what comes next in my story."

This is not your character arc, Elsie. More like a . . . character bump.

"Could there be a positive side?"

I cock my head. "Positive?"

"Now you don't have to juggle anymore. You can use your hands to . . . flip people off. Scratch your butt crack. Become a finger puppeteer." She shrugs. "If you woke up tomorrow and could choose anything, what would you do?"

My eyes, quicker than my brain, fall on the upper left corner of my computer, where my Word doc sleeps its neglected slumber. *I'd finish my work on two-dimensional liquid crystals*, I instantly think. But how, without the MIT job? And that ball has dropped, which means that—

Cece sighs. "Okay, you know what? That was a hard question. Let's just daydream about the future."

"Sure." I lean back in my seat. "Income inequality? Nuclear proliferation? Climate change?"

"I'm always up for discussing how rising sea levels will lead the merpeople to claim the lost city of Miami, but I was thinking more . . . next year. Money."

I sigh. "UMass has open instructor slots, and so does—"

"No. Listen, I don't want you to do that. I've been thinking about this, and . . . I think I can swing it." Her earnest, heartfelt look is only slightly undercut by the waving of a caesar crouton. "Kirk is giving me a job. He said he'll need me at least twice a week, and he wants to pay me like an employee. His team is actually drawing up a contract."

I frown. Why does Kirk crop up so much in conversation? And above all: "Where does Kirk get the money?"

"He's a scientist."

"As a scientist myself, let me ask you once again: Where does Kirk get the money?" A spine-chilling thought occurs to me. "Please tell me he's not Elon Musk."

"You *monster*. Take that back."

"He's the only rich scientist I can think of!"

"Kirk is Kirk, I promise! He'd never write petulant tweets about how the world is unfair to poor billionaires. To be honest, I doubt he knows what Twitter is. He's like . . ." Her eyes shine a little. "A total nerd, Elsie. In grad school he created this material that everyone wants, then he built a company around it with his friend who has an MBA. But the company is huge now, as in, *ridiculously* big. It has stocks and stuff." Cece's getting animated. Croutons fly all over the room. Hedgie has noticed. "So now he has all these functions and meetings he needs to go to, and he hates them, but he says that if I'm there, they're more bearable, even though I know nothing about science *or* money—"

"Hang on." I frown. "What's the name of the material?"

"I keep forgetting. Some kind of resistant blah synthetic blah fiber blah blah." She taps her lips with the chopsticks. "Taurus, maybe?"

I wish I were drinking, because this deserves a spit take. "Cece, are you fake-girlfriending the dude who invented *Tauron*?"

"Oh, yeah. That's what it's called."

"Tauron is literally *everywhere*." I blink. "He must be a millionaire."

"I think he is. And that's why you don't have to teach sixty-nine classes next year."

She gives me an expectant look till I sigh and mutter, "Nice."

"Thank you. Anyway, I'll cover rent. So you can work a reasonable amount. One or two classes. And the rest of the time you can stay home and do your research about sparkles."

"Crystals."

"Crystals. And we can spend our nights eating Gruyère and ranking Wong Kar-wai's movies from most to least cinematographically poignant."

Does she know how much you like Twilight*?*

I smile, trying to remember one single Wong Kar-wai movie. Pretty sure we did a two-day marathon three years ago, which I spent solving equations on my mind's blackboard while Cece was in full Stendhal syndrome. "*2046* would win."

She smiles dreamily. "Probably."

I don't like Kirk. No—I don't like the way Cece looks when she talks about him, because I've seen her act like that only about for-eign movies, or Sapir-Whorf, or hedgehogs. It just doesn't seem like a good idea to like one's fake boyfriend that much. But I don't have a chance to say it, because Cece is standing again, rummaging in the cupboard for wonton strips. And because my phone is buzzing with a text—the first I've ever gotten from this number:

Are you free tomorrow night?

17

DISPLACEMENT

WEAR BLACK JEANS.

A cute sweater.

Ankle boots.

I leave my hair down. Then I pull it up in a bun. Then I let it down again. Then I braid it.

Then I leave it down.

I haven't told Cece where I'm going, because she's not home, and I'm physically unable to send her a text explaining that:

I.

Am.

Going.

Out.

WithJackSmithTurner.

Maybe. I'm still not positive that the reason he wants to see me is *not* to stealthily substitute my insulin with Frappuccino. Maybe I should make a safety call—make the investigators' job easier when they find my corpse in a swamp. But the car is already there when I get downstairs, and I simply slip into the passenger seat.

The cabin smells like leather, Jack, and bad ideas. I should say something. *Hi, how are you? Did you have a good week? Favorite Teletubby? Off-year elections thoughts?* I've done this a million times—gone out with people. A million fake dates. Then why? Why? Why can't I . . . Why?

"I think," he drawls, "I just heard your head explode."

I turn to him. He's handsome in a near-painful way, and my head is still in mid-explosion.

"Want to go back up?" The smile. Uneven. Amused. All-knowing. "Try this another day?"

I shake my head before I change my mind. "I want to do this now." I swallow. Face straight ahead. "I think."

He starts the engine. "Look at you."

"Look at me?"

He puts his hand on the headrest of the seat to back out of the spot. His fingers brush against my hair, soft, distracted.

"Yeah. Look at you, telling the truth."

"TWO FRIENDS ARE IN TOWN FOR A CONFERENCE," HE TELLS ME, "and another friend is hosting a small get-together. I figured with witnesses you'd be more . . . relaxed."

He's probably right, but also: "I don't want to intrude."

"I'd love for you to meet them."

Is it a good idea, hanging out when his friends are around? I'm probably very lame in comparison. I'm just not that entertaining—

not at my best, and definitely not with Jack, who so far has gotten my worst. "Are all your friends scientists?" I ask.

"Some." A pause. "Jesus. I can't think of one who isn't."

I nod. It's truly hard to expand one's social circle. Academics become friends, hang out, and above all sleep almost exclusively with other academics. Because academia is a bit like the Olympic Village—sans opening ceremony with condom distribution.

We park in front of a narrow brownstone, and after ringing the bell at a yellow door, he turns to me. "Hey."

I turn, too. Under his coat he's wearing jeans and a dark henley, and he's big and attractive, and it occurs to me for the first time in years that nights in which people go out together—not *all* nights, but *some* nights, maybe *several* nights—don't just end with a hug and *good night*.

I shiver.

"Honesty," he reminds me. "You don't need to impress anyone. No need for the usual party tricks."

I smile. "I was going to carve a recorder out of a carrot and play it for your friends."

He gives me a long look, like I'm the single most charming person he's ever met. "Not gonna lie, that'd be pretty cool."

Even before I knew about his mother, Jack always seemed to me like a lone wolf, set apart from the rest of the Smiths. It's instantly clear, though, that his friend group is his chosen family. There are over fifteen people in the house, and not only are they all delighted to see him, they welcome me just as warmly. The single exception: Andrea, Jack's MIT colleague. She stares at me like a vaguely displeased gargoyle, probably feeling awkward about the fact that I didn't get the job.

"Beer?" Sunny, the engineer who owns the house, asks. She's a dark-haired ball of energy. "Wine?"

I'm ready to spend the rest of the night holding a drink I don't want just to avoid looking out of place, but Jack says, "I'll have one. Elsie doesn't drink."

I never told him, but of course he knows. "Anything else, then? Water? Soda? OJ? Maple syrup?" Sunny frowns into her fridge. "Milk?"

"Whole?" Jack asks.

"Two percent."

"Keep your white water."

"You spoiled little Smith brat, raised with unpasteurized emu tit juice." She punches his arm. "Remember when Caitie was pumping and kept her bottles in the fridge of the student lounge?"

"And Kroll used it."

"For his coffee." Sunny shakes her head. "Good times."

Jack has friends, inside jokes that go back a decade, and a whole group of smart, kind people who tease him *because* they care about him, and . . . I'm not sure what to do with this piece of information, aside from being mind-numbingly fascinated. I briefly wonder if they know about the article Jack wrote, whether they support him, what their opinion of theoretical physics is, and then force my brain to shut up for once. I should learn how to have fun at some point in my life.

One of the people visiting town is a biologist from Stanford. He's as tall as Jack—an impossibility, I thought, especially within the nerd community.

"This is Adam," Jack says after they shake hands warmly, in that affectionate but understated way of men who like each other a lot but will probably never openly admit it. Adam looks like he might be a few years older. Dark. Frowny. Intimidating, though the beautiful girl next to him looks anything but intimidated. "And this is—"

She takes a step forward and enfolds Jack in a tight hug. "Jack!"

He hugs her back with a smile. "Hey, Ol. Nice to see you're still putting up with this guy—thank you for your service. Elsie, this is Olive Smith—no relation to my terrible family, lucky her. She's Adam's . . . Adam, is she still your fiancée?"

Adam nods with a mildly irritated expression.

Jack grins. "Haven't picked a date yet?"

"She has not," Adam whines. Sternly, though.

"Ol. Put him out of his misery."

"At twenty-eight? What am I, a child bride?" Olive looks between me and Jack. "Have *you guys* picked a date?"

I wish to die on the spot. I wish to melt into the sweet respite of nothingness. "Oh, we . . ." I glance at Jack, hoping he'll come to my rescue. He just gives me a look halfway between pleased and amused, holds my eyes, and says, "Not yet." I step closer to pinch him hard in the ribs. He stops me with a hand on my wrist and a delighted smile.

"How did you and Adam meet?" I ask him in a desperate attempt to change the subject.

"In undergrad I did a summer internship at Harvard, in the lab where Adam was a Ph.D. student."

"He ran the worst Southern blot I've ever seen," Adam says.

"It was a rough three months. I was gently discouraged from going into biophysics. Then a few years later I moved to Pasadena, and he was in Palo Alto, and we started hanging out. Hiked our way around California. And then he introduced me to Olive when . . . Ol, how did you and Adam meet again?" he asks with the tone of someone who knows the answer full well.

She grins. "Why, Jack, *Adam* was a *tenured professor.* And *I* was but a *lowly student.*"

"*Graduate* student," Adam interjects, speaking to me. "And not *my* student."

"But in his department," Olive adds impishly. "It was all very, *very* scandalous."

Jack smiles. "You should sell the movie rights, Ol."

"I'm hoping for a Netflix miniseries. Something sexy like *Bridgerton*, you know?"

It's clearly a bit Jack and Olive do a lot. Adam lets out a long-suffering sigh. "Anyway." He changes the topic. "How are you, Jack?"

"*Very* entertained."

Jack and Adam are somewhere north of circumstantial friends. In a couple of minutes they are absorbed in conversation, talking about people, things, places I'm not familiar with. Olive and I gravitate toward each other, sitting on the couch while all around us Jack's friends laugh and joke and embody the epitome of successful adulthood.

"Do you also not know anyone else and feel like the dumbest person in the room?" she whispers at me.

I nod. Everyone here is a bit older, and I try not to imagine the academic positions they might have. "What do you do?" I ask Olive.

"Cancer biology. Just finished the first year of my postdoc. I'm probably going on the job market in the next couple." She makes a face, sipping on her beer.

"Are you planning on staying in California?"

"Would be nice, since my friends are there. But honestly, academic jobs are so rare, it'll be hard enough to make sure Adam and I are in the same city."

"Do you have a plan?"

She shakes her head. "The good thing is, Adam has grants. We're hoping that whatever institution wants me will take a look at the money and decide that we can be a package deal. But if they don't . . ." She shrugs. "We might have to negotiate a spousal hire."

I smile. "Then you'll set a date?"

She leans closer with a surreptitious expression. Her skin is 90 percent freckles, and I've known her for five minutes, but I want to be her friend. "I've set it already. We're getting married in April. During spring break. Adam just doesn't know it yet."

"How does that work?"

"So, he's into nature. Hiking, that stuff. I'm taking him to Yosemite, where a park ranger will marry us in a quick and painless ceremony. Then it's just going to be the two of us for a week. And the bears, I guess. Oh God, I hope the bears don't eat us." She shrugs the thought away. "Anyway, Adam doesn't love people, and we can always have a party later, but this . . . I think this is the kind of wedding he wants. The one we're meant to have."

I picture Olive and Adam, alone, trekking hand in hand under the ponderosa pines. It's not difficult. "Why don't you just tell him?"

"I should, right?" She laughs softly. "I just . . . I was in a pretty bad place when I met him. He did so much—still does, always taking care of me, and I . . . I want to take care of him for once, you know? Make him feel like I've got him."

I nod and then stare down at my empty palms.

When I really let go, I imagine that you let me take care of you, too.

"Have you and Jack been together for a while?" Olive asks, and I look up at her. I can tell that the Elsie she wants would say yes. That she loves Jack very much and likes the thought of someone who'll take care of him. But.

Honesty.

For a second, I picture myself blurting out the entire story: how I fake-dated *Greg*, then met *Jack*, then met *Jonathan*. But I doubt Olive is familiar with the concept of fake dating, so I sanitize my version. "This is the first time, actually."

It feels weird to say the opposite of what someone wants. And it feels downright horrible when Olive's response is a disappointed "Oh."

I swallow. "I'm sorry—"

"No, no." She smiles, reassuring. "*I'm* sorry about earlier. Asking if you're getting married."

I shake my head. "We're just . . . getting to know each other."

"That's great. It's nice to hear that he's over his I Don't Date, Let Me Set Boundaries and Make It Clear That This Is Just About Sex phase." Her impression of Jack sounds more like Vin Diesel, but it has me thinking: I have no idea what Jack wants from me. Olive is the second person to mention how important boundaries are to him. He hasn't set any, but he also said that he was attracted to me, and . . .

If what Jack wanted from me was sex . . . what then?

Honestly, no clue. I don't have much experience. Not because I ever bought into the idea that sex is something precious, but because it felt like a means to an end, a way to ensure that the person I was with was pleased with me. Sex never happened because of any attraction *I* experienced, but that's okay: maybe I never *craved* it, but I also never minded it. Because it wasn't *for me*.

With Jack, though . . . something's different. Perhaps because he sees more of me than anyone ever has. I find myself thinking about last Sunday by the car, over and over. Tethered on the edge of a kiss that might not come, tense, heated, spellbound.

There might be something here. Or it might be nothing. What's certain is that I'm more curious than ever. If something were to happen, it would be *for me*.

"Did you guys meet at work?" Olive asks.

"Kind of. I'm a physicist, too. Though I'm an adjunct."

"Ouch."

I laugh. "Yeah."

"You like teaching?"

"Nope. Lots of high-def pictures of butt rashes that are too deadly for people to come to class. Sifting through those doesn't leave time for research."

She laughs, too. "I bet. I did not like TA'ing. It's nice being a postdoc—none of the bullshit of being a grad student, none of the responsibility of being a faculty member. Just research."

"Sounds like a dream."

She gives me a surprised look. "You didn't do a postdoc?"

"There weren't any positions. But my Ph.D. advisor says it's for the best. I'll move to a faculty position earlier."

"But do you *want* to move to faculty earlier?"

"It's . . . complicated. But I trust him. I owe him a lot, so . . ." I sigh.

Olive scans my face, large eyes assessing, and then says, "In my experience, we all want to trust our mentors, but they don't always have our best interests in mind."

"In what way?"

"Just . . ." She chews on her lower lip, pensive. "Academia is so hierarchical, you know? There are all these people who have power over you, who are supposed to guide you and help you become the best possible scientist, but . . . sometimes they don't know what's best. Sometimes they don't care. Sometimes they have their own agenda." Her expression darkens. "Sometimes they're total shit-buckets who deserve to step on a pitchfork and die."

I wonder what happened to her. I even open my mouth to ask, but Adam turns to us, as if feeling the shift in her mood. "Olive, do you have pictures of the tux Holden bought for his wedding? Jack won't believe it's sequined."

Olive brightens. "It's *totally* sequined, and it's *amazing*."

We end up chatting, first the four of us and then others, too, for what feels like minutes but turns out to be hours. While Andrea is telling the story of how her advisor showed up completely sloshed at her thesis defense and started offering digestive cookies to the rest of the committee, the cushion next to mine dips and I hear, "Everything okay?"

It's Jack. Murmuring in my ear, arm resting behind me on the back of the couch. He's surprisingly close, but I don't pull back. "Your friends are fun."

"I figured you'd like them more than me."

"I kind of do." I smile, thinking about Millicent, Greg, Olive. Thinking that he has great taste in people. And then notice something on my thigh: a small pouch of almonds. "What's this?"

"Glycemic level control." His mouth quirks. "Or you can faint on me. Since it's a hobby of yours."

"Did you steal these from Sunny's cupboard?"

He gives me a look. "I shared an office with her for years, and she once left a urine sample for her doctor on her desk." He stares at my lips while I laugh silently. "I'm not going through her cupboards."

I shake my head. Out of the corner of my eye, I notice Olive and Adam looking at me—no, at *us*, in a way I cannot quite understand. I focus on my almonds, then go in search of a trash can for the wrapper, and . . .

"Elsie?"

Georgina Sepulveda is in the kitchen, beautiful and kick-ass. She's *tall*—I didn't fully grasp how tall when Jack was nearby, dwarfing her.

"So glad you're here. I've been wanting to talk to you, but Jack was the usual shitlet and refused to give me your number." She rolls her eyes. "At first I thought he didn't have it and just didn't want to admit it. But you're here, which means he was just hoarding it. Like a dragon. God, I *knew* he'd be like this when he found someone. You and I should become best friends just to spite him." Her smile is wide and warm, and it's instantly, violently, mortifyingly present in my mind that the last time we met, I acted like a toddler with little bitch disorder.

"I . . ." I look around like an idiot, in search of . . . what? A teleprompter? This is mortally embarrassing. "I didn't know you were here."

"Just got here. Faculty meeting ran late for no reason—the entire thing could be summarized in two fifteen-second TikToks." She shrugs, moving closer. I clutch my almond wrapper like it's a terry cloth monkey.

"Georgina—"

"George, please. Georgina is my mother. And my grandmother. My great-grandmother, too, probably. We should invest in a baby names book."

"Oh." I clear my throat. My contributions to this conversation are priceless. "Jack's in there, if you—"

"I know. Like I could miss him when he's standing next to Adam Carlsen. They're the Mount Rushmore of STEM academia. Anyway— will you have lunch with me next week? I want to chat with you, but not in Sunny's home." She shudders. "I can't be in here without thinking of the urine sample."

Professionally, my life sucks a bit. Psychologically, I'm not, as some would say, "healthy." Musically, I should hire a tuba to follow me around. But on the upside, I've been *killing it* in the lunch invite department.

"You want to chat with me," I repeat. Just to be sure.

"Yes. Partly because Jack is my closest friend, and it would bug him if I stole you from him even just a bit. But mostly because the last time we met, I acted like a total bitch, and I want to make it up to you."

What? "No, no, I'm the one who ran away like a lunatic. My first reaction to finding out that you'd gotten the job was unforgivable and incredibly messed up. *I* acted like a bitch—"

"Yes, you totally did." George's smile is triumphant. "To make it up to me, you will let me take you out for lunch."

"That's . . ." I slow-blink. "Very well played."

"Thank you." She dusts nonexistent specks off her shoulder, and I laugh.

"I see why Jack likes you so much."

"I see why Jack likes you more." Her smile softens. "Next Wednesday okay?"

I nod. "Sounds great."

Jack and I leave a few minutes later. I exchange numbers with Olive, and Sunny hugs me goodbye while Jack is getting the car, whispering that any urine sample rumors I might have heard have been greatly exaggerated. She also swears that if Jack and I break up, she'll side with me, because she already likes me more.

I laugh on the doorstep. "It makes me feel guilty for stealing your almonds."

"Oh, they must be someone else's. No nuts in this house—they're, like, so gross."

In the car, I'm contemplating the idea that Jack researched, bought, and packed a diabetes-friendly snack just for me when he asks, "Where to for dinner?"

"Oh." Something happy and surprised flips in my chest at the idea of the night not being over yet. "I like everything."

He merges into traffic. "Excellent. Some of my favorite stuff is everything. Now tell me what you want to eat."

I look at his near-perfect profile. He hasn't shaved in the last couple of days, looks a bit tired. I wonder if he's been up and about since morning. If he hasn't had anything since lunch. He's huge, probably always ravenous. Simple stuff, big portions.

"Burgers," I say.

He gives me a *Nice try* look. "Yes, Elsie, I do like burgers. That wasn't the question, though."

I scowl. How does he do this? How does he *always*—

"Want me to pull over so you can get out and stomp your foot a bit?"

I growl. Judging from the smile, he absolutely hears me.

Okay—what do I want? Well, cheese. I'm always in the mood for cheese. But cheese is not really a meal, and the places where it might be are usually too fancy, and—

"Say it," he orders.

"What?"

"What you're thinking."

"I'm not—"

"Say it."

"Really, I'm—"

"Say it."

"*Cheese*," I almost yell. Shocking myself.

Jack smiles, satisfied. "I know just the place."

"YOU'RE JOKING."

"Nope."

"We can't—not here."

"Why?"

"Because . . ."

Jack waits for me to finish the sentence. When I'm unable to, the ever-present lower-back hand nudges me inside the cozy heat of the restaurant.

Of *Miel*.

"This seems sadistic," I point out, "even for you."

"You underestimated me, then."

"Two?" The hostess greets us, chirpy. "Would you prefer a table or a booth?"

Jack looks at me like we're a drug cartel and I'm the ringleader who needs to sign off on any decision. Dammit, this honesty business is hard. Okay, so not the booth—Jack's legs are skyscraper long, so he'd probably hate it. But tables are less private, which he *also* might hate—

He leans into my ear. "Stop building observational models about what you think *I'll* like, and just be honest about—"

"*Booth*," I grunt out. The hostess makes an obvious mental note to tell our waiter that I'm a weirdo, but her "If you'll follow me" is impeccable.

"Excellent choice," Jack murmurs while we weave toward the table, and all I can think of is that Two-Weeks-Ago-Elsie, bright-eyed and future-hopeful, sat in this very restaurant across from Jack and contemplated slipping under the table to power-drill his knee-caps. Tonight-Elsie gapes at him as he tells the waitress, "I'll have your craft beer. And she'll have the cheese board."

I lift my eyebrow. "What happened to *me* asking for what I want?"

"The cheese board *is* what you want."

It is. But. "How can you be so sure?"

"Ikagawa ordered it the other night. I saw the way you looked at it."

"How's that?"

"Like people look at porn."

Laughter bubbles out of me. "Okay, you want me to be honest? I'm going to be honest."

"Go for it."

"Brutally honest." I take a deep breath. Maybe it's the booth, but it almost feels like we're alone in his apartment again. Just the two of us. Intimate. "Sometimes, when I can't sleep because I'm nervous, I look up cheese on Google Images and I just . . . scroll. I scroll infinitely. And I feel peace."

"That's nothing." God, his dimple. "George's entire YouTube history is pimple-popping videos."

I snort a laugh into my water. "By the way—she mentioned you wouldn't give her my number."

Jack's beer arrives. His tongue pushes against the inside of his cheek. "I had a very disturbing mental image."

"What mental image?"

"Of George reminding me daily for the next few decades that she got to take out the girl I liked before I ever did."

I laugh, picturing her starting her maid of honor speech with "*Webster's Dictionary* defines *sloppy seconds* as . . ." Then I realize who the bride would be in the wedding, and my face is suddenly cooked medium rare. Whoa.

"You look like that again."

"Like what?"

"Worried." He searches for words, like he's not sure himself. "Vigilant. Overthinking."

I play with the cloth napkin. "How can you always tell what's in my head?"

"Same way *you* can tell what's in everyone's head."

I frown. "I just look. Try to pay attention to what people want."

"That's what I do. Except that I don't care much about most people, but I can't stop paying attention to you." He shrugs. There is something so utterly, disarmingly honest about him. "So I look."

Is it really that simple? Is that what's happening here? "What am I thinking now?"

"You have questions."

I laugh. "That was a softball."

"It was. Just ask the questions."

"They're kind of . . ." I exhale a laugh. "They're not really just-casually-getting-to-know-each-other questions. They're not . . . normal."

"You're not a normal person," he says, in a way that feels like the opposite of an insult. "And I'd rather you ask than overthink."

I close my fingers around his glass, feeling the condensation pool in my palm. Then I pull my hand back into my lap, wet, cold.

Okay. "Back at Monica's place, you said that you don't date. And Olive told me the same . . ."

He laughs. "Olive?"

"We may have touched on your love life." I flush.

"Ah. Olive." He nods. "She and Adam are . . . I think she wants others to have what they have."

I nod. I've known her for two hours, but it's the impression I got.

"It's not a hard and fast rule—no commitment, no dating, no feeding past midnight. I haven't sworn it off because love is a capitalist construct or some bullshit like that." He shrugs. "But when I was younger, I was in a couple of relationships where the interest didn't match up, and . . . It's better to be up-front. So no one gets hurt."

"I see." I picture a boy being told by his mother that he's not her son anymore. Then growing up to hate the idea of telling a woman that she's not his girlfriend anymore. It makes sense, this determination of his. It also makes my heart heavy.

"What about you?" he asks.

"Me?"

"Do *you* date?"

I smile. "For a living."

"Right. How did *that* start?"

"Oh." I go back to tracing patterns on the glass. "In college. It's kind of a depressing story. Does not pair well with cheese." I let out a nervous laugh, hoping he'll laugh, too.

Instead he asks, "Why depressing?"

Honesty. *Honesty.* It's a thing that I can probably manage. "Because . . . I didn't know."

"You didn't know you were dating someone?"

"No." I swallow. "I didn't know it was fake."

His attention shifts. Still on me, still focused, but more cautious. Gentle. Land mine territory. "You didn't."

I've never spoken aloud about what happened, not even with Cece, because . . . I'm still not sure how it could have happened to *me.* It's been years, and it still doesn't feel like my story. I've always been so guarded. So careful-footed. And when I stumbled, I didn't just skin a knee. I fell facedown and knocked out all my teeth.

"When I was a sophomore, this guy I knew moved abroad. The place he rented was cheap, so I took over his rent. That's how I met J.J. He was the roommate." I push the glass away. "I'd seen him around the Physics Department, and I thought he was an okay guy. Though he *was* planning on becoming an experimentalist."

"Should have tipped you off."

I laugh. "We spent almost one entire year politely ignoring each other. Ideal roommate situation. Then he broke up with his girl-friend." I sigh. "It was messy. Twenty-year-old messy, you know? There were still feelings, but she'd met someone else, and . . . All I know is that a couple weeks later she came over to pick up her stuff, and she found J.J. and me having dinner together while watching something on TV. She went ballistic. She was *so* jealous, which was hilarious, since J.J. and I were sitting ten feet apart and I was having chickpeas—officially the least romantic food. But that's how J.J. got the idea that we should pretend to be together so she'd get even more jealous and . . . I don't know, race through Boston Logan to confess her undying love? It was a fuzzy plan. But I said yes, because . . ."

"Because you weren't any better than you are now at saying no?"

"Hey—no personal callouts." He smiles, and I continue. "We started the ruse, and . . . we didn't just fake it on campus, when she was around. He told everyone—his friends, my friends. And in my defense, which—maybe I have none, but we didn't talk much about the fact that it was *fake*. He brought me home to his parents for the holidays, we studied together, he taught me how to play Go."

Jack nods slowly. "How quickly did you get better than him?"

"Very to extremely. But I pretended I didn't, because he hated losing. He hated not feeling like the smartest person in the room, but he was good at hiding it. He was charming in public. But in private the insecurities came out, and . . ."

"Not so charming?"

"Not really. He was self-centered, but . . . you have to understand, I'd never had lots of friends. I was always the wallflower, trying not to get noticed, but all of a sudden I was at the center of someone's universe. We were together all the time. First just a few weeks, then six months. He started kissing me in private, too. Then more than kissing. Then he wanted to have sex."

"Did you?"

My mouth is dry. "Yeah. I did it."

"No—did you *want* to?"

"I . . . I didn't *not* want to." I trace my finger against the tablecloth. "Mostly, I wanted him to have a version of me he could enjoy."

Jack's eyes close, and I'm suddenly afraid of what I'll find when he opens them. Disgust. Pity, maybe. Judgment. But no: it's just that deep brown, the slice of color, and a bunch of other things I cannot recognize.

"It was Elsie and J.J. Everyone said how beautiful a couple we were, and I settled into that. I read the *Dune* books because they were his favorites. I told myself Dream Theater was good. I did his laundry. Cut my hair short because he liked bobs. I felt powerful, like I'd cracked how to be a social human being. I'd learned how to make people want me." I wet my lips. "Then his ex asked him to get back together."

Jack's jaw tenses. His neck tightens. "And he said that you had to go, because your relationship was fake."

I nod. "I wasn't even sure if I had the right to be hurt. It was just . . . confusing."

"Were you in love with him?"

I let out a small laugh and shake my head. "Not at all. And it should have made it better, right? That I didn't lose the love of my life, that he was just some guy I only liked because I knew how to please him. But then I realized why it hit me so bad." I have to stop.

Take a deep breath. "I'd tried *so* hard. Given my all to be the perfect Elsie he wanted, and . . ." It almost hurts too much to say it.

"You gave him a perfect version of you, and he still didn't want you," Jack says prosaically. Almost detached. Like I'm a gravitational singularity that can be explained, cataloged, predicted. I'm momentarily stunned by how right he is. Then I'm surprised that I'm even surprised.

"And what you took away from it was that you had to try harder."

I nod. "Pretty much." The tray of cheese arrives, but my stomach is sealed. "J.J.'s girlfriend wouldn't allow me to live in the apartment. And because the contract was in J.J.'s name, I had to move out. I didn't really have anywhere left to go, and . . . I'll spare you the details, but it was a mess. I missed tests, assignments. Didn't get enough credits to stay on my scholarship. My junior-year grades were shit—and the first thing on the transcripts I sent in for grad school applications. I'd wanted to become a physicist for a decade, and because of some . . . some *guy* who sucked at Go, I almost didn't." I force myself to reach for a piece of fontina, because—fuck J.J. It's delicious in my mouth. Rich and smooth, sweet and pungent. It makes me forget that I nearly bawled like a four-year-old in the middle of a fancy fusion restaurant. "But my mentor saved me."

Jack tenses. "Your mentor."

I nod, picking another cube. "Laurendeau." The guy whose career Jack accidentally ruined. I'm trying not to think about it—Jack's article, or what Dr. L. would say if he knew that I'm here with him. It seems like a good use of my well-honed compartmentalization skills. "He saw through the bad grades and the rec letters that said I was flaky. Told me I had potential. Accepted me into grad school. Everything I've accomplished, I owe to him."

ALI HAZELWOOD

Jack scans my face for a long time. Then he exhales slowly and nods once, as if coming to an arduous decision. "Elsie—"

"My turn to ask a question," I interrupt. I'm done talking about J.J. and Dr. L. "Since we're on the topic."

Jack hesitates, like he's not ready to let go of the subject. "What is it?"

"Olive also said something else. That when you *do* go out with women, it's usually to . . ." I can't bring myself to utter the words. But it doesn't matter, because Jack looks like he knows exactly what I want to say. I point back and forth between us. "Is that what you want?"

He doesn't answer immediately. Instead he studies me, stern, unreadable, impenetrable as he hasn't been in a while. And then, after a long beat of choosing words carefully, he slowly says, "You and I won't be having sex—"

"You guys ready to order?" The waitress interrupts us.

We don't go back to the topic. And I wonder why the knot of relief in my belly feels so much like disappointment.

18

FLUX

MY MAIN SENTIMENT GOING INTO LUNCH WITH GREG IS fear—closely followed by self-loathing, guilt, and an uncontrollable impulse to run back home and feed myself to Hedgie. Does he hate me? Does he hold me responsible for outing him? Does he want his money back? He deserves it. I'll sell a cornea. Or a foot. Whatever goes for highest.

As it turns out, I shouldn't have worried. Because Greg grins widely the moment he sees me, and then asks suggestively, "You and my brother, huh?"

"Oh, no. No, I . . ."

We're at our usual café, but even though today I could use some diversions, there are no screaming toddlers or projectile vomiting or tragic mishearings. Just the barista in a "Breathe If You Hate Tom Brady" shirt, me, and Greg's winky face. I silently wish for a tectonic earthquake, to no avail.

"We—Jack and I are just . . . hanging out."

There was dinner last Thursday, of course, which ended when he drove me home and answered my "Do you want to do this again?" with an infuriating "Do *you*?" And then the Saturday afternoon spent hunting down the *Murder, She Wrote* novelization for Millicent and bickering about the validity of string theory. ("It has produced no testable experimental predictions." "We are working on the math!" "Work away, but until you come to me with a substantial breakthrough, the multiverse is as scientific as the Great Pumpkin.") And last night, of course, when he drove me to a Northeastern lecture I was going to attend anyway. ("Or you can take the subway and we can meet there, if you enjoy watching people masturbate to Tropicana ads.") Afterward we spent one hour in his car, trash-talking the speaker for saying that the gravitational-wave experiment was a waste of money.

It's Tuesday now, and yes, I've seen Jack three times in the past week, but if I told Greg, he'd assume that we're a couple, which we aren't. We haven't even held hands, unless one counts that time I was complaining about the militarization of science and almost got run over by a Honda Civic. He'd grabbed my wrist and pulled me back and hadn't let go until he'd gotten me safely to the other side of the road. Plus half a block.

Whatever this is, it's slow—static, some would say. I may have found myself thinking about kissing. I may have found myself thinking about whether Jack is thinking about kissing. I may have been pitting seemingly conflicting things he's said—*You and I won't be having sex*; *The girl I liked*; *Really beautiful*; *It'll go away*—against each other in a March Madness–like bracket, trying to figure out how exactly he feels about me.

I guess I could ask. I will. Once I'm ready.

"It's not serious. We're just . . . getting to know each other, and—" Greg's eyebrow lifts, and I crumple. Spiritually. "I don't know. Maybe?"

He grins. "I had a feeling."

"A feeling?"

"He asked *lots* of questions about you. I thought he was just being his usual needlessly protective older brother self, but when we got into 'Does Elsie prefer winter or summer?' territory, I realized it was something else."

I scratch my temple. "You did mention that."

"I did?"

"The tooth. When you . . ."

"Oh. Yeah." He sighs. "You know, I actually had fun that night. Maybe I should incorporate more recreational drugs into my lifestyle."

"Greg, I feel like I unwittingly precipitated you having to come out to Jack, and I'm really sorry."

He shakes his head. "What's funny is, back at Woodacre, before the tooth decided to rot me from within, I had the thought that it was time for me to just ask Mom to leave me alone. Besides, I could have octuplets and Grandma would probably still leave everything to Monsanto just for spite. And Jack was never the issue. I'd been meaning to tell him for a long time, and it's nice that now he knows and doesn't treat me any different. Nothing's changed, except that he was torn up about not researching the aro/ace spec before and very, *very* apologetic for lusting after my 'girlfriend.'" He air-quotes the last part and then laughs a little. I want to spray about like a morning mist and disappear into nothingness.

"Greg, I . . ." *Honesty.* "I get it, I think. How you feel about relationships. Because I also am not quite sure what I want. And . . . I'd love to continue being friends."

"Good. Because now that I almost peed on you, we're bound for life." He grins. "Oh my God. You know what I just realized?"

"What?"

"That if you and Jack work out, Uncle Paul's going to ask you guys for threesomes till the day he dies."

I close my eyes. I might just be the one projectile-vomiting this time around.

LUNCH WITH GEORGE IS A TOTALLY DIFFERENT BEAST. I HAVE one hour between classes at UMass, and she agrees to meet me outside the building where I teach. Not sure why, then, I find her inside my lecture hall one minute before my eleven a.m. Intro to Physics is dismissed.

"Your essays on modern cosmology are due by—" I stumble when she slips inside, her purple coat a flash of color in the dull room. "By the end of the week. Two pages."

"Double spaced?" someone asks from the huddle of warm bodies that is the last row. Not sure why everyone seems to be willing to sell their soul to sit there, since I don't call on students, and as long as they're reasonably quiet, I pretend not to see when they're doing something else. I once had a guy hem curtains through Analytical Mechanics and never batted an eye.

He got an A-minus. Good for him, and for his windows.

"Single spaced. Twelve point." Groans arise. "Please do not insult my intelligence by using Algerian as a font. And do not set the margins to one point three inches hoping I won't realize, because I will check."

I will not check. In fact, I will barely skim the essays for keywords while Cece puts on some Noah Baumbach that is, unfortunately, not *Madagascar 3*. My students would find me *so* pathetic if they knew how desperately I hustle to give them all an A.

"And remember: in-text citations only from scholarly sources."

Raised hand. "What if my uncle—"

"Like I mentioned, while I'm very happy that your uncle minored in biology at the University of Delaware twenty-three years ago, I will *not* accept his Thanksgiving hot takes as a scholarly source. See you all next week."

"This looks like a fun way to spend your time on God's green earth," George tells me after joining me on the podium. "How many of these classes do you teach per week?"

"Oh, only four, five thousand?" She laughs, and I instantly feel guilty. I should be grateful that I have a job. The alternative is hypnotizing my pancreas into thinking it can make insulin and living off Wendy's ketchup packets. "But it's not that bad. The students are great, and—"

"Dr. Hannaway?" A sophomore runs toward me, sweater pulled down on her shoulder. "Could you check if this is just a pimple or—"

"We've been over it, Selina. I'm not *that* kind of doctor."

"Ah, right. My bad."

"No problem. Get it checked out at Student Health, okay?" I smile—externally. Internally, it's a bloodbath. "Please, don't say anything," I beg George.

"Let's go." She closes her hand around my elbow. "You deserve a twelve-course meal."

She takes me to a Turkish café near campus. "Very well," she says between dolmas. "I think we both know the reason I asked you here."

"Do we?"

"Of course." She leans forward, hands steepled, eyes burning into mine. "Jack's my closest friend. Hurt him, and I'm going full Tonya Harding. Though you're probably not as attached to your knees as Nancy was, so I'll do it on the knuckles. You won't be able to pick up chalk without experiencing agonizing pain. You'll have to hold it between your teeth, and all that hydrous magnesium silicate will fuck up your bowel movements forever." My blood drains. I'm planning to flee to a remote Latvian village, alter my fingertips with a cheese grater, dye my hair black, then blond, then back to brown again just to throw people off—when George bursts out laughing. "Oh my God, your *face*."

I blink at her.

"I'm sorry, that was *so* inappropriate. I just couldn't pass it up."

I blink again. "So you didn't want to meet because—"

"Nope, nothing to do with Jack. You can pull his heart out of his chest, grill it, and eat it with a side of creamed corn if you want. I mean, I *am* fond of him, but relationships are like assholes. Shouldn't go around and smell other people's, yada yada." Her smile is mischievous. "Sorry?"

I sip on my ayran. "It's okay. Just . . . Nancy Kerrigan is my cousin. And my father was diagnosed with chalk-induced lung disease."

She pales. "Oh my God, I'm *so* sorry. I didn't mean to . . . I feel horrible about—" She notices my small smile. "You just made that up, didn't you?"

I shrug, stealing one of her dolmas.

"Not only are you perfect for Jack, I think I might like you more than *he* does, and that's *a lot*. Anyway—this is why I asked you to meet." She moves my drink to the side. Then sets down a piece of paper.

She sips her water as I read and read—without understanding a single word. Mrs. Whitecotton from second grade would be *so* disappointed.

"Is this a . . . ?"

She nods.

"It's not . . . I didn't interview."

"But you did get to the final round of an MIT interview. Somebody who will remain nameless—let's just call them Jack—told me that over three hundred candidates applied. I'm going to trust that your credentials checked out and that you didn't try to spin an associate degree from Bible college into a physics doctorate."

"You . . . you are offering me a job? In your lab?"

"As a postdoc. There are two specific liquid crystals projects I'd have you work on."

"Jack put you up to this," I say. A little accusing.

"Nope. In my relationship with Jack, usually, and by 'usually' I mean *always*, *I* harass *him* into doing what I want."

She must be lying. "Listen, thank you. This is kind. But I already told him no. And now that he and I are kind of . . . It wouldn't be a good idea to—"

"Wait." She frowns. "What do you mean, you already told him no?"

"He already offered me the position."

"He *what*?" George explodes. The waiter and about fifteen other patrons turn to us. "Jack offered you a *job*?"

"You . . . didn't know?"

"That is so *inappropriate*." She is face-palming. Hard. "You don't offer *a job* to your brother's ex, whom you've been gone over for months." The face-palming graduates to both hands. "God. *Men.* Even the good ones are just—"

"Are you saying you didn't know?"

"Nope. And I didn't tell him I was planning to offer you a job. The funds come from my grants—this is *completely* separate from my work with him." She sighs heavily. "Listen, I'll be real: I didn't know who you were till last week. Aside from the girl Jack talks about when he gets drunk. But I looked up your stuff. Your work is *good*, and I could really use someone like you on my team. And before you ask—yes, so could Jack. But I'm *better*." She leans forward and points at a line in the contract. "It's a three-year position. I can pay you one point five times the NIH salary. Liquid crystals are a side project for me, so you'd be leading. First author on all publications. I know you don't have applied experience, but we need someone who knows the theory like the back of their hand. No teaching, no Algerian font— just research. Though if you want to keep pretending that you enjoy it, I'm sure we could find you a class."

What is *up* with all these people calling me on my bullshit lately? Am I suddenly giving off main character vibes? "And Jack, in all of this . . . ?"

"Is a nonentity. Don't get me wrong. I'm happy for you guys. Well, for him. He was starting to look miserable. All that broody, horny, guilty pining."

I clear my throat. "Would there be health insurance?"

"You don't have health insurance now?" I shake my head and she rolls her eyes. "Adjuncthood is the fucking eleventh plague of Egypt. Yes, of course, health insurance. You won't have to do this weird fake-dating thing."

Dignity: disintegrated. "Jack *told* you about that?"

"Oh." She winces. "Um . . . No. I could . . . read it in your face?"

Now I'm the one face-palming.

"Listen, he had to. Because I knew you as a librarian. But believe me, there's no judgment here—I put myself through my master's by working as a PA for one of Elon Musk's cronies. And to go back to the job—the most important thing is, three MIT theorists are going to retire within the next five years. You'd be first in line to replace them."

"There is no guarantee that—"

"There is no guarantee that we won't be suctioned off the surface of the earth by a demonically possessed vacuum cleaner." She hesitates for a second, as if deciding whether to add something. "Elsie, I know it can't be easy, accepting a job from someone who stole the one you wanted. But you got your Ph.D. less than a year ago. You're *young* to be competing for faculty positions. Honestly, I'm surprised you're adjuncting—research is your strong suit, and you should be focusing on building your CV, not checking students' zits."

It makes sense, and I want what she's offering—enough money to not worry about money, an office to neatly line up my Funko Pops, three years of peace of mind. But.

"Could I talk it through with my mentor?"

"Sure. Who are they?"

"Dr. Laurendeau at Northeastern."

It's a black cloud moment: one second George is all confident determination; the next she physically recoils, elbow knocking against the back of her chair. "*Christophe* Laurendeau? Does Jack know?"

"Yes. Why?"

"I . . . Nothing." She shakes her head. The light in her eyes has dimmed. "But you don't need to ask for his permission. This is *your* future. *Your* career. *Your* decision."

My career, yes. But I only have one because Dr. L. dragged me out of the pile. "When do you need an answer by?"

"I can wait for two, three weeks tops. After that, I'll have to start looking around to fill the position. Okay?"

ALI HAZELWOOD

I nod. *Just take the job*, a greedy, tired voice inside me insists. It craves those parmesan crisps that are five bucks a pop and is sick of reminding students to stop circling the Scantron bubble instead of filling it in. *Steal an ink cartridge from the Boston University printer and get yourself fired. Then you'll have no choice but to go work for George. Dr. L. will deal with the decision.*

"So," she asks, "aside from offering you a job, what other outrageous and utterly inappropriate things has Jack proposed to you? Marriage ceremony during faculty meeting? Retroactive hyphenation to Hannaway-Smith-Turner for all your academic publications? Naked cuddles in the MIT library?"

I almost spit my ayran all over her. But it's okay because she totally deserves it.

19

IMPEDANCE

ON FRIDAY NIGHT, I WEAR A DRESS.

Nothing fancy. It's a cable-knit sweaterdress my cousin handed down to Mom because it was too long, and Mom handed down to me because it was too small. I pair it with my one lipstick, my one tube of mascara, my one eye pencil, my one pair of thigh highs. I curl my hair all on my own, cursing softly whenever I burn the side of my hand, so Cece won't hear.

Reader: she hears anyway.

"This is such an M. Night Shyamalan plot twist," she tells me from the kitchen, where she's pouring milk into a bowl. "Do you see dead people? Oh my God—am *I* dead?"

"Shut up. I dress up all the time."

She waves her spoon at me. "Not for dates."

"Actually—"

"Not for *real* dates with your professional archnemesis and brother of the guy you used to fake-date, who you wished would incur a death by papercuts but now like enough to fix that cowlick on the back of your head."

I sigh. "Great synopsis of my life."

"Thank you. If you ever need a biographer . . ." She pours Cocoa Puffs *into* the milk, like the nonsensical creature she is. "Where are you guys going?"

"Dinner with his friends. He has this really active social circle that makes me look back to that summer when my best friend was a watermelon with googly eyes and feel absolutely devastated."

"In third grade?"

"High school."

"Ouch. Well, you have *me* now. Ready to call law enforcement if you're not back by eight thirty. May I? I've always wanted to report a missing person." She holds the spoon like a phone. "No, Officer, she didn't have enemies, but she *was* part of a weird sectarian conflict that only someone with a doctorate in physics could fully grasp. Last seen cavorting with a big dude in a Saint Patrick's Day Porta Potty. Yes, I'll hold."

I laugh. "Do text me before you call Liam Neeson. And I might be later than that, but I'm not spending the night."

"Ever?"

"Ever."

She gasps. The spoon clatters. "Are you not letting him smack the salmon because of the article he wrote? Is his seventeen-year-old self cockblocking him from the past?"

I frown—at her usage of *salmon* and at the reminder that why, yes, the guy I'm going out with *did* do that. And it's not that I ever forget. It's just that I truly cannot reconcile it—the way Jack is when we're together, kind and funny and even admiring of my work, and the fact that fifteen years ago—

"Elsie? Is that it?"

"No. No, he's just . . . not planning on having sex with me."

Her eyes widen. "Are *you* planning on having sex with him?"

Maybe. Probably. No. Should I? I want to. I'm scared. Maybe. "I have to go." I chew on the inside of my cheek and pick up my purse. Then stop at the door when Cece says, "Hey, Elsie?"

I turn around.

"You look pretty tonight." Her big eyes are warm. "Even more than usual."

I smile. I think I look medium as usual, but my heart feels open all of a sudden, open for Cece, this beautiful, odd person who cannot read analog clocks or tell the difference between left and right, who's been sticking with me through thin and thin and *thin* for the past seven years. For a moment, all I want is to open my mouth and say, *I hate art house movies. Could we watch a rom-com sometimes? Riverdale? Literally any Kardashian show?*

What comes out is "You look like a weirdo, pouring milk before the cereal, but I love you anyway."

I step out to her middle finger. Then my phone rings, and that's when my night collapses like an accordion.

In my defense, I pick up assuming it's Jack, calling to say that he's late, or that I'm late, or that someone hammered him in the frontal lobe and the resulting brain injury helped him realize that he doesn't want to see me ever again. A tragic miscalculation on my part, because:

"Elsie, finally. You need to come home *right now*."

"Mom?"

"Lance is now with Dana. And Lucas punched him after the soccer game. *Everyone* saw."

God. "But I talked to them last week. Lance said he wasn't interested—"

"He lied, Elsie. I'm disappointed in you for not picking up on it."

"I—" I exhale, stepping out of the building. "He seemed sincere."

"That's why you need to *come home* and help me sort this out. I have been so tense and jittery. My poor nerves."

"Mom, I can't. I don't have a car, for one. And I have classes."

"Just find a substitute teacher."

"That's not—I'm not—Mom." I spot Jack's car. It's freezing cold. Every instinct yells at me to first finish my conversation, but I cannot resist getting in. The seat is already heated, Jack's hair still shower damp, curling in soft wisps on his neck. He looks freshly shaved and smells divine—like soap they sell in fancy boutiques and the hollow of his throat when I slept nestled in his arms.

One minute, I mouth. He nods. Mom's going on about how Lance is misunderstood, Lucas is sensitive, Dad is busy with work, and the mean ladies at church are sure to be rejoicing in the downfall of the once-esteemed Hannaway household. Meanwhile, Jack studies me through my open coat. My dress hits only about midthigh when I'm sitting. His eyes follow the line of the hem, stop on my knees. Linger for a longer-than-polite moment. Then his Adam's apple bobs, and he turns away. His shoulders rise, then fall, and then he's driving out of the parking lot, looking anywhere but at me.

Oh.

"Mom, I have to go. I'll call them both tomorrow and talk them out of . . . illegal stuff, at the very least—"

"You can't solve this at a distance."

I sigh. "I'll do my best. Honestly, I'm not sure I can solve this at all. I'm not sure *anyone* can."

Mom gasps, outraged. "How can you be so *selfish*, Elsie?"

I exhale slowly. "I don't think I'm being selfish. I'll help as soon as I'm able, but they're both beyond listening to anything I—"

"Unbelievable," she says, and then . . . nothing.

Absolutely nothing.

"Jack?" I say.

"Yes?"

"If I'm talking with someone and out of the blue I hear the busy signal . . . what does it mean?"

He gives me a look. "Sounds like you already know."

"Oh my God." I'm dumbstruck. "My mom just hung up on me."

He nods. "Should I be shocked? Is that something that doesn't happen in functional families?"

"I . . . don't know. Does your father hang up on you?"

"Does my father have my number?"

I laugh, and we exchange a half-clueless, half-amused glance. Peas in a pod, really. "It's a first." My stomach feels heavy. "She usually likes me. Or pretends to, anyway."

Jack looks at me with his resting *I see you* face. I'm not used to Mom being *this* mad at me. It feels terrible, like my entire soul is passing a kidney stone, and suddenly the idea of going out to dinner holds zero appeal. *It'll be good*, I tell myself. *You like his friends. Laughter is the best medicine. Or opiates.*

"Want to tell me what happened?" he asks gently, twisting the car through Boston's narrow one-ways.

"My family is . . . embarrassing."

"More so than a dozen people in monogrammed shirts vulture-circling a ninety-year-old in the hope that she'll drop dead and a few wads of cash will roll in their direction?"

"My family would do the same, if there were any money to be had. If something happened to my grandma, my brothers would beat each other up over the six-pack of beer she left in the fridge."

"Is that what they're fighting about? Beer?"

"I wish. It's . . ." I roll my eyes. It sounds too stupid to bear. "A girl."

"A girl."

"Well, she's a woman now. But she was a girl when it all began."

He frowns. "How old are your brothers?"

"Older than me. And honestly, I blame this entire mess on traumatic encephalopathy. Both of them were on the football team getting their brains oatmealed, and there were seventy million cheerleaders they could have, I don't know, played D&D under the bleachers with, but no, they decided to choose the same one. Dana."

His mouth twitches. "I don't think that's what people do under the bleachers, Elsie."

"They're my brothers, okay? For the purpose of this conversation, they've been fighting over the exclusive right to attend Dana's decoupage classes. And the most ridiculous thing is, they fancy themselves in some kind of *Legends of the Fall* situation. They both think that the big love of their life is doomed to fail because of the machinations of their evil twin, but the truth is, it's so obvious from the outside that *no one* loves *anyone* here. Dana gets ninety percent of her dopamine from watching two guys fight over her. Mom only cares about what her cousin's husband's sister's nanny thinks, and is totally fine with them shanking each other as long as they do it privately. And the sad thing is, Lucas and Lance used to be best friends. They'd have fun trying to convince me that ChapStick was made of dromedary sperm and watching me gag. But by now . . . they've forgotten that they're brothers, forgotten why they liked Dana in the first place, and are just chickens pecking at each other's feed—like they're two hydrogen atoms, and Dana is the electron they constantly steal back and forth. But they're both nonmetals, and even though they wish they could pluck that electron out for good and keep it for themselves, nope, same electronegativity, sorry, it won't work. And we're back to square one *every six damn months.*"

"And where do you come in?" Jack asks, voice quiet in the car after my bout of yelling. I feel guilty for unloading my entire life story on him, like he's Oprah or something. I should be *fun.*

"Mom sends me in to broker peace." I squirm against the seat. Jack's eyes slide to my legs, or maybe they don't. The car is dark and I can't tell.

"Why?"

"What do you mean?"

"It sounds like your brothers are having issues with one another." I nod. "Why does she send *you*?"

"I—because—we—" It's such a *Why is the sky blue?* question. Scattering of solar light through the atmosphere, duh. "It's my family."

"It's your mom's family, too. And your dad's, and your brothers'. And yet they're fine with not addressing the issue and asking *you* to take care of it." He takes a right turn, and the lights of the truck coming toward us hit his jaw at the perfect, most handsome angle. There's the way he looks, his low voice, this smell of his. What does this man want with this? With *me*?

"I owe it to them."

"You do?"

"Yes. You don't understand—I was . . . I gave them lots of problems growing up. My diagnosis was such a hassle for them, and the medical care was so expensive. I owe it to them." My stomach drops. Now Mom is mad at me. I'm an ingrate.

"So, to summarize: Because your pancreas stopped producing insulin when you were a child, you now owe your family a doula-worthy degree of emotional labor?"

It sounds horrible, put like that. Downright horrifying. But. "Yeah, kind of."

"What does your family think of your job situation?"

"Oh, that." I shrug. "Not much." I don't plan to elaborate, but he's giving me a raised-eyebrow look, and I want him to check the road. "I don't tell them about that stuff."

"You don't tell them about your *life*?"

"It's not what I meant." Though I don't. "Just . . . I'm a first-generation college student."

"There are plenty of first-generation academics whose parents are supportive and engaged."

I roll my eyes. Because it's not like I don't know that he's right, or like my heart doesn't feel heavy at the thought. "Just go ahead and do it."

"Do what?"

"You're dying to armchair-psychologize me."

He doesn't even hide how entertaining he finds me. "Am I?"

"You obviously have an opinion."

"Hmm."

"Just say it."

"Say what?"

"That I don't tell my family about my job because I'm unable to let people know that I'm more than the sum of the ways I can be useful to them. That if I show my true self, with my needs and my wants, I risk being rejected. That I've wielded my ability to hide who

I am like an emotional antiseptic, and in the process I've turned myself into a puppet. Or a watermelon with googly eyes."

He maneuvers the car past the glow of the streetlights, and as the seconds pass in silence, I grow afraid that I've said too much, showed too much, been *me* too much. But then:

"Well." His smile is fond. Tender. "My job here is done."

I close my eyes, letting my forehead slide against the window— hot skin and cold glass. "I know how messed up I am."

"You do?"

"Yeah. I just . . . I don't know how to stop."

"Then maybe my job is not done. And you should stick around." I turn to check whether his expression matches his tone—a mix of teasing, sweet, amused, hopeful, other things I can never understand.

Then I notice where we are. "This is your apartment."

"Yup." He parks. No, he *reverse* parks. Without sweating or crying or a litany of *fuck shit fuck*. I hate him.

"Did you forget something?"

"Nope."

"Then why—?"

"I figured we'd take it easy tonight. Relax."

"What about your friends?"

"They can entertain themselves."

"But they're waiting for us."

"Nah. I texted them."

"When?"

"While you were comparing your brothers' relationship to a nonpolar covalent bond."

"I . . . Why?"

"Because you're obviously upset. And probably had a long week at work. And you had more-or-less nonconsensual lunches with two people whom I know to be giant pains in the ass. I think it's better if we stay in." He kills the engine. "Just us."

"But . . ." I look up at his building. Unlike mine, it doesn't look like it's twenty minutes from being condemned and thirty-five minutes from burning down due to exposed circuitry. "What are we even going to do?"

I hear the smile in his words. "I have a couple of ideas."

"SO, *BREAKING DAWN*'S THE FIRST ONE."

"What? No. *Twilight* is the first one. Otherwise it'd be the Breaking Dawn Saga."

"Right. Need a blanket?"

The lights are low, but Jack tracks my movements as I shake my head and fold my legs underneath me. The hot chocolate he made sits on the coffee table, right next to his Heineken, and I think I saw him raise the thermostat when we first came in, after he noticed me shivering in the chilly hallway. I'm overdressed, over-made-up, overcurled for a night on the couch. I don't care, though.

"Okay." He grabs the remote and sits next to me, near but non-threatening. Not close enough to touch, but the cushion shifts, and the air around me is warmer. Denser.

"I cannot believe you own a *Twilight* box set."

"I needed to see what the fuss is about."

"You bought the Blu-rays. Who buys Blu-rays?"

"People who can't find the VHS."

I study him. His odd, beautiful eyes. "How old are you, precisely?"

"Seventy-three."

I laugh. "No, for real."

"Seventeen."

"You're thirty-three, aren't you? Thirty-two. Thirty-four?"

"Wouldn't you like to know."

"Give me a hint. What do you remember most from your childhood? Slime? The DSL dial tone? Butterfly hair clips? People dying of the bubonic plague?"

"You can shit on my *Twilight Forever* box set all you want—I've seen the way you're eyeing it."

"With polite but detached interest?"

"With shameless, covetous lust for the 'Edward Goes to Italy' featurette."

I laugh again. It's nice, being here where it's warm. "So what do you know about the movies?"

He drums his fingers on his knee. "They have a bloodcurdling CGI kid named Elizabelle—"

"Renesmee."

"—and something about sparkly dermatology? Spider monkeys?"

"There's also vampire baseball."

"Encouraging."

"Okay, real talk." I turn a little toward him. "Are you going to hate this?"

"Probably. But no more than *2001: A Space Odyssey.*"

"What do *you* like?"

"Physics-defying car chases, mostly. People climbing buildings. Space monsters." He shrugs. "George calls them my 'white male rage' movies."

"Okay, well, we can watch one of those. *Avengers' Infinity Endgame* or something with The Rock. I mean, what about what *you* want?"

"What about that?"

"We never focus on that."

"That's because I have no issues asking for what I want."

"That felt like a backdoor brag," I mumble resentfully.

"It was fully front door."

I play with the hem of my dress. "I understand that this is about helping me reclaim my individuality, but if we're going to be friends, we should do stuff *you* like, too. Otherwise—"

"Elsie." Hands on my chin, he lifts it till my eyes are on his. "You're doing it. We're doing it." I keep looking until I cannot bear it anymore, then free myself.

"Okay, well." I swallow. Twice. "You still didn't need to buy the box set."

"I told you, I—"

"No, I mean . . ." My cheeks are warm. "It's streaming on Netflix. And on Prime."

I pluck the remote from his hand before he can ask me how I know. And then I ignore the amused way his eyes linger on me, and laugh over my hot chocolate at his soft comments: "Very green," or "They go to *high school*?" or "What's up with the ketchup bottle?"

About halfway through, I pry myself from the hormonal ride of paranormal teenage angst to look at Jack. He's studying the movie intently, watchfully, like it's a documentary on unparticle physics. "I promise I'm not going to quiz you afterwards," I tell him. "You can scroll on your phone. Fall asleep. Roll your eyes."

"Is that what people do when you watch *Twilight* with them?"

"I don't."

"You don't . . . ?"

"Watch it with anyone." I never spend time with people doing something *I* unabashedly enjoy. "I usually stream a cam version on my laptop and give off a dense, guilty aura. Once Cece came in in the middle of *Eclipse*. I turned off the monitor and swore I was mas-turbating to stepbrother hentai."

His mouth curves. "Not Bill Nye?"

"Didn't think of it." He looks back at the screen, but something's blossoming in my stomach, something heavy and uncomfortable, and when I say, "Hey," he turns to me again. "Thank you."

"For suggesting Bill Nye porn?"

"No. For . . ." I cannot put it in words. Until I can. "For wanting to know me enough to watch my favorite movie with me."

I lean forward, fully planning to kiss him on the cheek. But something happens once I'm inside his space, and . . .

Plans change. I linger.

Jack is warm. He smells nice and feels familiar, real like very little in my life does. So I stay. Just because it's that good. And I stay even when he turns toward me, and his mouth is so close to mine, I'm almost sure this is going to turn into something else. Into a *kiss*.

He exhales.

I inhale.

His hand rises. Grips the back of my head to hold me still. My eyes flutter closed. A tight flush spreads all over my stomach, skin on fire, heart pumping.

Finally, a kiss that I want. And oh, do I want *this* kiss. I want to—

"No," he says. His lips nearly move against mine. "No."

He lets go abruptly. I open my eyes and he's on the edge of the couch, feet away from me, facing away. "Jack?" His back is rigid.

He rubs his eyes, mumbling something that sounds a lot like "Too soon," and I'm suddenly cold and full of dread.

"I didn't mean to . . ." I reach out and lay my hand on his shoulder blade. He instantly moves away, and I realize it's the wrong way to ask for forgiveness for invading his personal space.

"Elsie, I need you to not touch me for a minute." He goes to stand by the window, rubbing his fingers over his mouth. On the TV, Bella is crying. I feel like crying, too. Mortified to the core. My embarrassment could power a midsized European country.

"I'm sorry," I say to his taut shoulders. "Maybe I . . ." *Honesty. When is honesty too much?* "I think I may be attracted to you."

"Fuck," he breathes out. He turns around, running a hand through his hair. I've never seen him openly show distress before. "Fuck," he repeats softly, and I'm lost. What did I do? I didn't mean to—

He takes a deep breath. Suddenly he's even more imposing. "I'm not going to fuck you," he promises me quietly, almost talking to himself.

"I . . ." Have no idea what to say to that. "I am . . ." Confused? Rejected, maybe? But I didn't ask him for *that*. He's assuming a lot based on a couple of seconds of proximity, and I'm tempted to point it out, which is why I shock myself when what I say is vaguely resentful. "Right. You mentioned before that you're not interested."

He lets out a laugh. "I never said that."

"At the restaurant, you said that you didn't want to have sex with me."

"I said that I wasn't *going* to have sex with you."

I frown. "That's the same thing."

"It's not."

My mind rushes to catch up. Then it does, and my entire body flushes with heat.

"Is that how you interpreted what I said?" He sounds incredulous. "Lack of interest?"

I shrug, like it doesn't matter. Like it didn't cut deep.

"You think I don't *want* to fuck you," he says, blunt as always.

"Why else?"

"Why else."

I clear my throat. "Why else won't you?"

Jack shakes his head. His jaw has a stubborn set, like this is a rule he's made for himself, something he's thought a great deal about. "It's what's best for you. For us. Right now."

"I'm sorry, did you . . ." I clear my throat. "Did you just *inform* me that we're not going to have sex, because it's what best for *us*?"

He nods once, like he would to a known, undisputed fact. *Water molecules slow down light.* And that's when I stand, indignant. "You understand that this should be the product of a dialogue between two people, right?" I'm barefoot. He's so much taller than me, my neck protests the unnatural angle. "You can't just hand out decisions without explanation—"

"I can, actually." The way he bends down can't be comfortable, either. We're sharing about two square feet of space. Cross-armed. Unsmiling. A second ago we were joking on the couch. What the hell?

"This is incredibly patronizing. You can't assume that you know what's best for—"

"Okay, then." He shifts forward, and I can feel every millimeter. "How do I make you come?"

I . . . must have misunderstood. "What?"

"What do you like when having sex? What do you want? What are your needs?" His eyes are pools of black in the dim lights. "How do I make you *come*?"

I shake my head. Edward is moving at light speed to save his love, and my mind is as slow as a slug. "Sorry?"

"You said it was patronizing of me not to discuss sex. So let's talk." This is the Jack from our first meeting: challenging, uncompromising, demanding. "Unless it makes you feel uncomfortable. A good sign that maybe it's best for you not to have it, either, but—"

"That's not it," I hurry to say. But maybe it is, a little. I don't talk about sex very much with people. Just Cece, and mostly in terms of what fourteenth-century nuns were supposedly up to when they should have been tending to the herb garden. But it has nothing to do with *comfort*. We don't talk about sex for the same reason we don't talk about stock dividends: we have very little of it.

"Then tell me," he repeats. His look shifts to something that's not quite daring. Like for once this is not a power play of his, and he genuinely wants to know. "How do I make you come?"

"This is such a *weird* thing to ask. I—" Light bulb: on. "Oh my God. You think I'm inexperienced." I laugh right in his face. "I'm not. I've had sex with J.J., like, a million times, in a million ways!" I add, just to get a reaction out of him. But Jack's reaction is infuriatingly nonexistent. "You think I'm lying?"

"I don't. If you told me you're a card-carrying member of the Orgy of the Month Club, I'd believe you. But since you have all that experience, you'll have no problem telling me: How do I make you come?"

I open my mouth and . . . immediately close it.

"I'm waiting, Elsie."

I hate him when he's like this. Just—smug and merciless and all-seeing and—

"Still waiting."

I look down at my feet, the stockings sheer around my toes, and all of a sudden I'm feeling just . . .

I'm embarrassed. I have no idea what to tell him, and for a second I consider lying. Pretending that I'm a fucking sex goddess. Twenty orgasms in a trench coat. But Jack is lie-repellant, and he'd know, and it'd be even more mortifying than the truth: I have no idea how he can make me come.

My mind turns to J.J., and here's a truth I'm not going to admit out loud in this fancy open-plan apartment: I don't even know if I have the *capacity* to like sex. I never wondered, because *me* enjoying something was never a priority.

"Is this something you do with every girl you sleep with?" I ask bitterly. "An entrance exam?"

"Sometimes."

"Sometimes?"

"Other times it's more trial and error."

Something heavy twists in my stomach. "And after that?"

"After that, I do what they like. Have them do what I like, if they're up for it."

Jealousy. That's the feeling—I'm jealous of these unnamed girls. In my mind they all look leggy, stunning, smart. Worthy of being fucked by Jack.

Unlike me.

I turn away and step to one of the million windows. I don't know how he stands it, the nakedness of this place. It's a fishbowl. He needs curtains.

"Elsie." He's behind me. I see his reflection in the glass, holding my eyes like in a mirror. "You have a pattern of doing things you don't enjoy for the sake of others, and I need to be sure the two of us don't fall into it. I need to know that you're not initiating anything with me because it's something you think I expect. And I need to be certain that you don't feel like you have to be some . . . fantasy lay whose only focus is *my* pleasure. That you're in a place where you're able to acknowledge and articulate your needs."

I let my forehead fall against the glass, watching my eyes cross over my nose.

"You should tell me what you're thinking," he says after a while, much more gentle than a minute ago.

"Why?"

"Because I want to know." He sighs. "And you promised you'd try."

Right. Yes, I did do that. Stupidly. "I'm thinking . . ." I turn around. Drum my nails against the windowsill and close my eyes when I can't bear to look at Jack. What am I thinking at any given time? The more I try to grasp my own mind, the faster it goes blank. "I'm thinking that two things can be true at once: you want to protect me, and also do it in a patronizing way. I'm thinking that by trying to respect me, you ended up making a decision for me—like everyone else before you. I'm thinking . . . that I don't really know you, not yet, but sometimes, when I'm with you, I feel like you know me better than I do myself." I swallow. "But I'm also thinking something else."

"What?"

I open my eyes. He is—I *want* him. For myself. I have no idea in what shape, timeline, texture, but I do. "I'm thinking that I don't know how you can make me come. But it would be fun to find out together."

I'm exhausted from all the thinking, overthinking, rethinking, unthinking. So for the first time in my life, I just let my mind white out. I step out of my head and into my body, savor the absence of formulas and prediction models, and just do it.

Grab the hem of my dress.

Take it off in one fluid motion.

Drop it until it crumples at Jack's feet.

It's a big gamble. I've never done anything this brave, stupid, reckless before, but this is Jack: having so many of my firsts. And it doesn't even matter if the second my clothes are off, I'm all out of courage. I stare at the fabric, too scared to move my eyes anywhere else, letting the tension stretch, the pressure build, till I hear a low "Elsie."

I glance up.

I'm not insecure about my body, probably because I am so busy being insecure about every little thing I do, say, broadcast. But if I were, if I had any doubts about whether I'm attractive, pretty, desirable enough to him, they'd dissolve like sugar in water.

Jack's cheeks are pink. His pupils fat, fixed at some point between my belly button and the elastic of my panties. At his sides, both his hands twitch, then clench into fists. "It's too soon," he says again. "We should wait till you're more comfortable around me."

"I'm at my most comfortable around you," I say. And then, because *honesty*: "And also at my least. But that's because you're an asshole, and unlikely to ever change."

He exhales a sharp laugh. I look at him looking at me, thinking that I might win this if I play it right. And then he says, "If we . . . We need rules," and it occurs to me that I've already won.

"I don't—"

"*I* need rules," he says firmly, in a tone that brokers no objection. He's staring at the swell of my breasts over my bra, mapping the edge of the simple black cotton. "You promise me you will—"

"Stop you if I need to. Tell the truth. Be honest." I nearly roll my eyes. He's right, but I'm impatient. Hot. Tingling with a sense of almost victory. Of possibilities.

His throat bobs. "We take it slow." He's starting to sound like he just finished a sprint. I consider making a CrossFit joke, but my mind's occupied. "We're not having sex. And clothes stay on."

I glance at my dress. "Should I put it back on?"

"Jesus." He licks his lips, steps closer. His hand lifts to hover somewhere around my waist but doesn't touch me. "*My* clothes stay on."

They won't. They can't, logistically. But he seems obsessed with being in control, so I say, "Suit yourself." I reach around behind my back to unclasp my bra. He stops me and shifts even closer.

"Leave that on."

I nod and bend down to roll off my thigh highs.

"Leave them on, too." His jaw works. "Please."

Oh.

"Okay." I clear my throat. My heart is pounding and he's flushed, and neither of us is doing anything. We're caught. Stuck in the transition. "Can we . . . I don't know. Can we kiss now? Or is it still 'too soon'—"

Jack is not clumsy, not ever, but the embrace somehow is. Too hurried, greedy, impatient, the momentum too strong when he presses me against the window. The cold glass bites into my skin, a heady contrast to the unyielding weight of his chest on my front. "Why are—?"

His mouth is on mine, and I'm overwhelmed, then dizzy, then confused. In my experience, kisses are brief, something to do before moving to other body parts, to the real thing. But Jack won't let this one end: his tongue presses against mine, strokes slowly, coaxes my jaw open. He kisses like he's already inside me. I don't know what to do about that, so the moment stretches endlessly, full and hot, until I cannot help squirming against him.

There is a couch nearby. A bed, countless chairs, an air mattress

I've heard tales of. We're here, though, the windowsill digging into my hips till he lifts me on top of it. He's still taller, bigger, stronger, but he yields a few inches of advantage and I arch into him, twisting to get closer.

"Wait. Wait, let me—" His fingers close on my wrists and draw my arms around his shoulders. His hand slips between my thighs, lifts one up to make room for his hips, and then we're locked together, finally close enough.

I moan into his mouth. He grunts and breaks the kiss. "Is this okay?" he pants. Something hard pushes against my stomach through his jeans. "Is this okay? Do you—"

"Yes."

"Thank fuck." He sweeps my hair away and holds his nose to the hollow of my throat. Inhales sharply. "You smell out of this world. I've been stuck on it since last summer, but it's gotten better, and—"

"Bed. We should go to bed."

"We're not going to bed." He nips my cheekbone, then licks the sting off, and we both moan at the feeling. "I'm not going to fuck you. We're just . . . making out. Fooling around. This is not . . ." He hooks his finger into the soft cup of my bra and lowers it. His forehead presses against mine and he looks down, to the hard point of my nipple. "Jesus," he mutters.

"I can take it off—"

"No." He groans softly and thumbs the pebble back and forth. Pinches it just this side of too much, making me gasp. "I'm not going to fuck you, but God, I could." His entire palm rubs against my breast, and my whimper is humiliating.

This is going to feel good. Really, really good. It's already much better than . . . than anything. Pulling embarrassing, unfortunate noises out of me.

"What do I do?" he asks, fitting his fingers in the dips of my ribs.

I look up at him, glossy-eyed, already a little dazed. "What?"

"What do you like?" He's looking down at my body like it's a beautiful space oddity, something belonging to a minor goddess, to be investigated in filthy, methodical, obscene ways. His hand traces my flat stomach. Skims the place where my thigh highs transition into tender skin. Brushes reverently against the pod right above my panties, like this little thing my life depends on is as much a part of me as my navel. J.J. asked me to take it off, said he found it off-putting. Made bionic woman jokes. And then there's Jack. Licking his lips and asking, "Where do I start?"

I have no clue. "Um . . ."

He kisses me again, this time slow and gentle, pulling back from that initial brink. He uncovers my other breast, and his fingers are back, playing with my nipple like it's an instrument. Liquid warmth hooks low in my belly. "Trial and error, then."

"What do you do with other girls?"

"Other girls?"

"Normal girls."

He laughs into my collarbone, then starts sucking on it. "Elsie."

"I just want to know. If I . . . if I weren't *me*, what would you do?"

"No." Against my sternum.

"I just—honesty, you said." He's licking the inside of my breasts like they're luscious, sweet fruits. I run my fingers in his hair, bow into him, beg, "Please."

He hums against my nipple. I wait for him to take it into his mouth, tense as a violin string, and when he doesn't, when he pulls back to stare at me, I nearly groan.

I do groan. A soft, miserable whine.

"If you were any other woman . . ." His palms stroke my knees, spreading my legs apart. "If you were anyone but you, I would take you to bed. And I'd fuck you everywhere you let me." His fingers are like electricity, climbing up my inner thighs, lighting up nerve endings. "I would go down on you, maybe while you're going down on me. And because your tits look like something I'll be dreaming about for decades, I'd ask for permission to come on them. Paint a picture." He reaches the elastic of my panties. I inhale, sharp. "I'd clean you up and feed you before taking you home, if you wanted me to." His thumb pushes the wet cotton to the side. Slides underneath. "But you wouldn't be you. And afterwards I wouldn't think of you very much."

He taps against my clit and I let out a moan. It's knee buckling, how good this feels, the rush of pleasure climbing down my spine.

"This is way too fast," he says hoarsely, but he's drawing slow circles around me. My pussy throbs in time with my heartbeat, and my nails dig hard into the windowsill. I am grateful for my black panties, which won't show how wet I am. For the low lights. I'm grateful that I can close my eyes, pretend he's not looking at me and seeing every little thing I'm made of. "Elsie, maybe you should ask me to stop."

"*Don't*. Whatever you do, please don't stop."

He laughs, breathless. "More? Less? What do you want?"

I want everything, and nothing will ever be enough. I'm empty and I ache and I'm clenching around nothing and—

"Elsie, what do you—"

"I don't *know*," I whine, burning, out of control. "I don't know, but please—can you—"

"Shh. It's okay." The thumb presses harder, and my head falls back against the window. "I barely know what I want from you, and I've had much longer to think about it." He's close, licking my neck and my nipples, scraping his teeth around my throat. It makes everything worse and so much better. "I don't know what I'm doing, either. Not with you. This is new."

My head is a jumbled mess of pleasure and panic. This is—oh *God*. "That's humble of you," I manage to push out. My hips shift, trying to meet him and get more friction. Jack sees me strain, and he does nothing. I hate him. I *hate* him, I hate him, I—

"There's something *really* humbling about having the face of your brother's girlfriend in your head every time you come."

Another whimper. Mine. "I was never his."

"I didn't know it. For months, I didn't know."

I want to ask him what he thought of. When it started. I just say, "I was sure you hated me."

He laughs, a little wistful, and leans in for a kiss against my temple. "I did sometimes. For making me hate my brother, just because *he* was the one who got to eat you out." His hand twists, and something in his grip changes: more points of contact, Jack parting my folds, the heel of his hand pressing against my clit. It's even better. So much better. "Should I put a finger inside you?"

A flush spreads up from my chest. My entire body is burning, a blend of embarrassment, heat, pleasure.

"I don't . . . I usually . . ."

I feel him nod against my cheek. "No, then."

"But . . ." Historically, penetrative sex has done very little for me. But then so has kissing or touching, and as I sit here, trembling from Jack's hand between my legs, I cannot help thinking that maybe there could be more to that. "Trial and error," I say, which makes him laugh, a deep rumble in his chest.

"You sure?"

I nod. And then his middle finger nudges at my opening, tapping gently while his thumb strokes my clit, and I think it's going to be a process, I think my body is going to have to work for it, but I'm wrong. He sinks inside me like a stone in water, gentle but not tentative, and it's tight, but the friction is good. He pulls back to hold my eyes, and we stay like that, both vaguely surprised, both not quite daring to breathe. Until he kisses my mouth and hooks his finger inside me.

I arch and contract around him. We both jolt.

"Fuck," he breathes out. "Here, huh?" He does it again, hitting a spot that's somehow indecently, massively perfect. My entire body blooms with heat, thrums from the intensity of it.

"Oh my *God*, Jack, you—"

He does it some more, and I lose any ability to speak. His kisses deepen, become more aggressive, but I am too lost in the pleasure shooting up to my brain, too uncoordinated to return them in any meaningful way. He realizes it, I think, because he groans in the back of his throat, and his other hand moves between my shoulder blades and he pulls me into his chest, a soft creature he scooped up from the floor, squirming under him, melting between his fingers, utterly defenseless. "I imagined being with you like this a lot. But, Elsie, this is unreal. You are *unreal*." His lips trail across my cheek. "When I get inside you, I'm going to lose my fucking mind," he pants against the shell of my ear, like it's too dirty to say out loud, even alone in a dark room.

"You *are* inside me—"

"You know what I mean." He bites my lobe. His hand caresses up and down my spine, a soothing touch that's the polar opposite of the slick mess between my legs. "Two?"

I swallow. My thighs are starting to tremble, and a frightening thought occurs to me: I might *come* from this. I might actually have an orgasm. I might lose all control and a fair bit of dignity, in front of someone else. In front of *this* someone else.

"Elsie? One finger okay? Or you want more?"

I don't know. No. Yes. I shake my head and blindly grab his arm, digging my nails into him. His biceps is an oak tree, no give to the heavy muscles, and I feel less stranded. Anchored.

I want more of this. Of Jack. But I'm already full, bursting at the seams. "You have really big hands," I say, and I *don't* say, *I like your hands. I love your hands. I watch your hands.*

"Okay." He wets his lips against mine. We're drawing a map together, of a place neither of us has visited. "Okay, let's stick with one."

"I think . . ." I cup his cheek. Make sure my eyes are on his. "I think we should go to bed. Have sex. Real sex."

He laughs, strained. "I think you should let me go on my knees and eat you out until tomorrow morning."

God. *God.* I shake my head, dizzy, warm, dazzled. "Let's just have sex. You—you can't be enjoying this," I tell him around a moan. I clearly am. Enjoying it.

"You sure?" He angles me a little, and there is no mistaking the hot bulge of his cock against my hip.

"Oh."

"Yeah."

"I'm not—I'm not even doing anything. If we went to bed, I could—"

"You make soft little sounds. You shift your hips when I do—ah, yes. This. And these tiny spasms around my finger, which make me think of you clenching around my cock. Given how tight you are, it isn't happening anytime soon, but—" He closes his eyes and takes a deep, undone breath. "Sorry."

His rhythm on my clit is picking up, and I'm fading fast, all shallow breathing and spotty vision. "Sorry?"

"Just trying to get a grip."

"You don't have to get a grip. You can take me upstairs and—"

My channel contracts around him and we both groan. "You sure you don't want two fingers, Elsie?"

I let my shoulders fall back against the window. It's wet with my sweat, not cold anymore. "We should try."

He watches himself this time. He stares at his index finger disappearing inside me alongside the middle, his other hand drawing calming patterns on my waist. I clench and gasp and twist on him, but he doesn't let up, keeps pushing in slowly, and after some resistance, I'm taking him, arching involuntarily to make room, letting out a final little noise of gratitude and disbelief.

"Jesus," Jack says. "*Fuck.*"

I'm getting used to it. This sense of being crammed with something hot and beautiful. I move experimentally. Squeeze around him till we both make sounds that belong to animals.

"Good?"

I nod. The edges of my vision are blurry. "Good."

His kisses are gentle pecks, almost chaste. Afterthoughts, punctuations to this lurid, soaking thing we're doing. "So maybe you like to be full," he says, voice husky.

I nod. Maybe I do.

"I will give you anything I have—anything you want, if you let me go down on you right now."

I lie back, enjoy the fullness, and try to decide in the mush that is my brain. "I've never done it," I whisper, and Jack must find the situation unacceptable, because he drops to his knees in front of me and inhales deeply against the crease of my abdomen.

It takes exactly two swipes of his tongue to send me to outer space. One around my opening, where he's stretching me too wide, and I think I'm going to die of embarrassment, of heat, of the liquid pressure that grows with each of his guttural groans. Then he moves up to my clit, and I know—I *know*—that nothing has ever felt like this in my life, that good things come sparingly, that I should try to make this last, but it's over before it starts. My body seizes and snaps and bursts into a bubble of simple, pure, physical pleasure that feels too intense to weather alone. My fingers pull Jack's hair too tight, dig in his scalp, and he keeps on eating at me, even when I'm coming down. His fingers stay deep inside, as if to give me something to contract around while I ride it out, and it's perfect, this. It's explosive, crashing, nuclear. Somewhere in the universe antimatter is being produced, and it's all because of this.

Because of us.

"I think I'm dying," I say the second I can breathe, completely serious. My heels are digging into his back, and wet noises rise up from where he's still running his tongue over me.

"I think I want to do this every day," he responds, kissing my pussy like he would my mouth. "Every day for the rest of my life."

His words barely register, the glow of pleasure scrambling my mind as he pulls out his fingers and stands to press a soft kiss on my jaw. He murmurs soothing praises and nuzzles the top of my head, like he knows how disoriented I feel. I think these are cuddles. They feel as good as the orgasm.

Then something occurs to me: I came. He didn't. I think of that moment of tense desperation just before, the fear of being stuck on the verge of pleasure, and I wonder if that's where Jack is at now. If that's how he feels, pulled too tight, too big for his skin.

"I want to have sex," I tell him for the millionth time, and it's true. I do. I want to see Jack come, for a whole host of reasons that have little to do with him. I'm utterly, purely selfish.

"Against tonight's rules," he mutters into my shoulder.

"So you're just going to stop?" I shift my thigh, and it's still there. His erect cock.

"I'm fine with—"

"Honesty," I cut in. We're both starting to wield the word like a weapon. "What do you want now? Putting aside your 'rules.'" I roll my eyes at the last word, which seems to amuse him. My stomach blooms with heat—a physical reaction to his dimple.

"I don't have to—"

"Honesty."

"Okay." He exhales and stares down at my body. Considers the possibilities. "I want to come on your stomach."

"Oh." I expected . . . I don't know what. Not this. "Is it a . . . kink you have?"

He shakes his head. "Not usually, no. But . . ." He looks past my eyes, uncharacteristically bashful.

"Honesty?" I request.

"I never thought of myself as the possessive type. But . . . you were someone else's for a long time. It drove me a bit crazy in my lizard brain."

I nod, thinking of my own vague jealousy. "I think you should, then."

He swallows. "Yeah?"

"Yeah." I bite back a smile. "Make sure your clothes stay on. Rules and all."

He gives me a dirty look. For a second I'm giggling on the high of teasing him, then there's his belt clinking undone, the catch of a zipper, brushes of fabric as he takes himself out, and the smile dies on my lips.

I am looking, and he isn't. He doesn't watch for my reaction. Just takes himself in hand, pumping up and down. His cock is hard, long and thick in a way I didn't think possible. I glance at the way he's stroking himself, then away to the couch, then at him again, and ask, "Doesn't it . . . get in the way?"

It's a mortifying question, and I want to air-fry myself out of this plane of existence the second it's out of my mouth, but Jack's not listening. His eyes move rapidly all over my body, like I haven't been almost naked in front of him for the past ten minutes. "You really are the most beautiful thing I've ever seen," he murmurs.

"You said you don't care. That you barely notice. That there are lots of beautiful women."

"I don't know." He's usually so confident, but right now he sounds as disoriented as I feel. "With you, I notice." He nips wet kisses down my jaw. "You think you can come again?"

Impossible to tell. I haven't come with another person before, and an improvement rate of 200 percent seems steep, but maybe? I'd rather be present for this, though. Study him. Know what Jack looks like when he's not fully in control. "I think I don't want to."

He nods, and what happens next is not really for me. He steps between my thighs and angles the underside of his cock so that it hits my clit. It has us both gasping, but it's about what *he* wants. As is the way he slots the head against my opening, and the long moment he leaves it there, grunting, a turning point in the multiverse, where two futures exist: one in which he pushes in and fucks me, the other in which he follows those inflexible rules of his.

Unfortunately, Jack Smith-Turner is a stickler.

It occurs to me that I could be doing this for him. I could be more than just a warm body and slender arms looped around his neck. "Should I—"

"Not tonight." His movements are picking up, knuckles brushing rhythmically against my slit. "I just want to look at you. Know you're here." He uses my slick to make himself wet, hard, fast pulls, and after just a handful of seconds I see the tension in his arms, the muted tremors in his fingers, how close he already is. "Shit, Elsie." His voice is urgent. A little desperate. His forehead presses against mine. "There were days, these last few months, when you were all I could think about. Even if I didn't really want to." Then a choked "Fuck" that feels like a rush of breath against my lips, and I know he's there.

I think he'll finish with a growl, make a mess out of me, maybe admire his handiwork, but that's not what happens at all. Instead he pulls back so that his eyes can hold my own till the very last moment, glassy and nearly all black. His free hand searches blindly, frantically. It grabs mine when he finds it, twining our fingers together in a tight grip, and that's when I know. When I realize deep in my belly that for Jack this is not about friction or about fucking. It's not even about coming, or about anything else I might have stupidly suspected.

This is about him and me. And the possibility of something that goes far beyond the both of us.

"Elsie," he mouths when he comes. He seems to retreat into himself, to dig deep into his head to deal with the shocking pleasure of it and avoid losing his mind, and all I need to do is hold him tight to remind him that yes. I'm here. With him.

I'm here.

It's downright terrifying, what this could be. What I want it to be. It makes me tear up, and then it makes me sob, and then it makes me clutch at Jack for dear life, the splotch of his semen sticking to his shirt and my stomach, pooling in my belly button. To his credit, he doesn't ask me what's wrong. He doesn't beg for explanations. He just holds me close, both arms wrapped around me, even when my tears morph into giggles, like I'm some crazy, unstable girl who doesn't know what to be or what to feel.

Wait. That's exactly who I am.

I laugh. Then I laugh some more. Then I cannot stop. The movie is over, "15 Step" by Radiohead bafflingly plays during the black-and-white end credits, and I'm laughing again.

"You're ruining the moment." His lips curve into my throat, winded like he just finished an Olympic race.

"I'm *so* sorry. I just—"

"What?"

"Just wondering if you still think it's 'too soon.'"

He slaps my butt. I yelp and then keep on laughing.

"Yes." He maneuvers back and angles my head so that I'm look-ing at him. "It's *really* soon. But the only person who can slow us down is you, so . . ."

"So what?"

He pushes a strand of sweaty hair behind my ear. His eyes are worried, and warm, and empty of everything that's not us. "Be gen-tle with me, Elsie. That's all I ask."

20

FALLING BODIES

From: SandraShuberton@gmail.com
Re: Thermodynamics Essay

Doctor Hannaway, ma'am, it's been 23 hours, have you graded my essay yet?

Saturday's a daze.

I shuffle around my room gingerly, full of distant stares and hands stopping midaction, like I cannot remember what I opened my closet for, how to squeeze the tube to get the right amount of toothpaste.

It's a first. I sense that some paradigmatic shift has happened within me, but I cannot justify it. Jack and I did a bunch of things that high schoolers today would barely consider a quarter of first base—so what? I try to cognitively reframe last night as two adults having casual fun, but my head is full of aggressive, intrusive, embarrassing thoughts that make it hard to concentrate on grading. As though the sheer nature of grading didn't do it on its own.

"When did you get back last night?" Cece asks when I emerge in the kitchen. As usual, she's engaged in a mix of activities: teaching Hedgie an obstacle course, listening to an audiobook on the women of the Plantagenets, making oatmeal.

I try to recall what the clock in Jack's car looked like when he dropped me off. The red numbers blinking at me in the dark, as if to say, *You should go.* And Jack leaning over the armrest for a kiss, then pulling me into his lap. Whispering, *Not yet.* "Around one."

"A record."

"We watched a movie," I tell her, to avoid saying, *I think I had the most soul-shaking night of my entire adult life, and it didn't even involve cheese.*

"What movie?"

"Um . . . a vampire movie."

"Oh my God. *Nosferatu: Eine Symphonie des Grauens?*"

". . . Yeah."

"Lucky you." She sighs. "Did you make out before or after Count Orlok awakens?"

"We didn't—" She points at my neck, and I turn to catch my reflection in the microwave. Dammit. "During."

She nods knowingly. "It's a horny movie, isn't it?"

I remind my brothers that if they go to jail for killing each other, their future lives will contain very little Dana and very copious amounts of toilet wine. In response I get called a bitch (Lucas), ordered to get a fucking life (Lance), and told, unceremoniously, "Humph" (Mom).

"They *did* agree to not run over the other if they meet at the farmers' market, so there's that."

"Glad to see you're doing your part for the family, Elsie," she says.

I think I'm forgiven. Because I did what I was told. There should be relief in that, but while Mom goes on about that Comic Sans inspirational quote my aunt posted on Facebook that may or may not be shade, I picture practicing honesty. *Mom, stop. This is messed up.*

I don't do it, though.

I often meet with Dr. L. on Saturdays, and I've been dying to discuss George's offer with him, but he's out of town. Instead I have lunch with Cece (a quinoa bowl—I snap a picture and send it to Greg, who replies with seven face-palming emojis in a row) and then spend the afternoon at the science fair, manning the UMass Physics Club stand alone because none of the students who were supposed to help showed up. I freeze my ass off, wonder if I should be worried about the group of kids who keep begging me to teach them how to build a catapult, then imagine doing this next year, all over again.

Then I imagine making my life about what *I* want.

When I get a text from Jack, my brain stops working.

JACK: Greg invited us to dinner. Want to go? We can stay in if you prefer.

He talks like his Saturday nights belong to me, even though this thing with us only just started, and my heart skips too many beats.

ELSIE: I'm at UMass doing unspeakable things till late. But I could join when I'm done.

JACK: Perfect.

I think of the word *honesty* a lot before adding:

ELSIE: I'd like to spend the night afterwards.

The reply takes a long time to come, and I find myself picturing answers. *It's too fast. Let's get back on track. Take it slow.*

But something has shifted. Maybe on the windowsill. Maybe when he nipped my chin after buttoning up my coat. Maybe in the parking lot, the moment he grabbed my hand and pulled me back into the car, telling me that I couldn't leave without telling him the ending of the movie. *Do they go to college? Does Edward ever see a dermatologist? Who wins the golden onion?*

His reply takes a long time to come, but I'm not surprised when it does.

JACK: Good.

BY THE TIME GREG OPENS THE DOOR, I'VE WORKED MYSELF UP to a state of panic.

"I thought coming empty-handed would be rude," I blurt out, "so I grabbed this. Because it was cheap, but not the cheapest." I hand him the bottle of red wine like it's a hot potato. "I didn't notice the name until I got on the bus, and . . ."

Greg looks down at the label, which proclaims "Ménage à Trois" in a sexy, flirtatious font. He snorts out a laugh.

"I swear, this is *not* a proposition."

"Noted." He hugs me, at once new and comfortingly familiar.

"I'll put this orgy invite in the fridge and go finish the food. Make yourself comfortable."

I claw out of my anxiety pit, take off my coat, then make to follow him into the kitchen, when—

Jack.

For no reason whatsoever, my heart jolts and I cannot breathe. Maybe there's something wrong with my cardiopulmonary health— is my entire body joining my pancreas and crapping out? Does nothing inside me *work* anymore? But really, it's not important. I don't care. *Jack* doesn't care. He stands just a few feet from the entrance, arms crossed, chestnut eyes full of warmth and amusement as he murmurs, "Looks like you and Uncle Paul have something in common, after all."

"I . . . He . . . It's a misunderstanding."

His mouth twitches. "When you said you wanted to spend the night, I didn't think you meant *here*."

I groan, covering my eyes with my hand. And when I feel Jack's heat, I know he has drifted closer, and I let myself sink into him.

"Hey," he says, lips against my temple, and suddenly everything feels a bit more right in the world. I want to kiss him, desperately, just as desperately as I don't want his brother to walk in on us kissing in his living room. So I pull back and open my mouth to say the first thing I can think of.

Then immediately close it.

Am I going insane? Is my brain leaking out from my ears? I can't say *that*. I'm not batshit—

"Honesty," he chides gently.

Crap. "I . . ." I swallow. Buck up. Take a deep breath. "I missed you." I rub my forehead. "God, I'm such a weirdo."

He nods slowly, as though mulling it over. Then offers, "I went to campus today to get work done. Instead I kept wondering how buck wild it would be if I asked you to move in."

I let out a surprised laugh. "You're a weirdo, too."

"Yeah."

"Have you ever . . . ?"

"Nope. Total first."

"What's wrong with us?"

His eyes hold mine, unyielding. "I think we both know what."

I laugh again. "What?"

"Come on, Elsie. You know where we're going, here."

I take a step back, nearly bumping into a fully assembled hutch. Panic bubbles as I track this conversation. I think I know what he's referring to, but . . . It's not possible. It might *feel* like that, but it's too fast.

"No," I say. And then turn away, dry mouthed, because he's giving me the look again, the one he reserves for when we both know I'm lying.

I'm afraid he'll be his usual merciless self, but he just nods, pushes a strand of hair behind my ear, and tells me, "It'll come to you." His touch lingers briefly, then his hand drops to his side just as Greg calls to tell us that dinner is ready.

"I'm a very mediocre cook," he warns me, and it's not a lie, but his mediocre food pairs perfectly with my mediocre wine, and even better with stories of his and Jack's mediocre childhoods. Teenage Greg, apparently, used to update every Facebook status with emo song lyrics. Jack had a skater phase *and* a man-bun phase (not overlapping). They once collaborated on a homemade mafia thriller titled *The Godson*, which Greg promises to show me. In exchange, I make them laugh with my weirdest fake-girlfriending stories, like the guy who had me learn sea shanties in preparation for our date, or the one who was afraid of wallpaper.

"This is . . . easy," I tell Jack when Greg gets a late-night work call. He's washing the dishes; I dry.

"What is?"

"Just . . ." I stare at his soapy fingers. "This. The three of us. I thought it'd be weird, but . . ." It's not.

"Why do you think that is?" he asks, with the tone of someone who already has the answer. I don't, though. It eludes me, even as Greg unearths *The Godson* for its first showing in two decades. After we hug him good night, I doze off inside the car. And once we're home, I hang my coat on *my* hook.

Is it messed up that I've started to think in those terms? If being somewhere three times were a sign of ownership, Cece and I would be the barons of Trader Joe's cheese aisle. But my peacoat always finds itself in the same spot—between a lightweight black jacket and the lanyard with Jack's MIT Physics Institute badge. The budding domesticity makes reaching for possessive pronouns that much easier.

"Want a hot chocolate?" he asks. He ventures deep inside the apartment, turning on just one light. His face is full of shadows, and I'm a little lost in them.

"No."

"Anything else?"

I shake my head and stifle a yawn. It's past two and all I want is a pillow, but I think we're about to have sex. That's what *spending the night* means, right? I should check Urban Dictionary.

"Let's go upstairs, then."

In his room, he hands me an extra-large hoodie and herds me

toward the bathroom. I change into it because I'm too tired to wonder why, because it's kind of comfy, and because maybe it fits into a kink of his. He did like lingerie. Sportswear might be the next logical step. Or tentacle dildos.

I use his mouthwash, scrub my face clean, then pad back into his room, hair up in a messy knot, the thick cotton hitting my thighs almost to my knees. I brush past Jack and his amused look and throw myself on *my* side of the bed—more unwarranted possessive pronouns—and sneak in a twenty-second micronap. Or maybe it's more like ten minutes, because when I next wake up, Jack blocks the night-light seeping in from the hallway. He smells like shower and toothpaste. And he's wearing plaid pajama bottoms and a *Toy Story* T-shirt.

"Cute," I say, closing my eyes again. "Did you notice Woody and Buzz's homoerotic undertones?"

"I thought they were very overt."

"Validating. Thank you. We're about to have"—I yawn—"sex, right?"

The mattress dips. "Sure." Under the down blanket, strong hands pull me closer, long legs tangle with mine, and we've done this before. It's comforting. Familiar. The word *mine* pops into my sleepy head again, and I let it float about longer than I should.

"Okay, good." I can't stop yawning, but I force my lids open. "I'm on the Depo shot. I get it from Planned Parenthood, otherwise I couldn't afford it."

"Planned Parenthood's good people."

"Yeah." I shift closer. He's hard against my stomach, but nothing about him broadcasts impatience. "We don't have to, like, use a condom. Unless you have pubic lice."

His cheek curves against mine. "I doubt condoms protect from pubic lice, sweetheart."

I doze off into a pillow that smells like shampoo and a hint of sweat and Jack's MIT office, thinking about the logistics of little critters jumping from one crotch to another, only to jolt awake mid-fading. "Don't let me fall asleep," I yawn into his neck. "We're supposed to be doing it."

"We are. We're going at it like animals. Just close your eyes."

I do. It's easier. "Is this another rule of yours? Are you into BDSM?"

"I do have a thing for consent. And my partners being awake."

I picture legions of beautiful, intelligent, curvy partners with advanced degrees. "What happened to the geologist?"

"Who?"

"She was your date the day I met you. Very nice. On the short side. Dark hair. I forgot her name . . ."

"Madeleine. She's currently in Europe for her sabbatical. Spain, I believe." He pushes a strand of hair behind my ear. "She's cool. You two would get along."

I'm marginally more awake. "Have you been with lots of women?"

"Mmm." The sound purrs through my skin and bones. "I don't know."

"How do you not know?"

"I have no idea what the parameters of 'lots' are."

"Between one hundred and three hundred and twelve." He slaps me gently on the ass. I chuckle and melt into him. "I'm not sure, either."

"Then we'll never know."

"But you do this a lot."

"I haven't in a while."

"Since when?"

"I think you know."

Oh. "You like sex," I say. Not a question.

"I do." He pauses. "But I'll also go months without thinking about it if I'm busy working on a grant or an experiment."

"Like your current sets of failed experiments?"

He laughs softly, pressing a kiss on my hair. "I've thought more about sex in the last six months than ever before."

"I hope you'll like it." I burrow further into him. "With me."

"I will."

"You can't know."

"I can." He rubs a hand up and down my back, like I'm a fussy pet in need of soothing. Maybe I am.

"Sexual compatibility is a thing. What if we're not . . ."

"Then we'll work on it."

"I don't want to be *work*. I don't want you to feel that I'm *work*."

He sighs. "Somewhere along the way your wires got crossed. Your brain decided that you're not worth people's time and effort, and that if you ask for anything, they won't just say no, they'll also leave you." He says it matter-of-factly, like he's Archimedes of Syracuse repeating his findings about upward buoyant forces to the acropolis for the tenth time. "That's not how love works, Elsie. But don't worry for now. I'll show you."

"But I—"

"Go to sleep."

"What? Why? No!" I try to move up, but his arms cage me tighter. "We should be having all the sex."

"In a minute. For now, just close your eyes and be silent for twenty seconds."

"Why?"

"It's a kink I have."

"You perv." Yawn. "What happened to anal play and bondage?"

"We'll get there. Are your eyes closed?"

I nod into his chest.

"Perfect. Now count to twenty in your head."

His breath is a soft, steady rhythm under my ear. I'm warm and safe, and I get only to thirteen before I'm lost to the world.

21

COMPLEX HARMONIC MOTION

M Y FIRST THOUGHT IS *I'M GOING TO BUY HIM CURTAINS.*
My second: *I'm going to do without cheese, insulin, and possibly toilet paper for the next six months. To save up. To buy him curtains.*

Blackout. Rod pocketed. Floor to ceiling.

It's unacceptable, falling asleep that late and then waking up at what—seven thirty? Eight? Nine? Just because some guy doesn't know that shades exist. Seems like a pretty simple concept to—

"I'll get you a sleep mask."

I open my eyes and I think, *Blue*. Which—less than one-eighth of his eyes is blue. It makes no sense. "How do you know what I was—?"

"Your frown woke me up," he says, voice rough with sleep. He shifts in a stretching yawn, and it's like a seismic event, a huge tectonic fault shifting under the crust of the earth. Because during the night, I ended up facedown on top of Jack.

"How?" I ask.

"You moved around a lot," he says. "Felt like the easiest way to keep you from kicking my shins."

"Wait—when did you—?"

"About five minutes after you fell asleep."

"Wow." I *should* move away. But he makes for a good bed, firm and bulky and warm. I'm groggy with sleep that was either not enough or too intense, and don't want to leave just yet.

For once, I feel myself, my body. Jack's hand is on my lower back, under the hoodie. My feet are wrapped around his shins. His mouth is several inches away, but also accessible, and I reach for it.

I aim for a simple peck, suspecting a mess of rotten-eggy morning breath, but there's none of that. He tastes like himself, familiar, and deepens the kiss into something gentle, slow, deliciously lazy. Time doesn't exist. This bed is the expanse of the universe. We're still dreaming, tucked safely inside our heads.

There is no urgency in him, no pressure point. Just the unhurried rhythm of his tongue against mine, leisurely patterns traced against my skin. His heartbeat speeds up but remains steady. His breathing grows shallow, but I know it only from the rise and fall of his chest against mine.

It's a good way to wake up. I want to wake up exactly like this again and again and again. I want to feel the blinding sunrays wash over us, and this new brightness inside me, fragile and scalding hot all at once.

Maybe that's why there are no curtains. In the light, it's easy to feel brave. All those things I'm scared of seem conquerable, and honesty is almost effortless.

"Jack?" I pull back, balancing on my palms, one on each side of his head. My hair has come undone and drapes around us like a shrine.

"Elsie." His palms come up to hold my face.

"I . . ." I'm not scared. I'm just *not*. "I lied."

His mouth quirks sleepily. "Which time?"

I glare. "I hate you."

"Sure." His thumbs swipe gently over my cheeks. Lovingly. Because that's what this is about. "What's this lie you speak of?"

"I said I didn't know. But I do."

"Know what?"

I swallow. "Where this is going. Where we're headed. The two of us."

Something thickens between us, dense and weighty. I know. He knows. We've acknowledged it. It's almost a sign, the universe's permission to move forward. Jack's eyes are warm and probing, and he says, "Come here."

I don't remember taking off my bra last night, but I must have, because when he tosses my hoodie to the floor, my too-pale skin is bare in the blinding light. I don't even want to ask him to look away.

Jack sees me. And it's okay.

"Come here," he repeats, and his mouth's on mine, insistent, brakeless this time. Like he's kissing me for now, for all the times he couldn't before, for later, too. Whatever it was that held him back yesterday, two nights ago, the past two weeks, it melts in the morning sun.

You, a voice suggests. *All those Elsies that aren't really you are what stood between him and this.*

I'm out of breath when he sits up to take his shirt off, and this—this is actually *new*. He's almost as undressed as I am, we're *equals*, and when he tries to pull me down to him, I shake my head and begin to inspect him. I sit astride his hips, riding him as though he were a mellow, compliant beast instead of the most dangerous thing in my life.

"I used to . . . Back before my interview, I used to try to picture them." I trace the inside of his elbow. "Your tattoos."

He *will* stay where he is, but he *can't* help touching me. His hand comes up to my rib cage, thumb stroking the outside of my breast. "How did you know I had tattoos?"

I swallow. "I could see the end of one."

"Ah." His thumb moves to my nipple, feathery light. I arch into the touch. "What did you think they were?"

"Barbed wire. A Bon Jovi quote. Elon Musk's face."

"Jesus."

I laugh, but I'm not breathing easily. "Sorry."

His tattoos are beautiful. The Dirac equation. The electron cloud. Beta decay. The Fibonacci spiral. Kinematic models, astral planes, Drake's formula, the molecular structure of MBBA. Black strokes of faded ink interlocked together in a beautiful painting. The entire foundation of modern physics is on his broad shoulder, wrapped around his large biceps. I trace every line of it, every curve and every corner, and he lets me explore. Vibrating with restraint, but he does. I've never been so selfish before, never taken up so much time for something that is only mine, and I think he knows. I think that's why he allows it.

"Remember how it was?" I ask. "Learning them for the first time? The Schrödinger equation. The standard model."

He nods. His throat bobs. He's hard under my core, patiently impatient. "Knowing that the universe can be made sense of."

"Made of patterns. Rules that can be learned, discovered, predicted."

"Find them out, and you'll know how to make the world into what you want," he says.

"Find them out, and you'll know how to make yourself into what the world wants," I say in return.

We regard each other for a moment. My hands are on him, and his hands are on me, and I'm thinking of two-, five-, ten-year-old Jack, alone in the world, calling someone Mom, being told not to. The only fair-haired Smith. I'm thinking of a young boy determined to shape his surroundings. He chose his own world in the end, didn't he? Greg. Millicent. His friends. He carved a place for himself.

And I'm certain he's thinking of me. All the Elsies I've created to fit all the worlds I've inhabited, all the people in them. He's stripping them off me one by one, like he has since the day we met.

We're not so different, you and I, I think, and then hear myself exhaling hard. I've been holding my breath without realizing it. "I know where we're going," I say again, feeling the certainty of it deep within my bones, like Dirac, like relativity, the strong interaction between quarks and gluons, and he takes it like what it is: permission to take charge, to roll us over, pin me underneath him.

He takes my panties off. Slides them under his pillow—hoarding, like a dragon. "You could be my entire world," he whispers in my ear before moving to my collarbone. "If you let me."

I stroke his hair. "I think I will."

"Then I'm sorry."

"What are you—ah, what are you sorry for?"

He's making room for himself between my legs, spreading them open, touching me there purposefully, exploringly, urgently, like he's looking for answers. Do I want this? Am I ready? Am I wet enough? *Yes.* Yes. I don't know.

"Because I'm never going to let you go."

I moan. His erection brushes against my stomach, and I reach down for him. I want to feel him, too. I want to touch him. But the second my hand closes around him through his pants, he seems to stutter. His expression blanks and then he inhales sharply. He is hard. He's *really* hard.

"Stop," he orders, choked.

I obey. But say, "Honesty? I'd like to keep going."

He's not sure whether to believe me. But he lets me push us on our sides, and when I slide my fingers past his waistband, he's still, motionless but for the movement in his throat.

"You don't like this?" I ask.

"I do," he rasps.

"You seem . . ."

"It's new for me, too."

I laugh softly. "Hand jobs?"

"Being with someone that I . . ." He doesn't finish. My fingers wrap around him, and his eyes drop shut. He seems to fall backward. Into himself. "Fuck."

I pump up and down, but it's weird, clumsy, with his pants on. He's too distracted by my touch, and I have to tug at the waistband several times before he understands that I want him to pull them down.

"Can you tell me? How do you like this?" I ask, adjusting my grip. I need two hands. Yes, it'll be better with two hands. Still an awkward position, but also intimate, how close we are. Nice. I smell him deep in my nostrils and he's good. So good.

"I like it too much, Elsie."

"No, I—" I shake my head against his chest. "Tell me how you do this. When you're alone."

"This is—fuck, it's good. Just . . . slow for now. Steady. And if you—the head—yes. Yes, *there*."

"What else?"

I hear him swallow. "Your voice."

"I . . . What?"

"Just speak."

"I'm not . . ." Laughter bubbles out of me. "I don't think I can do dirty talk."

"You can go with nematics. You can count to ten. I don't care, just—"

"I . . . I could talk about George's offer. How I've been seriously considering. If I accepted, we'd be working together. I'd be at MIT with you next year. I'd earn a livable amount of money, so maybe we could go to lunch together sometimes. I'd buy—"

He makes a deep, guttural sound. His hand moves down between our bodies, and I think he's about to shoo me away, but his head dips forward and his fingers tighten around his balls, then fist around mine. "I want to fuck you," he says into my hair. "Please, let me fuck you."

I simply nod.

It's beautiful, having him on top of me. He's so wide and heavy, I'd have expected feeling constrained, unpleasantly held down, but there's none of that. I wrap my arms around his neck, tip my chin up to kiss him, let him press me into the mattress and deliciously contain me.

And then, when his stomach slides across mine, I get a stab of panic.

"Wait."

He stops *instantly*. Looks down at me, watchful.

"If it's not good, we're going to work on it. Right?"

He laughs against my lips. "It's already the best sex I've ever had."

"But if—"

"Yeah." He eases my legs open, or maybe they spread all on their own. His cock pushes against my abdomen first and then slides down the wet mess of my folds, slots against my entrance. "We will."

It suddenly seems improbable that this is going to work. He's much bigger than J.J., and even though I was aware of this before, at some abstract, theoretical level, the practical implications are now glaringly obvious. This is a physical impossibility. That, or it's going to hurt like hell. And this is the part of sex I've always liked the least—someone pushing inside me, and me struggling to adjust, to keep up, to accept. I imagine it will be the same, and for a split second I wonder if *I* could bear it, not liking this. With Jack.

It's new, worrying about my own enjoyment. I'm contemplating it, vaguely dumbfounded, when something changes.

Jack presses into me.

The head of his cock slides inside, just one or two inches.

My body contracts around him in a small spasm.

I let out a choked cry, and he slurs something that sounds like "Fuck" against my cheek. I arch into him as air rushes out of my lungs, trying to get closer, trying to chase that feeling.

This is—nice. Really, *really* nice. *Unprecedentedly* nice. Maybe I'm just wet enough, maybe I'm more relaxed than ever, but he's not even halfway inside and I'm fluttering around him, the tingling of an orgasm already deep inside my belly.

"Holy fuck," Jack rasps, and helps me go after whatever this is. His hand slips between us, thumb pressing against my clit, and I tighten even more around him, a reedy whimper coming out of my throat, mixing with his loud groan.

My head whites out. I'm confused. Dizzy. I don't think I came, but this is good in a way I cannot even begin to parse. This feels right, and my body knows, because it welcomes Jack inside like I'm where he belongs.

So maybe you like to be full.

Yes. Yes. It appears that I *do* like to be full.

"Is it all in?"

He shakes his head. I consider laughing in his face, telling him that he's lying, but he's in no shape to do so. His eyes are glassy. The arm he's propped himself up on is shaking on the side of my head, like the effort to pace himself is somewhere above the realm of what's human.

"You're . . . big."

He nods, like he knows and it doesn't matter. My nipples are hard pebbles against the expanse of his chest, and the contact is exquisite. I could come just from this—rubbing myself against him.

I let out a reedy laugh. "Is this what sex feels like for normal people?" I ask, moving my hips, circling, tipping back and forth, just to see where this could end up going. The possibilities are tantalizing.

"No one has felt like this in all of history," he tells me, voice deep and shaky, and then he's kissing me hard, his tongue licking inside my mouth, and after a few seconds of that I'm softer, I'm open, I'm lost, and it takes only two upward thrusts, one forceful and the other almost accidental. Then I'm taking him right to the hilt, feeling his sack flush against me, and it feels like something dreamt, something meant to be.

"Fuck," he murmurs again, but I barely hear him. I focus on my own body, the way it's stretched full. I feel Jack in the bones of my skull, in the tips of my toes, and everywhere in between. I thrum, flutter gently around him, and even though I've never been this close to anyone else, it's still not enough. He must know, because he gathers me off the mattress in his arms. I am completely, utterly surrounded by him, by the perfect tension of this moment, and Jack begins to push in and out of me, in and out, delicious rhythm and drawn-out friction.

I cannot take it. It's too brilliantly, stupidly good. My head lolls back against his pillow, and his lips find my jaw, nip my chin, bite my neck. "I'm going to fuck you everywhere, Elsie." He licks the hollow of my throat. "Between today and the day we die, I'm going to fuck you *everywhere*."

I nod. Let him know that he can. There is a tight, liquid pool blooming inside my stomach, twitches of pleasure making their way down my limbs, surging up my spine. I reach for Jack again, pull him to me for the kisses I want, but it doesn't work. We're too raw, too new at this, too desperate to catch every drop of this. Our lips press together, then they pause, forgotten by both of us.

"Can you come like this?" he asks, his breath a hot wash against my ear.

I'm drifting away. I'll never hear his voice and not think of this. Of the deep, rough bite of it sinking inside my brain. Of the whispered *Yes* and *This way* and *Perfect* and—

"Elsie." His body trembles around mine. On the verge of tipping over. "Can you come this way?"

"I don't know. I—maybe?" I'm close, I think. About to snap. It's phenomenal, the way he hits everywhere inside me at once, a masterpiece of biology that something could work so gloriously, and I just need a little more—just a little *more*—

"Shit." His thrusts quicken, he buries his face in my throat, and I think he's getting close. I think he didn't expect it. He doesn't want to come, not yet, but this might be fully out of his control.

And it's what *I* want. To see him lost in something. "You're good. This is good," I urge him, and the word is such a paltry substitute when what I mean is *This is the best thing I've ever felt* and *Thank you* and *Whatever you want, really, whatever you want, just take it.*

"Fuck," he says again, and I see it in his face, the second it's all over for him. His hand closes around my hip, holding me to him while he presses as far as he can go, and then I feel his cock jump in quick, jerky movements. *"Elsie."*

I'm moaning. He's gasping. His skin slides against mine, sweaty, and my body clamps down on him. His back tenses into a slab, and I hold him while his hips turn erratic, then stop, then—

The heat spreading inside me comes to a halt. I watch Jack's eyes go blank, feel him bite my collarbone like I'm his anchor, like he wants to be reminded that I'm really here. The grunts he lets out come from somewhere deep inside him, somewhere I doubt he himself knows, and I hold him to myself until his orgasm dies down to a few clumsy, involuntary thrusts.

I'm still buzzing with thrumming, unsnapped tension. And it should be frustrating—it *is* frustrating that he came and I didn't, that there's heat pushing against the seams of me, simmering from within. But it was good anyway. And after a moment he pulls out, breaths rapid and choppy, and looks down at me. His expression is shaken, a little astonished.

"Shit," he breathes into my neck, his heart a drum against my skin. I cannot stop trembling. "I'm sorry."

"It's okay. I—"

He pushes my legs open with his palms, and I arch like a rainbow when he slides two of his fingers inside me, feeling blissfully full again.

He can kiss me properly now, soft, deep, hungry, and says, "Let me—I'm going to—"

He's more reptilian brain than anything else. I'm wet with his come and my own slick, and he draws fast, beautiful circles around my clit that immediately push me over the edge. I shut my eyes tight and come in strong waves, and when I do, he pushes inside me again, something delicious to clench around, something beautiful and grounding, and when we fall asleep like that, I think that wherever it is that we're going, maybe, just *maybe*, it might turn out to be a place I never want to leave.

22

CRITICAL MASS

WHEN I WAKE UP, THE SUN IS HIGH IN THE SKY, AND shadows have shortened to little stumps. It's the latest I've been in bed since that time I got the flu during freshman year and spent forty-eight hours hallucinating that my skin was an eggshell and my skeleton had finally grown enough to hatch out of it.

There are no nightmares today. Just a feeling of bone-deep rest and Jack's big body curved behind me, arms wrapped around my torso like a cross, securing me to him. It's not unlike the way I awoke exactly two weeks ago. Except that we're naked, our skin tacky. This time he *is* going to have to change the sheets.

Something nags at the back of my skull, telling me that I can't afford to waste time, that I should get out of bed and be productive—answer emails, clean the oven, buy a cemetery plot. I shush it and stretch in Jack's arms. He stays asleep, hard once again. I wonder if it's another peerection. If—

"A what?"

Oh shit. "Nothing." Did I say it out loud?

Jack's voice is a deep rumble. "Did you just—"

"No. Nope. I—"

I hide my face in my pillow. This is why I don't sleep in—if I get the amount of rest I actually need, my head-to-mouth filter stops working and—

Jack's hand slides down past my stomach. He starts grinding drowsily against my ass, and my mind blanks.

"Okay?" he asks, half-asleep.

"Please." I hook my foot behind his shin. He presses an open-mouthed kiss on the curve of my shoulder.

"You did say that we might have to work on the sex."

I stiffen. If it wasn't good, I said. Was it not good? I thought it was, but—what do I know? He's the expert here. "I'm sorry, I—"

"Elsie. Work on how little *I* last." He bites the spot where he kissed me, and then his cock is rubbing against me, breaching my entrance. He makes a few soft, grunt-like noises next to my ear, then presses to the hilt in one single push. I spasm around him, and the drag against my muscles is sun-extinguishingly good. It's still a snug fit, but I'm wet from his come, soft from sleep, and he slides inside like a dream.

He pinches my hard nipple, like he knows exactly what my body wants, even when I don't. His palm presses against my abdomen, and I wonder if he can feel himself move within me, if he can tell how full I am. His thrusts are long and slow, at once leisurely and forceful enough to shift my entire body closer to the headboard.

"Okay, okay, I—" He laughs ruefully, breathless against my throat, and I reach behind me. To touch his cheek, to hold on to him. "Maybe you should be in charge. Before I fuck you into the mattress again."

Shockingly, I'm still capable of blushing. "What do I—"

"Just—move." He presses a kiss where my neck meets my shoulder. "Do what feels good. Let me see you—yes. *Yeah.*"

I grind my ass against his abdomen, shallow, slow, awkward at first, because the position is weird and because what even am I doing? But my hips circle in a long, sinuous move, and something hits just right, and—

We gasp in unison.

"There?" he murmurs against my ear, angling my hips to give me even more. "That's how I make you come?"

My mind blurs. "You already made me come."

He makes a guttural noise. "I want to feel it. When my cock is inside you."

I moan, and then I'm not in charge anymore. The pleasure gushes inside me, scarily strong, quicker than I thought possible, unraveling like an avalanche. I squeeze his fingers and he squeezes back, and when my body clamps down on his, he *does* press me into the mattress, and he *does* fuck me like his control is not fully there, and he *does* say my name over and over, like a war chant. He smells like sex and our sweat and the best sleep I've ever had, murmurs sweet, filthy things in my ear, promises that he'll never let me go.

The sun is high in the sky, Jack is deep inside me, and I smile into the sheets for no particular reason.

I THINK I MIGHT BE HAPPY.

Though due to a lack of hands-on experience, I cannot be sure.

But in the bathroom, while chasing droplets down Jack's throat, my legs wrapped around his waist as he pushes me into the tiled wall, I wonder if maybe this is it. This warm, comforting weight glowing shyly behind my sternum could be something like hope.

Hope that there'll be more days like this one.

"Stop smiling like that," he whispers in my ear. The jet of the shower pounds over his back, and his lips taste like hot water. "Or I'll be on you all day."

I laugh into his neck and pretend I didn't hear him.

The clock in the bathroom, the one I imagine Jack curses at when he runs late in the morning, reads 12:37. I towel myself dry, buzzing with possibilities, with the tenuous, burgeoning impression that for once I'm not running away, but *heading* somewhere.

"Food," he tells me once I'm wearing my—his—hoodie and a pair of socks that won't stay up on my calves. His smile is handsome, self-deprecating. "I have these elaborate daydreams that I'm feeding you a five-course meal I hunted, field-dressed, and prepared all by myself," he says with a kiss on my forehead.

"Why?"

He gives me an arch look. "Don't ask *why*, like it's a rational impulse. So, what do you want?"

"What can you make?"

"Nothing." He shrugs at my startled laugh, then throws me over his shoulder to take me downstairs. I feel like a sparkly drink. "I'll learn. It's a new obsession for me."

I can't remember the last time I giggled this much.

The five-course meal turns out to be slightly burned grilled cheese with boxed tomato soup. I sit on *my* stool at the island, and he eats his own standing across from me. It's simultaneously the most ordinary and the best thing I've ever tasted.

On my phone there is a text from Cece, time stamp 9:23 a.m.

CECE: "I'll never spend the night at Jack's," she said. "I'm destined to die alone, strangled by the tumble of cobwebs that have overtaken my vulva due to sexual inactivity," she said.

I laugh, and Jack smiles just because of that, which is a little unlike him and also stupid. He's stupid. I'm stupid. We're stupid. Or maybe we're just sixteen. Jack Smith, Jack Smith-Turner, Jonathan Smith-Turner and I have had sex. More than once. *More* than more than once. And now we're having breakfast at one p.m. This is not my timeline, but I'll claim it anyway.

I tell him about the science of grilled cheese, the negative surface charge of the lipid molecules, stress and strain, the optimal pH, which should always be somewhere around 5.5. ("Manchego, then," he says. "Or mild cheddar. Gouda, too.") My heart is spinning dizzily at the thought of this man who knows the pH of different cheese types off the top of his head, when my phone beeps.

A reminder to change my insulin pod. I consider putting it off till I'm home, then look at Jack and think, *Honesty.* This day, this not-too-good soup, this man with a black-hole tattoo peeping out of his T-shirt sleeve, they are too good to not spend some honesty on.

"I'm going to need a few minutes upstairs," I say, hopping off the stool. "But I'll be back."

"What's going on?"

"Just need to change my insulin pod." I rummage in my purse and then hold my kit up triumphantly—a pale yellow bag with little hedgehogs Cece got me years ago. "Don't worry, you don't have to be there. I know people get squeamish. I'll do it in your bedroom—"

"Show me how you do it."

He puts down what's left of his sandwich. Washes his hands.

I laugh. "Why?"

"Because I want to know."

"Why would you—oh my *God*. You want to put high-fructose corn syrup in my insulin. Was this a long con to murder me?"

He smiles and shakes his head. "I'm starting to be partial to the way you bypass all rational explanations for everything I say, and dash straight to me being an unhinged serial killer."

"I think it's our thing."

His biceps bunch up when he leans his palms against the table. "Show me how it works," he repeats. It sounds like a soft order, and I answer with a soft question:

"Why?"

"Because I want to know these things."

There's something unsaid in this. *Because I want to know your life*, maybe, or *Because I want to know you*. My eyes fall on the kit, and I picture myself using words like *reservoir* and *expiration advisory* and *ketoacidosis*. Explaining how each component works. I've never said some of those words out loud. They live exclusively in *my* head, together with the rest of *my* problems.

Even Cece knows only the basics. But this is Jack. So I swallow. "Do you have any disinfectant?"

The dimple is back. "I thought you'd never ask."

Less than an hour later, I settle between his long legs on the couch, toes brushing against his calves, his hand splayed on my stomach under the hoodie. He refuses to watch the end of *Twilight* ("I think I've seen enough") but agrees with me that *New Moon* is the best in the series ("Relativistically"), curls around me for a two-hour nap during *Eclipse* ("You smell like me—you should always smell like me"), and then wakes up as the afternoon stretches into evening, just in time for Bella's unexpected pregnancy.

"This is *atrocious*," he says, laughing at every single thing the characters do.

"Shut up."

He laughs harder against my nape.

"Shut up—she could *die*!"

More laughter.

"It's about the hardships and sorrows of the universal human experience, *Jonathan*."

He nibbles on my ear a little too hard. "Still better than *2001*, *Elsie*."

"Obviously." Something occurs to me. "By the way, is Millicent okay?"

"Yup. Why do you ask?"

"It's Sunday. Shouldn't she be calling you with a vital emergency? Isn't the newspaper boy tossing the *Times* into her rosebushes or something?"

"Pretty sure newspaper delivery hasn't worked like that since the early 2000s. And she did her weekend routine yesterday. Sent a photo of an alligator coming out of a toilet in a Florida gas station. Claimed it was happening in her en suite."

"She knows how to send pictures?"

"Impressive, right?" He drums his fingers against my stomach. "I stopped by for lunch. Gave her the novel. Got scolded for not taking you."

"Oh." I flush. With . . . pleasure?

"Can't remember the last time she liked someone. Not that she'd admit to liking you."

I laugh. Then, after a few seconds, I hazard, "She told me she liked your mom."

There is a change in Jack, but not for the worse. He doesn't stiffen, just seems less relaxed, a little more on guard when he says, "I think so."

I'm encouraged. "She was a physicist, right?"

"Yeah."

"Theoretical?"

He lets out a deep, overacted sigh that lifts me up and down. "Unfortunately." I pinch his forearm in retaliation. Rudely, he doesn't notice.

I'm tempted to bring up the article. Find out how he could do something like that to his mother—to all of us—and demand that he take ownership of its consequences. But I also don't want to disrupt this . . . fragile, new, radiant thing we have. And after a bit of arm wrestling, the latter pull wins, and what I ask is "Do you have memories of her?"

I feel him shake his head. "She died too early."

"Did she"—I roll around till I'm facedown on top of him—"look like you?"

"There aren't many pictures. My family mostly scrubbed the house clean of them."

If he's bitter about it, I cannot tell. "When did you take her last name?"

He laughs softly. "That was Millicent's decision, actually. She had me legally change it when I was ten. I think she felt uncharacteristically guilty." He pushes a strand of hair behind my ear. "I do know that she was Swedish. Blond. Her eyes had the same weird . . ."

"Heterochromia?"

"Yeah. She was taller than my father. And kept some detailed diaries about her work. Millicent gave them to me when I started becoming obsessed with physics."

"Did she have any publications?"

His jaw works. "Just two. She got married halfway through her doctorate and didn't go back to work after she had me. Her diagnosis came quickly after." His tone is wary, like he's choosing his words carefully.

"Why didn't she go back?"

He exhales. "There were . . . issues. With the lead researcher of her group."

"Why?"

"They had some . . . disagreement over their joint research. He was intensely controlling. She refused to abide. You can imagine the rest." His face is blank. "Her diaries are . . . She wasn't well when she found out that she wouldn't be allowed back."

"That's bullshit. How dare he cut her out of her own research group?"

Jack doesn't respond. His pause feels a little longer than normal. "Her work was on semiconductors."

My eyes widen. It's not my field, but I know a bit about it, because it's one of the topics my mentor works on. I wonder if I read Jack's mom's papers years ago without even realizing it. An invisible string, tying us together. "Good stuff?"

"Very solid, yes."

"I bet she was great. I mean, she *was* a theoretical physicist."

"True. On the other hand, she did marry my dad."

"Good point. Maybe he used to be more . . . engaged with his surroundings?"

"Maybe. Maybe she needed a green card? Or the Smith money."

"She *was* a grad student. It's a move I can respect."

"For sure." His smile is fond. And has me asking, "Do you miss her?"

A long pause. "I don't think you can miss someone you've never met, but . . ." He organizes his thoughts. Orders his feelings. "It's easy to look at how dysfunctional my family is and laugh it off now that I have my own life. But when I was in my teens, there were times when things got really bad at home. And I'd read her diaries and think that maybe if she'd been around, everything could have been . . ." His throat works. "But she wasn't."

I've felt out of place my entire life, and nothing anyone ever said made me feel any less so. So I stay silent and just lean forward, hide my face in Jack's throat, press a kiss to his Adam's apple right as it moves. His hand comes up to cup my head, keep it there, and I feel him turn to the screen again. Bella's pregnancy complications are getting alien-like, and he groans into my hair.

"Elsie. I can't watch this."

"But it's the best part. The emotional roller coaster of her transformation. The inappropriate Jacob plotline. Her face when she drinks blood."

"No way."

"Fine. You may amuse yourself otherwise. But stay close, because you're a space heater disguised as an organic life-form."

"Perfect." He lifts me like I'm a pliant little thing, flips us around, braces himself over me. I can only watch him in confusion while he lowers himself down my body with a concentrated frown between his brows and then lifts my hoodie as though . . .

Is he . . .

He's not . . .

Is he actually?

"What are you doing?"

"You told me to amuse myself."

I sit up on my elbows. "I meant take another nap, or do today's Wordle—"

"Just watch your movie, Elsie."

"But—"

He takes my hips within his hands and holds me like I'm a precious artifact, at once firm and gentle. His kisses between my legs are long, savoring, messy, slow licks that have me arching up against the couch and trembling into his mouth. There is something shameless about this—the way he enjoys it, the sounds he makes, the fact that he seems to go away at moments, like he does this for his pleasure more than for my own.

"Oh," I say, clawing my nails into his scalp. His arms wrap around my thighs, palms holding my knees open, and for a while I manage to swallow down the begging, moaning sounds in my throat. Then no more. "Oh. *Oh, Jack*" and I come once, then once again, then some more, and then his shirt is off and he's above and inside me, patient thrusts as he kisses me endlessly and tells me how beautiful I am, how much he loves this. Breathless laughter against my gasps as he reminds me of when I was afraid that this wouldn't be good between us—that this resplendent, life-altering, unearthly sort of pleasure might not be enough.

"It was cute," he rasps in my ear, "how you thought that fucking you once would make me want to fuck you less."

I cling to the sweaty muscles of his back, feel my entire body shake, and when he orders, "Eyes on me," my lids flutter open and we both come. The pressure in my belly and chest is heavy, overwhelming, delicious, and my nails sink into his shoulders as the evening becomes night.

"Second time we do this with *Twilight* in the background," he says.

"I can't believe we missed the part when Bella beats up Jacob."

"Jesus, Elsie, what *is* this movie?"

The room is pitch black except for the glow of the TV. I laugh into Jack's skin, and it feels just like coming home.

HE WON'T LET ME LEAVE. THOUGH, TO BE FAIR, I'M NOT TRYING very hard.

"I have class at eight a.m. tomorrow."

"Doesn't matter."

"At Boston University."

"Still doesn't matter."

"I need to get to my place, get dressed, pick up my stuff, take the bus—"

"I'll drive you."

"Drive me where?"

"Anywhere."

I'm sitting on the counter while he chops carrots for the soup I'm craving. The recipe is pulled up on his phone, a bright-red ad for a couples' cooking class blinking at us from the counter. "You'd have to wake up at, like, six. I cannot ask you to do that."

He sets down the knife and comes to stand between my legs. Even like this, he's taller than me. I'm trying to resent him for that, but my heart has grown a million sizes in the span of the last seven days. It's about to float away into the sky.

"You don't have to ask." He kisses the tip of my nose, then my mouth, then my nose again. "Because I'm offering."

My heart swells some more. I'm running out of space. "What if I say no?"

"Don't do that. Okay?" I break into a smile, and his hand slides under my hoodie and up my waist.

I love this. Just as much as I thought I hated him. And Jack's right: this is going fast—too fast, maybe. But I wonder if certain relationships are living proof of Heisenberg's uncertainty principle: their position and their velocity simply cannot both be measured at the same time, not even in theory. And right now I'm too busy savoring *where* we are to consider anything else.

"What?" he asks.

I shake my head. "Just thinking."

"Thinking of . . . ?"

"You know, during my interview, I was picturing how it would be if I got the job. Working with you. And I had these painstakingly intricate fantasies."

His interest is piqued. "Did I pack you sandwiches in a *Twilight* lunch box?"

I laugh. "Oh, no."

"Were you wearing that red dress from Miel, and I bent you—"

"*No.*" I can *still* blush—amazing. "It was mostly me harassing you into quitting in disgrace."

"I see." He looks intrigued. "What were you going to do?"

"Oh, you know. Jell-O your office supplies. Spread the rumor that you poop in the urinals. Frame you for white-collar crimes. Those kinds of things." His expression is delighted. "I mean . . . I could still do it."

"You could."

"Some would say I should."

"Some would." He kisses the corner of my smile. "Maybe next year," he says, and it sounds low and hopeful, a promise nestled inside it, and I realize that I'd love to accept George's offer because I want to work with her, because I want to dedicate my brainpower to liquid crystals, because I want to *not* spend eleven-fifteenths of my time commuting between campuses, and because I want to have enough money to surprise Cece with little hats for her ugly, murderous quill-nugget. But this man, who was going to be the absolute worst part of my dream job, might still turn out to be the thing I want the most.

To no one's surprise, I end up staying. And because of what happens on the following day, it turns out to be a pretty good decision.

23

FREEZING POINT

GET DR. L.'S EMAIL—*UNFORTUNATELY, I AM OUT OF TOWN THIS week, but let us meet next Monday*—*before* a Physics 101 student ambushes me to tell me about this super-cool movie he just watched and ask me if one could theoretically invert time (damn you, Christopher Nolan), and *after* one of my chairs calls me to let me know that yes, there is an opening for me next year, but adjuncts will take a pay cut because of *something something* taxes, *something something* the dean, *something something* the exploitation of non-tenure-track faculty members is the backbone of the capitalist model of academia.

A boy with something that sounds a lot like the whooping cough hacks on me on the bus, icy, slippery rain starts falling the second I get off at my stop, and somehow only one of the gloves Cece knit for me in her short-lived craft phase can be found in my pocket. There is a lot going on. A lot. But I don't care. Because above Lance's toilet-paper-long text asking me to find out if Dana is going to that U2 concert with Lucas, there's another message: a picture of the Hadron Collider model I saw on Jack's desk, and then just five words.

Would look great in Jell-O.

I smile. Reply I'm thinking cherry and then make my way through UMass's Physics Department.

JACK: I forgot that every first Monday of the month we do this thing at George's. Want to come? Or I can pick you up, and we can make scientifically accurate grilled cheese and watch the Cullen family featurette at my place.

I'm grinning so hard, I almost run into the water fountain.

ELSIE: I need to grade twelve bajillion essays

JACK: Do what I do. Give them all As.

ELSIE: Do you really?

JACK: I sprinkle in four Bs and two Cs and call it a curve.

This time I do walk into the water fountain. A *different* one.

ELSIE: No wonder they kiss your ass so hard. Does the thing at George's have a dress code?

JACK: If it does, I plan to ignore it.

ELSIE: Henley?

JACK: What's a Henley?

ELSIE: It's the name of the shirts you wear every single day.

JACK: They have a name?

Wow. Men.

ELSIE: Text me George's address. I'll meet you there when I'm done.

GEORGE'S DOOR OPENS TO A ROUND YOUNG WOMAN WITH A knockout smile who hugs me warmly and welcomes me into the largest, most beautiful apartment I've ever seen.

"They're in the living room," she tells me over the chatter coming from down the hallway. There is a slight accent, and I remember George mentioning that her wife is a Greek finance guru. "I'm going upstairs to have an edible and listen to Bach with noise-canceling headphones. Have fun."

The first person I find is Andrea. She's in the kitchen when I walk by, transferring tortilla chips into a big bowl.

"Oh." She looks up at me. "You're . . . here." Her smile is surprised. Vaguely tense.

"Hi." I decide to step inside, hoping to project *This doesn't need to be awkward* vibes. "How are you?"

"Good." She crumples the empty chip bag. "It's cool that you're okay with being at George's place, considering."

"Oh." I flush. So much for not awkward. "Yeah. I—"

"Andy," someone behind me interrupts, "George wants to know if—" It's Jack, of course. Who stops midsentence just like I did, as if completely losing track of the rest of the world. "Dr. Hannaway. You're late." He says it like he's been waiting for me. Like he spent our time apart thinking about the moment he could tease me again, like I'm the first thing on his mind and the last thing he lets go of, and before I even know it, I'm matching his step forward, I'm pushing up on my toes, I'm pressing my lips to his, I'm smiling against his mouth.

It's such a small kiss, but my heart pounds, and so does Jack's when I lay my palm flat against his chest. I pull back, less than an inch, to look at his eyes. It's like the weekend changed something about the people we are. Something fundamental in the shape of my brain and his, too. His lashes are fanning down: he's staring at my mouth and angling his head again, and—

"What did George want to know, Jack?"

Shit.

I fall back onto my heels and turn to Andrea, mortified. I glance at Jack, expecting to find his usual unbothered self, but he's still staring at me, looking a little shaken, like I'm his magnetic north.

He clears his throat. "What wine you want."

"What are the options?"

He seems confused. "Ah, red. And . . ." He shrugs, one arm wrapping around my shoulders, like being in my space is second nature. It feels right.

"Let me guess." Andrea rolls her eyes. "White?"

"Sounds right."

She huffs, picks up the tortilla chip bowl, then steps right between us to march out of the kitchen. We watch her walk away, all blond waves and excellent posture, and then—Jack steps closer again. Very close. Maybe too close. He leans down to kiss my forehead.

"Hi."

I can't look away from his eyes. "Hi."

We stay like that, silent, for what's probably too long. I can smell his clean skin, his woodsy shampoo, the red flannel I chose this morning from his closet. I don't feel like saying anything, so I don't, not for a long time, not until he asks, "You ready to play?"

"Oh. Play . . . what?"

"You'll see." His smile makes my heart vibrate. "You'll love it, too."

He's right. Even if for a moment, after Jack's friend Diego has explained Blitz Go to me—"Usual rules, but ten seconds per move"— I consider asking to be left out of the tournament.

"That's very little time." I chew on my lip. "Maybe I shouldn't—"

"Just go with your instincts," Jack whispers in my ear. He can, because he's right behind me. Or maybe it's vice versa: I'm the one who's sitting between his open legs, because I've counted eighteen people in here, and not nearly enough seats. "She can sit here with me while I play my first match," he tells Diego. "To learn."

Everybody can see how Jack's hand slides under my shirt and flattens against my abdomen, a solid, pleasant weight against my skin. The way he forgets to move because he's busy staring at me. "Dude," Diego calls him out the second time it happens.

"Right," Jack says, unruffled, and I spend the next two turns blushing and fidgeting in his lap, till his grip tightens on me and his words in my ear are a distracted "Be good."

Something scalding and liquid blooms inside me.

Jack still wins. And I must get the hang of it, because I win mine, too. I win a practice match against George, who bought four types of cheese because Jack told her it's all I eat. I win against Sunny. I win against another person whose name I don't recall. I win against Andrea in just a handful of moves. "Easy to advance when you're the only sober person in the room," she mutters, some teeth behind it, but when I say "You're not wrong," she bursts into laughter and tips her glass at me, and I'm sure I imagined the hostility. There's wine, beer, shots, academic horror stories, a whiteboard in front of George's fireplace with the brackets written on it, and somewhere around midnight Blitz Go becomes my favorite thing in the world. I'm having fun. *Genuinely* having lots of fun.

When Sunny announces the final match, her words are slurred. A frame with George's wedding photo is poorly balanced on her head. "The two people who haven't lost a game yet are . . . Jack, of course—fuck you, Jack, for making our lives so boring, you periodic-motion poster child—and, drumroll please . . . Elsie! Elsie, please, at least once in my life I want the opportunity to see this smug-ass face lose at something."

"I lost at number of urine sample jars on my desk," he points out.

The frame drops softly into the carpet. Sunny grasps my hand. "Avenge me, Elsie. *Please.*"

I nod solemnly, taking a seat on the side of the black. Jack picks up a stone and leans back in the chair, eyes glued on me, the blue as bright as the sea, a small smile on his lips.

"And so we meet again," he says, loud enough for everyone, and I tune out the way his friends whistle and cheer for me, how they fall silent as we squeeze every last second from each turn. Whenever I look up, Jack's already looking at me. I remember the first time we played, at Millicent's house, and wonder if it was the first of many. Wonder if Jack owns a board. Wonder if he keeps it in his study. Wonder why, when he looks at me, I forget how scared I am to be seen.

Wonder why when I win, he seems as happy as I feel.

"Well played," he says, ignoring the way everyone is ribbing him for breaking his eight-month streak.

I nod. Suddenly, *again*, I'm all heartbeat.

I duck inside the bathroom, high on victory. When I slip out, George is right there, scaring the shit out of me. "*Jesus.*"

"I fully own that I followed you," she says, leaning casually against the wall.

"Were you listening to me pee?"

"No. Well, yes. But it wasn't the primary purpose. Just a pleasant bonus." She grins. "I thought I'd harass you about the job offer."

"Oh." I clear my throat. "I don't have an answer yet. Sorry."

Her eyes narrow. "Is Jack trying to influence you one way or the other? Because I will use the cattle prod on him. Oh, who am I kidding? Of course he'd try to convince you to take the job. I'm reasonably sure that ninety percent of his spank bank is fantasies of driving you to work and buying you a latte on the way."

"I'm sure he doesn't—"

"What are *your* thoughts?"

I swallow. Then I glance around the hallway, as though George's niece's macaroni art might hold the key to my academic future.

It does not.

"I . . ." I take a deep breath. "I would love to say yes."

George blinks. Then smiles. Then repeats, "Yes?"

"But"—I force myself to continue past her face-splitting grin—"I can't formally accept until I talk with my advisor. Don't worry, though," I add quickly, because her smile is fading fast. "I'm sure I'll get his approval next week! I'll explain how much I want to take the job, and he'll agree that it's the best choice."

George stares for a second, looking considerably less excited. "Okay." She nods. And when I'm about to leave, she adds, "For the record, I'd love to continue being your friend. Even if you end up not accepting." Her smile is a little strained. "Now peace out. I gotta pee, and no, you can't listen, you weirdo."

I'm making my way back to the living room, wondering why it feels like George just resigned herself to me not taking the job, when I overhear it.

"... slumming it with the theorists now?"

It's Andrea's voice from the kitchen, and I stop in the hallway. I can see only about half of Jack: broad back, light hair curling on his neck, large hands storing dirty dishes in the dishwasher. I should go in and help clean up, but something tells me to skulk around like I'm corporate-espionaging in a Bond movie.

"Excuse me?" he says, confused.

"So, does she know?"

"Who?"

"Elsie." A quarter of Andrea appears in my field of view. Just her smile, small and private, pointed up at Jack. "Does she know that you despise people like her?"

"Andy, are you drunk?"

"A bit." She laughs nervously. "Aren't you? Elsie must be rubbing off. She must be a great lay, if you fucked over Pereira and Crowley for her. I guess she's hot, in a bland way—"

"They fucked over themselves. And you should go back to the others," Jack says firmly. "You're more than a bit drunk if you think telling someone that their girlfriend is bland is a good idea."

"She's not your *girlfriend*."

"She is if she wants to be. She can be my damn wife if she wants to be." Jack's losing his usual cool. For all his commanding presence, he's rarely truly irritated, and Andrea knows this, too. There's a fracture on her face, masked by another weak laugh that hurts my ears.

"A *theorist*, Jack? You having a slow year?"

"Are you serious—"

"You lost to her at Go," she says, petulant even as she tries to keep her tone light. I should be offended by what she's saying, but something's stopping me. Something heartbreaking. "You *never* lose at Go. You said you'd *never* lose at Go."

"I never said that." Whatever I recognized in her tone, Jack did, too. His voice softens.

"I bet you lost on purpose. If that's how bad you want her—"

"She won it fair and square." They're talking about something else altogether. Something that has nothing to do with Go or anything that happened tonight. *She cares about him deeply*, I realize. *More than that*. "Even if I had lost to her on purpose—it has nothing to do with you."

"I think it does."

"Andy." He sighs. "I've been honest about how I feel. You said you understood—"

"Jesus, Jack. She's a *theorist*."

"She's a better scientist than you or I will ever be. You're hurt, and I'm trying to cut you some slack, but you're way over the line—"

"Why are you her champion now? You're *you* and—she *makes up* stuff. Is it because you're *sleeping* with her?"

"It's because I *know* her work."

"But you've been saying shit about people like her for fifteen years. You're the entire reason her field was discredited—you ruined careers, Jack. And now you're telling me *she* is the person you're willing to *feel* something for?"

"That's it," Jack orders. "I'm done."

"You—"

"I'm serious. We can talk about this when you're sober. But you need to give me some space before I say something I regret."

"If—"

"Andy."

A second later, Andrea appears in the hallway, eyes shining with tears. She looks at me for a painful, uncomfortable moment, then moves past without a word. I press my shoulders against the wall, trying to stop the centrifuge in my brain.

Does she know that you despise people like her?

He doesn't despise me. Does he? No. Honesty, right? No, Jack doesn't despise me.

But it's not surprising that Andrea would believe that. It's exactly where *I* believed he stood, approximately two meltdowns in his apartment ago. He's Jonathan Smith-Turner. What he did to theoretical physics one and a half decades ago is in the Library of Congress and has a Wikipedia entry.

"What are you doing?" George says, appearing in the hallway.

"Oh, nothing. Just . . . looking at this art." I point to a flower painting to my right.

"Do you want it? My wife made it with her ex at one of those paint-and-sip things. I've been trying to get rid of it."

I laugh shakily. "Um, maybe next time."

She enters the living room and I go to Jack, who's staring out the window, back stiff and muscles coiled.

"Grumpy because you lost?" I ask, even though I know he's not.

I just want to watch the tension leave his body. Because maybe it'll leave mine, too.

"Elsie."

I heard you, I should say. *Do you really despise—*

You said "girlfriend"—

What did she mean, when—

But there's no time. He leans forward, hands around my neck, and kisses me deep for a long time. People walk by, make jokes, give us looks, but he doesn't stop. I don't want him to, either.

"Everything okay?" I ask when he pulls back.

He looks away. Grabs his bottle from the counter and drains what's left. "Want to leave?"

"Yeah. Sure."

The ride to my place is quiet. I feel cold everywhere except on my knee—where Jack's hand rests, his grip just a bit tighter than casual. I'm not sure why I invite him upstairs. Maybe I know what needs to happen. Maybe I'm just trying to hold on to him, to prolong that point of contact.

Cece's not home, probably out on Faux business, and I'm vaguely relieved. Our place is messy, because the last time we cleaned was when Mrs. Tuttle came over to convince us that the green stuff on the wall was totally paint, totally *not* mold. I try to see the apartment through Jack's eyes, but to his credit he doesn't act too Smith about the conditions I live in. Instead, he does something so *Jack*, my chest almost explodes with it: he picks up the top of the credenza like it weighs nothing. His biceps strain against the flannel as he puts it where it belongs, perfectly centered on the bottom part.

Three seconds. For something Cece and I have been putting off for three years.

"Nice place," he says, dusting off his hands on his jeans.

I laugh softly. "It's not."

He leans against the table where I've worked, eaten, laughed, cried for the past seven years. "Then you really should move in with me."

I laugh again. I should thank him for the credenza. It's just . . .

"I wasn't joking. This place is . . ." There's a bug, belly-up on the floor. "Don't those live in tropical areas?"

"Mmm. Our working theory is that this place is a 4D nexus where multiple climate regions exist at once and . . . Were you serious? About moving in?"

He shrugs. "Would save you money."

"Pretty sure half of your rent is more expensive than half of this."

"I don't rent. So you wouldn't have to pay me. I don't care about that."

Right. He doesn't care about money. Because he has money. "I can't leave Cece," I say lightly. "Want to take her in, too?"

"I have an extra room."

I snort. And then realize the look he's giving me.

Like he's *serious* serious. And waiting for an answer.

"I can't move in with you," I tell him. "We're not even . . ." We're not even what? I look away. I feel like total shit, and I cannot understand if he's joking, though he must be, but he looks weirdly earnest, and . . .

A few steps over the cheap vinyl and he's standing right in front of me. I'm trapped between him and the kitchen sink, and strong fingers come up to my chin, angle it back.

"I think we *are*."

My heart trembles. That blue slice cuts into me like a knife, and what comes out of me is "Andrea wouldn't agree." I didn't mean to bring her up. In fact, I actively meant to avoid the topic forever. But I guess this honesty thing is a little addictive.

Jack closes his eyes and swears softly under his breath. "You heard her."

"I . . ." I free my chin, and he understands that I need space. He takes a step back, but I still cannot breathe. "I didn't mean to. I . . ." I exhale. "Yes, I did."

Jack sighs. "I'm sorry. I'll talk to her when she's calmed down."

I nod, and it should be the end of it—a resolution, nicely wrapped. Instead I hear myself ask, "What about Crowley and Pereira? And Cole. And the rest of your students. Will you talk to them, too?"

His lips press together, expression shifting to something opaque. Like he's bracing for something. "What is this, Elsie?"

All of a sudden, the million balls that have been lazily rolling around in the back of my head for the past two weeks are bouncing against my skull. And they *hurt*. "Do you know what the problem is? That these people—they admire you. They really, really like you. Your students, your colleagues, your friends. They all want to please you. And for most of them, pleasing you means showing that they dislike what *you* dislike. And just like that, everything goes back to that *Annals* article."

He exhales. "Elsie—"

"To be fair, I did the same." I begin pacing around the kitchen. "I like you so much, I've been avoiding thinking about it for as long as I could. And to give you credit, you're good at letting me forget. You never *feel* like the person who wrote it, which makes it easy to pretend that you didn't exist before I met you, that your past actions don't matter. But what Andrea said today . . . I owe it to my mentor to remember. I can't forget that Laurendeau was the editor of the *Annals* at the time. That he was censured. And . . ." I feel the same mix of anger and embarrassment I always do when I think about what happened. "The thing is, Jack . . . you go through life with your man-with-money confidence, never second-guessing your actions. But there were lots of unintentional victims to what you did—"

"Laurendeau wasn't that," he says flatly.

"Yes, he was. His career was hugely impacted by—"

"He wasn't *unintentional.*"

"He . . ." I stop pacing. The words don't immediately sink in. And when they do, I'm still left confused. "What?"

Jack wets his lips. "Laurendeau *was* the target."

"I don't understand."

"I wrote the article *because* I wanted Laurendeau's career to be over." His throat moves. "It was everything else that was unintentional."

My mind spins a million circles, then halts abruptly. "Everything else?"

"I didn't want to become the poster boy for the rift between theorists and experimentalists." He throws up one hand, impatient. For a moment I sense hesitation, but his eyes harden, stubborn in a way that's almost . . . young. Seventeen again. "I wasn't making a *statement.* All I wanted was Laurendeau out of physics—and I failed, clearly. Since after screwing over my mother, he's been busy fucking up the life of the single person I've ever been in love with."

What did he . . . His mother? The single person he . . .

"I—"

"He was my mother's main collaborator, Elsie. *He* was the reason she couldn't go back to work after I was born. *He* was the reason she felt—it was the most important thing for her, Elsie. Her work *defined* her, and he took it away and—" His voice rises and rises and then abruptly stops, like he suddenly realized how loud he had gotten.

"Why did he . . . ?"

"Because he was envious. Because he felt superior. Because of *control*. He's like that with you, too."

"What?" I shake my head. "No. No, he *helps* me."

"To the point that you don't feel allowed to accept your dream job without his permission? This is not a normal mentor-mentee relationship."

"You don't know what you're talking about." Jack simply doesn't get it. Dr. L. is the only reason I was able to get into grad school. The reason I was able to pursue my dreams. The reason I'm not currently unemployed.

Jack takes a step forward. "Laurendeau has isolated you and made it impossible for you to realize it. Just like he did with my mother." He rubs his forehead, and I wonder when he last talked about all of this. "It's all in her diaries."

"Oh my God." I cannot believe it. "Is that why you wrote the article? Because of those diaries?"

He exhales a humorless laugh. "No. I wrote it because I went to Northeastern and tried to report Laurendeau. I was told that I couldn't file a complaint, because I wasn't the victim. It fizzled into nothing. And Elsie, I was . . ." His eyes hold mine for a second, and I see everything. He was young and he was tired. He was sad. He was angry. He was lonely; he was alone; he was the odd Smith out. He was helpless. He wanted revenge. "*Then* I wrote the article." His big shoulders rise and fall. "I used what I knew of physics to make it believable, and I still didn't think it'd get accepted. But somehow it did, and when I read that Laurendeau was removed as editor . . ." He shakes his head. "It didn't make me feel any better about the fact that I couldn't remember shit of my mother, or about the things Caroline did to me." His eyes are full of sorrow. "So I stopped thinking about it. And whenever someone reminded me, I ignored them. Until I met you."

My expression hardens. "Because I kept bringing it up."

"No, Elsie." His voice is calm, firm. "Because the idea of Lauren-deau doing to you what he did to my mother terrified me."

I scoff. "Why didn't you warn me, then? We talked about him. About your mother. You had *countless* opportunities." There's a piece of me, somewhere in the back of my head, that knows how much Jack's admission of vulnerability must have cost. But the larger piece thought this was the first relationship in my life based on honesty, and now . . . I feel incredibly stupid. "You *lied* to me. Over and over."

"Would you have believed me if I'd told you?" he asks, taking a single step closer. "In fact, do you believe me *now*?"

"I . . ." I glance away, suddenly flustered. "I believe that *you* believe it. But . . . maybe you misinterpreted the diaries. It must have been a misunderstanding, because he would never . . . I owe him so much, and . . ."

Jack pinches the bridge of his nose. "This is *precisely* why I didn't tell you. You idolize him and weren't ready to hear *any* of this. If I'd brought it up, I would have hurt you, and you would have pulled back."

"That's not for you to decide! And anyway, why do you think *I* spent my life lying to people, Jack?" I explode. "Why do you think I never told Laurendeau that I hate teaching, or Cece that her movies are worse than a Windows screen saver, or Mom that I'm a real fucking human being? Because I'm afraid that if I *hurt* them with the truth, then they'll *leave* me. Why is it only a good excuse when it comes to *you*?"

I walk away from the table, away from Jack. Take a deep breath, willing myself to calm down, staring at the streetlights shining over the rooftop snow.

Jack lied to me. After everything, *he* was the one to lie to *me.* Not about a movie or wanting to get sushi—he lied to me about something huge.

"Here's what I think, Jack," I say into the Boston skyline, angry, dejected. "You enjoy calling people out on their bullshit, but no one ever calls you out on yours."

"*My* bullshit?"

I turn around, not sure what to say. And yet when I look at him, it's right there on my tongue.

"When you were a teenager, you did something impulsive out of anger, and that . . . *that*, I can understand. But after, you went on to have a brilliant career that gave legitimacy to your actions—and you still *never* bothered addressing them. Even after you grew up and should have known better." I wipe my cheek with the palm of my hand, because I'm crying. Of course I am. "Your actions . . . *your* actions hurt lots more people than Laurendeau. And while you didn't think much about the article, I thought about it every day for over a decade. It had terrible consequences for something that I really, *really* love, and you know what? I've done my best to avoid thinking about it, but I don't know if I can keep on doing that. I don't know if I can stop being angry at you. I don't know if I . . ." My voice breaks and my eyes flood, and I cannot bear to be here, with Jack, a second longer.

"Is that what you are? Angry?" His hand cups my cheek, forcing my eyes to his blurry face. "Or are you just scared? Because you've been more honest with me than ever before?"

"Maybe." I pull away and see it in the twitch of his fingers that he wants to chase me, but no. No. "Maybe I'm scared. And maybe you're a liar. Where does that leave us?"

He gives me a long, undecipherable look. "I don't know. Where?"

You know where we're going, here, he said, over and over. And I said no, and then I said yes, and it *is* where I want to be. But he asked me for honesty and lied in return, and he did beat everything I stand for to a pulp, and I just—

I need space. I need to think.

"You should leave, Jack."

He lets out a breath and moves closer. Like he wants to wrap himself around me. It's in the way his muscles coil, that impulse to take care of me. "Elsie, come on. You're not—"

"I am." I'm starting to sob. I want him to touch me, but I cannot stand for him to be here. "You always talk about what I want, Jack. You helped me learn how to ask for it. Well." I force myself to look him squarely in the eye and show him that I mean what I say, even though I'm not sure I do. There's a burning heat in my chest, scalding, painful. "Right now, I don't want to be with you. I need you to give me some space."

I see it in his eyes, the moment he realizes that I'm telling the truth. And the second he's gone, I feel it in my bones like nothing before.

24

ELECTROMAGNETISM

J ACK CALLS ME TWO DAYS LATER DURING MY OFFICE HOURS,
but I'm busy explaining to a UMass senior that if she truly must
paste an entire paragraph from Wikipedia into her essay, she should
at least take out the embedded hyperlinks. He tries again on Friday
night, when I'm grading the thermo papers that came in late, and
one last time on Saturday morning, while I'm in bed staring at the
popcorn ceiling, thinking about him anyway.

I never consider picking up. Not once. Not even when I cannot
sleep. Not even after being sullen tempered, distracted, inefficient for
the entire week because I cannot stop replaying my fight with him,
slicing it into pieces, retracing what I said, what *he* said, what our
positions are, what algorithms could be used to solve the mess we're
in and the things I feel. Not even when Cece comments on the newly
whole credenza, making me miss him in an angry, visceral way.

I need answers. On Monday morning my alarm goes off at five

thirty, but I'm already awake, just as I've been for the rest of the night. I dress quickly, without looking at myself in the mirror, and leave as quietly as I can, stopping only to give a suspicious Hedgie a handful of food pellets. It's early enough that the bus to Northeastern is semi-deserted—the driver, me, and a girl in scrubs. Her foot taps to music I cannot hear, and focusing on it makes the thought of what I'm about to do almost bearable.

Dr. L. isn't in his office yet. He arrives about twenty minutes later and finds me leaning beside his nameplate—a first in six years. I study his hands as he unlocks the door, wondering how to bring up Grethe Turner.

I heard from someone that—

I'm sure it's all a misunderstanding—

I know these are serious accusations, but—

Please, you wouldn't—

"What is it that you wanted to tell me, Elise?" The green chair feels prickly under my thighs. Dr. L.'s tone is, as usual, encouraging. Supportive. "You mentioned something about a job opportunity in your email. Where would that be?"

I had . . . not quite forgotten about George's offer, but the topic seems trivial, inconsequential compared to my need to know what really happened between Laurendeau and Jack's mother. Still, it's why I originally scheduled this meeting. Since I have no idea how to bring up the topic I want to, I clear my throat and start with what's easy.

"At MIT."

"Ah. I see." His thin lips stretch into a satisfied smile. "The department realized they made a mistake. I'm pleased to hear that—"

"No. I . . . That's not it. Georgina Sepulveda wants me to become her postdoctoral fellow. The position pays well, comes with health insurance, and George has a line of liquid crystal research."

His eyes widen, then instantly narrow. "Georgina Sepulveda stole your job, and you're thinking of working *for* her."

"She didn't *steal* my job." Irritation bubbles inside me, but I quash it down. "She deserved it. And I can learn a lot from her. Honestly, it feels like a perfect match, and I'm leaning toward accepting." Dr. L. says nothing and just stares at me. The satisfied smile is gone now, and I nearly shiver. "What do you think?"

He's quiet for a few more moments. Then he leans back in his chair, lips thin, and asks, "What is it that you are here for, Elise? My blessing to accept this position?"

I take a deep breath. Another. *Honesty*, I tell myself like a mantra. *Honesty. I can be true to myself. People who care will stay, even when I'm not the Elsie they want.* "Yes. I understand your reticence, and I respect your wisdom, but—"

"If you really understand, you will stop considering it at once."

My brain stumbles and goes blank for a minute. "I . . . What?"

"Setting aside the humiliation of working for someone who beat you to a job, I have researched Georgina Sepulveda. Not only is she an experimentalist, but she also frequently collaborates with Jonathan Smith-Turner."

I'm not sure what feels the most like a punch: Dr. L.'s cutting tone, or the shock of hearing him say Jack's name. "This has nothing to do with him. George is an established scientist in her own right, and—"

"Enough, Elise." He lifts his hand, as though I'm a well-trained pet who'll fall silent at a simple gesture. Suddenly he looks tired, as though exhausted by an unruly child's tantrum. "You will *not* accept this position."

I frown. For a long moment, I have no idea what to do. Because on one side, there's the simple semantic knowledge of what Laurendeau's Elsie should do: Agree. Apologize. Chalk her stubbornness up to meningitis, leave after some teary genuflections, and continue her life as it has been for the past six years. On the other, there's the Elsie *I* want to be.

And the things she chooses to say. "Dr. Laurendeau. I *will* accept the position if it's what I think is best." My voice comes out surprisingly firm. "And while I understand your reservations and appreciate your guidance, I will ultimately decide—"

"You silly, stubborn girl."

His tone, at once harsh and condescending, is like an ice bucket pouring over my head. "You have no right to talk to me this way."

Dr. L. stands slowly, as he often does during our conversations. For the first time in six years, I stand, too. "As your academic advisor, I can talk to you however I choose." He leans forward. I have to lock my knees to not step back. "If you are adamant that you wish to work under an experimentalist," he continues coldly, "perhaps we may review some of the physicists who approached me about you in the past, but—"

"What did you say?"

"I am open to reviewing other offers, but Dr. Sepulveda's is not—"

"Other . . . offers? You said there were no other offers."

"There were some. From experimental physicists. Absolutely *unacceptable*. However, they would still be better than working with—"

"But you never told me."

"Because they did not bear contemplating."

The room spins. Topples. Stops to a crack within me—a neat split. "You . . ." I cannot speak. Cannot find the words. "That—that was—it was for *me* to decide. You knew how much I was struggling financially. How little research I was able to do this past year. And you didn't tell me?"

His mouth twists into a downward line. "I am your mentor. It is my job to guide you toward what's best for you."

"You *overstepped*," I say, so forceful, so different from my usual soft *but*s or reluctant *yes*es that for a moment he looks taken aback. But he recovers quickly, and his smile is chilling.

"Elise, if it weren't for me, you wouldn't have entered graduate school. I *chose* you. Whatever career you have, you owe it to me, and you should be very careful not to forget it."

I cannot believe my ears. This time I do take a step back, and another one, and all of a sudden it dawns on me that . . .

"Jack was right about you."

"I have no idea who Jack is, nor do I care. Now, please, sit down. Let's discuss this civilly, and—"

"You *are* controlling. And manipulative." I try to swallow past the knot in my throat. "Jack was right. You really did ruin Grethe Turner's career."

His eyes narrow to bitter slits. "Ah. That's who Jack is, then." He shakes his head twice, like I've disappointed him profoundly. "You have been associating with Smith-Turner. The man who jeopardized the very existence of *your* field."

"What did you do to Grethe?"

"His mother"—Laurendeau rolls his eyes impatiently—"doesn't matter. Grethe Turner doesn't matter and never did. If anything, her behavior should be a warning to you: there is no room for silly, stubborn girls in physics. And why would you believe anything Smith-Turner has told you?" His nostrils flare. "The article he wrote was a malicious hoax that ruined and derailed several careers and made it exponentially harder for theorists to have their work funded. We became the laughingstock of the academic world."

"That's true," I bite out. "But it doesn't erase what *you* did to Grethe Turner—"

"Do *not* mention her to me again." Laurendeau's voice is harsher than I ever remember hearing it. "And show some gratitude to the person who has given you a career."

I shake my head, feeling close to tears. I won't cry here, though. "I thought you wanted me to be the best possible physicist."

"What I want, Elise, is for you to do as I say—"

A knock. The door opens before I can turn around.

"Dr. Laurendeau? I have something for you to sign . . . Oh, Elsie, haven't seen you in a while. How've you been?"

I recognize the voice from my grad school days—Devang, the department administrator. I turn and wave at him, feeling numb. My hand doesn't feel like mine.

"Come in, Devang," Dr. L. says.

I'm nauseous, dizzy.

For the past six years, I've tried to be the Elsie that Dr. L. wanted. Resourceful, hardworking, tireless. Everything I needed—money, insulin, time, rest, mental fucking space—everything I needed I put after my work. I followed his advice before anyone else's, thinking that he had my best interests in mind, thinking that he deserved an Elsie who strove for brilliance.

And all along, all he wanted was someone he could control.

"Would you rather I come back later?" Devang is asking.

"No," Dr. L. says, eyes looking into me, lips pinched tight, "Elise was just about to leave."

I hold his gaze, knowing the first time I was truly honest with him is likely going to be the last time I'll ever see him.

"Dr. Laurendeau," I say before turning around, "you should really start calling me Elsie."

25

DUCTILITY

From: michellehannaway5@gmail.com
Subject: WHY DON'T YOU PICK UP YOUR PHONE? IT'S BEEN
THREE DAYS.

[this message has no body]

. . . .

From: marioluvr666@gmail.com
Subject: Re: Death in the family can't come to class

hey mrs. hannaway what do you mean, *who* died? pretty
sure you can't ask me that, it's a HIPAA violation

. . . .

From: Dupont.Camilla@bu.edu
Subject: Re: Not who you think I am

Dr. Hannaway,

I apologize! I mixed you up with Dr. Hannaday, who teaches
my Shakespeare After Dark: Intercoursing the Bard class.
He's actually a man in his seventies with bushy sideburns
and chronic nostril boogers, so . . . Oops & lol. Thank you
very much for answering my questions anyway! I ran with
your idea of looking at how *Breaking Dawn* by Stephenie
Meyer is loosely based on *A Midsummer Night's Dream* and
actually got an A+! I attached the paper in case you're
interested (It's titled: *Twilight vs. Shakespeare: May the
horniest triumph*). Also I looked you up on the BU database,
and you teach *Intro to Thermodynamics*? I'm thinking of
signing up for your class next year! I have a STEM
requirement, and you've been so nice. If anyone can help
me understand stuff like gravity or long division, that's you.

Cam

. . . .

From: GreenbergBern@northeastern.edu
Subject: Formal complaint

Dear Elsie,

I wanted to thank you again for our conversation re:
your former advisor. The pattern of behavior you have

highlighted is highly concerning, and an investigation on the matter has started. For now, I want to reassure you that part of my commitment as the new Chair of the Physics Department here at Northeastern is to counteract the secretive, toxic, unregulated academic environment that made it possible for Dr. Laurendeau to isolate you through the years.

I will keep you updated,

Best,
Bernard Greenberg, Ph.D.

My decision is already made by Tuesday night, but it's not until Friday morning that I get on the subway and head toward Cambridge. I walk through Harvard Square, coat open in the middle of a delightfully sunny sixty-degree February day that's probably paid for by several yards of coral bleaching somewhere in the Red Sea. I feel much like I have for the rest of the week: raw, delicate, a little bumbling. As though I'm gingerly trying on someone else's life.

It's my first time in the building, but I find the office easily. When I knock, a voice yells from inside, "I'm not here! Don't come in! Go away!"

I laugh and open the door anyway.

"Oh my God, Elsie! Come in—I thought you were one of my colleagues. Or students. Or family members. Basically, anyone else." George seems overjoyed to see me. Her office resembles her: a little messy, but cozy and comfortable. She begins to move a stack of printouts from the chair, but I shake my head.

"No need. I don't really have time to stay. I wanted to talk to you in person. About the job."

"Oh." Her expression briefly shifts into a wince. Then reverts back to a small, reassuring smile. "You didn't have to come all the way over here for that. I totally understand that working for an experimentalist might not be your ideal career. And I have no doubt that you'll find a tenure-track position soon. And like I said, I think you and I should still—"

"Actually." I clear my throat. "I came here to accept."

She blinks. Many times. "To . . . accept?"

I take a deep breath, smile, and nod. "Yes."

"To accept . . . the job?"

"Yes."

"Yes?"

"Yes."

"To be clear: you're *taking* the job."

"Yes."

She screams. And hugs me tight. And after a startled moment, I hug her back. And about ten seconds into that, something breaks through the foggy haze of the past few days: I feel selfishly, beautifully happy. I just chose something *on* my own, *for* my own, without first building a sophisticated theoretical model of other people's advice, preferences, needs. Without the nagging feeling that the only path I could take was the one pre-trodden for me.

This decision is all mine.

"I wanted to tell you in person," I say when we let go. "And I wanted to thank you for the opportunity." My smile wobbles a little. I could get emotional, but not yet. First, I have things to say. "And I'd love to set up a meeting, maybe for the next week. I don't know if I mentioned it to you, but I've been working on several algorithms regarding the behaviors of bidimensional liquid crystals for . . . well, years now. Lots of incomplete projects I want to finish up. I'd love to tell you more about it. Get your input." I bite my lower lip. "Maybe it could be part of our collaborative research, too?"

"Yes. Absolutely, I'd love to hear all about it." She grins. And then, almost abruptly, doesn't. "I really didn't think you were going to accept."

I nod. "I know." My heart beats a little harder. "But in the end, it was an easy choice. Because I wanted to."

I leave with a promise to meet her for drinks next week when her friend Bee's in town. The ride back home is still delicate, but a little less raw. When I tap through my phone in search of a good song, the old notifications of Jack's unanswered calls stare back at me, unflinching.

He hasn't tried to contact me since the weekend, and I wonder if he's angry at me. I wonder if he's sad. I wonder if he's disappointed.

Then I remember: *I'm* angry. And sad. And disappointed. Yes, Jack was right about Laurendeau, but I'm still furious—at *both* of them. They lied, withheld information, presumed to know what was best for me, and a new, vengeful version of me revels in the way these two men who hate each other are now tangled up together in the expanse of *my* rage. Anger is not a new emotion *per se*, not for me, but for the first time in my life, I'm letting myself *experience* it.

Desirable Elsies were never allowed to acknowledge negative feelings. But the Elsie I'm discovering I am is in the eye of several, and instead of trying to channel, disassemble, toss, forget, bury, transform, choke, erase, disappear those feelings—instead of doing *any* of that, she just lets them be.

Breathes them in. Then out. Then in again.

The therapist I once talked with but never went back to, because the copay was too steep even with Dad's health insurance, would probably call this *wallowing*. Unhealthy. Destructive. But I'm not so sure.

I treasure my newfound feelings. Hoard them. Every once in a while I study them, turn them around, squint at them like they're a ripe piece of fruit, plucked from a mysterious tree that shouldn't even be growing in my yard. When I pop them in my mouth to swallow them whole, they taste at once bitter and delicious.

For reasons that probably have to do with dopamine and oxytocin and other stupid chemicals in my head, Jack is ubiquitous. A shadow in the Walgreens line while I buy my insulin, the tall man waiting at the bus stop, the deep chuckle on my way to the UMass faculty meeting. Solidly nowhere, vanishingly everywhere. But it's okay.

For the first time, when faced with a conflict situation with someone I care about, I don't feel the urge to smooth things over. And it's ironic, in an Alanis sort of way, that the main reason is Jack's very voice in my head, asking, *What do you want, Elsie?*

I want to claw at your face, Jack. And then I want to bite into your shoulder while you hold me tight. But I will settle for just being sustainedly, explosively angry.

So I let myself do just that, and it bleeds over to other things, too. I ignore Mom's panic about my brothers going into debt to out-truck each other. I say no to manning the table for the Physics Society at the Boston Extracurricular Fair. When Cece asks if there's something wrong (I've been distracted, too lost in thoughts of Jack acting like an entitled, irresponsible little shit for fifteen years and *then* having the gall to see through me and make me laugh like no one before) and offers to watch *Delicatessen* with me—"To relax a bit!"—I say, "No, thank you," then slip into my room with a block of cheese to comfort-read Bellice fan fiction.

It's a balmy Wednesday afternoon, I just spotted Jack in the crowd (it was a postmodern clothespin sculpture), my heart hurts with fury and something I won't allow myself to name, and I realize something: the last time I felt this low was after J.J. kicked me out and my entire life crumbled down like a shit cookie. Except that at the time, I walked away convinced that I needed to try harder to be the Elsie others wanted. This time . . .

What do you *want, Elsie?*

Maybe I'm not stumbling through someone else's life. Maybe I'm just living mine for the first time.

WHEN I GET HOME, CECE IS WEARING:

- a teddy
- an apron
- a single knee sock
- nothing else

She's cooking and swaying to the sound of something I cannot hear, occasionally breaking into off-key singing in the direction of Hedgie, who keeps on frolicking in a bowl of dry kitten food.

It's a lot of chaotic energy. Even for her.

When I step closer, she takes out one AirPod and grins. "Found ten bucks on the bathroom floor of Boylston Hall and went to the supermarket, baby! We're having tartiflette, but with no bacon and extra cheese—"

"I need to tell you something."

Her smile stays in place. "Shoot!"

"It'll take a few minutes."

"Okay." She takes out the other pod. "Shoot!"

I open my mouth and . . .

Nothing happens. Air comes in, doesn't go back out. I squeeze my eyes shut.

"No need to shoot if you don't want to." There's a tinge of worry in her voice. A line between her eyes. "You could fire or discharge or—"

"I want to. It's just . . ." *I'm not motorically able to.*

Which Cece might know, because she crosses her arms, tilts her head in that compassionate way of hers, and tells me, "Maybe if you say it in a funny accent, it'll be easier? May I suggest Australian? Not to be culturally insensitive, but those closed *e*'s are just—"

"I hated *In the Mood for Love*," I blurt out. "And I find very little enjoyment in Wong Kar-wai's filmography."

Cece startles. Physically. Spiritually. "But . . . but they are *amazing*."

"I know. Well—I *don't* know. They *look* like I should find them amazing, but to me they're just sad and kinda slow. Still better than the Russian ones from the seventies, which feel like rubbing brambles against my eyeballs, and I *really* think producers should stop giving money to Lars von Trier and instead pick a good charity. Even just flush it down the garbage disposal, honestly. And don't get me started about *2001: A Space Odyssey*—"

She gasps like this is a theater play. "You said you *loved* it!"

"I . . . Maybe. I mostly repeated things I found online."

She frowns at the backsplash tiles. "Your review *did* sound very similar to Roger Ebert's," she mumbles to herself.

"I hate all auteur-style movies." My mouth feels like a desert.

Then it gets even *drier* when Cece asks me with a scowl, "What do you like, then?"

I try to swallow. Fail. "*Twilight*'s my favorite."

Cece's eyes bug out. She opens her mouth. Closes it. Opens it. Closes it. Opens it one last time. "Which one?" she asks, sounding constipated.

"I don't know." I wince. "All of them. The fourth?"

Is that a whimper? Maybe. Yeah. And I don't know what I expected her reaction would be, but it was not this one. Not her glaring at me and then something hitting me hard on the forehead. And then again. And then—

"Is this—" I lift my hands and take a protective step back. "Are you throwing cheddar cubes at—"

"Damn *right* I am!" She takes a two-second break to turn off the stove and starts again. With improved aim and vigor. I back down till the counter stops me. "I *knew* you weren't watching hentai porn that time! I *knew* I saw that shovel-face guy on the screen, I knew it, I knew it, I—"

"Not the *cheese*, Cece!"

The stoning stops. And when I peek between my fingers, Cece is there, a bag of Great Value cubed cheddar clutched in her fist, staring at me.

Her eyes are brimming wet. "Why?" she asks, and my heart breaks, and I want to take it all back. It was a joke. I love Wong Karwai, and Kubrick is the best. I'm still the Elsie she wants, and tonight we can have a Jodorowsky marathon. It's such a small lie, in the grand scheme of our friendship.

Except that I've built my entire life on small lies. And over time, they've all grown to be huge. And the Elsie that Cece wants is, first and foremost, not a liar.

"Because I . . ." I shake my head. I cannot even say it. Oh God. Oh. God.

"Because," I try in a poor man's Australian accent, "I thought that if you knew we weren't into the same movies, then you . . ." I can't make myself finish.

A single tear slides down her cheek. "Please tell me you weren't afraid I wouldn't love you anymore."

I can only look at her, apologetic.

"Oh, honey."

My eyes are burning, too. "I'm so sorry."

"Elsie. Elsie." She takes one slow step toward me. Then another. Then two more and we're clutching each other in a way we haven't for a long time, ever maybe, and I'm thinking that she smells like cheese and flowers and something ineffably homey and comforting. "I will love you forever," she says into my hair. "Even if you're an animal with no taste."

"I know. I'm just . . ."

She pulls back to look at me. "Incredibly messed up?"

"Yeah." My laugh is wet. "That."

"It's okay. It's not like I'm any better," she says darkly. Her slight shoulders rise and fall. "Anything else you've been faking?"

"Not really." I scratch my nose. "Flushable wipes are not really flushable."

"Oh." She cocks her head. "Is that . . . something you were faking?"

"Not really, but you should stop using them."

"Okay." She nods. "My poor butt."

"Oh, and Hedgie and I hate each other."

Her eyes narrow. "Now you're making shit up."

"I call her the p-word when you're gone."

"The p-word?"

"Pincushi—"

"Don't you dare say it. We're her moms!"

"I consider myself more of an evil stepmother."

She slaps my arm. "Who even *are* you?"

I try to swallow, but my throat is stuffed full. So I settle for holding out my hand and meet Cece's eyes squarely for what feels like the first time.

"I'm Elsie. And I really like cheese, particle physics, and movies with sparkly vampires."

She takes it with a watery smile. "I'm Celeste." Her fingers are sticky, a little gross. I love her *so* much. "I'm sure that we'll be the best of friends."

26

LIQUID CRYSTALS

RINSE THE DIRTY CHEDDAR RESCUED FROM THE FLOOR, THINK-ing, *We should probably sweep more often; I hope we don't get tetanus*—just as Cece stands triumphantly with the last three blocks in hand and says, "This floor is surprisingly clean!"

I smile into the swirling drain.

"So." She leans against the sink, arms crossed. "How much of you coming out as a lying liar has to do with Jack?"

I sober up and kill the faucet. "It's not . . ." I shake my head. "It's a mess."

"What is?"

My heart wrings. "Everything."

"But you had your sex-cation the other weekend."

I heat up. "We didn't really . . ." I notice her raised eyebrow and abort my Deny the Obvious mission. "Have you seen Kirk recently?"

"This is such an unskilled deflection attempt, I'm just gonna pretend it never happened. So, what exactly *isn't* going on between you and the Jackster?"

"Whatever it seemed like . . . Wherever we were going, we . . ." I grab the dishcloth. We should probably clean that, too. "I think that might be nowhere."

"How come?"

I don't really feel like meeting her eyes. "He lied to me about something. And before you say anything—I know it's rich of me to call out people for lying. But."

"Hmm." She drums her fingers against the steel of the sink. "Does this have to do with the article?"

"Yeah." I sigh, folding the ratty cloth. "I'm done with sweeping stuff under the rug. If something makes me mad, I'm going to let myself be mad. And that article has been the ammo people use to make fun of my work for fifteen years, so—"

"No, I meant—the article he wrote today?"

I lift my eyes. "The what?"

"You haven't seen it?"

"Seen what?"

"The entirety of academic Twitter is talking about it. Even the humanities—and you know how busy we are begging our boards of directors not to shutter our departments. Did you really *not* see it? Jack published an article. Today. In *Annals of Theoretical Physics.*"

I'm positive that a mallard must have flown in and eaten Cece's brain.

"Wait—I was wrong," she admits, and I relax. "It's not an *article.* More like one of those op-eds?"

Maybe she's high? Has she been inhaling Tauron fumes? "There are no op-eds about science."

"There are op-eds about everything. Trout fishing, plasma cool-ant, velvet suits, the unbearable lightness of being—"

"Okay. Yes. But Jack didn't write an op-ed, and if he had, he wouldn't have published it in the *Annals*."

Her brow furrows stubbornly. She picks up her phone. Taps the screen a few times, muttering something about the incredulity of Thomas, then thrusts it in my face.

"Cece, I can't read anything that's one millimeter from my nose."

"Here." She drops the phone in my palm and goes back to the tartiflette. I let my eyes focus on the words and—

The floor wobbles. Jerks. Then it drops from underneath my feet.

On the home page of the journal that published Einstein, Feyn-man, Hawking, there is an open letter written by Jonathan Smith-Turner.

An open letter addressed to the scientific community.

I take a few steps back, stopping when my thighs hit the table. The words on the screen feel like something Jack is murmuring in my ears.

The last time I published in *Annals of Theoretical Physics*, I was seventeen years old, and motivated by something that had nothing to do with science: revenge.

My mother, Grethe Turner, has long since passed away, but she was a brilliant theoretical physicist. When I was in my mid-teens I started developing an affinity for physics my-self, and as a consequence I read her diaries and reached out to her former colleagues, hoping to get a better idea of what a career in physics might entail. That is how I discovered her awful experiences with her former mentor, who had forced her to leave academia.

That man was Christophe Laurendeau, and at the time he was the editor in chief of *Annals*. When I tried to report him for what he'd done to my mother, I was told that there were no grounds to open an investigation. So I took matters into my own hands.

I knew what kind of article Dr. Laurendeau would look upon favorably, and I knew from the grapevine that he was infamous for being lax when it came to the peer review of works that he believed would further his own scientific agenda. So I wrote something that would fit those criteria. Again: my aim was to sabotage Laurendeau's career, and as unethical as that may sound, it's something I stand by. He did suffer setbacks, and for several years he was unable to receive funding or mentor students—an outcome I cannot regret.

But that's not all that happened. After I exploited one specific weakness within one specific journal to target one specific individual, the scientific community began to use my article as an example of the decline of theoretical physics. And what I regret is that as it happened, I stayed silent.

For over fifteen years I did nothing to dispel the idea that I believed theoretical physics to be inferior. I became a symbol of the enmity between theoretical and experimental physics, and of that, I am ashamed. I am ashamed of how it must have made my theorist colleagues feel, and I am ashamed that I did not quell these assumptions for over a decade. Above all, I am ashamed that I put a person I deeply respect in the position of having to explain to me the consequences of my own actions because I was too proud, too angry, and too self-centered to realize them.

So let me send a message to anyone who still cites my article as a weapon in some petty war within our discipline: don't. I never believed that theoretical physics was less rigorous, or less important a field than experimental physics. And if you do believe that, you are mistaken, and you should read some of the most meaningful theory work of the past few decades. I am citing several below . . .

"Oh my God." My hands are trembling. My legs, too. And the floor, I'm pretty sure. "Oh my *God*."

"Yup." I look up. I'd forgotten Cece existed. I'd forgotten to breathe. I'd forgotten the rest of the world was a thing. "That's, like, the science equivalent of proposing with a flash mob."

"No." I shake my head forcefully enough to scroll out everything that's inside it. Mashed potatoes, probably. "He's not proposing. He's just . . ." I crumple in a chair.

"Finally reckoning with his decades-long evil legacy because he wants you to be his girlfriend who sends him cute little heart emojis and sixty-nines with him every other day?"

I shake my head again. The truth is, it *feels* like it. Like the letter is addressed to *me*. "No—he—he *doesn't*—"

"He does. He has *that* look. I can just tell he's into all sorts of filthy stuff." She grins. "Anyway, just from reading this, Madame Person He Deeply Respects, it doesn't feel like you two are going *nowhere*."

My mind is tottering in circles. No. Yes. "It's complicated."

"What is?"

"Jack. Jack is complicated." I massage my temples. "Or maybe not. Maybe he's not, but—*I* am complicated. Too complicated."

"Okay. Totally. I'm not going to spare your feelings and fib about how complicated you aren't. You did lie to me about liking David Lynch for seven solid years—unless you *do* like—"

"No."

"Right. Well, this man just wrote an op-ed that's gonna get the STEMlords to throw parsnips at him till the day he dies, and I'm pretty sure he did it for you, so that's something you might want to consider. I mean, he does look pretty sturdy. He can take a few parsnips. He could probably take a whole cauliflower field. Plus, the power of love will numb the pain—"

"Jesus." I cover my eyes. "Shit."

"Elsie?" She kneels in front of me. "What's the problem?"

"Everything."

"Right. But if you had to be specific . . . ?"

"He's right. He was right. I was mad because he lied, and he said that I was scared, and . . . I *am* scared. That I'm *too* messed up for him."

"For Jack?"

I nod into my hands. "I lie all the time about who I am. While Jack is just—"

"Oh, Elsie."

"He sees everything—"

"Elsie."

"—and he'll get sick of my bullshit—"

"Elsie?"

"—and he's way too tall for me—ouch!" My arms drop. There is a red bruise on the back of my hand. Another cheddar cube on the floor. "What the—"

"Stop whining all over my kitchen," she commands. "Fear aside, do you *want* to be with Jack? Do you *like* being with Jack?"

So much.

So, so much.

So, so, *so* much.

"I like it. But maybe I still shouldn't."

"There are things like that. That feel nice but are bad for you. Like MDMA, or Q-tips for ear cleanings. I don't think Jack qualifies, though."

"Why?"

Cece's eyes are earnest. Her fingers reach out for mine.

"You know me, Elsie: I *hate* giving credit to a dude who probably went to kindergarten at a French château. But you've been seeing him for, what, weeks? And I don't know what it is precisely that you two have been doing for each other. But he just let go of a very shitty thing he's been carrying around for half his life. And you . . . I feel like I know you better than I ever did before. And I'm thinking that maybe, I owe it a little bit to him."

I look at Cece, letting her words swirl around me in messy, complicated, unpredictable patterns. Then they settle inside my brain, and I can *taste* their truth.

Four weeks ago I was a different person.

No: four weeks ago I was an infinite number of different people. I've put myself in a hundred tiny boxes, played a thousand roles, sculpted myself in a million smooth lines. But for the first time in memory I'm fighting against that, and . . .

What do you *want, Elsie?*

I squeeze my hand tight around Cece's. Then I stand, pick up my coat, and run out the door.

THERE'S SOMETHING NEW ON THE DOOR OF JACK'S OFFICE.

Under the "Jonathan Smith-Turner, Ph.D." plaque and the "Physics Institute, Director" subplaque, someone taped a printout of the *Annals* article Cece showed me earlier today.

All two pages.

Including the citations.

One of which is an article of mine.

"Dr. Hannaway?"

I turn to Michi walking down the hallway. "Oh—hi."

"Hi!" She smiles widely at me. "Can I help you?"

"Oh, I was . . ." I point at the door, which looks a lot like I'm pointing at the paper. I quickly lower my hand. "I was looking for Jack."

"I think he went straight home after the faculty meeting."

Shit.

No. Not *shit*. This is good. I can go to his place. I know where he lives. I've basically lived there, too, for a couple of weekends. So this is perfect—it gives me more time to think about what I'm going to tell him, since I have no idea. Why *am* I here? Just swept by the currents, like a salmon during mating season.

I shoot Michi a quick smile and speed-walk down the hallway. I think she yells after me that she followed me on Twitter, but I don't stop to investigate. Instead I rehearse my conversation with Jack. *Hi. Hey. Oh, hello. I've seen the article* sounds like a good beginning. But I could also start softer. *I was just in the area, and my dog ran away. Will you help me find it? It's a black-and-white Newfie with a big lolling tongue, and yes, if I have to make up an imaginary pet, I'm going to choose a cute one—*

I'm thinking so hard, I barely register that someone is calling me. And it takes a "Dr. Hannaway, is that you?" for me to recognize the voice.

I turn around.

It's Volkov. And behind him, Ikagawa and Massey. At their side, Monica, Sader, Andrea, half a dozen more people whose names I don't remember from my interview, and behind, an entire head taller, a million miles wider, only just stepping out of the conference room . . .

Jack. Of course.

Michi was wrong. Faculty meeting only *just* ended.

"Dr. Hannaway," Volkov says fondly, like I'm his niece who should visit more often, and even though there are twenty people staring at me and I'd like to disappear into the woods, I actually lift my hand and smile weakly.

"Are you an ocean?" he asks. "Because you just . . . waved!"

Oh God. When did this become my life?

"Elsie?" Monica butts in warily. "Is everything okay?"

My heart slams with mortification. I bet she's afraid I'll make a scene. "Um, I . . ." *I got lost. Forgot my colonics paraphernalia in the bathroom a few weeks ago. Have you seen a Newfie?*

No. No. *Come on, Elsie. Honesty.*

"I need to talk to Jack," I say in my newly found firm voice.

Jack.

Who has, by now, noticed me.

And is coming toward me.

Standing in front of me.

Towering toweringly with a puzzled, towered frown directed at me.

Deep breaths. It's okay. This is fine.

"I didn't know you two talked," Monica says, looking skeptically between us.

"I learned a few years ago," Jack tells her calmly, staring only at me. She's little more than a fly buzzing around us. "And Elsie's in the process of mastering the art of speaking for herself."

I glare. His mouth twitches.

"Elsie, has Jonathan been bothering you? Because I—"

"No. Not at all. We . . ." I'm beet red. "We do *talk*."

Her eyes widen in surprise, then narrow in suspicion. "Does this *talking* you have been doing have anything to do with Jonathan's article?" she says. To whom, I'm not sure.

Jack keeps looking at me, silent for a stretched beat. "The article was overdue."

"It certainly was." Monica huffs. "Still, this seems . . . highly irregular."

"Not *highly*." He shrugs. "More like middle of the road."

She stiffens. "Jonathan—"

"Monica?" Volkov calls from behind. "Will you help us with the meeting minutes?"

She turns away with a threatening look at Jack, and suddenly I'm very, *very* aware that coming here might not have been my best idea. For a number of reasons.

"I'm sorry," I say.

He cocks his head. "Why are you sorry?"

"I don't know—I . . ." I gesture around us, then look, and it's a bad idea. People are lingering in the hallway, and I don't *think* they can hear us, but they're sure looking, and I wouldn't want to—

Wait.

No. I don't care about people and what they think. "I figured you'd be in your office."

"Nope. We could go," he offers. "Though if we disappear together into my office . . ."

I nod. Okay, so I do care *a bit* about what people think. Just the right amount. Maybe I don't want them to picture me bent over Jack's desk. Maybe I'm still confused. I'll think more on this later.

"Elsie?"

"Yes?"

He's laughing at me. And I hate it. And I love it. "What are you doing here?"

"I just . . ." I clear my throat. "I know we had a *really* bad fight. And I didn't answer your calls, because I was *really* mad. And I know you thought that that was it, and we would never meet again, but . . ."

"I didn't."

Oh. "Oh?"

"I was giving you the space you asked for." He looks patiently amused. "And there was something I needed to do."

"Right. The article. I know you wrote it because it was overdue, and not because of me, but—"

"Both."

"—I still wanted to . . . What did you say?"

"It was overdue. *And* I did it for you."

My mouth is sand dry. "For me."

He nods, and his amusement shifts into something more serious. "What you said was true. And it was the right thing to do. But also . . . Elsie, there's very little I wouldn't do for you."

My cheeks burn hot and ice cold. "I . . . Jack. I need to explain. I—"

My phone chooses the worst possible time to vibrate. I glance down at the screen—*Mom*—reject the call, and immediately look back up at Jack.

"Sorry, I . . . Honesty. We're doing this with *honesty*." I inhale. "I came because I have several honest things to say to you."

His mouth twitches. "Please, do."

"Right. Okay. Then . . . first of all, I hate that you didn't like *Twilight*, and it invalidates all your other opinions—in movies especially, but not exclusively."

More phone buzzing. Which I ignore.

"I see."

"You need to buy curtains, because your apartment is *way* too bright, *way* too early. And your grilled cheese is good, but it could be better if you added aioli."

"Of course."

"And—"

The iTwat buzzes again, and—*dammit*.

"Mom," I pick up. "Not now, please."

"Elsie. Finally. Your brothers have been giving me so many head-aches, and you've been AWOL. I need you to—"

"I said, not *now*," I repeat impatiently. "I'm in the middle of some-thing important. Lucas and Lance are adults—if they want to ruin their lives, by all means, let them. I don't care, and I don't care what Aunt Minnie says on Facebook. Please, stop calling me with any-thing related to that." I hang up.

Jack stares at me with a stony, impenetrable expression.

"Um, sorry about that."

"No problem. It was . . ."

I squeeze my eyes shut. "Unhinged?"

"I was going to say hot. Elsie, look at me." His tone is command-ing, but in a way I don't mind. "Why are you here?"

"Because I . . ."

I close my eyes for a moment. Take a million deep breaths.

"Because I accepted George's offer. And I'll be working here next year." His smile widens with undeniable happiness—then stops abruptly when I add, "And because I hate you, Jack." I feel something warm on my lips. Salty, too. "I hate you, and it's pretty annoying, since I think I might also . . ." I shake my head. "And you're right—I am *terrified*, scared shitless that the more you know me, the less you'll like me, and I just . . . I *loathe* it sometimes."

He gives me a confused, curious look. Like he knows that I'm complicated, but he doesn't mind. Like he'd rather spend the rest of his life studying an inch of me than discovering the mysteries behind the universe. "What do you loathe?"

"The way you seem to always get under my skin."

"Elsie." His eyes close for a brief moment. When he opens them, stars are born. "You think you don't live under mine?"

"I . . . I don't know, really. I don't *really* understand you. You didn't tell me about Laurendeau, and . . . you know everything about *me*, but I know next to nothing about *you*. I'm constantly showing myself, but you rarely reciprocate—some, sure, but so much stays hidden, and I'm not sure what . . ."

He moves closer. Cups my face. There are people all around us— Monica, Volkov, Andrea. Jack's current and my future colleagues are getting a show, but he bends down anyway, like my space is his own.

"Okay, then. Honesty." He tilts my face backward, lips brushing against my ears. "I want you, Elsie. All the time. I think of you. All. The. Fucking. Time. I'm distracted. I'm shit at work. And my first instinct, the very first time I saw you, was to run away. Because I knew that if we'd start doing this, we would never stop. And that's exactly how it is. There is no universe in which I'm going to let you go. I want to be with you, *on* you, every second of every day. I think—I *dream* of crazy things. I want you to marry me tomorrow so you can go on my health insurance. I want to lock you in my room for a couple of weeks. I want to buy groceries based on what you like. I want to play it cool, like I'm attracted to you and not obsessed out of my mind, but that's not where I'm at. Not at all. And I need you to keep us in check. I need you to pace us, because wherever it is that we're going . . . I'm here. I'm already right here."

Jack straightens. He takes a step back, an intense, calm look in his eyes. Like he's said what he meant to and could never regret it.

"That was . . ." I clear my throat. "Honest."

He's quiet for a moment and then nods. "It's what I want to be. With you. And I'm sorry I lied."

"I . . . It's okay. This once." I clear my throat. "What you—the things—the fact that—" I take a deep, decisive, mind-clearing breath. And then I finally say it. "I am, too."

His head tilts. "You're what?"

"Almost there. Where we're going . . . I'm practically there, really. It's like . . . an inch away. I just need to . . ." I take another breath, this time shuddering. "I just need to find my footing. Feel the ground."

He smiles, and my heart thuds. Somewhere in the Tadpole Galaxy, comets are born, stars spring into being, liquid crystals twist, align, queue up in tidy formations.

"I'm here," Jack says. We're alone in this hallway, me and him. Just the two of us, in any way that matters. "But take your time, Elsie. I'll wait for as long as it takes."

EPILOGUE

Eight months later

I HATCH THE PLAN ON A SUNDAY MORNING.

The sun is bright, the curtains nonexistent, and Jack's eyelids must be as blackout as ever, because I get in at least twenty minutes of intense plotting before he wakes up to pull me closer. Then his stubble brushes against my belly, and I tuck my plans aside, carefully stored in an uncluttered corner of my brain, and let myself giggle in his arms. "You seem pensive," he points out later, in the kitchen, but I distract him with a kiss; his mouth is syrupy sweet, and the smell of waffles thickens the early-morning fall air.

The diversion works.

It's a plan that will require practice and organization, a touch of logistical troubleshooting. The best option would be to recruit someone else to help me, but I don't know. I'd rather do this on my own.

Except that Jack and I spend Sunday night the same way we do every Sunday—falling asleep on the sectional while catching up on articles. Monday's spent at Millicent's with the rest of the family, which involves the usual routine: Greg and I chatting about the YA books we've been buddy-reading, Jack playing against his grandma at the Go board, and the rest of the family, Caroline included, respectfully avoiding mentioning that I went from dating one brother to the other. I'm not sure what went down there, or what prompted the Smith Cinematic Universe to suddenly grow boundaries. I suspect that some overdue stern conversations were had, threats were made, and people were encouraged to either shut the hell up or never show up at Millicent's again.

It worked.

Tuesday night is also a no-go, because I have therapy, which I now can miraculously afford. I've never been this healthy—mentally and physically. The wonders of having insurance.

". . . and most of the time I really, truly believe that he sees me for what I am, but sometimes there is this petrifying fear," I explain to Jada, "that maybe he doesn't. Maybe he's making a mistake? Maybe he'll change his mind? Maybe there's a deal breaker, and he's days, *seconds* away from discovering it?"

"And what do we do when we feel like that?"

"We buy five pounds of Whole Foods pecorino?"

Jada blinks at me, unamused.

I sigh. "We articulate our insecurities to our partner and listen to their answer."

But it's not easy, *articulating*. Getting easier, yes, but a few hours later, when I'm lying on the couch on top of Jack, all that comes out is "You're not going to suddenly realize that you don't really like me, right?"

He dips his chin to look at me. "If my feelings for you haven't changed after reading that Bella and Alice alphaverse fan fiction, I'm pretty sure we're golden."

"It's called omegaverse—and you said it was good!"

"I said it was *hot*," he corrects me. The blue slice darkens. "Actually, you should read it to me again. Now."

I roll my eyes. "No, it's just that . . . I promise I'm usually . . . But sometimes I feel like . . . I'm not sure that . . ." I fall silent. There are no right words to be found in me.

"Rough session with Jada?" Jack asks. And I nod till he holds me tighter. We watch one of his white male rage movies in silence, and between a car chase and a weird CGI monster and his hands anchoring me to him, I think that maybe there is no something, no deal breaker, no shoe that's about to drop.

Maybe it's just us.

So, Wednesday. Wednesday is supposed to be the day I execute my plan, but I wake up to the coolest email of my life.

From: editor@naturephysics.com
Subject: Article ID: 89274692

Dear Drs. Hannaway and Sepulveda,

Congratulations. I am pleased to inform you that following your revisions, your paper entitled "Supermolecular organization in lyotropic liquid crystals: a new theoretical framework" has been accepted for publication in *Nature Physics*. Below you will find additional information . . .

That night George's wife makes souvlaki to celebrate. It's delicious, but George and I are too busy reading and rereading the email and letting out annoying high-pitched screams to truly savor it. We are obnoxious but just cannot help ourselves.

"Should we break up with them?" I hear Dora ask.

"We certainly deserve better," Jack answers. But that night he hugs me from behind while I brush my teeth and whispers, "You are the most magnificent thing that ever happened to me," and I know it to be true.

I'm a mess. A work in progress. I'm two steps forward and one step back. I hoard my cheese, and I can't efficiently load the dishwasher, and I'm going to struggle with the truth until the day I croak.

Jack knows all of this, and he loves me. Not *anyway*, but *because*.

So the next day—that's the one. Thursday. It's cutting it close, but it works.

"How's the job?" Mom asks me on the phone while I'm on my way to my apartment.

"Good. Great, actually."

"And that boyfriend of yours?" It feels a little robotic—like a list of questions that she's written in her Notes app. But she's trying. And she hasn't demanded I take care of Lance and Lucas in a while. "Has he proposed yet?"

I laugh. "Mom, it's been less than a year."

"That's plenty of time!"

"I don't need him to ask me to marry him," I say, distracted, rummaging in my bag for the keys that I almost never use anymore. I hope I haven't left them at Jack's.

"Why not?"

"Because . . ." Ha! Found them. "Because I already know that he wants to."

Cece arrives just a couple of minutes after we hang up. "Does

Jack know *why* you're here?" she asks, cheeks bright from the cool breeze.

"Nope. I told him we were just hanging out. A last hurrah before we move out for real next month."

"Good idea." She watches me mix the powder in water. "Maybe I should have brought Hedgie? For girls' night? But Kirk'll enjoy some one-on-one time with her."

He won't, since he's as terrified of her as I am. I finally feel seen.

"It's a bit bittersweet that we won't renew the lease," I say.

"Don't worry." She grins. "I wrote down Mrs. Tuttle's HBO password."

I laugh and shake my head. "It's just the end of an era."

"It's not, because our new places are five minutes apart."

"Still." I glance around. "Maybe I'll miss the coconut crabs and the exposed wires." I go back to stirring, and we're quiet for a while. Then her shoulder bumps against mine. "Elsie?"

"Yeah?"

"FYI, you'll always be my favorite."

"You too, Cece." The red in the pot gets a bit blurry for a second. "You too."

The following morning, when Jack steps into his office, I'm already there. Waiting in the chair behind his desk.

"Well, well, well," he says. Surprised. Delighted. "Look who's—"

His eyes fall on the fruits of my labor: his little Hadron Collider model is . . . well, where it always is. Except today it's trapped in cherry Jell-O.

"Happy birthday," I say. I'm a little breathless. I still get knocked off my feet when I see him after a while. I wonder if it'll ever end. I wonder if all these beautiful, momentous things I feel for him will ever settle into something ordinary. I can't imagine they will.

"The Jell-O is my birthday present?" he asks, like he'd be over-joyed if it were.

"Nope." I point to the card next to it. "That's the present."

The dimple makes my heart skip a beat. "Is it another Wayfair gift certificate? To buy more curtains?"

I laugh and swivel around in his chair—faculty members *do* get better furniture than the postdocs. I listen to him tear open the plain envelope, and let my eyes roam out the windows, to the trees that are just about to turn red and yellow, to the students going about their lives, to the blue sky. Then I close my eyes and picture Jack's face as he reads my words.

Dear Jack,

I know I've been slow, but I just wanted you to know something: I'm right here. With you.

AUTHOR'S NOTE

LOVE, THEORETICALLY IS, BY FAR, THE MOST "ACADEMIC" book I've written. I'd been wanting to tell a love story set against the backdrop of academic politics for a while, and for this one I really let myself get into the weeds. Maybe a little too much? Sorry! But as usual, lots of elements were inspired by my own experience in the slightly cesspooly mess of the academe.

Academic job interviews can be just as exhausting, long winded, and soul crushing as Elsie perceives them to be. The feuds within disciplines, just as petty. The power mentors have over their mentees, just as absolute. The adjunctification of higher education, which strands instructors with no job or financial security, just as terrifying. The bogus article Jack wrote is very loosely modeled after a real event: the Sokal Hoax happened in 1996, when an NYU physics professor wrote and submitted a "nonsense" article to *Social Text*, a leading cultural studies academic journal, to make a point about its editorial sloppiness and lack of intellectual rigor. The article was accepted, and the controversies, implications, and academic infights that followed are history (and documented in the Wikipedia entry, if you feel like busting out the popcorn).

Either way, I hope you enjoyed this story. And if you're wondering why anyone would want to pursue a career in academia after all of this . . . well, there are tons of academics out there, loving their jobs—and yet wondering the very same!

ACKNOWLEDGMENTS

Is writing hard, or am I just bad at it? In this essay, I will—

To be honest, this whole publishing thing isn't getting any easier for me, and I'm still relying on several trillion people to help me get my work in shape. *Love, Theoretically* was, simultaneously, a book I really wanted to write and a book I really struggled to write (go figure!). I owe a lot to my editor, Sarah Blumenstock (thank you for letting me keep that chapter break; BTW, I'm still mad you didn't tell me about that panel), and to my agent, Thao Le (thank you for being the only one who laughs at my jokes!), who constantly support me in all my writerly endeavors and are the reason writing is such a joy for me. I'm truly honored to get to work so closely with two people I *like* so much. Also, all my appreciation to Liz Sellers for her precious input. To my beloved Jen, Lucy, Margaret, and Kelly, who slogged through lackluster versions of this manuscript: this is what you get for being friends with me, you're welcome (I'm so sorry—ILU).

Thank you to my (anonymous) authenticity readers for their important and difficult work. In addition, I'm incredibly fortunate to have the best people working on the art (Lilith, who consistently creates the covers of my dreams, and Rita Frangie and Vikki Chu), production editorial work (Lindsey Tulloch), and copy edits (Janice Lee) for my books. And, of course, the best marketing and publicity team. To Bridget O'Toole, Kim-Salina I, Kristin Cipolla, Tara O'Connor: Hi. I'm sorry if sometimes I go rogue, and I'm sorry about all the crying on Zoom. I truly appreciate you and everything you do for me, and it's possible that I don't deserve you, but please don't leave me. Also, special acknowledgments to my grandeditor, Cindy, and my grandpublicist, Erin.

I would also like to thank all the foreign publishing professionals who have acquired and published my books abroad. I am so honored that *The Love Hypothesis* has reached so many readers, and I owe it all to you! In particular, all my love to my team at Sextante/Arqueiro (and to Frini and Nana) for having me in Brazil and giving me the experience of a lifetime, and to my team at Aufbau (especially Stefanie and Sara) for fitting so many cat cafés and Motel Ones in my memorable Germany visit.

When people ask me for writing advice, what I always say is that what matters the most is having a good support network, and mine is fantastic. I owe so much to my Grems, the Berkletes, and all the friends who've been so supportive of me in the last two years. In particular, thanks to Lo, Christina, Adriana, and Elena for their constant friendship, mentorship, and guidance. (And okay, fine, thanks to my husband, too, for making really good dinners.)

Last, but very much not least: all my gratitude to anyone who has read something I've written, ever. Time is a finite and precious resource, and I'm constantly overcome with emotion that people choose to spend it on my words. So thank you, thank you, thank you.

Justin Murphy of Out of the Attic Photography

ALI HAZELWOOD is the *New York Times* bestselling author of *The Love Hypothesis* and *Love on the Brain*, as well as a writer of peer-reviewed articles about brain science, in which no one makes out and the ever after is not always happy. Originally from Italy, she lived in Germany and Japan before moving to the US to pursue a Ph.D. in neuroscience. She recently became a professor, which absolutely terrifies her. When Ali is not at work, she can be found running, eating cake pops, or watching sci-fi movies with her two feline overlords (and her slightly-less-feline husband).

CONNECT ONLINE

AliHazelwood.com
🐦 EverSoAli
📷 AliHazelwood
♪ @alihazelwood

Ready to find
your next great read?

Let us help.

Visit prh.com/nextread

Penguin
Random
House